CW01080406

LITTLE MACHINES

Little Machines

by Paul McAuley

Paul McAuley

LITTLE MACHINES

Paul McAuley

Introduction by Greg Bear

PS Publishing 2005

ISBN
1 902880 93 5 (Deluxe slipcased hardcover)
1 902880 94 3 (Trade hardcover)

PS Publishing LTD
Grosvenor House
1 New Road
Hornsea, HU18 1PG
ENGLAND

e-mail
editor@pspublishing.co.uk

Internet
http://www.pspublishing.co.uk

CONTENTS

INTRODUCTION

Y ou're looking at a collection of terrific short stories by one of our finest writers. Fair warning! There are some shocks in store. You may not come out the same at the other end of this highway.

But you probably knew that when you picked up the book, didn't you?

One difference between a short story and a novel is that fewer people take part in the writing of a short story. A novel accumulates over months and even years of work. The author goes through changes of personality, or at least of mood. Information, point of view, and opinion slowly alter. Ultimately, hundreds of subtly different people see the manuscript from different angles as the days and weeks move on. This way, a novel acquires that grand and somewhat lumbering wisdom. No single human moment is responsible for its wholeness and artistry.

A short story is quicker, more elfin. Only a week or two or three—sometimes a month—goes into the creation of most short stories. That does not mean that short stories are simpler or easier to write. The intensity requires more focus, more concentration. A single slip-up can be disastrous.

Though Paul McAuley specializes in rich and complex novels, he's an admirable writer of short fiction, as well, and this sampling demonstrates his prowess admirably. I've compared some of his work to a wild hybrid of Cordwainer Smith and E.M. Forster. But Paul is versatile. His style varies and can be difficult to label. It's all compelling, however, and convincing, as well. He knows his history, science, literature, and popular culture, and expertly weaves them all into his tales.

He's also great company on long trips. In 1997, Paul, Larry Niven, Gregory Benford, and I traveled to a scientific station near the little town of Abisko, north of the arctic circle, to attend a conference sponsored by the Swedish Academy and organized in part by John Casti of the Santa Fe Institute. We had a great time. Benford, McAuley, and I later—in 2001—walked across Philadelphia to see the historical sights, just a week or so before September 11th.

We're chums. So take my admiration with a grain of salt.

Or a speck of silica.

These stories are rich and strange, like pearls. Bits of irritating sand—angry bits, puzzled bits, Quixotic bits—have accumulated nacre, a polished, refractive coating of vision and speculation. There's something not right with the world, something intrinsically unfair and painful, yet fascinating...How does McAuley deal with it? By turning it upside down and inside out. Taking the rough shell and showing us the mother of pearl.

Just a few highlights:

Philip K. Dick achieves great success in publishing, but the world suffers for his gain.

Mutilated cows and alien abductions bring celebrity and fame. Which is worse, the bending of the truth, or the warping of dimensions?

Biopunks and DNA hackers hold a conference—in 2010—and Paul McAuley (so I presume) gives us his expert reportage.

Deeply embedded in all of Paul's stories is a sense of fair play combined with moral outrage. Good. We live in outrageous times.

Sometimes, science fiction and fantasy are the best and most devious ways to express that outrage. The sugar coating is that we're toying with reality like kids with Play-Doh.

Science fiction writers just never know when to stop turning the screw. These stories get under your skin. Under your shell.

Don't let me slow you down. Be brave. Read on.

And along the way, make some of your own pearls.

Greg Bear

THE TWO DICKS

P hil is flying. He is in the air, and he is flying. His head full of paranoia blues, the Fear beating around him like black wings as he is borne above America.

The revelation came to him that morning. He can time it exactly: 0948, March 20, 1974. He was doing his program of exercises as recommended by his personal trainer, Mahler blasting out of the top-of-the-line stereo in the little gym he'd had made from the fifth bedroom. And in the middle of his second set of situps something goes off in his head. A terrifically bright soundless explosion of clear white light.

He's been having flashes—phosphene afterimages, blank moments of calm in his day—for about a month now, but this is the spiritual equivalent of a hydrogen bomb. His first thought is that it is a stroke. That his high blood pressure has finally killed him. But apart from a mild headache he feels perfectly fine. More than fine, in fact. Alert and fully awake and filled with a great calm.

It's as if something took control of me a long time ago, he thinks. As if something put the real me to sleep and allowed a constructed personality to carry on my life, and now, suddenly, I'm fully awake again. The orthomolecular vitamin diet, perhaps that did it, perhaps it really did heighten synchronous firing of the two hemispheres of my brain. I'm awake, and I'm ready to put everything in order. And without any help, he thinks. Without Emmet or Mike. That's important.

By this time he is standing at the tall window, looking down at the manicured lawn that runs out from the terrace to the shaggy hedge of flowering bougainvilleas, the twisty shapes of the cypresses. The Los Angeles sky pure and blue, washed clean by that night's rain, slashed by three white contrails that make a leaning *A*.

A for affirmation, perhaps. Or *A* for act.

The first thing, he thinks, because he thinks about it every two or three hours, because it has enraged him ever since Emmet told him about it, the very first thing I have to do is deal with the people who stole my book.

A week ago, perhaps inspired by a precursor of the clear white flash, Phil tried to get hold of a narcotics agent badge, and after a long chain of phone calls managed to get through to John Finlator, the deputy narcotics director, who advised Phil to go straight to the top. And he'd been right, Phil thinks now. If I want a fed badge, I have to get it from the Man. Get sworn in or whatever. Initiated. Then deal with the book pirates and those thought criminals in the SFWA, show them what happens when you steal a real writer's book.

It all seemed so simple in the afterglow of revelation, but Phil begins to have his first misgivings less than an hour later, in the taxi to LAX. Not about the feeling of clarity and the sudden energy it has given him, but about whether he is making the best use of it. There are things he's forgotten, like unformed words on the tip of his tongue. Things he needs to deal with, but he can't remember what they are.

He is still worrying at this, waiting in line at the check-in desk, when this bum appears right in front of him, and thrusts what seems like an unraveling baseball under Phil's nose.

It is a copy of the pirated novel: Phil's simmering anger reignites, and burns away every doubt.

It is a cheap paperback printed by some backstreet outfit in South Korea, the thin absorbent paper grainy with wood specks, a smudged picture of a castle silhouetted against the Japanese flag on the cover, his name far bigger than the title. Someone stole a copy of Phil's manuscript, the one he agreed to shelve, the one his publishers paid handsomely *not* to publish in one of those tricky deals Emmet is so good at. And some crook, it still isn't completely clear who, published this cheap completely illegal edition. Emmet told Phil about it a month ago, and Phil's publishers moved swiftly to get an injunction against its sale anywhere in the USA. But thousands of copies are in circulation anyway, smuggled into the country and sold clandestinely.

And the SFWA, Phil thinks, the Science Fiction Writers of America, Emmet is so right about them, the Swine Fucking Whores of Amerika, they may deny that they have anything to do with the pirate edition, but their bleatings about censorship and their insidious promotion of this blatant violation of my copyright proves they want to drag me down to their level.

Me: the greatest living American novelist. Erich Segal called me that only last month in a piece in *The New York Review of Books*; Updike joshed me about it during the round of golf we played the day after I gave that speech at Harvard. The greatest living American novelist: of course the SFWA want to claim me for their own propaganda purposes, to pump my life's blood into their dying little genre.

And now this creature has materialized before Phil, like some early version or failed species of human being, with blond hair tangled over his shoulders, a handlebar moustache, dressed in a buckskin jacket and faded blue jeans like Hollywood's idea of an Indian scout, a guitar slung over his shoulder, fraying black sneakers, or no, those are his *feet*, bare feet so filthy they look like busted shoes. And smelling of pot smoke and powerful sweat.

This aborigine, this indigent, his hand thrust towards Phil, and a copy of the stolen novel in that hand, as he says, "I love this book, man. It tells it like it is. The little men, man, that's who count, right? Little men, man, like you and me. So could you like *sign* this for me if it's no hassle..."

And Phil is seized by righteous anger and great wrath, and he smites his enemy right there, by the American Airlines First Class check-in desk. Or at least he grabs the book and tears it in half—the broken spine yielding easily, almost gratefully—and tells the bum to fuck off. Oh, just imagine the scene, the bum whining about his book, his property, and Phil telling the creature he doesn't deserve to read any of his books, he is *banned for life* from reading his books, and two security guards coming and hustling the bum away amid apologies to the Great American Novelist. The bum doesn't go quietly. He screams and struggles, yells that he, Phil, is a fake, a sell-out, man, the guitar clanging and chirping like a mocking grasshopper as he is wrestled away between the two burly, beetling guards.

Phil has to take a couple of Ritalin pills to calm down. To calm his blood down. Then a couple of uppers so he can face the journey.

He still has the book. Torn in half, pages frazzled by reading and rereading slipping out of it every time he opens it, so that he has to spend some considerable time sorting them into any kind of order, like a conjuror gripped by stage flop sweat in the middle of a card trick, before he can even contemplate looking at it.

Emmet said it all. What kind of commie fag organization would try to blast Phil's reputation with this cheap shot fired under radar? Circulating it on the campuses of America, poisoning the young minds who should be drinking deep clear drafts of his prose. Not this... this piece of dreck.

The Man in the High Castle. A story about an author locked in the fortress of his reputation, a thinly disguised parable about his own situation, set in a parallel or alternate history where the USA lost the war and was split into two, the East governed by the

Nazis, the West by the Japanese. A trifle, a silly fantasy. What had
he been thinking when he wrote it? Emmet was furious when Phil
sent him the manuscript. He wasted no words in telling Phil how
badly he had fucked up, asking him bluntly, what the hell did he
think he was doing, wasting his time with this lame sci-fi crap?

Phil had been stuck, that's what. And he's still stuck. Ten,
fifteen years of writing and rewriting, two marriages made and
broken while Phil works on and on at the same book, moving
farther and farther away from his original idea, so far out now he
thinks he might never get back. The monster doesn't even have a
title. *The Long Awaited. The Brilliant New. The Great
Unfinished.* Whatever. And in the midst of this mire, Phil set aside
the Next Great Novel and pulled a dusty idea from his files—
dating back to 1961, for Chrissake—and something clicked. He
wrote it straight out, a return to the old days of churning out sci-
fi stories for tiny amounts of money while righteously high on
speed: cranked up, cranking out the pages. For a little while he was
so happy: just the idea of finishing something made him happy.
But Emmet made him see the error of his ways. Made him see that
you can't go back and start over. Made him see the depth of his
error, the terrible waste of his energy and his talent.

That's when Phil, prompted by a research paper he discovered, started on a high-protein low-carbohydrate diet, started
dosing himself with high levels of water soluble vitamins.

And then the pirated edition of *The Man in the High Castle*
appeared, and Emmet started over with his needling recrimina-
tions and insinuations, whipping up in Phil a fine hot sweat of
shame and fury.

Phil puts the thing back in his coat pocket. Leans back in his
leather-upholstered First Class seat. Sips his silvery martini. The
anger is still burning inside him. For the moment he has forgotten
his doubts. Straight to the top, that's the only answer. Straight to
the President.

After a while, he buzzes the stewardess and gets some writing
paper. Takes out his gold-nibbed, platinum-cased Cross fountain

pen, the pen his publishers gave him to mark the publication of the
ten millionth copy of the ground-breaking, genre-busting *The
Grasshopper Lies Heavy*. Starts to write:

> *Dear Mr President: I would like to introduce myself. I am*
> *Philip K. Dick and admire and have great respect for your*
> *office. I talked to Deputy Narcotics Director Finlator last*
> *week and expressed my concern for our country…*

♓

Things go smoothly, as if the light has opened some kind of path,
as if it has tuned Phil's brain, eliminated all the dross and kipple
clogging it. Phil flies to Washington, D.C., and immediately hires
a car, a clean light blue Chrysler with less than a thousand miles on
the clock, and drives straight to the White House.

Because there is no point in posting the letter. That would take
days, and it might never reach the President. All Phil would get
back would be a photograph signed by one of the autograph
machines that whir ceaselessly in some White House basement…

No, the thing to do is subvert the chain of command, the
established order. So Phil drives to the White House: to the White
House gate. Where he gives the letter to one of the immaculately
turned out Marine guards.

> *Because of an act of wanton piracy, Sir, the young people,*
> *the Black Panthers etc etc do not consider me their enemy*
> *or as they call it The Establishment. Which I call America.*
> *Which I love. Sir, I can and will be of any Service that I*
> *can to help the country out. I have done an in depth study*
> *of Drug Abuse and Communist Brainwashing*
> *Techniques…*

Phil walking up to the White House gates in the damp March
chill, handing the letter, written on American Airlines notepaper

and sealed in an American Airlines envelope, to the Marine. While still buzzing from the uppers he dropped in the LAX washroom.

And driving away to find the hotel he's booked himself into.

Everything going down smoothly. Checking in. Washing up in his room. Wondering if he should use the room menu or find a restaurant, when the phone rings. It's his agent. Emmet is downstairs in the lobby. Emmet wants to know what the hell he's up to.

And suddenly Phil is struck by another flash of light, igniting at the centre of his panic, and by the terrible thought that he is on the wrong path.

♓

Phil's agent, Anthony Emmet, is smart and ferocious and tremendously ambitious. A plausible and worldly guy who, as he likes to put it, found Phil under a stone one day in the early '50s, when Phil was banging out little sci-fi stories for a living and trying to write straight novels no one wanted to publish. Emmet befriended Phil, guided him, mentored him, argued with him endlessly. Because (he said) he knew Phil had it in him to be huge if he would only quit puttering around with the sci-fi shit. He persuaded Phil to terminate his relationship with the Scott Meredith Agency, immediately sold Phil's mainstream novel *Voices from the Street* to a new publishing outfit, Dynmart, guided Phil through endless rewrites. And *Voices*, the odyssey of a young man who tries to escape an unfulfilling job and a failing marriage, who is seduced by socialists, fascists and hucksters, but at last finds redemption by returning to the life he once scorned, made it big: it sold over two hundred thousand copies in hardback, won the Pulitzer Prize and the National Book Critics Circle Award, was made into a movie starring Leslie Carron and George Peppard.

But the long struggle with *Voices* blocked or jammed something in Phil. After the deluge, a trickle: a novel about interned

Japanese in the Second World War, *The Grasshopper Lies Heavy*, which received respectful but baffled reviews; a slim novella, *Earthshaker*, cannibalised from an old unpublished novel. And then stalled silence, Phil paralyzed by the weight of his reputation while his slim oeuvre continued to multiply out there in the world, yielding unexpected translations in Basque and Turkish, the proceedings of a symposium on the work of Philip K. Dick and Upton Sinclair, an Australian mini-series that blithely transposed the interned Japanese of *The Grasshopper Lies Heavy* into plucky colonial prisoners of war.

Phil hasn't seen his agent for ten years. It seems to him that Emmet still looks as implausibly young as he did the day they first met, his skin smooth and taut and flawless, as if made of some material superior to ordinary human skin, his keen black eyes glittering with intelligence, his black hair swept back, his black silk suit and white silk shirt sharp, immaculate, his skinny black silk tie knotted just so. He looks like a '50s crooner, a mob hitman; he looks right at home in the plush, candlelit red leather booth of the hotel bar, nursing a tall glass of seltzer and trying to understand why Phil wants to see the President.

"I'm on the case about the piracy," Emmet tells Phil. "There's absolutely nothing to worry about. I'm going to make this—" he touches the frazzled book on the table with a minatory forefinger, "—go away. Just like I made that short story collection Berkley wanted to put out go away. I have people on this day and night," Emmet says, with a glint of dark menace. "The morons responsible for this outrage are going to be very sorry. Believe me."

"I thought it was about the book," Phil says. He's sweating heavily; the red leather booth is as snug and hot as a glove, or a cocoon. "But now I'm not sure—"

"You're agitated, and I completely understand. A horrible act of theft like this would unbalance anyone. And you've been self-medicating again. Ritalin, those huge doses of vitamins..."

"There's nothing wrong with the vitamins," Phil says. "I got the dosages from *Psychology Today*."

"In a paper about treating a kid with schizophrenic visions," Emmet says. "I know all about it. No wonder you're agitated. Last week, I understand, you called the police and asked to be arrested because you were, what was it? A machine with bad thoughts."

Phil is dismayed about the completeness of Emmet's information. He says, "I suppose Mike told you about that."

Mike is Phil's driver and handyman, installed in a spartan little apartment over Phil's three-door garage.

Emmet says, "Of course Mike told me that. He and I, we have your interests at heart. You have to trust us, Phil. You left without even telling Mike where you were going. It would have taken a lot of work to find you, except I just happen to be in Washington on business."

"I don't need any help," Phil tells Emmet. "I know exactly what I'm doing."

But he's not so sure now that he does. When the light hit him he knew with absolute certainty that something was wrong with his life. That he had to do something about it. He fixed on the first thing that had come into his head, but now he wonders again if it is the right thing. Maybe, he thinks unhappily, I'm going deeper into what's wrong. Maybe I'm moving in the wrong direction, chasing the wrong enemy.

Emmet, his psychic antennae uncannily sensitive, picks up on this. He says, "You know *exactly* what to do? My God, I'm glad one of us does, because we need every bit of help to get you out of this mess. Now what's this about a letter?"

Phil explains with great reluctance. Emmet listens gravely and says, "Well, I think it's containable."

"I thought that if I got a badge, I could get things done," Phil says. The martini he's drinking now is mixing strangely with the martinis he drank in the air, with the speed and Ritalin he took in LAX, the speed he took just now in his hotel bedroom. He feels a reckless momentum, feels as if he's flying right there in the snug, hot booth.

"You've got to calm down, Phil," Emmet says. Candlelight glitters in his dark eyes as he leans forward. They look like exquisite gems, Phil thinks, cut with a million microscopic facets. Emmet says, "You're coming up to fifty, and you aren't out of your mid-life crisis yet. You're thrashing around, trying this, trying that, when you just have to put your trust in me. And you really shouldn't be mixing Ritalin and Methedrin, you know that's contraindicated."

Phil doesn't try to deny it; Emmet always knows the truth. He says, "It's as if I've woken up. As if I've been dreaming my life, and now I've woken up and discovered that none of it was real. As if a veil, what the Greeks call *dokos*, the veil between me and reality has been swept away. Everything connects, Emmet," Phil says, picking up the book and waving it in his agent's face. Loose pages slip out, flutter to the table or to the floor. "You know why I have this book? I took it from some bum who came up to me in the airport. Call that coincidence?"

"I'd say it was odd that he gave you the copy I gave you," Emmet says. "The agency stamp is right there on the inside of the cover." As Phil stares at the purple mark, he adds, "You're stressed out, Phil, and that weird diet of yours has made things worse, not better. The truth is, you don't need to do anything except leave it all to me. If you're honest, isn't this all a complicated ploy to distract yourself from your real work? You should go back to LA tonight, there's a Red Eye that leaves in two-and-a-half hours. Go back to LA and go back to work. Leave everything else to me."

While he talks, Emmet's darkly glittering gaze transfixes Phil like an entomologist's pin, and Phil feels that he is shriveling in the warm darkness, while around him the noise of conversation and the chink of glasses and the tinkle of the piano increase, merging into a horrid chittering buzz.

"I hate this kind of jazz," Phil says feebly. "It's so goddamn fake, all those ornate trills and runs that don't actually add up to anything. It's like, at LAX, the soupy strings they play there."

"It's just background music, Phil. It calms people." Emmet fishes the slice of lemon from his mineral water and pops it in his mouth and chews, his jaw moving from side to side.

"Calms people. Yeah, that's absolutely right. It deadens them, Emmet. Turns them into fakes, into inauthentic people. It's all over airwaves now, there's nothing left but elevator music. And as for TV... It's the corporations, Emmet, they have it down to a science. See, if you pacify people, take away all the jagged edges, all the individualism, the stuff that makes us human—what have you got? You have androids, docile machines. All the kids want to do now is get a good college degree, get a good job, earn money. There's no spark in them, no adventure, no curiosity, no rebellion, and that's just how the corporations like it. Everything predictable because it's good for business, everyone hypnotized. A nation of perfect, passive consumers."

Emmet says, "Is that part of your dream? Christ, Phil. We really do need to get you on that Red Eye. Away from this nonsense, before any real damage is done. Back to your routine. Back to your work."

"This is more important, Emmet. I really do feel as if I'm awake for the first time in years."

A man approaches their booth, a tall overweight man in a shiny grey suit and cowboy boots, black hair swept back and huge sideburns framing his jowly face. He looks oddly bashful for a big man and he's clutching something—the paperback of *The Grasshopper Lies Heavy*. He says to Phil, "I hope you don't mind, sir, but I would be honored if you would sign this for me."

"We're busy," Emmet says, barely glancing at the man, but the man persists.

"I realize that, sir, so I only ask for a moment of your time."

"We're having a business meeting," Emmet says, with such concentrated vehemence that the man actually takes a step backward.

"Hey, it's okay," Phil says, and reaches out for the book—the man must have bought it in the hotel shop, the price sticker is still on the cover—uncaps his pen, asks the man's name.

The man blinks slowly. "Just your signature, sir, would be fine."

He has a husky baritone voice, a deep-grained Southern accent.

Phil signs, hands back the book, a transaction so familiar he hardly has to think about it.

The man is looking at Emmet, not the signed book. He says, "Do I know you, sir?"

"Not at all," Emmet says sharply.

"I think it's just that you look like my old probation officer," the man says. "I was in trouble as a kid, hanging about downtown with the wrong crowd. I had it in my head to be a musician, and well, I got into a little fix with the law. I was no more than sixteen, and my probation officer, Mr. McFly, he straightened me right out. I own a creme donut business now, that's why I'm here in Washington. We're opening up a dozen new franchises. People surely do love our deep-fried creme donuts. Well, good day to you, sir," he tells Phil, "I'm glad to have met you. If you'll forgive the presumption, I always thought you and me had something in common. We both of us have a dead twin, you see."

"Jesus," Phil says, when the man has gone. The last remark has shaken him.

"You're famous," Emmet tells him. "People know stuff about you, you shouldn't be surprised by now. He knows about your dead sister, so what? He read it in a magazine somewhere, that's all."

"He thought he knew you, too."

"Everyone looks like someone else," Emmet says, "especially to dumb-ass shit-kickers. Christ, now what?"

Because a waiter is standing there, holding a white telephone on a tray. He says, "There's a phone call for Mr. Dick," and plugs the phone in and holds the receiver out to Phil.

Even before Emmet peremptorily takes the phone, smoothly slipping the waiter a buck, Phil knows that it's the White House.

Emmet listens, says, "I don't think it's a good idea," listens some more, says, "He's not calm at all. Who is this Chapin? Not one of—no, I didn't think he was. Haldeman says that, huh? It went all the way up? Okay. Yes, if Haldeman says so, but you better be sure of it," he says, and sets down the receiver with an angry click and tells Phil, "That was Egil Krogh, at the White House. It seems you have a meeting with the President, at 12.30 tomorrow afternoon. I'll only ask you this once, Phil. Don't fuck up."

⌘

So now Phil is in the White House—in the anteroom to the Oval Office, a presentation copy of *Voices from the Street* under his arm, heavy as a brick. He's speeding, too, and knows Emmet knows it, and doesn't care.

He didn't sleep well last night. Frankly, he didn't sleep at all. Taking a couple more tabs of speed didn't help. His mind racing. Full of weird thoughts, connections. Thinking especially about androids and people. The androids are taking over, he thinks, no doubt about it. The suits, the haircuts, the four permitted topics of conversation: sports, weather, TV, work. Christ, how could I not have seen it before?

He scribbles notes to himself, uses up the folder of complementary hotel stationery. Trying to get it down. To get it straight. Waves of anger and regret and anxiety surge through him.

Maybe, he thinks in dismay, I myself have become an android, dreaming for a few days that I'm really human, seeing things that aren't there, like the bum at the airport. Until they come for me, and take me to the repair shop. Or junk me, the way you'd junk a broken toaster.

Except the bum seemed so real, even if he was a dream, like a vision from a reality more vibrant than this. Suppose there is another reality: another history, the real history. And suppose that history has been erased by the government or the corporations or whatever, by entities which can reach back and smooth out the actions of individuals which might reveal or upset their plan to transform everyone and everything into bland androids in a dull grey completely controlled world...

It's like one of the weird ideas he used to write up when he was churning out sci-fi stories, but that doesn't mean it isn't true. Maybe back then he was unconsciously tapping into some flow of greater truth: the truth he should deliver to the President. Maybe this is his mission. Phil suddenly has a great desire to read in his pirated novel, but it isn't in his jacket pocket, and it isn't in his room.

"I got rid of it," Emmet tells him over breakfast.

"You got rid of it?"

"Of course I did. Should you be eating that, Phil?"

"I like Canadian bacon. I like maple syrup. I like pancakes."

"I'm only thinking of your blood pressure," Emmet says. He is methodically demolishing a grapefruit.

"What about all the citrus fruit you eat? All that acid can't be good for you."

"It's cleansing," Emmet says calmly. "You should at least drink the orange juice I ordered for you, Phil. It has vitamins."

"Coffee is all I need," Phil says. The tumbler of juice, which was sitting at the table when he arrived, seems to give off a poisonous glow, as of radioactivity.

Emmet shrugs. "Then I think we're finished with breakfast aren't we? Let's get you straightened out. You can hardly meet the President dressed like that."

But for once Phil stands his ground. He picked out these clothes because they felt right, and they're what he's going to wear. They argue for ten minutes, compromise by adding a tie Emmet buys in the hotel shop.

They are outside, waiting for the car to be brought around, when Phil hears the music. He starts walking, prompted by some

unconscious impulse he doesn't want to analyze. Go with the
flow, he thinks. Don't impose anything on top of it just because
you're afraid. Because you've been *made* afraid. Trust in the
moment.

Emmet follows angrily, asking Phil what the *hell* he thinks he's
doing all the way to the corner, where a bum is standing with a
broken old guitar, singing one of that folk singer's songs, the guy
who died of an overdose on the same night Lenny Bruce died, the
song about changing times.

There's a paper cup at the bum's feet, and Phil impulsively
stuffs half a dozen bills into it, bills which Emmet snatches up
angrily.

"Get lost," he tells the bum, and starts pulling at Phil, dragging
him away as if Phil is a kid entranced beyond patience at the
window of a candy store. Saying, "What are you thinking?"

"That it's cold," Phil says, "and someone like that—a street
person—could use some hot food."

"He's isn't a person," Emmet says. "He's a bum—a piece of
trash. And of course it's cold. It's March. Look at you, dressed like
that. *You're* shivering."

He is. But it isn't because of the cold.

March, Phil thinks now, in the antechamber to the Oval
Office. The Vernal Equinox. When the world awakes. Shivering
all over again even though the brightly lit anteroom, with its two
desks covered, it seems, in telephones, is stiflingly hot. Emmet is
schmoozing with two suits—H.R. Haldeman and Egil Krogh.
Emmet is holding Haldeman's arm as he talks, speaking into the
man's ear, something or other about management. They all know
each other well, Phil thinks, and wonders what kind of business
Emmet has, here in Washington, D.C.

At last a phone rings, a secretary nods, and they go into the
Oval Office, which really is oval. The President, smaller and more
compact than he seems on TV, strides out from behind his desk
and cracks a jowly smile, but his pouchy eyes slither sideways
when he limply shakes hands with Phil.

"That's quite a letter you sent us," the President says.

"I'm not sure," Phil starts to say, but the President doesn't seem to hear him.

"Quite a letter, yes. And of course we need people like you, Mr. Dick. We're proud to have people like you, in fact. Someone who can speak to young people—well, that's important isn't it?" Smiling at the other men in the room as if seeking affirmation. "It's quite a talent. You have one of your books there, I think?"

Phil holds out the copy of *Voices from the Street*. It's the Franklin Library edition, bound in green leather, his signature reproduced in gold on the cover, under the title. An aide gave it him when he arrived, and now he hands it to the President, who takes it in a study of reverence.

"You must sign it," the President says, and lays it open like a sacrificial victim on the gleaming desk, by the red and white phones. "I mean, that's the thing isn't it? The thing that you do?"

Phil says, "What I came to do—"

And Emmet says, "Of course he'll sign, sir. It's an honor."

Emmet gives Phil a pen, and Phil signs, his hand sweating on the page. He says, "I came here, sir, to say that I want to do what I can for America. I was given an experience a day ago, and I'm beginning to understand what it meant."

But the President doesn't seem to have heard him. He's staring at Phil as if seeing him for the first time. At last, he blinks and says, "Boy, you do dress kind of wild."

Phil is wearing his lucky Nehru jacket over a gold shirt, purple velvet pants with flares that mostly hide his sand-colored suede desert boots. And the tie that Emmet bought him in the hotel shop, a paisley affair like the President's, tight as a leash around his neck.

He starts to say, "I came here, sir," but the President says again, "You do dress kind of wild. But that I guess is the style of all writers isn't it? I mean, an individual style."

For a moment, the President's eyes, pinched between fleshy pouches, start to anxiously search Phil's face. It seems that there's something trapped far down at the bottom of his mild gaze, like a prisoner looking up through the grill of an oubliette at the sky.

"Individual style, that's exactly it," Phil says, seeing an opening, a way into his theme. The thing he knows now he needs to say, distilled from the scattered notes and thoughts last night. "Individualism, sir, that's what it's all about, isn't it? Even men in suits wear ties to signify that they still have this one little outlet for their individuality." It occurs to him that his tie is exactly like the President's, but he plunges on. "I'm beginning to understand that things are changing in America, and that's what I want to talk about—"

"You wanted a badge," Haldeman says brusquely. "A federal agent's badge, isn't that right? A badge to help your moral crusade?"

Emmet and Haldeman and Krogh grinning as if sharing a private joke.

"The badge isn't important," Phil says. "In fact, as I see it now, it's exactly what's wrong."

Haldeman says, "I certainly think we can oblige, can't we, Mr. President? We can get him his badge. You know, as a gift."

The President blinks. "A badge? I don't know if I have one, but I can look, certainly—"

"You don't have one," Haldeman says firmly.

"I don't?" The President has bent to pull open a drawer in the desk, and now he looks up, still blinking.

"But we'll order one up," Haldeman says, and tells Emmet, "Yes, a special order."

Something passes between them. Phil is sure of it. The air is so hot and heavy he feels that he's wrapped in mattress stuffing, and there's a sharp taste to it that stings the back of his throat.

Haldeman tells the President, "You remember the idea? The idea about the book."

"Yes," the President says, "the idea about the book."

His eyes seem to be blinking independently, like a mechanism that's slightly out of adjustment.

"The neat idea," Haldeman prompts, as if to a recalcitrant or shy child, and Phil knows then, knows with utter deep black conviction, that the President is not the President. Or he is, but he's long ago been turned into a fake of himself, a shell thing, a mechanical puppet. That was what I was becoming, Phil thinks, until the clear white light. And it might still happen to me, unless I make things change.

"The neat idea," the President says, and his mouth twitches. It's meant to be a smile, but looks like a spasm. "Yes, here's the thing, that you could write a book for the kids, for the, you know, for the young people. On the theme of, of—"

"'Get High on Life'," Haldeman says.

"'Get High on Life'," the President says. "Yes, that's right," and begins a spiel about affirming the conviction that true and lasting talent is the result of self motivation and discipline; he might be one of those mechanical puppets in Disneyland, running through its patter regardless of whether or not it has an audience.

"Well," Haldeman says, when the President finishes or perhaps runs down, "I think we're done here."

"The gifts," the President says, and bends down and pulls open a drawer and starts rummaging in it. "No one can accuse Dick Nixon of not treating his guests well," he says, and lays on the desk, one after the other, a glossy pre-signed photograph, cuff links, an ashtray, highball glasses etched with a picture of the White House.

Emmet says, "Thank you, Mr. President. Mr. Dick and I are truly honored to have met you."

But the President doesn't seem to hear. He's still rummaging in his desk drawer, muttering, "There are some neat pins in here. Lapel pins, very smart."

Haldeman and Emmet exchange glances, and Haldeman says, "We're about out of time here, Mr. President."

"Pins, that's the thing. Like this one," the President says, touching the lapel of his suit, "with the American flag. I did have some..."

"We'll find them," Haldeman says, that sharpness back in his voice, and he steers the President away from the desk, towards Phil.

There's an awkward minute while Egil Krogh takes photographs of the President and Phil shaking hands there on the blue carpet bordered with white stars, in front of furled flags on poles. Flashes of light that are only light from the camera flash. Phil blinks them away as Emmet leads him out, through ordinary offices and blank corridors to chill air under a grey sky where their car is waiting.

"It went well," Emmet says, after a while. He's driving the car—the car Phil hired—back to the hotel.

Phil says, "Who are you, exactly? What do you want?"

"I'm your agent, Phil. I take care of you. That's my job."

"And that other creature, your friend Haldeman, he takes care of the President."

"The President, he's a work of art isn't he? He'll win his third term, and the next one too. A man like that, he's too useful to let go. Unlike you, Phil, he can still help us."

"He was beaten," Phil says, "in 1960. By Kennedy. And in 1962 he lost the election for governor of California. Right after the results were announced, he said he would give up politics. And then something happened. He came back. Or was he brought back, is that what it was? A wooden horse," Phil says, feeling hollow himself, as empty as a husk. "Brought by the Greeks as a gift."

"He won't get beaten again," Emmet says, "you can count on that. Not in 1976, not in 1980, not in 1984. It worked out, didn't it—you and him?" He smiles, baring his perfect white teeth. "We should get you invited to one of the parties there. Maybe when you finish your book, it'll be great publicity."

"You don't want me to finish the book," Phil says. He feels as if he's choking, and wrenches at the knot of his tie. "That's the point. Whatever I was supposed to do—you made sure I didn't do it."

"Phil, Phil, Phil," Emmet says. "Is this another of your wild conspiracy theories? What is it this time, a conspiracy of boring, staid suits, acting in concert to stifle creative guys like you? Well, listen up, buddy. There is no conspiracy. There's nothing but a bunch of ordinary guys doing an honest day's work, making the world a better place, the best way they know how. You think we're dangerous? Well, take a look at yourself, Phil. You've got everything you ever dreamed about, and you got it all thanks to me. If it wasn't for me, you'd be no better than a bum on the street. You'd be living in a cold-water walk-up, banging out porno novels or sci-fi trash as fast you could, just to keep the power company from switching off your lights. And moaning all the while that you could have been a contender. Get real, Phil. I gave you a good deal. The best."

"Like the deal that guy, the guy at the hotel, the donut guy, got? He was supposed to be a singer, and someone just like you did something to him."

"He could have changed popular music," Emmet says. "Even as a donut shop operator he still has something. But would he have been any happier? I don't think so. And that's all I'm going to say, Phil. Don't ever ask again. Go back to your nice house, work on your book, and don't make trouble. Or, if you're not careful, you might be found dead one day from vitamin poisoning, or maybe a drug overdose."

"Yeah, like the folk singer," Phil says.

"Or a car crash," Emmet says, "like the one that killed Kerouac and Burroughs and Ginsberg in Mexico. It's a cruel world out there, Phil, and even though you're washed-up as a writer, be thankful that you have me to look after your interests."

"Because you want to make sure I don't count for anything," Phil says, and finally opens the loop of the tie wide enough to be able to drag it over his head. He winds down the window and drops the tie into the cold gritty wind.

"You stupid bastard," Emmet says, quite without anger. "That cost six bucks fifty. Pure silk, a work of art."

"I feel sick," Phil says, and he does feel sick, but that's not why he says it.

"Not in the car," Emmet says sharply, and pulls over to the kerb. Phil opens the door, and then he's running and Emmet is shouting after him. But Phil runs on, head down in the cold wind, and doesn't once look back.

He has to slow to a walk after a couple of blocks, out of breath, his heart pounding, his legs aching. The cold, steely air scrapes the bottoms of his lungs. But he's given Emmet the slip. Or perhaps Emmet doesn't really care. After all, he's been ruined as a writer, his gift dribbled away on dead books until nothing is left.

Except for that one book, Phil thinks. *The Man in the High Castle*. The book Emmet conspired to suppress, the book he made me hate so much because it was the kind of thing I was meant to write all along. Because I would have counted for something, in the end. I would have made a difference.

He walks on, with no clear plan except to keep moving. It's a poor neighborhood, even though it's only a few blocks from the White House. Despite the cold, people are sitting on the steps of the shabby apartment houses, talking to each other, sharing bottles in brown paper bags. An old man with a terrific head of white hair and a tremendously bushy white moustache sits straight-backed on a kitchen chair, smoking a cheap cigar with all the relish of the king of the world. Kids in knitted caps and plaid jackets bounce a basketball against a wall, calling to each other in clear, high voices. There is warm yellow light at most windows, and the odors of cooking in the air. A good odor, Phil thinks, a homely, human odor. A radio tuned to a country station is playing one of the old time ballads, a slow, achingly sad song about a rose and a briar twining together above a grave.

It's getting dark, and flakes of snow begin to flutter down, seeming to condense out of the darkening air, falling in a slanting rush. Phil feels the pinpoint kiss of every flake that touches his face.

I'm still a writer, he thinks, as he walks through the falling snow. I still have a name. I still have a voice. I can still tell the truth. Maybe that journalist who interviewed me last month, the one who works for the *Washington Post*, maybe he'll listen to me if I tell him about the conspiracy in the White House.

A bum is standing on the corner outside the steamed window of a diner. An old, fat woman with a mottled, flushed, face, grey hair cut as short as a soldier's. Wearing a stained and torn man's raincoat that's too small for her, so that the newspapers she's wrapped around her body to keep out the cold peep between the straining buttons. Her blue eyes are bright, watching each passerby with undiminished hope as she rattles a few pennies in a paper cup.

Phil pushes into the diner's steamy warmth and uses the pay phone, and then orders coffee to go. And returns to the street, and presses the warm container into his sister's hand.

RESIDUALS

With Kim Newman

O
n his way out, the motel guy switches on the TV and the AC without bothering to ask if I want either. The unit over the door rattles and starts to drip on the purple shag carpet. On a dusty screen, a cowboy hunkers down over the Sci-Fi Channel station ident, squinting from under a Stetson. It ought to be like looking at myself, because the cowboy is supposed to be me. But it's not.

The Omega Encounter is always playing somewhere on a rerun channel, I guess, but here and now it's like an omen.

I'm still living off the *Omega* residuals because it's *my* version of what went down, officially adapted from the "as told to" book Jay Anson did for me. Nyquist sold *Starlight*, the book Tom Fuckin' Wolfe wrote with him, for twenty times as much to Universal.

There's a little skip where there used to be a shot of a flyblown, bloodied rubber cow carcass. It could be a censor cut or a snip to reduce the running time. When E.W. Swackhamer directed *Omega*, there were thirteen minutes of commercials in an hour of TV; now there are eighteen, so four minutes of each hour have to be lost from everything made before the nineties.

I don't unpack, except for the bottles of Cuevero Gold Tequila I bought at the airport, and sit up on the bed, watching two days of my life processed and packaged as a sixteen-year-old movie of the week.

It's gotten to the part where I find the first of the mutilated cattle. I'm showing one to Mr Nyquist, played by Dennis Weaver the way he plays McCloud, shrewd and upright. To tell the truth Nyquist was always half drunk even before it all started, and had a mean streak in him that was nothing to do with drink. The bastard would hit Susan when he was in the bag, going off like a firecracker over the slightest thing and stomping out, banging the screen door hard, leaving her clutching her cheek and me looking down at my dinner. He was crazy even then, I guess, but still able to hold it down.

The movie makes me a lot more talkative than I ever was around Nyquist. Susan is Cybill Shepherd in her post-*Last Picture Show*, pre-*Moonlighting* career slump. I am Jan-Michael Vincent in his post-birth, pre-death career trough.

I watch until I follow the slime trails in the grass and see the lights of the mothership off in the distance hovering above the slough, and then I flip channels because I can't stand to watch anymore.

They didn't have the budget to do the aliens right on TV and only used long shots, but I still don't want to watch. I can take the expensive computer-controlled models in the movie because they're too real in the way Main Street on Disneyland is too real. So perfect a reproduction it doesn't fool anyone for a second. But show me a couple of out-of-focus midgets jumping around inside silvered plastic bags in slow motion with the setting sun behind them, and my imagination fills in the blanks. The sour reek. And the noise the things made as they hopped around, like they were filled with jello and broken bones.

QVC is less of a blow to the heart. I drink tequila out of the bathroom glass and consider calling a toll-free number to order a zircon chandelier. Then I drink some more and decide against it.

Despite Steven Spielberg, Harrison Ford (as Nyquist), and five million preinflation bucks of ILM, *Starlight: The Motion Picture* was a box office disappointment. By the time the effects were developed, *Omega* had spun off a mid-season replacement series with Sam Groom (as me) and Gretchen Corbett that got cancelled after three episodes. The aliens were old news, and everybody knew how the story came out. In *Starlight*, I'm rewritten as a codger farmhand who sacrifices himself for Boss Man Ford, stealing the film with a dignified death scene. Richard Farnsworth got an Oscar nomination for Best Supporting Actor, but lost out to the gook in *The Killing Fields*.

I give up TV and call my agent, using the room phone because my mobile doesn't want to work out here in the desert, all that radar, or the microwave signals they send to the secret Moon colony (ha ha), and I tell him where I am. He says to watch my ass, and that when I get back he thinks he might have another hardware store commercial lined up ("Fix your Starship, lady?"). It's just for New York cable but it'll pay the rent a while. He doesn't think I can pull off this reunion, is what it is, and I tell him that and then I hang up and I watch an old *Saturday Night Live* for a while.

I was on one show for about five minutes, in a Conehead episode with Dan Ackroyd and Jane Curtin. Can't hardly remember that night—I was drunk at the time—but now I guess those five minutes are always showing somewhere, just like everything else that ever went through a transmitter. If aliens out there have been monitoring our broadcasts like they did in old movies to explain why they speak perfect English, just about the first question we'd ask them was if they taped those lost episodes of *The Honeymooners*. I watch Chevy Chase do Gerry Ford falling over just about everything in the studio set, and drink some more tequila and fall asleep a while.

It's been a long day, the flight out from New York delayed two hours, then a long drive through Los Angeles, where I've never driven because I was chauffeured around when all the deals were in the air, and which is ten times more packed with traffic than I remember, and out into the high desert along Pearblossom Highway with all the big trucks driving in bright sunlight and blowing dust with their headlights on.

The phone wakes me up. I use the remote to turn down Dave Letterman, and pick up. A voice I haven't heard for twenty years says, "Hello, Ray."

⋈

At first, only the *Enquirer* and the *Weekly World News* were interested. But when the reports came back and the FBI slapped a security classification on them, and Elliot Mitchell started making a fuss because he was transferred to the Texas panhandle and his field notes and his twenty rolls of film and six hours of cassette recordings were "lost", *Newsweek* and *Rolling Stone* showed up. Tom Wicker's piece in *Rolling Stone* said it was all part of a government plot stretching back to Roswell, and that the US Army was covering up tests with hallucinogenic weapons.

Then the artefacts went on view, and ten types of expert testified they were "non-terrestrial". It wasn't a government conspiracy any more, it was a goddamn alien invasion, just like Nyquist and me had been saying. Mitchell had rewritten his field notes from memory, and sent photocopies to *Science* and *Nature*. He even got his name as discoverer on the new hyperstable transuranic element, which along with the bodies was one of the few tangible residues of the whole thing. I wonder how he felt when Mitchellite was used in the Gulf War to add penetrative power to artillery shells.

Then the *Washington Post* got behind the story, and all the foreign press, and the shit hit the fan. For a while, it was all anybody talked about. We got to meet President Carter, who made a statement supporting our side of things, and declared he would see that no information was withheld from the public.

I was on *The Tonight Show* with Johnny Carson, back when
that meant something. I did Dick Cavett, *CBS News* with Walter
Cronkite, *60 Minutes* with Mike Wallace, *NBC Weekend News*
with Jessica Savitch. Me and Nyquist were scurrying to get our
book deals sorted out, then our screen rights. People were
crawling all over, desperate to steal our lives, and we went right
along with the feeding frenzy.

We wrapped each other up with restraints and gag orders, and
shot off our mouths all the time. Mitchell was out of the loop:
instead of deals with Hollywood producers and long lunches with
New York publishers, he got tied up in a civil liberties suit because
he tried to resign from the US geological survey and the government wouldn't let him.

Then the Ayatollah took the hostages, and everyone had
something else to worry about. Carter became a hostage in his
own White House and most of the artefacts disappeared in the C-
130 aircrash conspiracy theorists said had been staged by FBI
black ops. Reagan never said anything on record, but the official
line changed invisibly when he became President. The reports on
the reports questioned the old findings, and deposits of
Mitchellite showed up on Guam and somewhere in Alaska.

I did *Geraldo* with Whitley Strieber and Carl Sagan, and came
off like a hick caught between a rock and a hard place. I had
started drinking by then, and tried to punch out one or the other
of them after the show, and spent the night in a downtown
holding tank. I faced a jury of sceptics on *Oprah* and was cut to
pieces, not by reasoned scientific arguments and rationalizations,
but by cheap shot jokes from a studio audience of stand-up
wannabes.

I told my side of it so many times that I caught myself
using exactly the same words each time, and I noticed that
on prerecorded shows, the presenter's nods and winks—always
shot from a reverse angle after the main interview—were
always cut in at exactly the same points. An encouraging dip of
the head laced with a concerned look in the eyes, made in reaction

to a cameraman's thumb, not an already-forgotten line from me.

Besides *The Omega Encounter* and *Starlight*, there were dozens of books, movies, TV specials, magazine articles, a Broadway play, even a music album. Creedence Clearwater Revival's "It Came Out of the Sky" was reissued and charted strongly. Some English band did a concept album. John Sladek and Tom Disch collaborated on a novel-length debunking, *The Sentients: A Tragi-Comedy*. That's in development as a movie, maybe with Fred Ward.

Sam Shepard's *Alienation*, which Ed Harris did on Broadway and Shepard starred in and directed for HBO, looked at it all from the dirt farmer's point of view, suggesting Nyquist and me were looking for fresh ways of being heroes since we'd lost touch with the land. The main character was a combination of the two of us and talked in paragraphs, and the scientist—Dean Stockwell on TV—was a black-hatted villain, which displeased Mitchell no end. He sued and lost, I recall.

By then I was looking at things through the blurry dimple at the bottom of the bottle, living off the residuals from commercials and guest appearances in rock videos and schlock direct-to-video horror movies shot by postmodernist *auteurs* just out of UCLA film school, though I recall that Sam Raimi's *The Color Out of Time* was kind of not bad.

Then I read in *Variety* that Oliver Stone has a treatment in development raking the whole thing all up, blaming it on J. Edgar Hoover, Armand Hammer and Henry Kissinger. There was an article in *The New York Times* that Norman Mailer had delivered his thousand-page summation of the phenomenon, *The Visitation*. And that's where I got the idea to get in touch with Mitchell and make some cash on the back of Stone's and Mailer's publicity, and maybe Mitchell had been reading the same articles, because before I can begin to think how to try and track him down, he calls me.

⋉

I drive past the place I'm to meet Mitchell and have to double back, squinting in the glare of the big rigs which roar out of the darkness, all strung up with fairylights like the spaceship in *Closer Encounters*. I do what sounds like serious damage to the underside of the rental when I finally pull off.

The ruins are close to the highway, but there's a spooky feel which makes me leave the car's headlights on. Out across the dark desert basin, where the runways of Edwards Air Force Base are outlined in patterns of red and green lights a dozen miles long, some big engine makes a long drawn out rumble that rises to a howl before cutting out.

I sit in the car and take a few pulls on my bottle to get some courage or at least burn away the flutter in my gut, looking at the arthritic shapes Joshua trees make in the car headlights. Then I make myself get out and look around. There's not much to the ruins, just a chimney stack and a line of pillars where maybe a porch stood. People camping out have left circles of ash in the sand and dented cans scattered around; when I stumble over a can and it rattles off a stone I realize how quiet the desert is, beyond the noise of the trucks on the highway. I get a feeling like the one I had when the three of us were waiting that last night before we blew up the mothership, and have to take another inch off the level of the tequila to calm down.

That's when my rental car headlights go out and I almost lose it, because that's what happened when they tried to kidnap me, the lights and then the dashboard of my pickup cutting off and then a bright light all around, coming from above. That time, I had a pump action shotgun on the rack in the cab, which is what saved me. Now, I have a tequila bottle with a couple of inches sloshing in it, and a rock I pick up.

A voice behind me says my name, and I spin and lose my balance and fall on my ass, the tequila bottle emptying over my pants leg. A flashlight beam pins me and behind it Elliot Mitchell says, "This was the last socialist republic in the USA, did you know that? They called the place Llano del Rio. This was their meeting hall. They built houses, a school, planted orchards. But the government gave their water rights to the local farmers and they had to move out. All that's left are the orchards, and those will go because they're subdividing the desert for housing tracts to take LA's overspill."

I squint into the light, but can't see anything of the man holding it.

"Never put your faith in government, Ray. Its first instinct is not to protect the people it's supposed to serve, but to look after its own self. People elect politicians, not governments. Don't get up. I'm happier to see you sitting down. Do you think you were followed here?"

"Why would I be followed? No one cares about it any more. That's why I'm here."

"You want to make another movie, Ray? Who is it with? Oliver Stone? He came out to see me. Or sent one of his researchers anyway. You know his father was in the Navy, don't you, and he's funded by the UN counterpropaganda unit, the same one that tried to assassinate Reagan. The question is, who's paying you?"

"Crazy Sam's Hardware back in Brooklyn, if I do the ad."

I have a bad feeling. Mitchell appears to have joined the right-wing nuts who believe that little black helicopters follow them everywhere, and that there are secret codes on the back of traffic signs to direct the UN invasion force when it comes.

I say, "I don't have any interest except the same one that made you want to call me. We saved the world, Elliot, and they're ripping off our story..."

"You let them. You and Nyquist. How is old Nyquist?"

"Sitting in a room with mattresses on the walls, wearing a backwards jacket and eating cold creamed corn. They made him the hero, when it was us who blew up the mothership, it was us who captured that stinking silver beachball, it was us who worked out how to poison most of them."

I put the bottle to my lips, but there's hardly a swallow left. I toss it away. This isn't going the way I planned, but I'm caught up in my anger. It's come right back, dull and heavy. I say, "We're the ones that saved Susan, not her lousy husband."

"We didn't save her, Ray. That was in your TV movie, *The Omega Encounter*. We got her back, but the things they'd put inside her killed her anyway."

"Well, we got her back, and if fuckin' Doc Jensen had listened we *would* have saved her, too."

I sit there, looking into the flashlight beam with drunken tears running down my face.

"How much do you remember, Ray? Not the movies, but the real thing? Do you remember how we got Susan out of the mothership?"

"I stay away from shopping malls, because they give me flashbacks. Maybe I'm as crazy as Nyquist. Sometimes, I dream I'm in one of those old-fashioned hedge mazes, like in *The Shining*. Sometimes, I'm trying to get out of the hospital they put us in afterwards. But it's always the same, you know?"

Mitchell switches off the flashlight. I squint into the darkness, but all I see is swimming afterimages.

"Come tomorrow," Mitchell says, and something thumps beside me.

It is a rock, with a piece of torn paper tied to it. Under the dome light of the rental car, I smooth out the paper and try to make sense of the map Mitchell has drawn.

)(

Two days. That's how long it took. Now, my life is split into Before and After. What no one gets is that the thing itself—the event, the encounter, the invasion, the incursion, the whatever—was over inside two days. I've had headcolds and bellyaches that lasted a whole lot longer. That's what marks me out. When I die, my obits will consist of three paragraphs about those two days and two sentences about everything else. Like I said about Jan-Michael, I have a post-birth, pre-death rut for a life. Except for those two days.

After about a decade, it got real old. It was as if everyone was quizzing me about some backyard baseball game I pitched in when I was a kid, blotting out all of the rest of my life—parents, job, marriages, kid, love, despair—with a couple of hours on the mound. I even tried clamming up, refusing to go through it all again for the anniversary features. I turned my back on those two days and tried to fix on something else worth talking about. I came close to making it with Adrienne Barbeau, didn't I? Or was it Heather Locklear? Or maybe it was only in one of the scripts and some actor played me. I was doing harder stuff than alcohol just then.

That phase lasted maybe three months. I was worn down in the end. I realized that I needed to tell it again. For me, as much as for everyone else. I was like those talking books in that Bradbury novel—yeah, I admit it, I read science fiction when I was a kid, and doesn't that blow my whole story to bits, proving that I made it up out of half-remembered bits of pulp magazine stories—my whole life was validated by my story, and telling it was as necessary to me as breathing. Over the years, it got polished and shiny. More than a few folks told me it sounded like Bradbury.

"A million years ago, Nyquist's farm was the bottom of the ocean," I would always begin, paraphrasing the opening of my book. "Susan Nyquist collected seashells in the desert. Just before I looked up and saw the spinning shape in the sky, I was sifting through the soft white sand, dredging up a clam-shaped rock that might once have been alive..."

No, I'm not going to tell it all again here. That's not what this is about at all.

Do you know what a palimpsest is? It's old parchment that has been written on once, had the writing rubbed out, and been written on again. Sometimes several times. Only, with modern techniques, scientists can read the original writing, looking under-neath the layers.

That's my story. Each time I've told it, I've whited out the version underneath. It's built up, like lime on a dripping faucet. In telling it so many times, I've buried the actual thing.

Maybe that's why I've done it.

Regardless of the movies, it wasn't a B picture, with simple characters and actions. Okay, there were aliens (everyone else calls them that except Strieber, so I guess I can too), a woman was taken, and we poisoned most of them and dug out dynamite and blew up their spaceship (I've never liked calling it that—it was more like one of Susan's shells blown up like a balloon, only with light instead of helium or air). We saved the world, right?

Or maybe we just killed a bunch of unknowable Gandhis from the Beyond. That's what some woman accused me of at a book-signing. She thought they'd come to save us, and that we'd doomed the world by scaring them off.

That gave me a shock. I tried to see the story the way she might.

It didn't play in Peoria. The woman—pink bib overalls, bird's-nest hair, Velma-from-*Scooby-Doo* glasses, a *Frodo Lives!* badge—hadn't seen the visitors, the aliens.

She hadn't seen what they'd done to Susan.

But I was up close.

The little fuckers were evil. No, make that Evil. I don't know if they were from outer space, the third circle of Hell, or the Land of Nod, but they weren't here to help anyone but themselves.

What they did to the cattle, what they did to Susan, wasn't science, wasn't curiosity. They liked taking things apart, the way Mikey Bignell in Third Grade liked setting fire to cats, and Mikey grew up to get shot dead while pistol-whipping a fifty-two-year-old married lady during a filling station hold-up. If the visitors ever grow up beyond the cat-burning phase, I figure they could do some serious damage.

I am not just trying to justify what we did to them.

Now, without trying to tell the story yet again, I'm tapping into what I really felt at the time: half-scared, half-enraged. No Spielberg sense of wonder. No TV movie courage. No Ray Bradbury wistfulness.

"Inside, the ship was all corridors and no rooms, criss-crossing tunnels through what seemed like a rocky rubber solid stuff. Mitchell went ahead, and I followed. We blundered any which way, down passages that made us bend double and kink our knees, and trusted to luck that we'd find where they'd taken Susan. I don't know whether or not we were lucky to find her or whether they intended it. I don't know if we were brave and lucky, or dumb rats in a maze.

"Mitchell claims the thing told us where to go, flashed a floor-plan into our minds, like the escape lights in an airliner. I guess that's his scientific mind talking. For me, it was different. I had a sense of being myself and being above myself, looking down. We didn't take a direct route to Susan, but spiralled around her, describing a mandala with an uneven number of planes of symmetry. It was like the New Math: finding the answer wasn't as important as knowing how to get there, and I think Mitchell and I, in our different ways, both flunked."

I didn't say so in the book, but I think that's why what happened to Susan afterwards went down. When we dragged Susan, alive but unconscious, out of the hot red-black half-dark at the heart of the ship we were too exhausted to feel any sense of triumph. We went in, we found her, we got her out. But we didn't get the trick quite right."

Here's how I usually end it:

"Mitchell was shouting as he ran toward us with two of the things hopping after him. The reel of wire was spinning in his hands as he ran. Nyquist was shaking so bad he couldn't even aim his rifle, much less shoot, and I grabbed it from him"—in his version, he gets both of the critters with two shots, bing-bang— "and drew a bead, worried that Mitchell would zig-zag into the line of fire. I don't amount to much, and while I can't shoot good enough to take the eye out of the eagle if you toss a silver dollar in the air, nine times out of ten I'll at least clip the coin. My first shot put a bullet into the alien that was gaining on Mitchell. Pink stuff burst out of the back of it in midleap, and it tumbled over, deflating like a pricked party balloon.

"It was a couple of hundred yards away, but I gagged on the stink, and Nyquist started to throw up. The second critter was almost on Mitchell when I fired again, the hot casing stinging my cheek as I worked the bolt, and fired, and fired, and kept shooting as Mitchell threw himself down in a tangle of wire while the thing went scooting off back toward the ship. My hands were shaking, and I sliced my thumb when I trimmed the wires back to bare copper. Mitchell snatched them from me and touched them to the terminals of the truck's battery.

"We didn't have more than a dozen sticks of low grade dynamite for getting out tree stumps, and Mitchell hadn't had time to place them when those things came scooting out like hornets out of a bottle. And Mitchell hadn't even wanted to do it, saying that the ship must be fireproofed, like the Apollo module, or it wouldn't have survived atmospheric entry. But it was our last best hope, and when the sticks blew the ship went up like a huge magnesium flare. I put my hands over my eyes, and saw the bones of my hands against the light. The burst was etched into my eyeballs for months. It hardly left any debris, just evaporated into burning light, blasting the rock beneath to black crystal. You can still see the glassy splash where it stood if you can get the security clearance. There was a scream like a dying beast, but it was all over quickly. When we stopped blinking and the echo was dead, there was almost nothing where the ship had been. They were gone."

Is that an ending? If it is, what has the rest of my life been? An epilog, like on some Quinn Martin series episode, with William Conrad reporting that I am still at large, still running off my mouth, still living it down?

Or has it just been an interlude before the sequel?

♓

I wake up the next morning with the shakes. There's not even fumes left in the tequila bottle I clutched to my chest all night, and nothing but warm cans of Dr Pepper's in the motel vending machine, so I drive the mile into town and buy a twelve pack of Bud, giving thanks to California's liberal liquor licence laws. I'm coming out of the 7-11 when two men in sunglasses fall in step with me either side, and I don't need to see their badges to know what they are.

They make me leave my beer in the car and take me across the dusty highway to the town's diner, an Airstream trailer with a tattered awning shading one side. The older guy orders coffee and pancakes, and grins across the table while his partner crowds me on the bench. I can't help looking through the greasy window at my car, where the beer is heating up on the front seat, and the older guy's grin gets wider. He gets out a hip flask and pours a shot into my coffee and I can't help myself and guzzle it down, scalding coffee running down my chin.

"Jesus," the young guy, Dale Bissette, says, disgusted. He's the local field agent, blond hair slicked back from his rawboned face. He hasn't taken off his mirrorshades, and a shoulder harness makes a bulge under his tailored suit jacket.

"Judge not," the other guy says, and pours me another shot, twinkling affably. He has curly white hair and a comfortable gut, like Santa Claus's younger brother. He has hung his seersucker jacket on the back of his chair. There are half-moon sweatstains under his arms, and sweat beads under his hairline. "Ray's living out his past, and is having a hard time with it. Am I right, or am I right?"

I ignore the rye whiskey in the coffee mug. I say, "If you want to talk to me, talk to my agent first. Murray Weiss, he's in the Manhattan White Pages."

"But you're one of us," the older guy says, widening his eyes in mock innocence. "You got your badge, when? '77? '78?"

It was 1976, and I'm sure he damn well knows it, done right out on the White House lawn, with a silver band playing and the Stars and Stripes snapping in the breeze under a hot white sky. The Congressional Medal of Honor for me and Nyquist, and honorary membership of the FBI. I'd asked for that because if it was good enough for Elvis it was good enough for me. It was the last time I saw Nyquist, and even then he was ignoring me with the same intensity I'm right now ignoring that rye.

I say, "Your young friend here was polite enough to show me his badge. I don't believe I know you."

"Oh, we met, very briefly. I was part of the team that helped clean up." He smiles and holds out his hand over the coffee mugs and plates of pancakes, then shrugs. "Guerdon Winter. I'll never forget that first sight of the crater, and the carcass you had."

"You were all wearing those spacesuits and helmets. 'Scuse me for not recognising you."

The FBI agents looked more like space aliens than the things we killed. They cleared out everything, from the scanty remains of the mothership to my collection of tattered paperbacks. I still have the receipts. They took me and Nyquist and Mitchell and put us in isolation chambers somewhere in New Mexico and put us through thirty days of interrogation and medical tests. They took Susan's body and we never saw it again. I think of the C-130 crash and I say, "You should have taken more care of what you appropriated, Agent Winter."

Guerdon Winter takes a bite of pancake.

"We could have had that alien carcass stuffed and mounted and put on display in the Smithsonian, and in five years it would have become one more exhibit worth maybe ten seconds' gawping. The public doesn't need any help in getting distracted, and everything gets old fast. You know better than me how quickly they forget. You're the one in showbiz. But we haven't forgotten, Ray."

"You want me to find out what Mitchell is doing."

"Mitchell phoned you from a pay phone right here in town ten days ago, and you wrote him at the box number he gave you, and then you came down here. You saw him last night."

Dale Bissette stirs and says, "He's been holed up for two years now. He's been carrying out illegal experiments."

"If you were following me you could have arrested him last night."

Guerdon Winter looks at Dale Bissette, then looks at me. He says, "We could arrest him each time he comes into town for supplies, but that wouldn't help us get into his place, and we know enough about his interrogation profile to know he wouldn't give it up to us. But he wants to talk to you, Ray. We just want to know what it is he's doing out there."

"He believes you have the map," Dale Bissette says.

I remember the scrap of paper Mitchell gave me last night and say, "You want the map?"

"It isn't important," Guerdon Winter says quickly. "What's important is that you're here, Ray."

I look out at my rental car again, still thinking about the beer getting warm. A couple of Mexicans in wide-brimmed straw hats are offloading watermelons from a dusty Toyota pickup. One is wearing a very white T-shirt with the Green Lantern symbol. They could be agents, too; so could the old galoot at the motel.

I know Dale Bissette was in my motel room last night; I know he took Mitchell's map and photocopied it and put it back. The thing is, it doesn't seem like betrayal. It stirs something inside me, not like the old excitement of those two crystal clear days when everything we did was a heroic gesture, nothing like so strong or vivid, but alive all the same. Like waking up to a perfect summer's day after a long uneasy sleep full of nightmares.

I push the coffee away from me and say, "What kind of illegal experiments?"

⋈

If Mitchell hadn't been a government employee, if they hadn't ridiculed and debunked his theories, and spirited him off to the ass end of nowhere—no Congressional Medal ceremony for him, he got his by registered mail—if they hadn't stolen the discovery of Mitchellite from him, then maybe he wouldn't have ended up madder than a dancing chicken on a hotplate at the state fair. Maybe he wouldn't have taken it into his head to try what he did. Or maybe he would have done it anyway. Like me, he was living in After, with those two bright days receding like a train. Like me, he wanted them back. Unlike me, he thought he had a way to do it.

Those two agents don't tell me as much as I need to know, but I suspect that they don't know what it is Mitchell is doing. I have an idea that he's building something out in the desert that'll bring those old times back again.

Driving out to Mitchell's place takes a couple of hours. The route on the map he gave me is easy enough: south along Pearblossom's two-lane blacktop, then over the concrete channel of the aqueduct that carries water taken from Washington State— did you see *Chinatown*? yeah, there—and up an unmade track that zigzags along the contours of the Pinon Hills and into a wide draw that runs back a couple of miles. The light in the draw is odd. Cold and purple, like expensive sunglasses. Either side of the road is nothing but rocks, sand, dry scrub and scattered Joshua trees.

I start to feel a grudging sympathy for Agent Bissette. No matter how he hangs back, it's impossible to tail a car out here without your mark knowing. I have the urge to wait for a dip that puts me momentarily out of his sight and swerve off into a patch of soft sand, sinking the rental like a boat in shallows, creating another unexplained mystery.

Mitchell's place is right at the top of the draw, near the beginning of the tree line. In the high desert, trees grow only on the tops of the mountains. The FBI agents park under a clump of stunted pines and let me go on alone. I'm lucky they didn't want me to wear a wire. They'll just wait, and see if I can cope with Crazy

Elliot. For them, it'll be a boring afternoon, with maybe an exciting apprehension about nightfall.

Me, I'm going back to the Days of Sharp Focus.

♓

The rye in the coffee has burned out and I've not touched the soup-warm beer on the passenger seat. I can feel the heat steaming the booze out of my brain. I'm going into this alone.

I get out of the rental, aware of Winter and Bissette watching me through the tinted windshield of their Lincoln Continental. Of Mitchell, there's not a trace. Not even footprints or tyre tracks in the sandy track. I crouch down, and run a handful of warm sand through my fingers, making like an Indian tracker in some old Western while I ponder my next move.

There are tine-trails in the sand. The whole area has been raked, like a Japanese garden. I can imagine Mitchell working by night, raking a fan-shaped wake as he backs toward the paved area I see a dozen yards away.

I walk across the sand, and reach the flagstones. This was the floor of a house that's long gone. I can see the fieldstone hearth, and the ruts where wooden walls had been.

Beyond the stone is a gentle incline, sloping down maybe twenty feet, then levelling off. Down there, protected from sight, Mitchell has been building. I look at his paper, and see what it means. The FBI think it's a circuit diagram, but it really is a map. Mitchell has made himself a maze, but there's nothing on his map that shows me how to get through it.

I know now where the old timbers of the house have gone. Mitchell has cannibalized everything he could carry off within a mile, and some things I would have sworn you'd need a bulldozer at least to shift, but he must have had a few truckloads of chicken-wire, wood and just plain junk hauled out here. The archway entrance is a Stonehenge arrangement of two '50s junkers buried hood-first like standing stones, with their tailfins and clusters of egg-shaped rear lights projecting into the air. A crosspiece made of three supermarket shopping carts completes the arch.

There are other old cars parked and piled in a curving outer wall, built on with wire and wood. And all over the place, sticking up through the sand, are sharp spars and spines that sparkle in the sun.

I know that glittery look, a glinting like the facets of an insect's eye or 1970s eye make-up under fluorescent disco lights. It's Mitchellite.

I walk up to the gateway and stop, careful not to touch the spars. They dot everything—stone, wood, metal—like some sort of mineral mould. Crusty little alien points that seem to be growing out of the ordinary Earth stuff. About ten years ago, a couple of crazy English physicists claimed you could use Mitchellite to get unlimited energy by cold fusion and end up with more Mitchellite than you started with, but they were debunked, defrocked and for all I know defenestrated, and that was the end of it. But maybe they were right after all. It looks like the Mitchellite is transmuting ordinary stuff into itself.

There's an iron crowbar, untouched by Mitchellite, propped against a stone. I pick it up, heft it in my hands. It has a good weight. I always felt better with a simple tool, something you could trust.

Planks are set between the half-buried cars, a path into the interior of the maze. They are pocked with Mitchellite spars that splinter the rotten wood from the inside. I smash down with the poker and split a plank, scraping away bone-dry wood fragments from the Mitchellite nerve-tangles that have been growing inside, sucking strength from the material.

It looks fragile, but it doesn't crumple under my boots.

On the other side of the arch hangs a shower curtain that leaves a three-foot gap beneath it. I push it aside with the crowbar and step into the maze.

The structure is open to the sky, mostly. The walls are of every kind of junk, wood, lines of rocks or unmortared concrete blocks,

even barbed wire, grown through or studded with Mitchellite. A
few yuccas rise up from the maze's low walls, their fleshy leaves
sparkling as if dusted with purplish snow. The floor is made of
Mitchellite-eaten planks. There are stretches of clean, unmarked
sand. But by each of them is propped a rake, for obscuring foot-
prints. By the first rake is a pane of glass in the sand, and in the
hollow under the glass is a handgun wrapped in a plastic baggie,
and a handwritten note. *In case of F(B)IRE smash glass.* So that's
what the crowbar is for. I leave the gun where it is and turn and
stare at the maze again.

After a while I fish out the map and look at it. It takes me a
while even to work out where I am, but with a creepy chill I
realise I'm standing on the spot where Mitchell has drawn a stick
figure. In the center of the map is a white space, where there's
another, bigger stick figure. Dotted throughout are smaller
figures, drawn in red. I know what they're supposed to be. Some
are drawn over black lines that represent walls.

I call out Mitchell's name.

The maze funnels my own voice back to me, distorted and
empty.

⑄

"Ray, come on, what are you waiting for?"

It was obviously a doorway. Mitchell bent down low—the
round opening was the creatures' size—and squeezed into the
ship.

I hesitated, but thought of Susan, and the things that had taken
her.

"I'm coming, Mitchell."

I followed the geologist. Inside, was another world.

⑄

"I'm coming, Mitchell."

I know at once what he's done. This isn't really a maze. It's a model, twice as big again as the real thing, of the aliens' ship.

My knees are weak and I'm shaking. I'm back on the mandala path. I'm above myself and in myself, and I know where to go. I know the route, just as I know the ache that sets into my knees after a minute, an ache that grows to a crippling pain. Just as I remember finding Susan. And finding out later what they'd done to her.

Mitchell took the lead, that time. I followed, forgetting Nyquist chicken-heartedly frozen at the entrance, not daring to go further.

Remembering, I follow Mitchell's lead again. Around and inwards, a spiral across a DNA coil or a wiring diagram, a bee-dance through catacombs. The route is a part of me.

The deeper inside the maze I get, the more Mitchellite there is. The original wood and stone and wire and concrete have been almost completely eaten out. Purple light glitters everywhere, dazzling even through my sunglasses. Without them I'd be snow-blind in a minute.

When the process is finished, when there's nothing more of Earth in the maze, will this thing be able to fly? Will Mitchell carry the war to the enemy?

"Ray," someone—not Mitchell—shouts, from behind me.

It's the FBI. I thought I was supposed to haul Mitchell out on my own. Now the pros are coming in, I wonder why I've bothered.

I feel like a sheep driven across a minefield. A Judas goat.

I got into the maze and I'm still alive, so Guerdon Winter and Bissette know it's safe.

I turn, shading my eyes against the tinted glare that shines up from everything around me. The agents are following my foot-prints. Bissette doesn't duck under the crossbar of an arch nailed up of silvery grey scraps of wood, and scrapes his forehead against a Mitchellite-spackled plank.

I know what will happen.

It's like sandpaper stuck with a million tiny fishhooks and razorblades. The gentlest touch opens deep gashes. Bissette swears, not realizing how badly he's hurt, and a curtain of blood bursts from the side of his head. A flap of scalp hangs down. Red rain spatters his shades.

Bissette falls to his knees. Guerdon Winter plucks out a handkerchief from the breast pocket of his sweat-stained seersucker jacket. A bedsheet won't staunch the flow.

"You can't go on," Guerdon Winter tells the junior agent, who can't protest for the pain. "We'll come back for you."

Naturally, Guerdon Winter has his gun out. When Mitchell and I went into the mothership, we didn't even think of guns. I left my shotgun in the pick-up, and Nyquist held on to his rifle like it was a comforter blanket and wouldn't give it up to us. Some heroes, huh? Every single version of the story rectifies the omission, and we go in tooled up fit to face Bonnie and Clyde.

The FBI has made a bad mistake.

They've changed the story again. By adding the guns, and maybe themselves, they've made me lose my place.

I don't know which way to go from here.

My feet and my spine and my aching knees were remembering. But now the memory's been wiped.

Bissette is groaning. His wound is tearing worse—there are tiny particles of alien matter in it, ripping his skin apart as they grow—and the whole right side of his head and his suit-shoulder are deep crimson.

"Ray," prompts Guerdon Winter. There's a note of pleading in his voice.

I look at the fork ahead of us, marked with a cow's skull nodding on a pole, and suddenly have no idea which path to take. I look up at the sky. There's a canopy of polythene up there, scummy with sand-drifts in the folds. I look at the aisles of junk. They mean nothing to me. I'm as blank as the middle of the map Mitchell gave me.

Then Winter does something incredibly stupid. He offers me a hipflask and smiles and says, "Loosen up Ray. You'll do fine."

I knock the flask away, and it hits a concrete pillar laced with Mitchellite and sticks there, leaking amber booze from a dozen puncture points. The smell does something to my hindbrain and I start to run, filled with blind panic just the way I was when I followed behind Mitchell, convinced alien blimps would start nibbling at my feet.

I run and run, turning left, turning right, deeper and deeper into the maze. The body remembers, if it's allowed. Someone shouts behind me and then there's a shot and a bullet spangs off an engine block and whoops away into the air; another turns the windshield of a wheelless truck to lace which holds its shape for a moment before falling away. I leap over a spar of Mitchellite like an antelope and run on, feeling the years fall away. I've dropped the map but it doesn't matter. The body remembers. Going in, and coming out. Coming out with Susan. That's the name I yell, but ahead, through a kind of hedge of twisted wire coated with a sheen of Mitchellite, through the purple glare and a singing in my ears, I see Mitchell himself, standing in the doorway of a kind of bunker.

)(

He's older than I remember or imagined, the boy scout look transmuted into a scrawny geezer wearing only ragged oil-stained shorts, desert boots, and wraparound shades, his skin tanned a mahogany brown. I lean on the crowbar, taking great gulps of air as I try and get my breath back, and he looks at me calmly. There's a pump action Mossbauer shotgun leaning on the wall beside him.

At last, I can say, "This is some place you got here, Elliot. Where did you get all the stuff?"

"It's a garden," Mitchell says, and picks up the shotgun and walks off around the bunker. He has half-healed scars on his back. Maybe he brushed a little too close to something in his maze.

I follow. The bunker is a poured concrete shell, a low round dome like a turtle shell half-buried in the dry desert dirt. There's a battered Blazer parked at the back, and a little Honda generator and a TV satellite dish. A ramp of earth leads up to the top of the bunker, and we climb up there and stand side by side, looking out over the maze. It extends all around the bunker. The sun is burning over our shoulders, and the concentric spirals of encrusted junk shimmer and glitter, taking the light and making it into something else, a purple haze that shimmers and glitters in the air, obscuring more than it reveals.

"How long have you been doing this, Elliot? It looks like you've been here years."

Elliot Mitchell says, "You ever been to South America, Ray? You should have. They're very big on flying saucers in South America. Out in Peru there are patterns of stones in the deserts that only make sense from the air. Like landing strips, parking aprons."

A chill grips me. "You're building a spaceport?"

"We never had any evidence they came from outer space," Mitchell says.

"What are you saying, they're from Peru? There's some bad shit on Earth, but nothing like those things. What are you doing here, Elliot? Trying to turn yourself into one of them? Listen, if you've found anything out, it'll mean a shitload of attention. That's what I..."

"More chat shows, Ray? More ten line fillers in *Time*? I had some guy from the *National Enquirer* a month or so. He tried to get in. Maybe he's still in here, somewhere."

I remember the red marks on Mitchell's map, in the otherwise blank space of the maze.

I say, "You let me in, Elliot."

"You understand, Ray. You were there, with me. You know what it was like. Only you and me really know what it was like."

I see why he wants me here. Mitchell has built this for a purpose, and I'm to tell the world what that is. I say, "What are you planning, Elliot? What are you going to do with all this?"

Mitchell giggles. "I don't control it, Ray. Not any more. It's more and more difficult to get out each time. When we went to get Susan, where did we go?"

He's setting me up for something. I say dumbly, "Into the ship. That's how I knew to get to you here. This is like the ship."

"It's how I started it out. But it's been growing. Started with a bare ounce of Mitchellite, grew this garden over the template I made. Now it grows itself. Like the ship. We went in, and we went somewhere else. Not all the way because it hadn't finished growing, but a good way. Back towards where they came from. Wherever it was."

"You're saying the ship didn't come from Outer Space?"

"It *grew* here. Like this." Mitchell makes a sweeping gesture with the shotgun, including everything around him. He's King of the Hill. "Once a critical density had been reached, the gateway would have opened, and they would have come through."

"They *did* come through. We poisoned them, we shot them, we blew up their fucking ship—"

"Mitchellite is strange stuff, Ray. Strange matter. It shouldn't exist, not in our universe, at least. It's a mixture of elements which all have atomic weights more than ten times that of uranium. It shouldn't even get together in the first place without tremendous energies forcing the quarks together, and it should fly apart a picosecond after its creation. But it doesn't. It's metastable. It makes holes in reality, increases quantum tunnelling so that things can leak through from one universe to another. That's how they probed us. Sent a probe through on the atomic scale and let it grow. Maybe they sent millions of probes, and only one hit the right configuration. Before we sent up astronauts, we sent up chimps and dogs. That's what they did. They sent through seeds of the things we saw, and they lodged and grew.

"In the cows."

)(

Great chunks had been ripped out of the cows I found. Nyquist
thought it was chainsaw butchers, until I dug around and found
the blisters inside the meat. Like tapeworm cysts. And Susan,
Susan, when we got her out...

)(

"In the cows," Mitchell says. "That was the first stage. And then
they took Susan. That was the second stage. First chimps, then the
astronauts. But we stopped it."

"Yeah. We stopped it."

Mitchell doesn't hear me. He's caught up in his own story.

He says, "They gave the first *astronauts* ticker tape parades
down Wall Street, but what happened to the chimps? First time
around they picked us up and husked us of our stories and forgot
us. *Second* time is the ticker tape parade."

)(

Susan never came around. That was a blessing at least. Doc Jensen
wouldn't believe me when I told him that I figured what had
happened to the cattle was happening to her. Not until that night,
when the things started moving under her skin. He tried to cut
them out then, but they were all through her. So I did the right
thing. Doc Jensen couldn't, even though he saw what was inside
her. He'd still stuck with his oath, even though he had a bottle of
whiskey inside him. So I did what had to be done, and then we
went out and blew up the ship.

)(

Mitchell tells me, "You have to believe it, Ray. *This* time
they won't forget us. This time we'll control it. They tried to

discredit me. They stole my records, they said I was as crazy as Nyquist and tried to section me, they made up stories about finding terrestrial deposits of Mitchellite. Well, maybe those were real. Maybe those were from previous attempts. It's a matter of configuration."

He gestures with the shotgun again, and that's when I cold cock him.

He thought I'd be on his side. He thought I wanted nothing more than fame, than to get back the feeling we had in those two days. He was right. I did. His mistake was that he thought I'd pay *any* price. That, and forgetting to put on a shirt.

The crowbar bounces off his skull and he falls like an unstrung puppet. I kick the shotgun off the domed roof and then he looks up at me and I see what he's done to himself. The sunglasses have come off, and his left eye is a purple mandala.

When I finish, there isn't much left of the top of his head. In amongst the blood and brains: glittering purple-sheened strands, like cords of fungus through rotten wood. A couple of the things inside him try to get out through the scars on his back, but I squash them back into Mitchell's flesh.

♓

After I kill Mitchell I take the gasoline from his generator and burn the dome without looking to see what was inside it, and smash as much of the whole center of the maze as I can. I work in a kind of cold fury, choking in the black smoke pouring out of the dome, until I can hardly stand. Then I toss the crowbar into the flames and walk out of there.

There's no sign of the FBI agents, although their car is still there when I get out. Winter and Bissette are still in Mitchell's crystal garden spaceport; incorporated. I hope to God they're dead, although it isn't likely. But the maze has stopped growing, I know that. The light's gone from it. There's a cell phone in the glove compartment, and I use the redial button and tell the guy on the other end that Winter and Bissette are dead, that the whole place has to be destroyed.

"Don't go in there to look for them. Burn it from the air, it would give them a kindlier death. Burn it down and blow it up. Do the right thing. I made a start. They won't come back."

When I say it, for the first time, it sounds finished.

17

It seemed to 17 that her family had been labourers in the Factory forever. Her mother claimed that her great-great-great-grandparents had worked in the original Factory, and that they had helped in the reconstruction after the One Big One; her most treasured possession was a photo of men and women in rags standing in knee-deep mud in front of a hillside of trees all knocked down in the same direction.

17 had worked since she could walk, when her mother had taught her how to grade waste paper. Then she had cycled with the kids from her rack, chasing heavy metal residues in the flues of the refineries, harvesting mussels in the sewers for their metal-rich shells, sorting through the spill heaps. She had run with the same pack for ten years, had been boss for the last three, but at last she had realized that she wasn't interested in them any more. They were just kids. So she had picked a fight with the next oldest, a lanky boy called Wulf, had beaten him bloody and had told him that he was boss now, and had walked away.

That was last winter. Since then she'd been a free labourer, turning up each day at the canal junction by the cooler stacks, waiting with the others until the shift foremen arrived and made their pick. It was hard, dangerous work. The men went to the refineries or foundries. 17 mostly cleaned the spinners, clever machines which built up hundreds of different things using frames and cellulose spray. The spinners never stopped, their spray heads chattering away right above her while she dug out mounds of stinking cellulose that had accumulated beneath the frames. Blood worms lived in the stuff, thin red whips a metre long that stung bad if they lashed your skin. Rat-crabs too, and roaches and black crickets.

Her mother disapproved. It was time she settled down, her mother said, time she got herself a man and made babies.

They had terrible rows about it. 17 argued that she could do what she wanted, but she knew that if she stayed a free labourer sooner or later she'd get hurt. And if she got hurt bad, she'd be sent to work the tanks where wood pulp was dissolved in acid. Most people didn't last long there; fumes ate their lungs, blinded them, ulcerated their skin until gangrene set in. But it was that or ending up as a breeder like her mother, blown up by having kids one after the other, or becoming some jack's troll. She'd already had a taste of that, thanks to Dim, the prime jack of her rack. She'd messed around with the other kids of her pack, but Dim had shown her what real sex was like. She swore she'd kill him or kill herself if he or any other man ever tried it again.

Then Doc Roberts came, and everything changed forever.

⚓

Doc Roberts was ex-Service, come to the Factory to stretch his pension by leechcraft. He rented a shack on the roof of one of the racks at the edge of the quadrant. He filled it with sunlamps and plants and hung out a shingle announcing his rates.

17 went to see him the second decad after he arrived.

"You're not sick and you're not pregnant," Doc Roberts said, after a rough, cursory examination. "Why are you here?"

"You went up," 17 said, staring at him boldly. She had seen him gimping around the market in his exoframe, but he seemed much taller in his little shack. He was very thin inside the frame, like a cartoon stick man. No hair, his scalp seamed with lumpy scars, his face burned brown and leathery: he looked like one of the turtles that swam in the canal by the cooler outlets.

It was hot and steamy in his shack. The glossy leaves of plants shone in vivid greens and oranges under the rack of purplish sunlamps. There was a shelf of books over his cot, a toilet connected to a tank of spirulina, a glass-fronted cabinet where he kept his pharmaceuticals.

Doc Roberts said, "I upped and I reupped. More than twenty years, girly. It made me what I am."

"I want to go."

"That's a hard road. Stay in the dirt. Find a man. Have babies."

"No! Kill myself first!" Suddenly, amazingly, she was crying. She made fists, knuckled tears. "You tell me. Tell me how. How to get out and up."

Doc Roberts sort of leaned into his frame, the way an ordinary man might slump in a chair. He looked at her—really looked. She looked right back. She knew he hadn't had many customers. Breeders looked after each other and their kids; free labourers paid to get their lumps and wounds hacked and sealed at the Factory dispensary.

He said, "What's your name?"

She said defiantly, "17."

She'd chosen it herself. She liked the way it screwed up the system. Clerks would ask if it was her given name, and she'd say no, it was what she called herself. Was she her mother's seventeenth kid, the clerk would want to know, and she'd say no. Her age? She didn't know, fifteen maybe. What was her real name then? 17, she'd say, stubborn, defiant. That was what she was. 17. She had started calling herself that a little while before she'd left the cycling pack, had beaten any kid who called her different until it stuck. Her mother called her 'Teen, a compromise.

Doc Roberts didn't question it. He put his turtle head to one side and said, "You pay me, 17, and I'll give you some teaching. How does that sound?"

That was how it began. She took up cycling again to pay him. Mercury chases were the best. She knew the tunnels under the Factory as well as anyone. She knew where the heavy silvery stuff collected, always came back with twice as much as anyone else. But it was dangerous. Not just because mercury and other heavy metals could give her the shakes or the falling sickness, but because sooner or later a gang of jacks or a pack of kids would find her down there and beat her and maybe kill her for her gleanings.

She surprised Doc Roberts by being able to read (she had learnt from the brief captions under the cartoon notices the bulls pasted everywhere), and he soon discovered her knack of being able to multiply and divide long numbers without really thinking about it.

"You're an idiot savant," he said.

"You mean like a dummy? I'm no dummy."

"Maybe not. But you have a trick in your head. You can do something that takes most people a lot of brain hurt as naturally as breathing."

"It'll help me pass the tests?"

"You're bright, 17. I'll teach you as long as you want to keep paying me. When you're ready, you should buy a test that will find out just how bright you are."

"Would it cost more than learning about the up and out?"

"Maybe. If you're real bright the bosses might pay for some of it. They need bright people. Intelligence is precious, as precious as mercury or silver or copper or chrome. The bosses need bright people for all kinds of things, a lot of them better than going up."

"You mean like whores? I don't think so."

A few girls and one boy from her rack had gone that way. You saw them sometimes, visiting their families. The last one to come visiting, a girl, had worn silver boots, silver panties, and a very short open mesh dress, nothing else. 17 had looked at herself afterwards and knew she'd never make the grade—wide hips, no breasts, a blob of a nose. Besides, the best a whore could hope for was to become the plaything of one of the Factory bulls until her looks gave out and she was sent to work the Meat Rack.

Doc Roberts said, "I mean like all kinds of things. If I'm right about you, 17, you're going to go far and fast."

"Maybe I wouldn't mind a bit of whoring with you, Doc. Would be a lot easier than cycling."

Doc Roberts gave her one of his sharp looks. He said, "I upped and reupped. Radiation took care of that itch. I only want money off you, 17."

"I'll pay. I want out, Doc. I want it terrible bad."

Doc taught her more than math. He showed her what the world beyond the Factory was like. 17 had never been outside the Factory, and now she hungered for escape the way an addict has the jones for ripple or meth or smack. Doc taught her the true name of the world and the true name of its sun, explained its history.

17 had thought that the world was called the World; that its sun was called the Sun. Doc told her that the world was really called Tierra; the sun was a star called Delta Pavonis.

"We came from a long way away," Doc said. "So far away you have to measure the distance in years." It took two days to explain Einsteinian relativity, and the reason why nothing could go as fast as light. "That's why our ancestors came as zygotes in the seeder ship," he said.

"Was it big?" 17 had a hazy idea of something as big as the Factory falling towards a star that swelled like a balloon to become the sun.

"Oh no. In travel mode it was not much bigger than you or me. It had a light sail for braking that spread out for thousands of kilometres, but that was only a few molecules thick."

Explaining all this took more days, extra lessons after the lessons 17 bought with her cycler money.

Doc told her, "When the seeder hit dirt it built the first Factory, and that built us and cows and wheat and all the other stuff we eat."

"Like porridge and yeast?"

"Porridge is edible plastic. Yeast, I don't know where yeast came from. Maybe we brought it here, maybe it's native. Some of my plants came on the seeder ship, 17. See the thin green ones? That's wheat grass. I pulp it and drink the juice. That's from Earth, like you and me and cows. The other plants, the orange and red ones, are native. We got rid of most of the native life, but there's still a lot around in unlooked corners."

"Bugs and haunts."

"Yes. I suppose you might have seen one, now and then."

"Seen plenty of bugs, but never yet a haunt. They say there's maybe one down in the tunnels, 'cause a couple of kids went missing. Bugs though, I know about those. These from blood-worms." She showed him the welts.

"I suppose the haunts get in through the vents of the main cooling plants, or along the slurry pipes from the mines," Doc said. "They are tough things because this world is a hard place to live. You know why?"

17 nodded. She had learnt it last week. "Because there's no broom in the system. No Jupiter to sweep up comets that fall from the Oort Cloud. That's why the Service and Comet Watch is important, else the world would get hit bad every hundred years. But why is it that way, Doc? Why are all the big planets near our sun?"

"No one really knows. Maybe the primordial disc from which the planets condensed was spinning slowly, so the big planets formed close in and locked up most of the heavy metals in their cores. But that's only a theory."

"Well, they should know why. It's why cycling is so impor-tant, like they always tell us. Why heavy metals cost so much. They don't pay well for cycling, though. They should, don't you think?"

"That's economics, not orbital mechanics, 17. But I suppose it does all fit together."

Doc was constantly amazed by 17's ignorance and by her eagerness to learn. She knew about the One Big One, but had thought it had wrecked only the Factory, not the whole world. She hadn't known about the settlement of Tierra, the rise of the Syndic and the reason why people went up, hadn't even known that the world was just one of a dozen inhabited worlds. She was like a plant that will push up concrete slabs and break apart the seams between steel plates to get at light. She was hungry for everything he could give her. He watched her work out from first principles why orbits are elliptical. She soaked up Newtonian mechanics, tensor calculus, n-body interactions. He didn't spend any of the money she gave him. She would need it later, when she got out into the world.

♓

People began to notice that she spent a lot of time with Doc Roberts. 17's mother said that she shouldn't start thinking that she was more than she was, and they had a furious argument, with her mother stirring yeast soup all the time and the latest baby crawling around. 17 stormed out, and then Dim cornered her in the market.

"Tell me why you go wi' that old cripple-man," he said. He was running solo, her one piece of good luck. He had tattoos all over, wore only ripped shorts and a harness to show them off, and to show off his steroid-enhanced muscles, too. He stank of sweat and the goo he put on his skin rash. People avoided looking at the two of them; Dim had a hard rep.

"He good to me," 17 said.

"He not a real man, so how can that be?" Dim said. His spittle sprayed her cheeks. "They cut it off when they go up. Or do you do it with his rack?"

"You dumb as a worm," 17 told him. "Hung like one too. What you have isn't anything. I didn't even feel it."

"You getting a filthy tongue, girly. You getting above yourself."

Dim tried to put his hand over her mouth, but she bit his thumb and got away from him. He shouted after her. "Me and my jacks will find you in the tunnels, quim! We ream you both ends!"

The next day, someone saw a haunt in the sewers, stooping over a kid it had just killed. The day after, Doc told her that some of the bosses were coming to hunt the haunt, that it would be a chance better than any test.

"You shine in this, 17, and they'll take notice. How well do you know the tunnels?"

"I know 'em good. Better than anyone. You think you get me work with these bosses?"

"I have a little pull. I'm part of the Syndic, 17, but at a low level, about the same as the Factory bulls. The bulls work for the turf bosses. Above them are the ward bosses, and above *them* are the big capos. The higher you are, the more you see. The capos see a long way. They give up some of what they have to make sure the world holds together so they can keep what they have. That's why we have Comet Watch and all the rest of it."

"And one of them will help me?"

"They're coming here to hunt for a haunt, not for little girl geniuses. But you shine, maybe one of them will notice, and he'll ask me about you."

"Will he put me in the Service? Will he send me up?"

"Maybe he'll find you something better than that. You've a mind, 17. It shouldn't be wasted in the Service." Doc lifted an arm with a whine of servo motor. Loose skin hanging off bone, like the old women who sorted rags. He said, "Look at me. This is what happens to people in the up and out. Muscle wasting, decalcification of bones, circulatory collapse. Radiation fries gonads, so the Service sterilizes its recruits so they won't sire monsters. And radiation gives you cancers. These scars on my face, they're where keloid growths were cut away. I lost a metre of gut, too."

"But it's still better than the Factory."

"That's true," Doc said. "They made me a citizen, they gave me medical training and the rest of my education. But you can't keep reupping. For one thing, the Syndic doesn't want people living permanently in the up and out because they don't want to lose control. Suppose people decided to aim comets at the world instead of deflecting them? You get upped and if you do good you can reup, but after that they won't let you out of the well again. For another, it makes you bad sick, like I said. I'm forty-two, 17, and I got maybe five more years left to me."

17 started to say that most in the Factory didn't expect to make it to forty, but she saw he wasn't listening.

"A mind like yours," he said, "it should burn for a hundred years. That's what a boss can give you, if he sees what you are."

Almost every free labourer and jack signed up for the hunt; hardly any made the cut. But 17 did, and she had learned enough to thank Doc even though she thought she would have made it without his help. Dim wasn't on the list; none of the jacks were. She saw him one time afterwards, and couldn't resist taunting him. She would be safe from him for the next decad, because there was a lot of training to be done.

)(

One of the junior bulls took charge of them. Divided them into groups of three, told them they were bait runners now. They would go ahead of each boss, flush out anything bigger than a rat-crab and drive it towards the guns. If the bosses didn't find the haunt, at least they'd get their jollies blasting bugs. He taught them signals made up of long and short whistle blasts; taught them how to use proximity radar and flash guns. But he spent most of the time teaching them etiquette.

"Never look one of the bosses in the eye," the bull said. "Never speak unless you are spoken to, and always answer at once. If you don't know the answer, say so. Say *I don't know boss.* Go on, try it."

The bait runners gave up an uncoordinated mumble.

"Smarter. Quicker."

I don't know boss!

"Fucking awful," the bull said. "A bunch of crickets could do better." He was a tall man with a pot belly and a bald patch he tried to hide by combing his glossy black hair sideways. There were sweat patches on his white shirt under his arms. He strutted down the line, staring fiercely at the men and women, striking any who dared meet his gaze. 17 looked at her feet, trembling with fear and anger. When he reached the end, he turned and yelled, "You all listen up! The people coming here are some of the most important on the planet. They can erase the Factory at a whim. I have ten days to bring you to some sort of civilized behaviour. You will give up everything you have to make sure the bosses get their jollies. If it comes to it, you will lay down your lives to save theirs. If they ask you to cut off your dicks you will cut off your dicks. If they ask you to cut out the hearts of your children you'll do it at once, and willingly. And you will sing loud and clear when I ask or I'll send all of you to the mines. Let's hear it once again!"

They all sang out.

I DON'T KNOW BOSS!

Doc fed 17 private information about the visiting bosses. He had pics of each boss, and told 17 which family they belonged to, how they stood in the complicated hierarchies. They were all men, all very young. None of them seemed to have proper jobs. They climbed mountains around the North Pole, sailed catamarans in the southern ocean, spent their winters on the wide, white beaches of the Archipelago. They all looked the same to 17. Tanned skin, broad white smiles, buzz cut blond hair, good cheekbones, firm jaws. She was good with numbers, not people. She still hadn't got their names straight in her head when they arrived.

The whole Factory got the day off. For the first time in a hundred years the machines were stood down. The silence hummed in 17's head. She wondered if it was like the silence of the up and out. The foremen handed out flags and streamers and people waved them as the cavalcade of limousines swept through main drag to the compound where the bulls lived.

There were fireworks that night, fans of coloured stars exploding under the dome. Calcium-red, copper-green, sodium-yellow, cobalt-blue. The next day the hunt started.

♓

17 was teamed with a couple of older men who made it clear they had no time for her. She didn't care. She knew she could shine only by herself, not part of a team. She knew every bit of the sewer tunnels, didn't need to look at the corroded plates that marked every intersection as she blew through the perimeter of the area assigned to her team, making a wide arc that pivoted on one of the Factory's waste treatment plants. There were always plenty of mussel beds and pack crab nests there, and she had a feeling that the haunt would need something to eat other than the three kids it had snatched.

It was dark and warm in the tunnels. Only a few of the lights worked, a broken chain of dim red stars stretching away under the low curved roof. 17 sloshed through knee-deep scummy water. Water fell thunderously in one of the tunnels; huge islands of stiff foam whirled on the currents. Pack crab nests bristled along the waterline there, built of scraps of plastic and metal. The entrance hole of each nest was blocked by the swollen claw of its resident; desperate cyclers risked getting bitten or poisoned to tear up the nests for the scrap they contained. Barnacles floated their feathery sieves on the water, snatched at her wet suit. She edged past a reef of razor-edged mussels, paused at a Y junction.

One way led to the cooling water inlet complex, the other to the labyrinthine drains beneath the pulp holding tanks. Something was moving towards her, coming towards the junction. She put her head close to the water, heard slow sloshing footsteps and jammed herself against the wall, ready to blow her whistle. But it was something stranger and more fearsome than the haunt or any bug.

It was one of the bosses.

"Hey," he said breathlessly. "I saw some sign back there. Parallel scrapes on the bricks of the roof? New, cut right through the black slime stuff. My proximity radar gives too many signals because of the currents, but it must be close, don't you think?"

17 nodded. She had forgotten all of the bull's etiquette lessons.

The boss grinned. "That's why you're here, right? You're not on my team, but you guessed it would hang around here, you took a chance to grab some glory."

She nodded again. The boss was taller than Doc, well muscled and lithe, and impossibly young. His black and pink wetsuit was clean and new, not a rip or patch on it. His gun was slung on one broad shoulder, his breathing apparatus on the other. His grin was very white in his tan face; his hair was so blond it was as white as new paper. She could smell his cologne through the stink of the tunnels.

He said, "I'll bet you know every centimetre of this place. We'll clean up. Raphe *will* be pissed. Where do you think it might be?"

17 pointed down the tunnel that led towards the cooling water inlet.

"You lead on," the boss said. He kept talking as they sloshed through the water, moving with the current. "You've lived here long? No, wait, I bet you've lived here all your life. You know, I've been further north than this, but it's bleaker around here than at the pole. Just the forests and the sea, and the sea is covered with ice pack. And the mines further inland. I saw the pipes that carry the ore slurry from the air, like black snakes through the forest. That was before the weather closed in. Sleet *and* lightning? I suppose it's the iron in the rock. I'm not surprised the place is domed; only haunts and ghouls and bugs could live outside. Now, where do we go from here?"

They had reached another Y junction. Both tunnels sloped steeply upward away from them. The inlet complex, which fed seawater to the cooling system from concrete surge baffles, was half as big as the Factory itself. 17 had never been this close to the outside before, didn't know where to go next, but she didn't want to look stupid and pointed to the left-hand tunnel. But they had gone only a little way when it split again.

The boss saw her confusion, and said gently, "I'll go right and you go left. We'll meet back here in ten minutes. Oh, I bet you don't have a watch. Here."

He stripped the black chronometer from his wrist. "I have a chip," he said. "This is just jewellery."

17 took it. It was very heavy. The casing was titanium or chrome steel or some other impossibly rare alloy. The crystal beneath which black numbers counted the seconds was a cultured diamond.

The boss said, "I don't know your name."

"Katrina."

She said it without thinking.

The boss made a funny little bow. "Katrina, I'm pleased to be hunting with you. If you see anything, blow hard on your whistle and I'll be right there."

Two minutes into the tunnel, she knew that the haunt was close. Pack crab nests crushed. Fresh scrapes from the thing's spines on the ceiling, on the walls. A breeze chilled her face. It smelled as fresh as the boss, clean and wild. The smell of outside. The light ahead was daylight.

The haunt was at the screens at the end of the tunnel. It had already twisted aside the first set, was prying at the second. It was silhouetted against the thin grey daylight. Thousands of white flakes—snow—blew around it.

It turned on her with a swift liquid grace, opening its mandibles wide. It was as tall as the boss and thinner than Doc. Its long body was articulated in a dozen places. Its carapace was red and gold. Fringes of bronze hair grew thickly at the joints and at the bases of its spines. Its dozen limbs were as thin as wire and impossibly long.

It had a terrible beauty.

17 froze, one hand on her utility belt. Flares, the proximity radar, a flash gun useless in daylight, her whistle. Nothing else, not even a pry bar. She could have burnt it with a flare, but she knew that would only enrage it, not kill it. It didn't matter if a few bait runners were killed as long as the bosses got their sport.

When she did not move, the haunt turned back and started to pry at the screen again. It was working at the bolts, she saw, trying to turn them against beds of corrosion. It was trying to get out.

Pipes hung from the ceiling in an overhead maze. Rotten lagging hung from them in leprous sheets. 17 ran forward, jumped as the haunt whirled again, grabbed a pipe with both hands and swung through ninety degrees, right over the thing's head. The soles of her boots crashed into the screen; a whole edge popped free. The haunt slashed at her, catching several of its wire-thin claw-tipped limbs in her wet suit; frantic with fear, she twisted free and kicked and kicked at rusty mesh. The haunt squalled, then flung the length of its body forward.

Hanging upside down from the pipe, 17 saw the haunt smash against the screen and knock it free and fall away, but she could not believe it was gone. Snow and wind blew around her. She was still hanging there when the boss came back and found her.

He helped her down. He saw the signs of the haunt and leaned at the edge of the opening, looking down. 17 trembled with cold and spent fear. She was convinced that the boss would kill her, but when he turned he was grinning. He said that the hunt itself was more fun than killing some poor bug, and then he was gone, running into the darkness beneath the Factory. 17 followed as best she could. She had twisted her ankle when she had kicked out the screen.

She didn't see him again. By the time she had made her way to the mustering point, the bosses were flying back to the city. She racked her equipment and went to find Doc to tell him that she had failed, and found the worst thing of all.

♓

Doc was lying battered and bloody in his broken exoframe amidst the ruin of his indoor garden. He was dead. A motor in the exoframe kept trying to lift his left arm, whining and relaxing, whining and relaxing. 17 tore out wires until it stopped. Books lay everywhere, torn and soaked with water leaking from a broken irrigation pipe. All the sunlamps had been smashed. The glass front of the pharmacy cabinet was smashed; the shelves were empty.

17 saved a few of the books, picking them at random, and left Doc for the Factory cops to find. They came for her a few hours later, but she knew they couldn't pin Doc's death on her because she had been down in the tunnels. They questioned her anyway—Doc had been a citizen, after all—but the beating was routine and in the end they let her go. One told her that Doc had probably been killed by some junkie looking for a high, but she knew better.

♓

She knew even before she saw Dim. It was the next day. He was whistling and hooting amongst his jacks while she waited with the other free labourers.

After a shift spent reaming out the pipes that carried cellulose sludge from one settling tank to another, she paid to get real clean, bought gloss and perfume from the store. The perfume stung her skin. It smelt more strongly of roses than any rose had ever smelt.

Dim was hanging with his jacks in his usual bar. She ignored him but knew he'd come over.

He did.

"I hear some junky did your cripple-man lover, girly-girl. You don't worry. Dim'll see to all your needs."

17 endured the touch of saliva spray on her face, the smell and heat of him. She found it amazingly easy to smile.

Dim said, "How did the cripple-man do you? Not good I bet. I bet you come looking for me to show you how all over again." This last said loudly, for his jacks to hear. He acknowledged their whistles and hoots with a casual bow. "I got what you want," he told 17, his voice close and hoarse in her ear. "Prime worker meat, hot and hard."

17 put her hand between his legs, squeezed what was there and walked right out, her heart beating as quickly as it had when the haunt had turned to face her.

Dim followed her through the market, shoved her into a service entrance behind one of the stalls. "Not here," she said. "I know a place."

"I bet you do. But we ain't going to any of your secret places." He was breathing heavily. She let his hands do things.

"You didn't come armed," he said. "You know what's right for you."

"I know."

"That junky who did your cripple-man did you a favour. You wait here."

He was back two minutes later with tubes of vodka. "We go to my place," he said, and held her wrist tight. She didn't resist.

It was an upper bunk in the men's dorm. She felt the brush of the eyes of every man who turned to watch as Dim walked her down the narrow aisle. She got up on the bunk. The mattress stank of Dim and stale marijuana. There was a TV hung on a stay in one corner, a locker at the foot of the mattress.

She started to pull at her belt while Dim velcroed the curtains together. When he turned she snapped her wrist and at the same time thrust her hand forward; the long sliver of memory plastic she'd ripped from her belt stiffened when she snapped it, went into his eye and punched through the thin bone behind it. Blood burst hotly over her fingers. He shivered and fell on her with all his weight, dead as poor Doc. She found the card that opened his locker, shoved his body through the curtains and dropped all the vials and capsules and hypos on top of it, swung down and walked out, looking straight ahead.

No one tried to stop her.

Thirty days later she was five thousand kilometres away, under a hot blue sky on the roof of the Service induction building. She was in a line with two hundred fresh recruits, waiting for the shuttle copters that would take them out to boot camp. She was wearing the cleanest dungarees she had ever worn, crisp and sky blue, polished boots, a padded impact helmet with its silvered visor up.

Doc Roberts had wanted to change her orbit by a close encounter with one of the bosses, the way ships gained delta vee by swinging past a planet, but she knew that this was her true vector. She would fly it as true and straight as she could, climb as high as she could. She had only her hunger. The rest she had left behind. She was no longer 17. She was a recruit, newly born into the world.

The sergeant addressed the line. He was a veteran, his face like a leathery mask, one eye socket empty. His exoframe was just like Doc's. "You're in the Service now!" he yelled. His amplified voice echoed off into the sky. "You're going up and out, beyond the ken of mortal men. You're meat in a can. Everything human will be burnt away. You don't want that then step out of line now!"

No one did. The Service's psych profiling was very good.

"Close up and straighten up," the sergeant yelled.

Moving in unison with her fellow recruits, she snapped down the visor of her helmet. She was no longer 17. She had left that behind with everything else. 518972 was stencilled in black above her visor. That was her number now.

ALL TOMORROW'S PARTIES

And with exactly a year left before the end of the century-long gathering of her clade, she went to Paris with her current lover, racing ahead of midnight and the beginning of the New Year. Paris! The 1er arrondissement: the early Twentieth Century. Fireworks bursting in great flowers above the night-black Seine; a brawling carnival under a multicoloured rain of confetti filling the Jardin des Tuileries and every street from the Quai du Louvre to the Arc de Triomphe.

Escorted by her lover (they had been hunting big game in the Pleistocene era taiga of Siberia; he still wore his safari suit, and a Springfield rifle was slung over his shoulder), she crossed to the Palaeolithic oak woods of the Ile de la Cité. In the middle of the great stone circle, naked druids with blue-stained skins beat huge drums under flaring torches, while holographic ghosts swam above the electric lights of the Twentieth Century shore. Her attentive lover identified them for her, leaning against her shoulder so she could sight along his arm. He was exactly her height, with piercing blue eyes and a salt-and-pepper beard.

An astronaut. A gene pirate. Emperor Victoria. Mickey Mouse.

"What is a mouse?"

He pointed. "That one, the black-skinned creature with the circular ears."

She leaned against his solid human warmth. "For an animal, it seems very much like a person. Was it a product of the gene wars?"

"It is a famous icon of the country where I was born. My countrymen preferred creatures of the imagination to those of the real world. It is why they produced so few good authors."

"But you were a good author."

"I was not bad, except at the end. Something bad always happened to all good writers from my country. Sometimes slowly, sometimes quickly, but without exception."

"What is it carrying?"

"A light sabre. It is an imaginary weapon that is authentic for the period. Back then, people were obsessed with weapons and divisions. They saw the world as a struggle of good against evil. That was how wars could be called good, except by those who fought in them."

She didn't argue. Her lover, a partial, had been modelled on a particular Twentieth Century writer, and had direct access to the appropriate records in the Library. Although she had been born just at the end of the Twentieth Century, she had long ago forgotten everything about it.

Behind them, the drums reached a frenzied climax and fell silent. The sacrificial victim writhed on the heel stone and the chief druid lifted the still beating heart above his head in triumph. Blood ran down his arms. It looked black in the torchlight.

The spectators beyond the circle clapped or toasted each other. One man was trying to persuade his companion to fuck on the altar. They were invisible to the druids, who were merely puppets lending local colour to the scene.

"I'm getting tired of this," she said.

"Of course. We could go to Cuba. The ocean fishing there is good. Or to Afrique, to hunt lions. I think I liked that best, but after a while I could no longer do it. That was one of the things that destroyed my writing."

"I'm getting tired of you," she said, and her lover bowed and walked away.

She was getting tired of everything.

She had been getting tired of everything for longer than she could remember. What was the point of living forever if you did nothing new? Despite all her hopes, this *faux* Earth, populated by two billion puppets and partials, and ten million of her clade, had failed to revive her.

In one more year, the fleet of spaceships would disperse; the sun, an ordinary G2 star she had moved by the pressure of its own light upon gravity-tethered reflective sails, would go supernova; nothing would be saved but the store of information collected and collated by the Library. She had not yet accessed any of that. Perhaps that would save her.

She returned to the carnival; stayed there three days. But despite use of various intoxicants she could not quite lose herself in it, could not escape the feeling that she had failed after all. This was supposed to be a great congress of her own selves, a place to share and exchange memories that spanned five million years and the entire Galaxy. But it seemed to her that the millions of her selves simply wanted to forget what they were, to lose themselves in the pleasures of the flesh. Of course, for the many who had assumed bodies for the first time to attend the gathering, this carnival was a genuine farewell to flesh they would abandon at the end of the year.

On the third day she was sitting in cold dawn light at a green café table in the Jardin des Tuileries, by the great fountain. Someone was sculpting the clouds through which the sun was rising. The café was crowded with guests, partials and puppets, androids and animals—even a silver gynoid, its face a smooth oval mirror. The air buzzed with the tiny machines which attended the guests; in one case, a swirling cloud of gnat-sized beads *was* a guest. After almost a century in costume, the guests were reverting to type.

She sipped a citron pressé, listened to the idle chatter. The party in Paris would break up soon. The revellers would disperse to other parts of the Earth. With the exception of a small clean-up crew, the puppets, partials and all the rest would be returned to store.

At another table, a youthful version of her erstwhile lover was talking to an older man with brown hair brushed back from his high forehead and pale blue eyes magnified by the thick lenses of his spectacles.

"The lions, Jim. Go to Afrique and listen to the lions roar at night. There is no sound like it."

"Ah, and I would love that, but Nora would not stand it. She needs the comforts of civilization. Besides, the thing we must not forget is that I would not be able to see the lions. Instead I think we will drink some more of this fine white wine and you will tell me about them."

"Aw hell, I could bring back a living lion if you like," the younger man said. "I could describe him to you and you could touch him and smell him until you got the idea."

Both men were quite unaware that there were two lions right there in the park, accompanying a naked girl child whose feet, with pigeon's wings at the ankles, did not quite touch the ground.

Did these puppets come here every day, and recreate for the delectation of the guests a conversation first spoken millions of years ago? Was each day to them the same day? Suddenly, she felt as if a cold wind was blowing through her, as if she was raised up high and naked upon the pinnacle of the mountain of her great age.

"You confuse the true and the real," someone said. A man's voice, soft, lisping. She looked around but could not see who amongst the amazing people and creatures might have said such a thing, the truest, realest thing she had heard for... how long? She could not remember how long.

She left, and went to New Orleans.

Where it was night, and raining, a soft warm rain falling in the lamplit streets. It was the Twentieth Century here, too. They were cooking crawfish under the mimosa trees at every intersection of the brick paved streets, and burning the Maid of New Orleans over Lake Pontchartrain. The Maid hung up there in the black night sky—wrapped in oiled silks and shining like a star, with the blue-white wheel of the Galaxy a backdrop that spanned the horizon—then flamed like a comet and plunged into the black water while cornet bands played *Laissez le Bon Temps Rouler.*

She fell in with a trio of guests whose originals were all less than a thousand years old. They were students of the Rediscovery, they said, although it was not quite clear what the Rediscovery was. They wore green ("For Earth," one said, although she thought that odd because most of the Earth was blue), and drank a mild psychotropic called absinthe, bitter white stuff poured into water over a sugar cube held in silver tongs. They were interested in the origins of the clade, which amused her greatly, because of course she was its origin, going amongst the copies and clones disguised as her own self. But even if they made her feel every one of her five million years, she liked their innocence, their energy, their openness.

She strolled with her new friends through the great orrery at the waterfront. Its display of the lost natural wonders of the Galaxy was derived from records and memories guests had deposited in the Library, and changed every day. She was listening to the three students discuss the possibility that humans had not originally come from the Earth when someone went past and said, looking right at her, "None of them look like you, but they are just like you all the same. All obsessed with the past because they are trapped in it."

A tall man with a black, spade-shaped beard and black eyes that looked at her with infinite amusement. The same soft, lisping voice she had heard in the café in Paris. He winked and plunged into the heart of the white-hot whirlpool of the accretion disc of the black hole of Sigma Draconis 2, which drew matter from the photosphere of its companion blue-white giant—before the reconstruction, it had been one of the wonders of the Galaxy.

She followed, but he was gone. She looked for him everywhere in New Orleans, and fell in with a woman who before the gathering had lived in the water vapour zone of a gas giant, running a tourist business for those who could afford to download themselves into the ganglia of living blimps a kilometre across. The woman's name was Rapha; she had ruled the worlds of a hundred stars once, but had given that up long before she had answered the call for the gathering.

"I was a man when I had my empire," Rapha said, "but I gave that up too. When you've done everything, what's left but to party?"

She had always been a woman, she thought. And for two million years she had ruled an empire of a million worlds—for all she knew, the copy she had left behind ruled there still. But she didn't tell Rapha that. No one knew who she was, on all the Earth. She said, "Then let's party until the end of the world."

She knew that it wouldn't work—she had already tried everything, in every combination—but because she didn't care if it worked or not, perhaps this time it would.

They raised hell in New Orleans, and went to Antarctica.

It was raining in Antarctica, too.

It had been raining for a century, ever since the world had been made.

Statite sails hung in stationary orbit, reflecting sunlight that bathed the swamps and cycad forests and volcanic mountain ranges of the South Pole in perpetual noon. The hunting lodge was on a floating island a hundred metres above the tops of the giant ferns, close to the edge of a shallow viridescent lake. A flock of delicate, dappled *Dromiceiomimus* squealed and splashed in the shallows; giant dragonflies with wings as long as a man's arm

flitted through the rainy middle air; at the misty horizon, the
perfect cones of three volcanoes sent up threads of smoke into the
sagging clouds.

She and Rapha rode bubbles in wild loops above the forests,
chasing dinosaurs or goading dinosaurs to chase them. Then they
plunged into one of the volcanoes and caused it to erupt, and one
of the hunters overrode the bubbles and brought them back and
politely asked them to stop.

The lake and the forest were covered in a mantle of volcanic
ash. The sky was milky with ash.

"The guests are amused, but they will not be amused for ever.
It is the hunting that is important here. If I may suggest other
areas where you might find enjoyment..."

He was a slightly younger version of her last lover. A little less
salt in his beard; a little more spring in his step.

She said, "How many of you did I make?"

But he didn't understand the question.

They went to Thebes (and some of the hunting party went
with them), where they ran naked and screaming through the
streets, toppling the statues of the gods. They went to Greenland,
and broke the rainbow bridge of Valhalla and fought the trolls
and ran again, laughing, with Odin's thunder about their ears.
Went to Troy, and set fire to the wooden horse before the Greeks
could climb inside it.

None of it mattered. The machines would repair everything;
the puppets would resume their roles. Troy would fall again the
next night, on schedule.

"Let's go to Golgotha," Rapha said, wild-eyed, very drunk.

This was in a bar of some Christian-era American town.
Outside, a couple of the men were roaring up and down the main
street on motorcycles, weaving in and out of the slow-moving,
candy-coloured cars. Two cops watched indulgently.

"Or Afrique," Rapha said. "We could hunt man-apes."

"I've done it before," someone said. He didn't have a name,
but some kind of number. He was part of a clone. His shaved head

was horribly scarred; one of his eyes was mechanical. He said, "You hunt them with spears or slings. They're pretty smart, for man-apes. I got killed twice."

Someone came into the bar. Tall, saturnine, black eyes, a spade-shaped beard. At once, she asked her machines if he was a partial or a guest, but the question confused them. She asked them if there were any strangers in the world, and at once they told her that there were the servants and those of her clade, but no strangers.

He said softly, "Are you having a good time?"

"Who are you?"

"Perhaps I'm the one who whispers in your ear, 'Remember that you are mortal.' Are you mortal, Angel?"

No one in the world should know her name. Her true name.

Danger, danger, someone sang in the background of the song that was playing on the jukebox. *Danger*, burbled the coffee pot on the electrical coil behind the counter of the bar. *Dan-ger* ticked the mechanical clock on the wall.

She said, "I made you, then."

"Oh no. Not me. You made all of this. Even all of the guests, in one way or another. But not me. We can't talk here. Try the one place which has any use in this *faux* world. There's something there I'm going to steal, and when I've done that I'll wait for you."

"Who are you? What do you want?"

"Perhaps I want to kill you." He smiled. "And perhaps you want to die. It's one thing you have not tried yet."

He walked away, and when she started after him Rapha got in the way. Rapha hadn't seen the man. She said the others wanted to go to Hy Brasil.

"The gene wars," Rapha said. "That's where we started to become what we are. And then—I don't know, but it doesn't matter. We're going to party to the end of the world. When the sun explodes, I'm going to ride the shock wave as far as I can. I'm not going back. There's a lot of us who aren't going back. Why should we? We went to get copied and woke up here, thousands of years later, thousands of light years away. What's to go back for? Wait! Where are you going?"

"I don't know," she said, and walked out.

The man had scared her. He had touched the doubt that had prompted her to organize the gathering. She wanted a place to hide so that she could think about that before she confronted him.

Most of the North American continent was, in one form or another, modelled after the Third Millennium of the Christian Era. She took a car (a red Dodge as big as a boat, with fins and chrome trim) and drove to Dallas, where she was attacked by tribes of horsemen who rode out of the glittering slag heaps of the wrecked city centre. She took up with a warlord for a while, grew bored, poisoned all his wives and seduced his son, who murdered his father and began a civil war. She went south on horseback through the alien flower jungles that had conquered Earth after humanity had more or less abandoned it, then caught a *pneumatique* all the way down the spine of Florida to Key West.

A version of her last lover lived there, too. She saw him in a bar by the beach two weeks later. There were three main drugs in Key West: cigarettes, heroin, and alcohol. She had tried them all and decided she liked alcohol best. It helped you forget yourself in an odd, dissociative way that was both pleasant and disturbing. Perhaps she should have spent more of her long life drunk.

This version of her lover liked alcohol, too. He had thickened at the waist; his beard was white and full. His eyes, webbed by wrinkles, were still piercingly blue, but his gaze was vague and troubled, and he pretended not to notice the people who looked at him while he drank several complicated cocktails. She eavesdropped while he talked with the barkeep. She wanted to find out how the brash man who had needed to constantly prove himself against the world had turned out.

Badly, it seemed. The world was unforgiving, and his powers were fading.

"I lost her, Carlos," he told the barkeep. He meant his muse. "She's run out on me, the bitch."

"Now, Papa, you know that is not true," the young barkeep said. "I read your article in *Life* just last week."

"It was shit, Carlos. I can fake it well enough, but I can't do the good stuff any more. I need some quiet, and all day I get tourists trying to take my picture and spooking the cats. When I was younger I could work all day in a café, but now I need— hell, I don't know what I need. She's a bitch, Carlos. She only loves the young." Later, he said, "I keep dreaming of lions. One of the long white beaches in Afrique where the lions come down at dusk. They play there like cats, and I want to get to them, but I can't."

But Carlos was attending to another customer. Only she heard the old man. Later, after he had gone, she talked with Carlos herself. He was a puppet, and couldn't understand, but it didn't matter.

"All this was a bad idea," she said. She meant the bar, Key West, the Pacific Ocean, the world. "Do you want to know how it started?"

"Of course, ma'am. And may I bring you another drink?"

"I think I have had enough. You stay there and listen. Millions of years ago, while all of what would become humanity lived on the nine worlds and thousand worldlets around a single star in the Sky Hunter arm of the Galaxy, there was a religion that taught that individuals need never die. It was this religion which first drove humanity from their home star into the wide sea of the Galaxy. Individuals copied their personalities into computers, or cloned themselves, or spread their personalities through flocks of birds, or fish, or amongst hive insects. But there was one flaw in this religion. After millions of years, many of its followers were no longer human in form or in thought, except that they could trace back, generation upon generation, their descent from a single human ancestor. They had become transcendents, and each individual transcendent had become a clade, or an alliance, of millions of different minds. Mine is merely one of many, but it is one of the oldest, and one of the largest.

"I brought us here to unite us all in shared experiences. It isn't possible that one of us could have seen every wonder in the Galaxy, visit every world. There are a hundred billion stars in the Galaxy. It takes a year or two to explore the worlds of each star, and then there is the time it takes to travel between the stars. But there are ten million of us here. Clones, copies, descendants of clones and copies. Many of us have done nothing but explore. We have not seen everything, but we have seen most of it. I thought that we could pool all our information, that it would result in...something. A new religion, godhead. Something new, something different. But instead of fusion, there is only confusion; instead of harmony, chaos. I wonder how much I have changed, for none of these different people are much like me. Some of them say that they will not return home, that they will stay here until the sun ends it all. Some have joined the war in China—a few even refuse regeneration. Mostly, though, they want to party."

"There are parties every night, ma'am," the barkeep said. "That's Key West for you."

"Someone was following me, but I lost him. I think he was tracing me through the travel net, but I used contemporary transport to get here. He frightened me and I ran away, but perhaps he is what I need. I think I will find him. What month is this?"

"June, ma'am. Very hot, even for June. It means a bad hurricane season."

"It will get hotter," she said, thinking of the machine ticking away in the core of the sun.

And went to Tibet, where the Library was.

For some reason, the high plateau had been constructed as a replica of one of the great impact craters on Mars. She had given her servants a lot of discretion when building the Earth; it pleased her to be surprised, although it did not happen very often.

She had arrived at the top of one of the rugged massifs that defined the edge of the crater's wide basin. A little shrine stood close by: a mani eye painted on a stone pillar, a heap of stones swamped with skeins of red and blue and white and yellow prayer

flags ravelling in the cold wind. The scarp dropped away steeply
to talus slopes and the flood lava of the crater's floor, a smooth,
lightly cratered red plain mantled with fleets of barchan dunes.
Directly below, nestling amongst birches at the foot of the scarp's
sheer cliff, was the bone-white Library.

She took a day to descend the winding path. Now and then
pilgrims climbed past her. Many shuffled on their knees, eyes
lifted to the sky; a few fell face-forward at each step, standing up
and falling again at the point where their hands touched the
ground. All whirled prayer wheels and muttered their personal
mantras as they climbed, and few spared her more than a glance,
although at noon, while she rested under a gnarled juniper, one
old man came to her and shared a heel of dry black bread and
stringy dried yak meat. She learned from him that the pilgrims
were not puppets, as she had thought, but guests searching for
enlightenment. That was so funny and so sad she did not know
what to think about it.

The Library was a replica of the White Palace of the Potala. It
had been designed as a place of quiet order and contemplation, a
place where all the stories that the clade had told each other, all the
memories that they had downloaded or exchanged, would be
collected.

Now, it was a battleground.

Saffron-robed monks armed with weaponry from a thousand
different eras were fighting against black man-shaped androids.
Bodies of men and machines were sprawled on the great steps;
smoke billowed from the topmost ranks of the narrow windows;
red and green energy beams flickered against the pink sky.

She walked through the carnage untouched. Nothing in this
world could touch her. Only, perhaps, the man who was waiting
for her, sitting cross-legged beneath the ruin of the great golden
Buddha, which a stray shot from some energy weapon had decap-
itated and half-melted to slag. On either side, hundreds of candles
floated in great bowls filled with water; their lights shivered and
flickered from the vibration of heavy weaponry.

The man did not open his eyes as she approached, but he said softly, "I already have what I need. These foolish monks are defending a lost cause. You should stop them."

"It is what they have to do. They can't destroy us, of course, but I could destroy you."

"Guests can't harm other guests," he said calmly. "It is one of the rules."

"I am not a guest. Nor, I think, are you."

She told her machines to remove him. Nothing happened.

He opened his eyes. He said, "Your machines are invisible to the puppets and partials you created to populate this fantasy world. I am invisible to the machines. I do not draw my energy from the world grid, but from elsewhere."

And then he leaped at her, striking with formal moves millions of years old. The Angry Grasshopper, the Rearing Horse, the Snapping Mantis. Each move, magnified by convergent energies, could have killed her, evaporated her body, melted her machines.

But she allowed her body to respond, countering his attacks. She had thought that she might welcome death; instead, she was amused and exhilarated by the fury of her response. The habit of living was deeply ingrained; now it had found a focus.

Striking attitudes, tangling in a flurry of blows and counterblows, they moved through the battleground of the Library, through its gardens, down the long talus slope at the foot of the massif in a storm of dust and shattered stones.

At the edge of a lake that filled a small, perfectly circular crater, she finally tired of defensive moves and went on the attack. The Striking Eagle, the Plunging Dragon, the Springing Tiger Who Defends Her Cubs. He countered in turn. Stray energies boiled the lake dry. The dry ground shook, split open in a mosaic of plates. Gradually, a curtain of dust was raised above the land, obscuring the setting sun and the green face of the Moon, which was rising above the mountains.

They broke apart at last. They stood in the centre of a vast field of vitrified rock. Their clothes hung in tatters about their bodies. It was night, now. Halfway up the scarp of the massif, small lightnings flashed where the monks still defended the Library.

"Who are you?" she said again. "Did I create you?"

"I'm closer to you than anyone else in this strange mad world," he said.

That gave her pause. All the guests, clones or copies or replicants, were of her direct genetic lineage.

She said, "Are you my death?"

As if in answer, he attacked again. She fought back more forcefully than before; when he broke off, she saw that he was sweating.

"I am stronger than you thought," she said.

He took out a small black cube from his tattered tunic. He said, "I have what I need. I have the memory core of the Library. Everything anyone who came here placed on record is here."

"Then why do you want to kill me?"

"Because of who you are. I thought it would be fitting, after I stole this, to destroy the original."

She laughed. "You foolish man! Do you think we rely on a single physical location, a single master copy? It is the right of everyone in the clade to carry away the memories of everyone else. Why else are we gathered here?"

"I am not of your clade." He tossed the cube into the air, caught it, tucked it away. "I will use this knowledge against you. Against all of you. I have all your secrets."

"You say you are closer to me than a brother, yet you do not belong to the clade. You want to use our memories to destroy us." She had a sudden insight. "Is this war, then?"

He bowed. He was nearly naked, lit by the green light of the Moon and the dimming glow of the slag that stretched away in every direction. "Bravo," he said. "But it has already begun. Perhaps it is even over by now; after all, we are twenty thousand light years above the plane of the Galactic disc, thirty-five thousand light years from the hub of your Empire. It will take you

that long to return. And if the war is not over, then this will
finish it."

She was astonished. Then she laughed. "What an imagination I
have!"

He bowed again, and said softly, "You made this world from
your imagination, but you did not imagine me."

And he went somewhere else.

Her machines could not tell her where he had gone; she called
upon all the machines in the world, but he was no longer on the
Earth. Nor was he amongst the fleet of ships that had carried the
guests—in suspended animation, as frozen embryos, as codes
triply engraved in gold—to the world she had created for the
gathering.

There were only two other places he could be, and she did not
think he could have gone to the sun. If he had, then he would have
triggered the machine at the core, and destroyed her and everyone
else in the subsequent supernova.

So she went to the Moon.

She arrived on the farside. The energies he had used against her
suggested that he had his own machines, and she did not think that
he would have hidden them in full view of the Earth.

The machines which she had instructed to recreate the Earth
for the one hundred years of the gathering had recreated the
Moon, too, so that the oceans of the Earth would have the necessary tides; it had been easier than tangling gravitic resonances to
produce the same effect. It had taken little extra effort to recreate
the forests that had cloaked the Moon for a million years, between
the first faltering footsteps into space and the abandonment of the
Earth.

It was towards the end of the long Lunar night. All around,
blue firs soared up for hundreds of metres, cloaked in wide fans of
needles that in the cold and the dark drooped down to protect the
scaly trunks. The grey rocks were coated in thin snow, and frozen
lichens crunched underfoot. Her machines scattered in every

direction, quick as thought. She sat down on top of a big rough boulder and waited.

It was very quiet. The sky was dominated by the triple-armed pinwheel of the Galaxy. It was so big that when she looked at one edge she could not see the other. The Arm of the Warrior rose high above the arch of the Arm of the Hunter; the Arm of the Archer curved in the opposite direction, below the close horizon. Star clusters made long chains of concentrated light through the milky haze of the galactic arms. There were lines and threads and globes and clouds of stars, all fading into a general misty radiance dissected by dark lanes that barred the arms at regular intervals. The core was knitted from thin shells of stars in tidy orbits concentrically packed around the great globular clusters of the heart stars, like layers of glittering tissue wrapped around a heap of jewels.

Every star had been touched by humankind. Existing stars had been moved or destroyed; millions of new stars and planetary systems had been created by collapsing dust clouds. A garden of stars, regulated, ordered, tidied. The Library held memories of every star, every planet, every wonder of the old untamed Galaxy. She was beginning to realize that the gathering was not the start of something new, but the end of five million years of Galactic colonization.

After a long time, the machines came back, and she went where they told her.

It was hidden within a steep-sided crater, a castle or maze of crystal vanes that rose in serried ranks from deep roots within the crust, where they collected and focused tidal energy. He was at its heart, busily folding together a small spacecraft. The energy of the vanes had been greatly depleted by the fight, and he was trying to concentrate the remainder in the motor of the spacecraft. He was preparing to leave.

Her machines rose up and began to spin, locking in resonance with the vanes and bleeding off their store of energy. The machines began to glow as she bounded down the steep smooth slope towards the floor of the crater, red-hot, white-hot, as hot as the core of the sun, for that was where they were diverting the energy stored in the vanes.

Violet threads flicked up, but the machines simply absorbed that energy too. Their stark white light flooded the crater, bleaching the ranks of crystal vanes. A hot wind got up, raising dozens of quick lithe dust-devils.

She walked through the traps and tricks of the defenses, pulled the man from his fragile craft and took him up in a bubble of air to the neutral point between the Moon and the Earth.

"Tell me," she said. "Tell me why you came here. Tell me about the war."

He was surprisingly calm. He said, "I am a first generation clone, but I am on the side of humanity, not the transcendents. Transcendent clades are a danger to all of the variety within and between the civilizations in the Galaxy. At last the merely human races have risen against them. I am just one weapon in the greatest war ever fought."

"You are my flesh. You are of my clade."

"I am a secret agent. I was made from a single cell stolen from you several hundred years before you set off for this fake Earth and the gathering of your clade. I arrived only two years ago, grew my power source, came down to steal the memory core, and to assassinate you. Although I failed to kill you before, we are no longer in the place where you draw your power. Now—"

After a moment in which nothing happened, he screamed in frustration and despair. She pitied him. Even though all the power, the intrigues and desperate schemes his presence implied were as remote from her as the politics of a termite nest, she pitied all those who had bent their lives to produce this poor vessel, this failed moment.

She said, "Your power source is not destroyed, but my machines take all its energy. Why did your masters think us dangerous?"

"Because you will fill the Galaxy with your own kind. Because you will end human evolution. Because you will not accept that the Universe is greater than you can ever be. Because you refuse to die, and death is a necessary part of evolution."

She laughed. "Silly little man! Why would we accept limits? We are only doing what humanity has always done. We use science to master nature just as man-apes changed their way of thinking by making tools and using fire. Humanity has always struggled to become more than it is; it has always been ready to travel to the edge of the world, and step over it."

For the first time in a million years, those sentiments did not taste of ashes. By trying to destroy her, he had shown her what her life was worth.

He said, "But you do not change. That is why you are so dangerous. You and the other clades of transhumans have stopped humanity evolving. You would fill the Galaxy with trillions of copies of a few dozen individuals who are so scared of physical death that they will do any strange and terrible thing to themselves to survive."

He gestured at the blue-white globe that hung beneath their feet, small and vulnerable against the vast blackness between galaxies.

"Look at your Earth! Humanity left it four million years ago, yet you chose to recreate it for this gathering. You had a million years of human history on Earth to choose from, and four and a half billion years of the history of the planet itself, and yet almost half of your creation is given over to a single century."

"It is the century where we became what we are," she said, remembering Rapha. "It is the century when it became possible to become transhuman, when humanity made the first steps beyond the surface of a single planet."

"It is the century you were born in. You would freeze all history if you could, an eternity of the same thoughts thought by the same people. You deny all possibilities but your own self."

He drew himself up, defiant to the last. He said, "My ship will carry the memory core home without me. You take all, and give nothing. I give my life, and I give you this."

He held up something as complex and infolded as the throat of an orchid. It was a vacuum fluctuation, a hole in reality that when inflated would remove them from the Universe. She looked away at once—the image was already burned in her brain—and threw him into the core of the sun. He did not even have a chance to scream.

Alone in her bubble of air, she studied the wheel of the Galaxy, the ordered pattern of braids and clusters. Light was so slow. It took a hundred thousand years to cross from one edge of the Galaxy to the other. Had the war against her empire, and the empires of all the other transcendents, already ended? Had it already changed the Galaxy, stirred the stars into new patterns? She would not know until she returned, and that would take thirty-five thousand years.

But she did not have to return. In the other direction was the limitless Universe, a hundred billion galaxies. She hung there a long time, watching little smudges of ancient light resolve out of the darkness. Empires of stars wherever she looked, wonders without end.

We will fight the war, she thought, and we shall win, and we will go on for ever and ever.

And went down, found the bar near the beach. She would wait until the old man came in, and buy him a drink, and talk to him about his dream of the lions.

INTERSTITIAL

Echo huddled under his thin blanket, clutching the pillow to his head and feigning sleep as footsteps marched down the aisle towards his bunk. His chip told him it was just after three in the morning. He was horribly tired, his blood glucose low, his muscles poisoned by fatigue. Ever since the Copernicus Alliance had taken Little Tokyo, some four hundred hours ago, South Pole had been on a war footing. Purity squads had rounded up and executed recalcitrant techs in an orgy of self-righteousness. The upper levels had been evacuated, the greenhouses stripped, the defense systems mobilized. After finishing a twenty-hour shift, Echo had collapsed into his bunk without even making a stop at the canteen, but he was too wired to sleep.

The footsteps drew closer and closer, undeniably vectoring on Echo's bunk. His heartbeat spiked as the thin Mylar curtain he had tacked up for privacy was ripped aside. Light washed red across his squeezed eyelids. Someone spoke into his ear: a harsh and familiar voice, the voice of his brother, Captain Achilles.

"Rise and shine, Dave, you unrecycleable piece of shit. Time to go to work."

Echo was eighteen, the median age for techs. He had been working since age twelve; only his eldest brother still used his birth name. Captain Achilles had five years on him, a grizzled veteran who had survived two skirmishes with patrols from the Copernicus Alliance. He had been a bully when both of them were being raised by their dam, and was a bully still. He pulled Echo out of his bunk into the freezing dark of the dorm, told him to leave his boots because there was no time to put them on, and to leave the rest of his stuff as well.

Captain Achilles was bulked out by an armoured p-suit with a chameleon paint-job, its helmet hung from the utility belt. Echo was wearing only thin underalls, and because it was the middle of the long lunar night, power in the dorms was strictly rationed. It was easily ten below freezing; the cold of the floor scorched the tender soles of his bare feet. Echo said, between clenched teeth, "You fucker," and was rewarded with a cuff to the back of his head.

"I got you a prime job," Captain Achilles said, pushing Echo ahead of him between tiered bunks. He was a very tall man, with close-cropped hair and a long thin face whose pronounced chin always looked swarthy. He added, with calculated nastiness, "You're going to love it."

Echo knew that Captain Achilles was crazy. All soldiers were stone-cold crazy. It was the price of eternal pumped-hard vigilance, overdoses of testosterone and steroids, and the combat programmes in their heads. Since they weren't yet officially at war, this had to be some deeply dangerous bad-ass mission, just the kind of thing a soldier would love. He said, "Oh shit. You bastard. You're putting me on the front line."

"You techs are all the same. Snivelling worms with no guts."

"You mean no backbones," Echo said, which earned him another cuff. By now they were bouncing along narrow corridors lit only by red emergency lights, as if Echo were a virus being chased down a capillary by an implacable leucocyte. The cuff knocked Echo to the floor. He ricocheted back up, and before he could wipe his bloody nose was caught in the back of the neck by Captain Achilles and pushed on.

"You will do your job and you will do it well," Captain Achilles said, "and you will do it without smart chat or asking damn fool questions. I'll make the family proud of you yet."

"They'll weep crocodile tears and forget me as soon as I've been recycled."

"Survive this, you'll be a hero. You owe me big, little brother. Just for once, you'll be doing a real man's job."

"Can I at least ask if we are at war?"

"Not yet. Soon. We've already pulled a move on that pirate's nest of slant eyes and traitors, and if we're lucky they'll try and retaliate. *Then* we'll be at war. Meanwhile, Dave, you've been selected for special duties."

A phrase which jammed an icicle in Echo's heart. Soldiers loved special duties. It meant high danger and almost certain death. It was the one thing that techs tried to avoid at all costs. He said, "Let me guess. We've taken Little Tokyo from the Copernicus Alliance."

"Who told you that?"

"I worked it out just this minute."

"Yeah?" Captain Achilles clearly didn't believe this. "You're in the army now, bro. No need to think."

Echo said, "Thinking is what I do for a living. I'm right, aren't I?"

"We took it fifty hours ago, and secured the perimeter. It's ours, bro. There's stuff they missed, and that's why worms like you are needed. This is a chance to make the family look good, Dave boy. A chance to redeem yourself."

"I'm needed for defense work. That's more important than some special op."

"I know what you were working on. Those old pop-up radar-guided missiles? Last ditch stuff we will never need because we are strong and we will keep the enemy far below the horizon at all times. This is special, bro. This will make you famous."

Captain Achilles shoved Echo through a pressure curtain into the brilliant glare of a staging lock. It was almost completely filled with a dozen soldiers in p-suits, and the coffin-shaped metal boxes which contained their gear. The soldiers all gave Echo the cold eye, as if wondering exactly what his guts might look like, and where would be the best place to draw them out. This was the Greek crew, Captain Achilles' command, with names like Perseus, Andromeda, Jason, and Alexander stitched to the breasts of their p-suits. Most likely, they were already running their combat programmes, and Echo tried to avoid making eye contact as, cold and miserable, he climbed into his borrowed suit. It was ill-fitting, the extension joints at elbows and knees loose and baggy, and it stank. The left knee joint was stiff and gave him a comical limp; the helmet visor was scuffed, and half the functions were redlined.

Echo hooked up his backpack, and followed the soldiers through the airlock into a bus. Captain Achilles sat beside him, slipped him a tube of fish paste, and whispered, "You're replacing a casualty on the tech team out there. Don't fuck up and you'll make me proud."

Echo sucked down paste and spluttered, "What kind of casualty?"

"The bitch went crazy. Tried to kill a couple of my men. Can you believe that? They iced her ass straight away, of course."

"Of course they did. It's what soldiers do."

Captain Achilles thrust his face close to Echo's. His eyes were bloodshot and he reeked of male aggression. A hectic butterfly rash from steroid overdose stippled his nose and cheeks. He grinned and said, "You better believe it, little bro."

Echo could feel his cells bloom gratefully as the protein in the fishpaste began to enter his starved system. It was laced with testosterone and steroids and oestrogen suppressant, all going straight to work on him too. He had squeezed the plastic tube flat; now, he unzipped the seam with a thumbnail and licked up the last smears of paste.

Captain Achilles, watching in disgust, said, "Don't they feed you in your nasty little warren?"

"Of course not. Soldiers get all the real food."

"We need it to keep strong and fit."

"And stupid. I bet your people didn't even try and find out why that poor tech went crazy before they iced her."

Captain Achilles gave Echo a tab. "That's your job, bro. Stay sharp and do good work and maybe you'll get back in one piece."

♓

The tab, high-grade military issue meth, was kicking in when the bus boosted with a bone-deep roar and bruising acceleration. The meth gave everything a harsh, heightened edge; Echo's thoughts tumbled like a rain of razor blades. His p-suit couldn't access the bus's video system, but he was right in the back of the cargo tube, and by pulling his harness to its full extension he could lean over and look out the scratched port.

The full Earth hung in the black sky, white as a sunblinded eye, bright enough to cast shadows across the heavily cratered terrain that was unravelling below the bus's keel. Echo activated the scope on the suit's teevee system, was rewarded with a fuzzy, upside down view of Earth's ice-covered disc. He could just make out the belt of volcanoes along the equator, tiny blotches against a uniform white so blinding it was like staring at the sun.

Fifty years ago, a robot probe, the last sent from the Moon to Earth, had discovered that bacteria and algae were still living around the volcanoes, in hot springs and in water trapped under fresh lava fields. Apart from a few species clinging to deep sea hydrothermal vents, this was the only surviving life on Earth. Humanity's survival on the Moon was just as precarious. When the sun's luminescence had begun to decline, and ice had spread towards the equator from the north and south poles, reviving old space flight technologies had taken second place to fighting for dwindling habitable territory. Grandiose plans to crash comets into the atmosphere and raise the carbon dioxide partial pressure to stimulate greenhouse warming had come to nothing.

In the end, only a few thousand people had escaped the great winter. Those in the Yankee Mars base had died out within thirty years, and for two centuries the two dozen bases on the Moon had fought savage wars over dwindling resources. Now, after the Copernicus Alliance had destroyed Little Tokyo, the last humans alive were in two bitterly opposed bases, one at the South Pole, the other buried deep below the surface of Mare Insularum. Enriched by the biomass looted from Little Tokyo, the Copernicus Alliance would be urging its population to make babies, and would turn those babies into hardwired warriors. In less than ten years they would be ready to begin a final war against South Pole—so South Pole would have to strike first. Of course, soldiers had never needed an excuse to go to war. It was what they were programmed to do.

Echo soon tired of staring at Earth, and withdrew into his own reveries. Despite the blast of meth, he actually fell asleep, and woke only when the bus blew its retrojets and more or less crash-landed near the wreckage of Little Tokyo. All flights were like this: fast and low to escape any autonomous missiles the enemy might have scattered across the surface.

Captain Achilles kicked Echo to his feet, ordered him to pull on his gloves and fasten his helmet, kicked him through the bus's airlock. Like all bases, Little Tokyo had buried itself deep underground, beneath rubble berms and heavy slabs of concrete, but the Copernicus Alliance's burrowing warheads had blown it open like so many hammers smashing into a clam shell. Bits of blackened concrete were strewn for kilometres across the trampled and blasted moonscape. There were pits everywhere, brimful of inky shadows, and the raw scars left by the strip-mining equipment that had pulled out every kilogram of steel from the reinforced concrete and ripped up the solar farm and the greenhouses. The entire population had been killed, either in the bombardment or in the desperate hand-to-hand fighting afterwards, and the corpses had been rendered for their organics on the spot.

The Alliance had completely withdrawn from the wrecked and looted base sixty hours ago, leaving only boobytraps for the scouting party from South Pole to deal with.

"We probably haven't found them all, so watch where you walk," Captain Achilles said as he manhandled Echo towards a rover, where two soldiers were waiting for them. "I don't want to have to go back and find another tech to take your place."

"I appreciate the sentiment. If the base has been stripped, why am I here?"

"Those sons-of-bitches didn't find everything. Get in."

As soon as Echo had clambered into the back of the rover, beside his brother, it accelerated down a ramp of compacted soil into a wide cut-and-cover tunnel. They drove recklessly fast, in complete darkness. From his p-suit's GPS, Echo estimated that they had gone twenty kilometres when the headlights and brakes kicked on simultaneously and the rover slewed to a halt in front of a standard airlock that protruded from a rubble wall.

Echo was shoved inside by the two soldiers and Captain Achilles, and they all cycled through into normal pressure and a chilly but survivable temperature. Menaced by the soldiers' assault rifles, Echo was ordered to strip off his p-suit. Shivering, his nose itching from the wet ash smell of moondust, Echo was pinioned by a soldier while Captain Achilles used a pressure gun to blast a capsule under the skin of his forearm.

"You're going to find out what they're doing down there," Captain Achilles said. His voice was rendered flat and metallic by his p-suit's external speaker; his face was barely visible behind his gold-filmed visor. "Once you're done, pinch the capsule hard; that will activate the radio transmitter."

"Why don't you go down there yourself?"

"Because they'd attack us and we'd have to kill them," Captain Achilles said. "And we don't want them dead because they haven't finished work yet."

Echo tried to smile, although he knew it must look hideously false. "You're scared, aren't you? Scared of techs. You don't understand what we do."

"The people down there have gone crazy. That's why we don't understand them. My advice is that you don't go crazy too."

The soldier who was holding Echo turned him around and shoved him into a bucket elevator strung on a jury-rigged winch. Captain Achilles said, "Work good, bro. Be a man. Do our family proud," and thumbed a fat red button at the end of a hanging cable.

The winch hummed and the bucket fell into a narrow shaft towards a promise of light far below.

Ж

It fell a long way: at least a kilometre. Echo's ears popped twice, adjusting to the increase in air pressure. It grew noticeably warmer; still below freezing, but no longer dangerously so. Echo began to think he might at least live through the ride when the elevator dropped into a huge chamber.

It was a deep cylindrical excavation with what looked like a missile or chimney rising from the rubble floor and reaching all the way to the roof. There were banks of blazing lights, and the bare rock walls had been sealed at tremendous expense with spray-on construction polymer. The missile tube or chimney or pillar—perhaps it was some kind of huge hydraulic ram, Echo thought—was shiny black, and scratched and hatched all over, as if attacked by a gang of graffiti artists armed with jack-hammers. It was rooted in a jumble of raw rock, with bits of kit—cylinders of polymer mix, ration packs and water kegs, a microwave, a recycling toilet—scattered around. Scaffolding rose up around it, clever, lightweight plastic stuff that constantly shifted and shivered, balancing out the load of the four people who were climbing down to meet Echo, their shadows cast hugely across polymer-sprayed walls.

There were just four techs working on what they called the Artifact: Basic and Syntax, Slash and Port. Syntax was their leader. She explained that it was their mission to understand what the Artifact was trying to tell them.

Echo craned to stare up the dizzying perspective of the pillar's glistening black length. It was clad in some kind of seamless stone coat and radiated an evil cold; he had burnt his hand when he had touched its flank. He said, "You're trying to figure out how it works?"

"In a way," Syntax said. She was a grizzled oldster of forty odd years, almost bald, her face scarred where cancers had been removed, steel plates instead of teeth showing when she cracked a smile. Like the others, she had the shiny-eyed look of someone who has spent far too long on meth. "The marks dug into its surface are code. We're reading it, piece by piece."

"It's a message," one of the other techs said.

Echo laughed. "Like a time capsule? Why would Little Tokyo go to all the expense of burying a time capsule?"

Syntax said, "Little Tokyo didn't make it; they found it. It's a time capsule all right, from the very deep past."

"You mean the American Empire?"

Syntax flashed her steel teeth. "Hardly. As near as we can tell, it's seven hundred million years old."

)(

After a scout patrol had discovered the entrance to the tunnel, Syntax's small crew of techs had been hijacked from the library and put to work on the Artifact. They were all wired with meth so they could work twenty hours a day, snatching sleep when they fell from exhaustion, sucking food from cold packs while they worked. One woman had gone bugfuck crazy and had jumped on the bucket elevator after it had brought down a case of rations; it had come right back down with her bullet-riddled body, and the others had buried her at the base of the Artifact.

None of the techs trusted Echo because he was so obviously a
spy. He didn't blame them. He knew that if he didn't readily give
up whatever he learned here, it would be tortured out of him by
his brother. The other techs were even more cynical about their
fate. They believed that once they had finished translating the
Artifact they would all be killed.

"Like Egyptian slaves who constructed the tombs of
pharaohs," Syntax told Echo. "Soldiers don't think techs are
human. They'll kill us and bury us all when we're done, so we
can't squawk about what we've discovered."

She set him to translating a huge block of glyphs carved high
up on the Artifact. Her crew had already worked out that the
strings of dots and dashes carved deep in the black granite column
were binary code, but no one would tell Echo whether they had
translated any of it, or what they had found.

He quickly became as obsessed as the others. All techs loved
crypto—it tickled their maths programmes. Echo worked until
he dropped from exhaustion, ate only when the pain in his
stomach cut through his focused concentration. The cold,
bone-dry air sucked moisture from his skin, and although he
was constantly taking sips from a bladder of distilled water, his
mouth felt as if it had been packed with salt. His world shrank
to the problem at hand. He hardly noticed the other techs,
working away on their separate projects above and below him like
monks in isolated carrels. When Port and Slash had a fight over
use of one of the computers, he watched for a few minutes
and went back to work as soon as Syntax swarmed down to break
it up.

Echo took pics of every square centimetre of the glyphs,
loaded them into one of the disposable computers, ran dozens of
decryption programs, started writing his own when nothing out
of the box cracked the code. He began to think that he had been
given a piece of junk info to keep him harmlessly busy, but there
was also a nagging sense that he was missing something familiar
and obvious.

On one of his food breaks, he noticed that Basic, the youngest of the techs, was picking about amongst the rubble at the base of the Artifact, catching and zapping the tiny motile cameras which the soldiers used to spy on them. Echo joined in, taking pleasure in outsmarting the cameras' hardwired cockroach evasion routines. After a while, Basic said that she was only doing it because it helped her think. Even if they got all the cameras, the soldiers would just send down more.

Echo smiled, tasting blood as his dry lips cracked. "Maybe there's a better way. You got any construction polymer kit left?"

His voice was a rusty croak; he hadn't spoken since Syntax had showed him where to start work—more than thirty hours ago. He wondered if the war with the Copernicus Alliance had begun. Somehow, it didn't seem to matter.

The girl shrugged. "Sure, I guess."

Basic would be pretty, Echo thought, if she was given a couple of baths and about a month's sleep and another month on a proper diet, if her stringy hair was washed and cut and the sores on her face treated. Techs weren't allowed to have children—that was the prerogative of successful soldiers—but there were plenty of unofficial marriages amongst them. For the first time, he was aware that he stank like a pharm goat, that his underalls clung greasily to his greasy skin.

He said, "There's this neat trick I know. Want to help?"

He showed Basic how to mix up the ingredients of construction polymer in proportions that were radically different from the instructions. Sprayed on to the plastic liner of the crypt, the stuff stayed sticky, a trap for the roving cameras. Then he and Basic went on a serious bug hunt, and the other techs joined in. When the soldiers realized what was happening, more cameras were sent crawling down the walls, but these were trapped in the wide sticky band of polymer. Then the soldiers tried dropping cameras, but the five techs methodically stomped or zapped the hapless critters before they could find shelter. After that, a few cameras were lowered on diamond thread, but any that were dropped too low could be zapped, and the rest were too high up to be able to see much.

After the great bug hunt, the other techs still maintained a frosty politeness towards Echo, but they relaxed their rule about discussing their work. Sometimes they even talked to each other instead of using their covert librarian finger language, and Echo (who knew the basics of finger language, but couldn't follow their practiced, high-speed flurries) began to pick up clues about the Artifact.

It was a chunk of basaltic granite, shaped by some high temperature process that had fused its exterior to a glassy sheen as hard as diamond. A mining team from Little Tokyo had found it by accident, while digging for the remnants of an iron meteorite. After Little Tokyo had been overrun, the Copernicus Alliance had either failed to find the Artifact, or hadn't realized what it was. Since most of the Alliance's population was soldiers, the latter was most likely.

Hundreds of thousands of glyph strings had been cut into the Artifact's surface. The shortest ones had been deciphered—basic stuff about Earth and the Solar System, biochemistry, fundamental mathematical principles. There were pictures, too, decoding into one hundred ninety-two by one hundred ninety-two pixel grids. Echo persuaded Slash, a dour young man with a badly scarred bald head, to show him a map extracted from one patch of code, although it didn't look like any map of Earth Echo had ever seen.

"That's how it was back then," Slash said. "All the continents were lined up in this single band along the equator. It confirms the dating we got from thermoluminescence and radon decay."

Echo was struck with a sideways bit of associational logic. "Show me where you got this from," he said.

An hour later, he had cracked the chunk of code he had been assigned.

It was a movie, highly compressed by pasting every bit of non-moving background into each frame instead of generating fresh code, and recycling common motion elements from a palette stuck at the front end, mixed up with instructions on polygon types, greyscales, and scan rates.

It ran for just under a minute, black and white, fourteen frames a second, one hundred ninety-two scan lines, as low rez as stone age teevee. Echo looped it and played it over and over. He fell asleep with it still playing, woke to find the other techs watching it raptly.

It showed a thing like a half-squashed crab built out of bubblewrap sidling up to the camera, slowly turning on a fringe of tiny legs. At what might be its front end was a bug face above a rack of crushing and chiselling and biting mouthparts like an organic Swiss Army knife; the camera or whatever had taken the movie zoomed jerkily in on the mouthparts at the end, as if their frantic twitching was significant.

"There's your alien," Echo said.

"It isn't an alien," Basic said abstractedly, pushing greasy hair away from her eyes as she leaned in, watching the loop start over. "Look at that recycled critter dance."

"It doesn't seem to have eyes," Echo said.

Slash tapped the screen of Echo's computer. "There are apertures all around the rim of the shell. Like pinhole cameras. We have the gross morphology of the boogers from other chunks of code."

"Just stills," Port said, giving Echo a challenging look. He was a rangy fellow with a wolfish look, pale as a ghost, long wispy hairs at the corners of his mouth. "Stills and diagrams."

Echo said, "I'm not pissed. I know you held stuff back from me, and I would have done the same in your place. So you call these things boogers?"

The other four techs looked at each other. Syntax said, "There have to be dozens of loops like this in the code. You did good, Echo."

"I didn't think it would look like a crab," Echo said.

"It doesn't," Slash said. "Not exactly."

"Well," Echo insisted, "it isn't a very alien-looking alien."

The other four techs looked at each other again.

Echo said, "I'm not getting out of here alive, right? I might as well know what I'm gonna die for."

Syntax said, "It isn't exactly an alien. It came from Earth, just like us. It seems that everyone got the history of life on Earth wrong."

Syntax did most of the explaining, with the others chipping in now and then.

The great winter was not the first time Earth had been covered in ice. There had been another great winter seven hundred million years ago, caused by an accident of geology rather than a dip in the sun's luminescence. Breakup of the Earth's only land-mass at that time, a vast equatorial supercontinent, had exposed huge areas of what had been interior desert to oceanic rainfall, and chemical weathering of the exposed rocks had locked atmos-pheric carbon dioxide into carbonates. The catastrophic drop in carbon dioxide partial pressure had meant that less infrared radia-tion was trapped by Earth's atmosphere. As the mean global temperature fell, ice had begun to spread outwards from the poles, and because ice reflected sunlight, there had been runaway, unstoppable glaciation, ice spreading south and north across open water and reflecting back more sunlight which cooled the Earth so the ice could spread some more. In only a few decades the whole Earth had been covered in ice and all higher forms of life had been wiped out, including the boogers and their nascent civilization.

Because there was no rainfall and no weathering of rocks, carbon dioxide released by volcanoes had slowly built up in the atmosphere. At last, after millions of years, the equator had warmed enough to begin to melt the ice, allowing water vapour back into the atmosphere. And because water vapour is even better at trapping infrared radiation than carbon dioxide, the global temperature had quickly risen to forty or fifty degrees Centigrade, generating vast hyperhurricanes and continent-sized storms of acidic rain, which had rapidly weathered newly exposed rocks and removed excess carbon dioxide, cooling the Earth and allowing life to flourish once more.

And evolution had begun all over again.

"It was always thought that it took three and a half billion years of evolution before multicellular life arose," Syntax said, "and another half billion years to evolve intelligence. But there was an entire multicellular evolutionary epoch before our own, wiped out by a great winter whose end was the trigger that started our own epoch. Wiped out so thoroughly that not even a fossil was found. The glaciers scraped at least fifty metres of rock from the surface of the land, and acidic rain eroded at least as much again."

"No animals with backbones or carbonate shells seem to have evolved during the boogers' epoch," Basic said. "Only soft-bodied animals which rarely fossilize. The boogers' shells were made up of millions of cells of pneumatically inflated polymer film."

Slash said, "The boogers' epoch was probably started by the end of a previous great winter, coincident with the appearance of oxygen-evolving photosynthesis. There were at least five cycles of great winters and acidic hothouses. There might have been two or three evolutionary epochs while Earth's atmosphere was still mostly methane."

"Unlikely," Port said. "Biochemistry adapted to reducing atmospheres is too low energy for multicellular life."

"Life that we know about," Slash said sharply, obviously reiterating an old argument.

Syntax hushed them, and told Echo, "The boogers developed spaceflight once their great winter started. In only ten years or so they were more advanced than we ever were."

"But they died out," Echo said.

Syntax nodded. "They left the Artifact as a monument to their epoch. There are maps on it which suggest that there are dozens of other Artifacts on the Moon, probably copies of this one."

Basic said, "The boogers accepted their fate. Only single-celled bacteria and algae survived their great winter. Those were our ancestors. Everything else died out."

"Except maybe the Ediacara," Port said.

"We can never prove that," Slash said.

Port told Echo, "The Ediacara were this very weird group of multicellular animals that were around just after the end of the Precambrium—at the end of the boogers' great winter. They were nothing like any other known phylum—those evolved later, in the so-called Cambrium explosion which gave birth to every modern multicellular phylum. The Ediacara could be a relic of the boogers' epoch. They could have survived around hydrothermal vents."

"But we'll never know," Slash said.

"And we'll never not know either," Port said, glaring at him.

Basic told Echo, "The soldiers wanted us to find records of technology that could be used against the Copernicus Alliance, but there's nothing like that here."

"It's no more than a greeting," Syntax said. "A message sent into the future in case intelligent life evolved again. The boogers didn't think like us. They accepted that life was a precarious thing, able to exist only in those interstices of a planet's history between catastrophic events. They were fatalists."

"I think they were a lot like us," Basic said. "People put messages from Earth on early deep space probes like Pioneer and Voyager. Those were sent into interstellar space rather than the future, but the intention was exactly the same."

"In the end it doesn't matter," Port told Echo. "We can't get out of here."

"When the soldiers realize that there's nothing useful here they'll kill us," Slash said, "but they'll let you live."

"Nothing useful?" Echo laughed, and tasted blood from his split lips. "You're thinking like soldiers. I don't blame you. The soldiers took over long ago. We all think like them now, and all we think about is survival."

"You're working for the soldiers," Slash said. "Don't deny it. You're a spy. That's why you were sent here."

"My brothers and sisters are all soldiers," Echo said. "All of them are ashamed that I became a tech, but my oldest brother took it personally. That's why he sent me here. He wanted me to do a soldier's job because that might make me into a soldier. But once you've been made over into a tech that's what you are."

Echo tapped his head. "At first you run the programmes, but pretty soon they start running you. It's the same with soldiers. They can't help what they are because they were made that way, but it's our fault that we let them take over. I looked up the records once. Hardly anyone does that now. We're too focused on the present, on survival. In the last two hundred years the proportion of soldiers increased every time we've gone to war against another base, and remained at the same high level after the war ended, until the next war pushed the proportion even higher. The soldiers are in charge now, but we were in charge before the wars began. We used to set the agenda.

"And you know what? Even now we're stronger than soldiers. We face up to the truth. We can see what has happened to the human race. As resources decreased, aggression between the bases increased. It was inevitable. We'll fight the Copernicus Alliance and either they'll beat us or we'll beat them, but in the end it won't matter who wins. Because after the last battle there will be no more resources to grab, and the victorious base will dwindle and die out, or tear itself to pieces in civil war. We'll have lost everything that makes us human. We'll have become as mindless as a nest of ants. Maybe we can't survive until the Earth warms again, but we can die with dignity. That's what I've learned here. We'll beat the soldiers, and we'll build our own Artifact. And in half a billion years perhaps some new species will understand what we achieved. What we were."

The other techs were smiling. Echo felt blood heat his face as his sudden passion turned to embarrassment. "Shit," he said, crestfallen. "You already know that."

"We're techs too," Syntax said.

"The woman who died," Echo said. "She wasn't crazy, was she?"

"We drew lots," Port said.

"And she lost."

"No," Syntax said gently. "She won. We knew the soldiers would send down a replacement because we were one person short of a squad. That's how soldiers think. And we knew that they would send down a spy."

"Someone with a way out," Port said.

"Of course, we weren't sure if he would help us," Slash said.

"We knew we could get him to help us," Basic said, "because he would be a tech, just like us."

Echo put his hand over the bruise on his forearm, where the capsule had been inserted. "Of course I'll help you. Just tell me what I have to do."

)(

When everything was ready, when everyone was in position and the lights had been turned down, Echo pinched the capsule in his arm. There was a moment of sharp pain as its acid leaked out and created a charge to power the tiny radio transmitter. Echo sat on a cold slab of rock in the semi-darkness, and waited.

An hour passed. Halfway through the second, dozens of diamond wires dropped down almost to the ground, some with cameras at their ends, some with glaring lights that spun like mad stars. Ten minutes later, the bucket elevator came into view high overhead, descending past the black flank of the Artifact. Echo stood up and backed away as it fell towards him.

Captain Achilles swung over the edge of the bucket before it grounded, surprisingly agile considering he was wearing an armoured p-suit and toting an assault rifle. His voice blared at full volume through the p-suit's external speaker.

"Where are they! Are they dead?"

Echo raised his hands. He felt very calm, although his heart was beating quickly and lightly. Its rapid pulse tremored in his fingertips. He said, "Not exactly."

Slash and Port stood up behind Captain Achilles, throwing off their dust-covered blankets, raising their hoses. Captain Achilles managed to half-turn before they started to spray him; arms already stuck to his sides, he fell beneath falling sheets of hardening polymer. Echo bounded forward and ripped the antenna from his backpack.

The first part was over.

The five techs, working with feverish haste, blinded the cameras with polymer, loaded kegs of polymer mix into the bucket elevator, packed them with crude gunpowder made from rations burned to charcoal, nitrates from the recycling toilet, and sulphur from a couple of lamp batteries. Slash and Port lashed themselves to the underside of the bucket with strips torn from their underalls and, with practiced synchronization, Echo pressed the return button in the same moment that Syntax lit the gunpowder-soaked fuse.

The fuse fizzled merrily as the elevator slowly rose towards the slot in the chamber's roof. Echo found that he was counting silently, and wondered if they'd got the fuse length right. It had been difficult to work out how the elevator's travel time would be affected by its load. Too long, and the soldiers would have time to stifle it; too short, and the surprise package would blow prematurely.

He was still counting when the elevator, with the two half-naked men swinging beneath it, vanished into the shadows high above. A minute passed. Echo began to think that it had all gone wrong—and a dull thud shook dust from the roof. He and Syntax and Basic whooped and hugged each other, broke apart when they heard a ragged burst of gunfire.

Silence. Then a body dropped out of the darkness, slammed against the black flank of the Artifact and tumbled down, arms and legs akimbo, landing with a horrible wet broken noise on a slab of rock. It was Port. He had been shot in the chest and face. The three techs were still staring at him when the bucket elevator started back down. Slash was standing on a freeform sculpture of solidified polymer. Only then did they know that they had won.

)(

"We'll kill all of you," Captain Achilles told Echo.

The techs had used solvent to clean polymer from his rifle, and more solvent to free him. They had made him shuck his p-suit at gunpoint, and then had tied him up. He lay on the ground in his underalls, arms lashed behind his back, legs drawn up because his ankles were tied to his wrists. He glared up at Echo and said, "Kill me now, bro. Because I surely mean to kill you."

Echo said, "We'll leave you and the other two here, at the bottom of the shaft, no p-suits, no way of contacting the outside. Just like you left us. The rest of your soldiers will come and find you, sooner or later, and meanwhile you could do worse than study the Artifact, and think about everything I've told you."

"Those lies aren't worth a second's thought," Captain Achilles said. "How do you know your new friends are coming back? They've left you here with me, Dave boy, because you're a spy."

"They'll be back."

Echo was guarding the soldiers who had been caught like flies in amber when the construction polymer had been blown all over the platform at the top of the shaft. One had managed to half-free his arm in the instant before it solidified around him, and he had shot Port. At first, Slash had wanted to kill the two soldiers for that, but his anger had quickly subsided into sullen determination. Techs weren't killers. He and Syntax had taken the soldiers' p-suits and had driven off in the rover to steal the bus. Syntax had been a mechanic before she had been transferred to the library. She and Slash would fly it in over the top of the chamber, blast into the cut-and-cover tunnel and bring in spare p-suits.

"If they do manage to steal the bus, they'll run away," Captain Achilles said, "but most likely they're already dead. Free me, bro, and I'll save your ass when my people come looking for me."

"They'll come back," Echo said.

"Suppose they do. What will you do if you reach South Pole? Kill all the soldiers?"

"There won't be many soldiers left at South Pole," Echo said. "There's a war on. And if we have to fight, we'll be fighting inside the base, a place techs know better than soldiers. That's what happened at Little Tokyo, isn't it? After its techs found out what the Artifact was for, they rebelled against the soldiers, and the Copernicus Alliance saw its chance and finished them all off. And now the same thing is happening at the Alliance's base, because their techs found out about the Artifact too.

"You thought you could contain us, bro, but you were as wrong as all the other soldiers. We're going to tell the other techs about what we found here, and we're going to ask them whether they want humanity to die out in a futile war, or whether we should work on a suitable memorial instead. You could help. All the soldiers could help. Once the war against the Copernicus Alliance is over, there will be no more enemies to fight, nothing more for you to do. Tell me that you'll think about helping me and I won't leave you here."

Captain Achilles made a tremendous effort and managed to arch his back so he could spit at Echo. He missed, and glared at Echo with a mad, bloodshot eye.

"That's what I thought," Echo said sadly. "Soldiers can't help being soldiers. It's all they can do."

"You're as crazy as the others."

High above, shadows swayed across the flank of the Artifact as the elevator descended towards them. Echo stood up.

"Here come my people," Captain Achilles said. "Last chance to ask for my help, bro."

"I don't think so," Echo said.

"If you're so sure, why are you holding on to the rifle like that?" Captain Achilles laughed. "Suppose you get out of here, suppose you even get to South Pole. I bet you don't even know how you're going to get past security."

Basic leaned out of the swaying bucket, waving madly. Echo waved back, and threw the rifle away. "We're techs," he told the soldier. "We'll think of something."

HOW WE LOST THE MOON,
A TRUE STORY BY FRANK W. ALLEN

You probably think that you know everything about it. After all, here we are,
barely into the second quarter of the first
century of the Third Millennium, and it's being touted as the
biggest event in the history of humanity. Yeah, right. But tossing
aside such impossibly grandiose claims, it was and still is a hell of
a story. It's generated millions of bytes of web journalism (two
years later, there are still more than two hundred official web sites,
not to mention the tens of thousands of unofficial newsgroups
devoted to proving that it was really caused by God, or aliens, or
St Elvis), tens of thousands of hours of TV and a hundred
schlocky movies (and I do include James Cameron's seven-hour
blockbuster), thousands of scientific papers and dozens of thick
technical reports, including the ten million page Congressional
report, and the ghostwritten biographies of scientists Who Should
Have Known Better.

Now you might think that I'm sending out my version
because I was either misrepresented or completely ignored in all
the above. Not at all. I'll be the first to admit that my part in the
whole thing was pretty insignificant, but nevertheless I was there,
right at the beginning. So consider this shareware text a footnote

or even a Tall Tale, and if you like it, do feel free to pass it on. But
don't change the text or drop the byline, if you please.

♓

It began in the middle of a routine calibration run in the Exawatt
Fusion facility. All the alarms went off and the AI in charge shut
everything down and sent in the maintenance robots. The robots
couldn't find any evidence of physical damage, but the integrity
and radiation alarms kept ringing, and analysis of experimental
data showed that there had been a tremendous fluctuation in
energy levels just *after* the fusion pulse. So the scientists sent the
two of us, Mike Doherty and me, over the horizon to eyeball the
place.

You've probably seen a zillion pictures. The Exawatt was a
low, square concrete block half-buried in the smooth floor of
Mendeleev crater on the Moon's farside, surrounded by bulldozed
roadways and cable trenches, the two nuclear reactors that
powered it just at the level horizon to the south. It used a thousand million times more power than the entire US electrical grid
to fire up, for less than a millisecond, six pulsed lasers focused on
a target barely ten micrometres across, producing conditions
which simulated those in the first picoseconds of the Big Bang,
before symmetry was broken. Like the atom bomb a century
before, it pushed the envelopes of engineering and physics. The
scientists responsible for firing off the first atom bomb believed
that there was a slight but definite chance that it would set fire to
the Earth's atmosphere; the scientists running the Exawatt
thought that there was a possibility that it might burst its containment and vaporize several hundred square kilometres around it.
That's why they had built it on the Moon's farside, inside a deep
crater. That's why it was run by robots, with the actual labs in a
bunker buried over the horizon.

That's why, when it went wrong, they sent in a couple of
GLPs to take a look.

We went in an open rover, straight down the service road. We were wearing bright orange radiation-proof shrouds over our Moon suits, and camera rigs on our shoulders so that the scientists could see what we saw. The plant looked intact, burning salt-white in the glare of a Lunar afternoon, throwing a long black shadow toward us. The red and green perimeter lights were on; the cooling sink, a borehole three kilometres deep, wasn't venting. I drove the rover all the way around it, and then we went in.

The plant was essentially one big hall filled with the laser pumping assemblies, huge frames of parallel colour-coded pipes each as big as one of those old Saturn rockets and threaded through with bundles of heavy cables and trackways for the robots that serviced them. We crept along the tiled floor in their shadows like a pair of orange mice, directing our camera rigs here and there at the request of the scientists. The emergency lights were still strobing and I asked someone to switch them off, which they did after only five minutes' discussion about whether it was a good idea to disturb anything.

The six laser focusing pipes, two metres in diameter, converged on the bus-sized experimental chamber. Containment was a big problem; that chamber was crammed with powerful magnetic torii that generated the fields in which the target, a pellet of ultracompressed metallic hydrogen, was heated by chirped pulse amplification to ten billion degrees Centigrade. It was surrounded by catwalks and hidden by the flared ends of the focusing pipes, the capillary grid of the liquid sodium cooling system, and a hundred different kinds of monitoring devices. We checked the system diagnostics of the monitors, which told us only that several detectors on the underside had ceased to function, and then, harangued by scientists, crawled all around the chamber as best we could, sweating heavily in our suits and chafing our elbows and knees.

Mike found a clue to what had happened when he managed to wriggle into the crawlspace beneath the chamber, quite a feat in a pressurized suit. He had taken off his camera rig to do it, and it took quite a bit of prompting before he started to describe what he saw.

"There's a severed cable here, and something has punched a hole in the box above it. Let me shift around… Okay, I can see a hole in the floor, too. About two centimetres across. I'm poking my screwdriver into it. Well, it must go all the way through the tiles, I can't see how deep. Hey, Frank, get me some of that wire, will you?"

There was a spool of copper cable nearby. I cut off a length and passed it in.

"You two get on out of there now," one of the scientists said.

"This won't take but a minute," Mike said, and started humming tunelessly, which meant that he was thinking hard about something.

I asked, because I knew he wouldn't say anything otherwise, "What is it?"

"Looks like someone took a shot at this old thing," Mike said. "Shit. How deep does the foundation go?"

"The concrete was poured to three metres," someone said over the radio link, and the scientist who'd spoken before said, "It really isn't a good idea to mess around there, fellows."

"It goes all the way through," Mike said. "I wiggled the wire around and it came back up with dust on the end."

"This is Ridpath," someone else said. Ridpath, you may remember, was the chief of the science team. Although he wasn't exactly responsible for what happened, he made millions from selling the rights to his story, and then hanged himself six months later. He said, "You boys get on out of there. We'll take it from here."

Five rolligons passed us on our way back, big fat pressurized vehicles making speed. "You put a hair up someone's ass," I told Mike, who'd been real quiet after he crawled out from beneath the chamber.

"I think something escaped," he said.

"Maybe some of the laser energy was deflected."

"There weren't any traces of melting," Mike said, with a preoccupied air. "And just a bit of all that energy would make a hell of a mess, not leave a neat little hole. Hmm. Kind of an interesting problem."

But he didn't say any more about it until a week later, about an hour before the President went on air to explain what had happened.

)(

The Moon was a good place for work back then. It was more or less run by scientists, the way Antarctica had been before the drillers and miners got to it. There were about two thousand people living there at any one time, either working on projects like the Exawatt or the Big Array or the ongoing resource mapping surveys, or doing their own little thing. Mike and I were both part of the General Labour Pool, ready to help anyone. We'd earned our chops doing PhDs, but we didn't have the drive or desire to work our way up the ladder of promotion. We didn't want responsibility, didn't want to be burdened with administration and hustling for funds, the inevitable lot of career researchers. We liked to get our hands dirty. Mike has a double PhD in pure physics and cybernetics and is a whizz at electronics; I'm a run-of-the-mill geologist who is also a fair pilot. We made a pretty good team back then, and generally worked together whenever we could, and we'd worked just about every place on the Moon.

When the President made the announcement, we'd moved on from the Exawatt and were taking a few days R&R. I'd found out about a gig supervising the construction of a railway from the South Pole to the permanent base at Clavius, but Mike wouldn't sign up and wouldn't say why, except that it was to do with what had happened at the Exawatt.

We'd been exposed to a small amount of radiation when we'd gone into the plant—Mike a little more than me—and had spent a day being checked out before getting back on the job. The scientists were all over the plant by then. The reaction chamber had been dismantled by robots, and we brought in all kinds of monitoring equipment. Not only radiation counters, but a gravity measuring device and a neutrino detector. We helped bore a shaft five hundred metres deep parallel to the hole punched through the floor, and probes and motion sensors and cameras were lowered into it.

Mike claimed to have worked out what had happened as soon as he stuck the wire in the hole through the foundation, but he wouldn't tell me. "You should be able to guess from what they were trying to measure," he said, the one time I asked, and smiled when I called him a son of a bitch. He's very smart, but sort of fucked up in the head, antisocial, careless of his appearance and untidy as hell, and proud that he has four of the five major symptoms of Asperger's Syndrome. But he was my partner back then, and I trusted him; when he said it wasn't a good idea to take up a new contract, I nagged him for a straight hour to explain why, and went along with him even though he wouldn't. He was spending all his spare time making calculations on his slate, and was still working on them at the South Pole facility.

I raised the subject again when news of the special Presidential announcement broke. "You'd better tell me what you think happened," I told Mike, "because I'll hear the truth in less than an hour, and after that I won't believe you."

We were in an arbour in the dome of the South Pole facility. Real plants, cycads and banana plants and ferns, grew in real dirt around us; sunlight poured in at a low angle through the diamond panes high above. The dome capped a small crater some three hundred metres across, on a high ridge near the edge of the South Pole-Aitken basin and in permanent sunlight, the sun circling around the horizon once every twenty-eight days. It was hot and humid, and the people splashing in the lake below our arbour were making a lot of noise. The lake and its scattering of atolls took up most of the crater's floor, with arbours and cafés and cabins on the bench terrace around it. The water was billion-year-

old comet water, mined from the regolith in permanently shad-
owed craters. A rail gun used to lob shaped loads of ice to supply
the Clavius base in the early days, but Clavius had grown, and its
administration was uncomfortable with the idea of being
bombarded with ice meteors, which was why they wanted to
build a railway. In the low gravity, the waves out on the lake were
five or six metres high, and big droplets flew a long way, changing
shape like amoebae, before falling back. People were body surfing
the waves; a game of water polo had been going on for several
days in one of the bays.

I'd just been playing for a few hours, and I was in a good
mood, which was why I didn't strangle Mike when, after I asked
him to tell me what he knew, he flashed his goofy smile at me and
went back to scratching figures on his slate. Instead, I snatched the
slate from his hands, held it over the edge of the arbour, and said,
"Tell me right now, or the slate gets it."

Mike scratched the swirl of black hair on his bare chest and
said, "You know you won't do it."

I made to skim the slate through the air and said, "How many
times do you think it would bounce before it sank?"

"I thought I'd give you a chance to work it out. And it isn't as
if there's anything we can do. Didn't you enjoy the rest?"

"What's this got to do with not taking up that contract?"

"There's no point building anything any more. You still
haven't guessed, have you?"

I tossed the slate to him. "Maybe I should pick you up and
throw you in the lake."

I meant it, and I'm a lot bigger than him.

"It's a black hole," he said.

"A black hole."

"Sure. My guess is that the experiment caused a runaway
quantum fluctuation that created a black hole. It had to be bigger
than the Planck size, and most probably was a bit bigger than a
hydrogen atom, because it obviously has been taking up other
atoms easily enough. Say around ten to the power twenty-three

kilograms. The mass of a big mountain, like Everest. The magnetic containment fields couldn't hold it, of course, and it dropped straight out of the reaction chamber and went through the plant's floor."

I said, "The hole we saw was a lot bigger than the width of a hydrogen atom."

"Sure. The black hole disrupted stuff by tidal force over a far greater distance than its Swartzschild radius, and sucked some of it right in. That's why there was no trace of melting, even though it was pretty hot, and spitting out X-rays and probably accelerated protons too—cosmic rays."

I didn't believe him, of course, but it was an interesting intellectual exercise. I said, "So where did the mass come from? Not from the combustion chamber fuel."

"Of course not. It was a quantum fluctuation, just like the Universe, which also came out of nothing. And the Universe weighs a lot more than ten to the power twenty-three kilograms. Something like, hmm—"

"Okay," I said quickly, before Mike lost himself in esoteric calculations. "But where is it now?"

"Well, it went all the way through," Mike said.

"Through the Moon? Then it came out, let's see—" I tried to visualize the Moon's globe "—somewhere in Mare Fecunditas."

"Not exactly. It accelerated in free fall toward the core, went past, and started to fall back again. It's sweeping back and forth, gaining mass and losing amplitude with each pass. That's what the President is going to tell everyone."

I thought about it. Something just bigger than an atom but massing as much as a mountain, plunging through the twenty-five kilometre thick outer layer of gardened regolith, smashing a centimetre wide tunnel through the basalt crust and the mantle, passing through the tiny iron core, gathering mass and slowing, so that it did not quite emerge at the far side before falling back.

"You were lucky it didn't come right back at you," I said.

"The amplitude diminishes with each pass. Eventually it'll settle at the Moon's gravitational centre. And that's why I didn't want to sign the contract. After the President tells everyone what I've just told you, all the construction contracts will be put on hold. What you should do is make sure we're first on the list for evacuation work."

"Evacuation?"

"There's no way to capture the black hole. The Moon, Frank, is fucked. But we'll get plenty of work before it's over."

He was half-right. The next day, after the President had admitted that an experiment had somehow dropped a black hole inside the Moon, a serious problem that would require an international team to monitor, we were both issued with summonses to appear at the hastily set up Congressional enquiry.

⋈

It was a bunch of bullshit, of course. We went down to Washington, D.C. and spent a week locked up in the Watergate hotel watching bad cable movies and endless opinion shows, with NASA lawyers showing up every now and then to rehearse our Q&As, and in the end we had no more than half an hour of easy questions before the committee let us go. Our lawyers shook our hands on the steps of the Capitol, in front of a couple of bored video crews, and we went back to Canaveral and then to the Moon. Why not? By then Mike had convinced me about what was going to happen. There would be plenty of work for us.

We signed up as part of a roving seismology team, placing remote stations at various points around the Moon's equator. The Exawatt plant had been dismantled and a monitoring station built on its site to try and track the period of the black hole, which someone had labelled Mendeleev X-1. Mike was as happy as I had ever seen him; he was getting some of the raw data and doing his own calculations on the black hole's accretion rate and orbital path within the Moon. He stayed up long after our work day was over, hunched over his slate in the driving chair of our rolligon, with sunlight pouring in through the bubble canopy while I tried to sleep in the hammock stretched across the cabin, my skin itching from the Moon dust which got everywhere, our Moon Suits propped in back like two silent witnesses to our squabbling. His latest best estimate was that the Moon had between two hundred and five thousand days before it was eaten up.

"But things will start to get exciting before then."

"Excitement is something I can do without. What do you mean?"

"Oh, it'll be a lot of fun."

"You're doing it again, you son of a bitch."

"You're the geologist, Frank," Mike said. "It's easy enough to work out. It's just—"

"Basic physics. Yeah. Well, you tell me if it's going to put us in danger. Okay?"

"Oh, it won't. Not yet, anyhow."

We were already picking up regular moonquakes on the seismometer network. With a big point mass swinging back and forth through it, the Moon's solid iron core was ringing like a bell. There were some odd subsidiary traces too, smooshy echoes as if spaces were opening in the mantle—hard to believe, because pressure should have annealed any voids. I was pretty sure that Mike had a theory about these anomalies, too, but I kept quiet. After all, I was the geologist. I should have been able to work it out.

Meanwhile, we toured west across the Mare Insularium, with its lava floods overlain by ejecta from Copernicus, and on across the Oceanus Procellarum, dropping seismometers every two hundred kilometres. We made good time, speeding across rolling, lightly cratered landscape, detouring only for the largest wrinkle ridges, driving through the long day and the long, Earth-lit night into brilliant dawn, the sun slowly moving across the sky toward noon once more. The Moon had its own harsh yet serene beauty, shaped mainly by vulcanism and impacts. Without weather, erosion took place on geological timescales, but because almost every feature was more than three billion years old, gravity and ceaseless micrometeorite bombardment had smoothed or levelled every hill or crater ridge: it was like riding across an infinite plain gentled by a deep blanket of snow. We rested up twice at unmanned shelters, and had a two-day layover at a roving Swedish selenology station which had squatted down on the mare like a collection of articulated tin cans. A week later, just after we had just picked up fresh supplies from a rocket lofted from Clavius, we felt our first moonquake.

It was as if the rolligon had dropped over a kerb, but there was no kerb. I was in the driving chair; Mike was asleep in the hammock. I told the AI to stop, and looked out through the canopy at the 180 degree panorama. The horizon was drawn closely all around. An ancient crater dished it to the north and a few pockmarked boulders were sprinkled here and there, including a fractured block as big as a house. Something skittered in the corner of my eye—a little rock rolling down the gentle five degree slope we were climbing, ploughing a meandering track in the dust. It ran out quite a way. The rolligon swayed gently from side to side. I found I was gripping the padded arms of the chair so tightly my knuckles had turned white. Behind me, Mike stirred in the hammock and sleepily asked what was up; at the same moment, I saw the gas plume.

It was very faint, visible only because the dust it lofted caught the sunlight. Gas plumes were not uncommon on the Moon, caused by pockets of radon and other products of fission decay of unstable isotopes overpressuring the crevices where they collected. Earth-based astronomers sometimes glimpsed them when they temporarily obscured surface features while dissipating into vacuum. This, though, was different, more like a heat-driven geyser, venting steadily from a source below the horizon.

I told the AI to drive toward it. Mike leaned beside me, scratching himself through his suit of thermal underwear. He smelled strongly of old sweat; we hadn't bathed properly since the interlude with the Swedes. I had a sudden insight and said, "How hot is the black hole?"

"Oh, the smaller the black hole, the more fiercely it radiates. It's a simple inverse relationship. It was pretty hot to begin with, but it's been getting cooler as it accretes mass. Hmm."

"Is it still hot enough to melt rock?"

Mike's eyes refocused. "You know, I think it must have been much bigger than I first thought. Anyway, anything that gets close enough to it to melt is already falling toward the event horizon. That's why there was no trace of melting or burning when it dropped out of the reaction chamber. But there's also the heat generated by friction as stuff pours toward its gravity well."

"Then it's remelting the interior. Those anomalies in the seismology signals are melt caverns full of lava."

Mike said thoughtfully, "I'm sure we'll start picking up a weak magnetic field soon, when the iron core liquefies and starts circulating. Of course, the end will be pretty close by then. Wow. That thing out there is really big."

The rolligon was climbing a long gentle slope toward the top of a curved ridge more than a kilometre high, the remnants of the rim of a crater which had been mostly buried by the fluid lava flow which had formed the Oceanus Procellarum. I told the AI to stop when I spotted the source of the plume. It was a huge, fresh-looking crevice that ran out from a volcanic dome; gas was jetting out of the slumped side of the dome like steam from a boiling kettle. Dust fell straight down in sheets kilometres long. Already, an appreciable ray of brighter material was forming on the regolith beneath the plume.

"We should get closer," Mike said. He was rocking back and forth in his chair like a delighted child.

"I don't think so. There'll be plenty of rocks lofted along with the gas and dust."

We transmitted some pictures, then suited up and went outside to set up a seismology package. The sun was in the east, painting long shadows on the ground, which shook, ever so gently, under my boots. With no atmosphere to scatter the light, shadows were razor-sharp, and colour changed as I moved about. The dusty regolith was deep brown in my shadow, but a bright blinding white when I looked toward the sun, turning ashy grey to either side. The gas plume glittered and flashed against the black sky. I told Mike that it was probably from a source deep in the megaregolith; pressure increased in gas pockets with depth. A quake, probably at the interface between the megaregolith and the rigid crust, must have opened a path to the surface.

"There'll be a lot more of these," Mike said.

"It'll blow itself out soon enough."

But it was still venting strongly when we had finished our work, and we drove a long way north to skirt around it, with Mike scratching away on his slate, factoring this new evidence into his calculations.

♓

We were out for another two weeks, ending our run in Lunar night at the Big Array station at Korolev. It was one of the biggest craters on the farside, with slumped terraced walls and hummocky rim deposits like ranges of low hills. Its floor was spattered with newer craters, including a dark-floored lava-flooded crater on its southern edge which was now the focus of a series of quakes of steadily increasing amplitude. Korolev station, up on the rim, was being evacuated; the radio telescopes of the Big Array, scattered across the farside in a regular pattern, were to be kept running by remote link. Most of the personnel had already departed by shuttle, and although there were still large amounts of equipment to be taken out, the railway that linked Korolev with Clavius had been cut by a rockslide. After a couple of spooky days resting up in the almost deserted yet fully functional station, Mike and I went out with a couple of other GLPs to supervise the robots that were clearing the slide and relaying track.

It was a nice ride: the pressurized railcar had a big observa-
tional bubble, and I spent a lot of time up there, watching the
heavily cratered highland plains flow past at two hundred kilometres an hour. The Orientale basin dominated the west side of the
Moon, a fissured basin of fractured blocks partly flooded with
impact melt lava and ringed round with three immense scarps and
an inner bench like ripples frozen in rock. The engineers had cut
the railway through the rings of the Rook and Cordillera
Mountains; the landslide had blocked the track where it passed
close to one of the tall knobs of the Montes Rook Formation, a ten
kilometre high piece of ejecta which had smashed down onto the
surrounding plain—the impact really had been very big.

A slide had run out from one of its steeply graded faces,
covering more than a kilometre of track, and we were more than a
week out there, helping the robots fix everything up. When we
finally arrived at the station in Clavius, it was a day ahead of the
Mendeleev eruption and the beginning of the evacuation of the
Moon.

⊁

The whole floor of Mendeleev crater had fractured into blocks in
the biggest quake ever recorded on the Moon, and lava had
flooded up through dykes emplaced between the blocks. Lava
vented from dykes beyond the crater rim, too, and flowed a long
way, forming a new mare. Other vents appeared, setting off
secondary quakes and long rock slides. The Moon shivered and
shook uneasily, as if awakening from a long sleep.

Small teams were sent out to collect the old Rangers, Lunas,
Surveyors, Lunokhods and descent stages of Apollo LEMs from
the first wave of lunar exploration. Mike and I went out for a last
time, to Mare Tranquillitatis, to the site of the first manned lunar
landing.

When a permanent scientific presence had first been established on the Moon, there had been considerable debate about

what to do with the sites of the Apollo landings and the various old robot probes and other debris scattered across the surface. There had been a serious proposal to dome the Apollo 11 site to protect it from damage by micrometeorites and to stop people swiping souvenirs, but even without protection it would last for millions of years, everyone on the Moon was tagged with a continuously monitored global positioning sensor so no one could go anywhere near it without being logged, and in the end the site had been left open.

We arrived a few hours after dawn. A big squat carrier rocket had gone ahead, landing two kilometres to the north, and the robots were already waiting. There were four of us: an historian from the Museum of Air and Space in Washington, a photographer, and Mike and me. As we loped forward, an automatic beacon on the common band warned us that we were trespassing on a UN heritage site, reciting the relevant penalties and repeating itself until the historian found it and turned it off. The angular platform of the lunar module's descent stage sat at an angle; one of its spidery legs had collapsed after a recent quake focused near new volcanic cones to the south-east. It had been scorched by the rocket of the ascent stage, and the gold foil which had wrapped it was torn and tattered, white paint beneath turned tan by exposure to the sun's raw ultraviolet. We lifted everything, working inwards toward the ascent stage: the Passive Seismometer and the Laser Ranging Retro reflector; the flag, its ordinary, wire-stiffened fabric faded and fragile; an assortment of discarded geology tools; human waste and food containers and wipes and other litter in crumbling jettison bags; the plaque with a message from a long-dead president. Before the descent stage was lifted away, a robot sawed away a chunk of dirt beside its ladder, the spot where the first human footprint had been made on the Moon. There was some dispute about which print was actually the first, so two square metres were carefully lifted. And at last the descent stage was carried off to the cargo rocket, and there was only a litter of cleated footprints left, our own overlaying Armstrong's and Aldrin's.

It was time to go.

)(

As the eruptions grew more frequent, even the skeleton crews of the various stations were evacuated, leaving a host of robot surveyors in close orbit or crawling about the troubled surface to monitor the unfolding disaster. Mike and I left on one of the last shuttles, everyone crowding to the ports as it made a single low orbital pass before lighting out for Earth.

It was six months after the Mendeleev X-1 incident. The heat generated by the black hole's accretion process and tidal forces had remelted the Moon's iron core; pockets of molten basalt in the mantle had swollen and conjoined. A vast rift had opened in the Oceanus Procellarum, splitting the nearside down its north-western quadrant and raising new scarps as high and jagged as those in an old Chester Bonestell painting. The Orientale basin had flooded with lava, and the fractured blocks of the Maunder formation were sinking like foundering ships as new lava flows began to well up. There was much less volcanic activity on the farside, where the crust was thicker, but the Mare Ingenii collapsed and reflooded, forming a vast new basin which swallowed the Jules Verne and Gagarin craters.

It took two more months.

As the end neared, the Moon's surface split into short-lived plates afloat on a wholly molten mantle, with lava-filled rifts opening and scabbing over and reopening along their edges. There were frantic attempts to ensure that the population of the Earth's southern hemisphere would all be able to reach some kind of shelter, for the Moon would be in the sky above the Pacific in its final hour. Those unlucky or stubborn enough to remain outside saw the Moon rise for the last time, half-full, the dark part of her disc riven with glowing cracks which spread as the black hole sucked in exponentially increasing amounts of matter. And then there was a terrific flare of light, brighter than a thousand suns.

Those witnesses who had not been blinded saw that the Moon was gone, leaving shells of luminous gas expanding away from a short-lived accretion disc as ejected material spiralled back into the black hole, which, although it massed the same as the Moon it had devoured, had an event horizon circumference of less than a millimetre.

The radiation pulse was mostly absorbed by the Earth's atmosphere; the orbit of the space station had been altered so that it was in opposition when the Moon vanished. I was aboard it at the time, and spent the next six months helping repair satellites whose circuits had been fried.

There are still tides, of course, for the same amount of mass still orbits the Earth. Marine organisms that synchronize their reproduction by the Moon's phases, such as horseshoe crabs, corals and certain marine worms, were in danger of extinction until a cooperative mission by NASA and the Russian and European space agencies lofted a space mirror that reflects the same amount of light as the Moon, and even goes through the same phases. There'll be a big problem in 5×10^{43} years, when by loss of mass through Hawking radiation the black hole finally becomes small enough to begin its runaway evaporation. But long before then the Sun will have evolved into a white dwarf and guttered out; even its very protons will have decayed. The black hole will be the last remnant of the Solar System in a cooling and vastly expanded Universe.

There are various proposals to make use of it. A Korean company has proposed that it would make the ultimate garbage disposal device (I want to be well away from the Solar System if they try that). A group of scientists at Cal Tech think that it could be turned into an interstellar signalling device; if it can be made to bob in its orbit (perhaps by putting another black hole in orbit around it), it will produce sharply focused gravity waves of tremendous amplitude. Meanwhile, it will keep the physicists busy for a thousand years. Mike is working at one of the stations which orbit beyond its event horizon. I keep in touch with him by email, but the correspondence is becoming more and more infrequent as he vanishes into his own personal event horizon.

As for me, I'm heading out. The space programme has realigned its goals; it turns out that the black hole retained the Moon's rotational energy, so slingshot manoeuvres around it can accelerate spaceships to any destination in the Solar System. There are plenty of other moons out there, and most are far more interesting than the one we lost.

For Stephen Baxter

UNDER MARS

Four in the afternoon, and at last it's the end of Bill "Buzz" Brown's shift on the Marsport shuttle ride. The other steward, Cristal, hands out lollipops to half a dozen fretting kiddies while Buzz does his bit about how there might be a bumpy ride ahead because there's a dust storm in the upper atmosphere, "So make sure those seatbelts are done up tight, folks," and then zones out in his bucket seat, his long fingers surreptitiously kneading a scrap of paper, Homer's mysterious message, while the shuttle bucks and slews, red light flaring through the viewscreen portholes and most of the guests yelling and screaming gleefully as they get into the spirit of the ride.

The biggest screams of all, as usual, are for the final moments when the shuttle rolls through twenty degrees (the viewscreens make it seem steeper) as it shoots past a cruel mountain peak and uncoiling rock snakes spitting great washes of fire that clear to show the white dome of Marsport like a ripe boil on the cratered red plain. A minute later the shuttle shivers and settles. The seatbelt lights go out and there's a scattering of applause that quickly dies down as everyone starts to get up. Buzz Brown is on his feet a scant moment before the guests, a tall, tanned, twenty-five-year-old in a purple jumpsuit trimmed with gold, his crisp crewcut bleached almost white by Florida sun. With the mike cable whipped once around his forearm, he delivers the last line in his script, "All you folks be sure to remember to take your stuff along with you, and have yourselves a fine time in Marsport," not much caring that the guests are too busy getting ready to leave to pay any attention to him. He and Cristal work the clunky, old-fashioned airlock doors, say goodbye to the disembarking guests, police the seats, finding nothing but candy wrappers and waxed paper cups half-full of melting ice, a well-chewed soft-toy and a pair of cheap sunglasses not worth keeping, and exit through the curtained door that ostensibly leads to the cockpit.

The two stewards taking the next shift are already climbing the steep metal ramp between the big hydraulic rams at the front of the shuttle's cradle. One of them stops to ask Buzz if he's holding, and Buzz tells him what he's been telling everyone else these past few days, that's he's out but he's going to connect soon, and escapes down the ramp.

Cristal dumps the bag of trash in one of the pneumatic tubes that sucks everything straight to the central incinerator, lifts off her blonde wig and shakes out her shag-cut black hair and says, "How about me, sweetie? I need some of your candy too, and you've been telling me you're out for three days now. What's going on?"

"Nothing's going on," Buzz tells her, although he himself does not believe it. "I'm seeing Homer in a couple of hours, he got in contact with me just this morning. Everything's going to be fine."

Homer is Buzz's source, his one-time roommate at Florida State. It was Homer's idea to drop out of college and work here ("What else are you going to do with your media studies degree, except ask people if they want fries with their burgers a couple of hundred times a day?"), and Homer's idea to supplement their meagre wages by selling speed he cooks up in his apartment's kitchenette. Half the park's workers get by on speed or coke;

because of their just-above-minimum wages, most casual temps need a lot of overtime, and need to keep the bounce in their steps and the smiles on their faces. Dealing home-cooked crank isn't how Buzz planned his life to turn out, but he thinks of it as a public service, part of the lubrication that keeps the park moving; a semi-official position even, since the management turns a blind eye to it—there's no blood or urine testing, and most leads and line managers aren't averse to the odd pill or snort. You can get fired for half a hundred infractions, for not smiling enough, for being too friendly to a guest, for not black-bagging a costume properly when carrying it to and from work, so a tentacle tip or an antenna sticks out in full view, but no one has ever been sacked for getting high.

Homer's speed is prime stuff, and he and Buzz have a nice little business going, but just lately Homer has been increasingly evasive whenever Buzz has asked him when he's going to cook up a fresh batch. Buzz feels pushed into a corner by Homer's intransigence and the demands of his customers, feels the same claustrophobic oppression, a sick clutching pressure on his heart, he gets when he's stuck on a level of a virtual game with energy levels draining fast and no obvious way out. Last evening, when Homer didn't answer his phone, Buzz finally nerved himself up to drive over to his apartment building. Homer didn't answer the bell, and his window, which Buzz could see through the closed gate, beyond the little courtyard swimming pool, remained stubbornly dark. But just this morning a tech stopped Buzz as he was coming through the employees' entrance and pressed a note into his hand: a brief message, in Homer's childish, backward slanting scrawl, telling Buzz to meet him in the Bradbury section canteen at six p.m.

Cristal says, as she and Buzz enter the service tunnel, "I need a little pick-me-up right now. I'm double-shifting, another eight hours waitressing on the strip, and then tomorrow morning I'm doing auditions."

"You go for it," Buzz says absent-mindedly, still thinking about the note. Maybe it's nothing more than the delivery of a fresh batch of speed, but Buzz can't shake the feeling that Homer is up to something, that he's about to try and persuade Buzz to take another wrong turning in his life.

"I will. This ride isn't where this girl is going to spend the rest of her life. I'm a comedic actress. I should at least be out on the strip in Marsport doing one-on-one routines with the guests, but the spot I'm going for?" Cristal lifts her slim arms above her head, does a shimmy step. "It's the coolest: one of the Princesses in the Barsoom section."

Buzz has to smile at her burlesque. "You're a natural," he tells her.

"Eight years of dance classes, I don't intend to waste them. And there's no way I'm casual temping for ever. I was laid off seven weeks before my last rehire. If I get the Barsoom gig, I'm going to make it my own, and then I'm on the road to a full time job and all those yummy benefits. So I just need a little lift, sweetie, a little something to put a spring in my step."

"Like I said, I'm out until maybe later this evening."

Cristal looks at him. She's a tall, willowy girl, with a long, mobile upper lip that lifts now in amusement. "You're too nice a guy to be a dealer, Buzz. You can't lie to save your life. I know you took a little lift from your own personal supply before the shift, I know you're holding out on me. How about I take you to this thing I know about? It's this bunch of musicians, and I can promise they know how to party. Someone's birthday or divorce, I forget which, tomorrow night." Cristal puts a little bump and grind into her walk. "It could be fun."

She's just twenty, pretty under the pancake and thick blue eyeshadow in a corn-fed teeth-'n-'tits Kansas kind of way, but Buzz has a rule not to mess around with the people he deals to, and he says, "I don't think so."

Cristal's face hardens. "Well, maybe I don't need your stuff. I hear there's something new coming in."

Buzz has heard the rumours too. It's another reason why he's been trying so hard to get hold of Homer. On impulse, he says, "You can have what I've got, but it isn't much."

"Don't do me any favours."

"This is a favour," Buzz protests. "I'm down to dust. But step into my office, and I'll see what I can do."

Between two green-painted dumpsters, out of sight of the tunnel security cameras, Buzz takes from the pouch hung inside the pants of his purple jumpsuit the very last glassine envelope. Cristal digs into it with a long pinkie nail, lifts the nail to her nose, sniffs up the crest of white powder, shudders with delicate pleasure.

"Buy a full bag tomorrow," Buzz tells her, "and we'll call it even."

"You're a doll," Cristal says, and treats him to a nailful. As he bends to sniff, she adds, "I'll be thinking of you when I get that gig."

"Knock 'em dead," Buzz tells her. He means it, but he feels a prick of jealousy too. She's moving on, and it seems he'll be here for the rest of his life.

In the men's locker room, he strips off his skanky costume and throws it into a hamper, and feels the speed coming on as he showers. A sudden dryness in the throat, a tightening of the skin over his face, a sharpening of the lights and the hiss and needle-point kiss of the shower. The crushing weight of his anxiety recedes a little. Maybe things will work out, he thinks, as he dresses in a clean white T-shirt and red jeans and straps on his watch, a good Timex some guest left behind a few months ago. He looks at the message on the scrap of paper for about the fiftieth time, and decides to catch Homer, who plays the child-emperor of Mars, at the end of the Bradbury section's five o'clock parade. If Homer is playing one of his silly mind-games, Buzz is going to put his own spin on it.

The park is divided into twelve sections, like a neatly sliced pie, the hotels spaced around the perimeter, a fifty-metre-high scale replica of Olympus Mons at the centre. Each section is its own little kingdom, with its own tunnel complex, its own set of locker rooms and break areas, its own cafeteria. Section crews don't mix. Company policy encourages fierce loyalty to your own crew, a divide-and-rule strategy that's created a dozen little rival factions. Sometimes there are even *West Side Story*-style rumbles and spats between crews; last year, one of the Barsoom crew was knifed by a jealous boyfriend when he hassled a Marsport bar girl. Buzz has been ripped off a couple of times when he's dealt with people from other crews, and feels a flutter of apprehension under the speed's steely rush as he rides a service lift topside. In this part of the Florida panhandle, the limestone is saturated with water only a couple of feet below the surface, so the park is raised up like an ant mound, and its underground tunnels and service areas are actually the ground floor. Buzz comes up at the far edge of Marsport's geodesic dome, the first sunlight he's seen for more than nine hours blazing through its translucent panes, and makes his way through a crowded fast-food area to the mock airlock that links Marsport's dome with the Face of Mars section.

Buzz puts on his shades, strides quickly along the empty walkway. The air is hot and sultry; the sunlight brassy. The red rocks and the red sands, the three rough, red pyramids and the Face itself, tilted at a viewable angle, glow like heated iron. From this aspect, the mock-up of Olympus Mons has the profile of a cowled nun.

In five minutes, Buzz is on the other side, amongst the limpid canals and crystal towers of the Bradbury section, making his way through increasingly dense crowds to the central canal. Men and women and children in shorts and T-shirts, slacks and sports shirts, pack the bleachers. Baseball caps, sunglasses, sneakers. Children ride their fathers' shoulders or clutch their mothers' legs. Almost every adult is watching through the viewfinder of a video or still camera the dancers and musicians in skintight silvery costumes and weird masks who swirl along either side of the wide canal, where decorated barges linked nose to tail smoothly plough the limpid water.

Buzz discovers that he is grinding his teeth. He pops a stick of gum in his mouth and drops the wrapper; it's barely touched the tiles when a little maintenance robot, a slipper-sized silver teardrop, scoots over and snatches the scrap of paper in its jaws and scoots away.

The child-emperor of Mars, a small skinny silvery figure with a flowing purple robe and a huge fantasticated mask and head, stands at the centre of a giant crystalline flower on the last barge. As the barge glides past, Buzz sees with a stir of alarm that something's wrong. The child-emperor is sort of slumped in his cloak, and he isn't waving at the guests. Buzz keeps pace with the barge, threading through the crowds, following the last of the dancers around the barrier that shields the working part of the canal from the view of the guests, that separates the magic from the mundane.

In the backstage zoo, dancers are shucking their masks, hanging towels around their shoulders, lighting cigarettes; assistants are leaping onto the barges, helping actors disengage their headpieces. A locker room smell of sweat and talcum powder mingles with the hot oil and ozone of working machinery.

When the child-emperor's barge comes gliding under the arch of the false bridge, Buzz jumps aboard and shakes the slight, silver-clad figure's shoulders, but gets no response. Homer must have fainted inside his costume, something that happens all the time; it can get as hot as a hundred thirty degrees inside the heavy costume heads, under the brutal Florida sun. Buzz finds the latches which hold the mask and head to the costume's metal shoulder rack. A steel pole runs up the back of the costume to the top of the head, and when the latches snap open the emperor slides down the pole into Buzz's arms. It isn't Homer.

A moment later, a tech jostles Buzz aside. "You go on down to the cafeteria," the man says.

"What's going on?"

The tech bends over the impostor emperor, anoints the paper-white face with water from a spray bottle. "Go on down," he says. "People are waiting for you."

)(

The Bradbury section cafeteria, like all the other staff cafeterias in the park, is a charmless bunker carpeted in astroturf, with arctic air-conditioning and tired fluorescent lighting. Tables and chairs scattered amidst stands of fake tropical plants; a long row of vending machines that sell everything from cola to enchiladas; a gaming area at the back, with pool tables, virtual reality machines, and a dart board. Buzz is scanning the groups of actors in half costume, techs in taupe coveralls, teenage sales persons, reception-ists and restaurant staff in red jeans and white T-shirts, when someone calls his name.

It's Wolfie Look, the kingpin of the Bradbury section, a beefy, fortysomething redneck with a shaved scalp and bad skin, a wet black cheroot plugged into his grin. He runs the section's garage, and runs the numbers and drug rackets too. He's lounging at a table with half a dozen of his cronies, all of them, like Wolfie Look, maintenance gangers. Homer is sitting in the middle of them, looking very small.

Buzz ignores Wolfie Look and says, "What's up, Homer?"

"He's been a bad boy," Wolfie Look says.

Buzz ignores him, and tells Homer, "You weren't answering your phone for about a week, and then you ask me to come all the way over here. What's up?"

"Be cool," Homer says. He has a pockmarked face and coke-bottle-end glasses, and is the only person Buzz knows who came to work in the park because it is the next best thing to going to Mars. His half of the college room he shared with Buzz was covered with photographs of red, rocky panoramas taken by robot surveyors; he even persuaded Buzz to join the Mars Society, a group of monomaniacs who make endless, deeply detailed plans for terraforming Mars. Homer is a very scientific boy, but he's also deeply lazy, and he hides his laziness with an affected contempt for the straight world.

"There aren't any secrets between me and Homer," Wolfie Look says. "Not any more. Isn't that right, boys?" There's a murmur of agreement, and Wolfie Look tells Buzz, "I knew you'd be along, speedo, chasing after that home-brewed crank your pal puts out, and here you are."

"Talk to me, Homer," Buzz says. "What have you got yourself into? Who was that guy who took your place? And why did he take your place? What's going on?"

"You'll see why I had to take time out," Homer says, "if you'll just sit down and listen."

"The guy fainted, Homer," Buzz says. "If the parade lead finds out what's going on, he'll can the substitute and he'll can you, too."

"Don't you worry about that," Wolfie Look says, with a smile that shows half a dozen gold teeth. He shifts his cheroot from one corner of his mouth to the other, pushes out a chair with his foot, and tells Buzz, "Take a load off."

Buzz knows that Wolfie Look's good ol' boy act masks a devious and dangerous mind, and says warily, "I just want a quick word with Homer, then I'll be gone."

"Oh, I don't think so, speedo. For one thing, this isn't your turf, and for another Homer's business is my business now." Wolfie Look raps the table. There are gold rings on every one of his fat, dirty fingers. "You sit down. I'll tell you what's going down."

Buzz sits.

"What it is," Wolfie Look says, "is that Homer here is in the hole with me for about five thousand dollars."

"Five thousand three hundred and forty," one of his cronies says.

"There you go," Wolfie Look says. "So the deal is that either Homer does some business for me, or I break his arms and legs."

"He isn't interested in selling crank," Homer says. "Frankly, nor am I, not any more."

Buzz says, "Then I don't know why I'm here," and pushes back his chair. The speed has made him bold.

"You came because I asked you to," Homer says. "This is a great opportunity. We're getting into the big time."

"Your pal's right," Wolfie Look says, his smile stretching as wide as a frog's. "I can supply you with something far superior to home-brewed crank. Focus. You might even have heard of it."

"Focus?"

"Trust me," Homer says. "We'll clean up on this stuff."

"First of all you have to do a little job for me," Wolfie Look says. "Think of it as an initiative test."

♓

"I knew you'd come in with me," Homer says happily. "You won't regret it."

"You'd better tell just how you got so deep in the hole," Buzz says. "Five thousand dollars? I know you're not a betting man, Homer."

"It was this stuff," Homer says. He twirls the plastic bag, printed with the park's logo, that's weighted with the package Wolfie Look gave them.

"Focus?"

"Yeah. Focus. The stuff we're muling."

Buzz steps around a guest, four hundred pounds of Midwest beef crammed into Bermuda shorts and a *War of the World*s T-shirt, who's standing in the middle of the path and panning his video camera up the side of one of the crystal towers. He tells Homer, "I wish you wouldn't call it that. It makes us sound like criminals."

"That's what we are, Buzz," Homer says. "Let's face it, that's what we've been since we started up our little business. And now we're in with the big boys," he says, and gives the plastic bag an extra-wide twirl.

"Jesus, Homer. Aren't you being, I don't know, a little insouciant about this?"

"You think someone will guess that I'm carrying a half kilo of an illegal drug in this plastic bag? No way."

A couple of guests glance at them.

"Keep your voice down," Buzz says, feeling sweat prick his whole skin. "Be cool."

"I am cool!" Homer shouts. "I'm the king of the world! I'm the emperor of Mars!"

"Okay, okay. Jesus. Maybe you'd better tell me what this Focus shit does."

"It concentrates the mind wonderfully," Homer says.

"Like an impending execution?" Buzz's jaws ache; he's been manically chewing the same stick of gum for twenty minutes now. He spits the flavourless wad into his hand, drops it into one of the flower-shaped crystal waste-bins, which in a tiny, tinny tinkle says *thank you*. Buzz unwraps a fresh stick and tells Homer, "You spent five thousand dollars on this stuff? No wonder you weren't answering your phone. Not to mention getting around to making up your orders."

"I was on Mars."

"You're on Mars now."

"No, seriously. That's what Focus does."

"It takes you to Mars. Right."

"It puts you wherever you want to be."

"This is a VR thing, isn't it?"

"Not exclusively," Homer says. "That's why Wolfie Look is going to clean our clocks."

"And it does what? Makes you dumb enough to believe VR is real?"

They walk through a crystal gateway into the next slice of the park's pie. Red rocks and red sand dunes saddle away into the *trompe l'oeil* distance of a painted backscene. Signs point towards the Viking landing site, the secret flying saucer factory, the Mars landing simulation, the life on Mars display.

"It works in here," Homer says, tapping his head. "Focus makes the impossible real. It suspends disbelief. It makes fake reality as real as you and me. I was plugged into one of the NASA rovers, Buzz, travelling through Nirgal Vallis. I was on Mars."

"You're on Mars right now," Buzz says, turning in a circle with his arms out, taking in the red sands (dyed Florida beach sand fixed into shape with resin), the pockmarked red rocks (each hand-carved from Arizona sandstone), the red crags (ditto).

"I never did try it in the park," Homer says, "but I'm told it works just as well here as with VR."

"You're serious about this stuff, aren't you?"

"It's the real deal. When we're done with this little job we'll try it out. You and me, what do you say?"

"I'd say you've done so much of this stuff you don't know what's real or not any more. Hey! Quit it!"

Because Homer has grabbed Buzz's arm, is steering him off the main path.

"I want to show you something," Homer says.

Buzz pulls free. "Man, what's wrong with you?"

"It won't take but ten minutes," Homer says stubbornly.

Buzz knows better than to argue. It's always been this way: Homer making up his mind, and Buzz going along with it. Homer is the go-getter, the man with the plan; Buzz is the sidekick.

The path winds between bigger and bigger rocks, dives into an artfully simulated crevice in the arc of a crater's rampart wall. The room beyond is low-ceilinged, red lit, and, apart from a bored docent lounging in the far corner, completely deserted. Tall glass cylinders are scattered across the black rubber floor, and Homer walks straight across the room to the largest, in which a red lump of rock half a metre high sits on a black display stand.

"There," Homer says. "That there is real."

"Come on, Homer. It's just plastic. A model."

"I know that. I'm not fried. But it exists. It's sitting on Mars right this moment, in one of the canyons in Deuteronilus Mensa. A robot took twenty-eight days to scan that rock right there on Mars, and a laser stereolithograph used the information to build it up out of polymer. Look at it, Buzz. It's a fossilized stromatolite, just like the ones found in three-billion-year-old sedimentary rocks on Earth, which in turn are just like living stromatolites found in certain shallow bays of the Australian coast. See the striations, like pages in a book? Each one is a layer of sediment trapped and stabilized by a year's-worth of growth of mat-forming microorganisms. There was life on Mars, once upon a time. This is the hard evidence."

"Look around you, Homer," Buzz says, exasperated. "We're the only people here. No one cares about the real Mars because no one but a bunch of robots is ever going there."

"I've been. That's the point. That's what Focus does."

"You'd rather be a robot than the emperor of Mars."

"It was like I grew into it. Like the way you grow into the corners of your car when you drive, only more intense. It was as if I was right there."

"You always were a scientific boy, Homer, but don't you think you're taking this a little too far?"

"When did you get so cynical, Buzz? You used to love this place as much as me."

"I guess when I realized I'm just another temp loser pissing away his life smiling and greeting in a second rate amusement park. Are you done with your little lesson here? We've a job to do."

"I just want you to know that I know what I'm doing. You've got to think of it as a career opportunity."

"It's working for a redneck drug dealer, is what it is."

"Wolfie is smart, in his own way," Homer says, rooting in the plastic bag. "He wants the whole park, and with this stuff he's going to get it, too. This is the real deal, Buzz."

"He certainly has you by the balls. You'll be paying off your debt forever."

"I'll play Wolfie Look's game for now, but I have a plan, Buzz, don't you worry. I'm going to analyze the hell out of this shit. I'm going to figure out how to synthesize it and then I'm going to undercut that shit-kicker until he squeals for mercy. You and me, Buzz, what do you think?"

"I think you're crazy. What are you doing?"

Homer has pulled out the package. A dozen medium baggies, each stuffed rigid with white powder and bound together by duct tape and saran wrap.

"Christ," Buzz says. "It might as well have *Dangerous Drugs* written all over it in big red letters."

"You just need the tiniest snort," Homer says, pulling at an edge of duct tape like a child impatient with the wrapping of a present, "and it all becomes real."

Buzz grabs at the package. "If Wolfie Look's guy finds he's short, Wolfie really will break your arms and legs."

"Just one tiny snort," Homer pleads. "I want to see how real hyperreality can get."

There's a glint of wildness in Homer's eyes that alarms Buzz. He manages to snatch the package away, leaving Homer with a long curl of silvery tape in his hand. Behind them, someone says, "Can I help you guys?"

It's the docent, a tanned teenage boy in red jeans and a white T-shirt. Homer grabs the package from Buzz, drops it in the plastic bag, and says, "We were just going."

"I thought maybe you might give me a taste," the boy says. His crew cut hair is dyed yellow, as bright as a sunflower.

"There is something I can give you," Buzz says, and spits the wad of gum in the boy's hand and closes his fingers around it. "Take care of that, will you? I don't want to mess up your nice display."

⊁

Buzz and Homer pass through the *War of the Worlds* section, where amniotronic walrus-like Martians with wise, friendly faces disgorge scientific nuggets amidst fantasticated steampunk machineries, their earnest discourses mostly ignored by guests, who prefer the Battle of Dorking arena. They pass through the Malacandrian section, its bosky dells amidst giant celery trees populated by hundreds of cute amniotronic animals, a queue of parents and children for the *It's All One World* ride snaking around a dozen turns, neatly corralled by railings. And then, through a crumbling stone archway hung with green and red and gold banners, they enter the Barsoom section.

Wolfie Look told them to drop off the stuff in one of the taverns. They try to look as inconspicuous as possible while drinking root beer from paper cups at a wooden table in a corner of a big open space bounded by half-ruined arches and crowded with guests, while a trio of huge, green-skinned, four-armed amniotronic musicians play a selection of Beatles tunes. Homer, the plastic bag planted firmly between his feet, keeps glancing at his watch; they're waiting for the tavern to empty when the show begins, when John Carter and his band of red Martians fight the yellow Martians and rescue Dejah Thoris and her handmaidens. Barsoom is packed with guests waiting to see the spectacle, as Buzz can't resist pointing out.

"Disney has Tarzan, we have the nearly nude Princesses of Mars."

Homer shrugs. "The dads love them, the daughters want to be them."

"Did you ever think it would come to this, Homer? Two grown men play-acting a Mars shuttle flight attendant and the child-emperor of Mars."

"I wanted to be an astronaut," Homer says. "That's all I ever wanted to be when I was a kid. I went to space camp every year. I majored in physics and maths. I even thought that being not so tall would be a help. Most astronauts aren't exactly endowed in the vertical direction."

"Except no one goes into space any more."

"The first time I took this stuff, Buzz, it really did put me there. It was like finding the place you've belonged to all your life. It was like going home. It's the new thing. It beats speed hollow."

"We're still young. We've still got our looks. We could do anything out in the world."

But Homer isn't listening. Buzz turns and sees what he's staring at: two rent-a-cops are threading through the crowded tables at the far side of the tavern, followed by a yellow-haired boy.

Homer and Buzz make it out into the crowded street by keeping a family group, from grandmother to two-year-old riding her father's shoulders, between themselves and the rent-a-cops.

"This isn't good," Homer says. He's clutching the plastic bag close to his chest.

"Where are we going?"

"We'll find a phone and make a new rendezvous," Homer says, and plunges purposefully into the crowds.

Technicians are roping off the wide avenue where the show will take place. People are camped along its edge, on the kerb, under clustered palm trees and banana plants. Homer and Buzz badge themselves into the staging area behind a false stone wall. It's a chaos of buffed bodybuilders in metal-leaf kilts and red skin-paint, handmaidens in long black wigs and spray-on flesh-coloured bodysuits decorated with scales at appropriate places, lizardmen and apemen, their big false heads in one hand and cigarettes or paper cups of iced water in the other, leads with clipboards and stopwatches trying getting everyone into line, technicians talking into headsets. The actor who plays John Carter is standing in a corner, wearing a red kilt and a big brass belt and staring manfully into the far distance as his muscular torso is sprayed with glycerin by a pert teenage girl. A tech is checking the systems of the amniotronic model of a giant, shag-furred, fanged dog, typing instructions into the laptop which is plugged into the thing's back, making each of its five pairs of legs flex in turn.

Buzz follows Homer through this melee towards the office area at the back, but they're only halfway there when one of the leads challenges them. As Homer shoves the man out of the way, a rent-a-cop comes running, pushing through startled actors. Buzz and Homer dodge around a train of prop carts and hurry down the stairs to the service tunnels. Turning left and right at random, they run past a row of steel trash cans, past someone trundling a rack of costumes, past locker rooms and a canteen, and run up a ramp and come out into the staging area, deserted now apart from techs standing in the bright sunlight at the far end. The cheers and laughter of the crowd are a dull roar through the fake stone wall. They have run in a circle.

Homer bends over and breathes hard, hands on knees.

Buzz says, "All we have to do is get out of the section."

"We have to get out of the park. And how are we going to do that? Listen."

Shouts sound faintly in the tunnel at the bottom of the ramp.

"They must have tracked us on the security cameras," Homer says.

"We're not finished yet," Buzz says. "Give me the bag."

"Don't be dumb."

"Give it to me. They don't know what's in it. If they don't have any hard evidence, all they can do is fire us."

The shouts are closer now. Suddenly, half a dozen rent-a-cops turn the corner, start running up the ramp towards them. Homer throws the plastic bag to Buzz, and Buzz takes it and runs, charging across the staging area, dodging startled techs and running out into sunlight and loud cheers, and people dancing all around him.

He's come out through an archway into the middle of the staged fight. The actor playing John Carter is duelling with a warrior with lemon-yellow skin. The nearly nude princesses of Mars are in a pen on a rough wooden wagon in the centre of the wide, white avenue, stagily menaced by lizardmen. Two white apes are chasing each other in circles. Red-skinned swordsmen are trading sword-blows with their yellow-skinned counterparts. And a couple of rent-a-cops are pushing through the guests pressing up against the red rope stretched on the other side of the avenue.

Buzz picks up a sword that lies beside a "dead" yellow-skinned warrior, who opens an eye and whispers fiercely, "What the fuck are you doing?" The sword is made of a light, pliable alloy, but it makes a satisfactory swish as Buzz runs forward, hacking the air. Guests cheer, thinking this is part of the show, a Keystone Cops comedy routine. The air prickles with camera flashes as Buzz drives the rent-a-cops back against the rope, then dodges a trio of bare-chested red Martians who try and bring him down. He tries to climb over the rope, but a guest built like a quarterback enters into the spirit of things and pushes him back.

John Carter has, on schedule, finished off his opponent and sent the lizardmen running, and is now hacking at the big rope around the nearly nude princesses' cage. The rope, held only by a twist of nylon wire, parts as it is supposed to. The princesses rush into John Carter's arms, all long limbs and spangles and toothy squeals of delight.

Overhead, a crane lowers the flier that will carry them off, a wooden platform on a raft of inflated bladders, its gossamer propeller spinning in a rainbow blur.

The rent-a-cops regroup and rush at Buzz. He turns and runs at the flier, swinging the plastic bag around his head like David confronting Goliath. And lets it go. A rent-a-cop jumps for it, misses. It soars through the air, hits the whirling propeller. There's an explosion of white, thinning immediately as it's blown over Buzz and the actors and the rent-a-cops and the guests.

The air seems to brighten. Everything swims into focus and is intensified, from the grains of dust hung in the sunlit air to the pull of Buzz's sheathed muscles, and every moment is as separate and intense as the sunstruck dust grains. One half of Buzz's brain is trying to tell the other half that it's just the drug, but the urgent reality of the world shuts out this sensible advice. He's on Mars.

The red and yellow warriors redouble their fight. Dejah Thoris and John Carter, the Red Princess and the Swordsman of Mars, kiss and rekiss. Guests lower their cameras, look around themselves as if for the first time. Everyone is on Mars, in a terrible and strange city on the floor of a lost, dry sea.

Buzz runs down the ancient avenue. Crowds of Martians part before him. He runs through the ancient gate and runs on across the red sands of Mars. He's free, and so full of sudden joy that gravity seems to lessen with every step he takes.

DANGER—HARD HACK AREA

Many people predicted that VirCon 2010, the first open meeting of the biopunk movement, would end badly: in mass arrests; in a riot; in some horrible mixture of serious weirdness and wholesale violation of civil liberties. In truth, it was as privately exciting and as publicly dull as any science conference. From their besieged underground culture, from garages and basements and bedrooms, the clandestine surfers of the new wave in biology are emerging blinking into daylight and, dare one say, into respectability.

But the meeting, held in a dilapidated midtown New York hotel, was not without friction. Despite the rule, rigorously enforced by the conference's organizers, that no biological material could be brought in, there was a ruthless but futile inspection by officers of the Food and Drug Agency. Several people suspected of being undercover federal agents or snoops from biotech companies were summarily ejected, and the press was barred, which led to strange scenes outside the hotel, as TV journalists were videoed typing into laptops to communicate with conference delegates in the hotel lobby.

I was allowed to cover the event from the inside because of the contacts I made while writing an article on the pursuit and arrest of Kevin "Freaky-Deaky" Miles, the man who, in the ultimate biopunk brag, claimed to have turned the Amazon rainforest luminescent, and because I'm a science fiction writer, and the biopunks love sf.

The delegates themselves were mostly young white males under twenty-five, dressed in everything from no-style baggies and T-shirts through goth black and multiple piercings, to business suits. All had self-inflicted gene hacks: feathers or scales instead of hair; bands of chromatophores on their foreheads; motile tattoos. And of course, unlike the pasty-faced, acne-ridden, overweight cliché of computer hackers, the biopunks were bursting with rude health, their skin and eyesight perfect, their muscle definition superb, their energy seemingly boundless.

That energy was needed: the convention operated on a twenty-four-hour basis, and no one seemed to need any sleep. The biopunks took over the hotel's conference rooms and its second and third floors, talking over laptops displaying DNA source codes, poking through half-dismantled sequencers and synthesizers in the tech room, attending sessions on resetting metabolic clocks, overwriting junk DNA, constructing artificial metabolisms, perturbing quantum effects in microtubules, and, of course, on meme viruses.

In many ways it was rather like a science meeting in the so-called Golden Age of science, before research was taken over by big business and commercial confidentiality strangled open exchange of ideas. Biopunks are scornful of secrecy. They are pathological braggers. Their standing depends on letting everyone know what they have done; their entire culture is based on the idea of "open source", from pirated genomes placed on servers in Cuba, Costa Rica, North Korea and Finland, to sequences and hacks disseminated in philes and ezines with titles like *Mad Cow*, *Triplet Threat*, and *They're Made Out Of Meat*. The only differences between biopunk and mainstream science are that biopunk science stands or falls not by peer review prior to publication but by its utility, and that almost every biopunk uses their hacker handle rather than their real name.

One major exception to the last is the grey eminence of the biopunk ethos, Professor Jack Lovegrove, who attained legendary status after he was fired from the University of Kansas for teaching a practical course in evolution and was jailed for distributing pirate DVDs containing the entire sequence of the human genome.

"Garage science is the wave of the future for biology," Lovegrove told me, in a brief interview. "The big companies are tied down by class action suits and vicious regulations imposed by frightened, short-sighted politicians. Twenty years ago, DNA had to be cut by expensive enzymes and sequenced one base-pair at a time. Now, the kind of sequencer found in any general practitioner's surgery can be modified to run in parallel, and keeping the human genome copyrighted is a joke. Anyone here could sequence it in a couple of days, starting with just one of their own cells."

Lovegrove's keynote address, "Posthumanism and how to achieve it", was packed out, but he was at pains to point out to me that most of his ideas were in the "golden vapourware" stage.

"We're interested in radical ideas, not frost-proofing strawberries or making beef-flavoured potatoes. Rumours that these kids have found the cure for cancer and the key to immortality and boosting intelligence are a crock. If some biopunk had done any one of those things, he would have bragged about it, and then set up his own company, or sold out to Cytex or Dow.

"Of course, biopunks are trying out radical techniques on themselves, but medical science has a long and honourable history of self-experimentation. This is no secret society of immortal, hyperintelligent supermen—just idealistic kids who love science and believe that information and exchange of ideas should be free and unregulated, not locked up by copyright and litigation. All our ideas are discussed openly, although not everyone will be able to understand them."

As for the idea that biopunks are using meme viruses to modify human behaviour, Lovegrove was scathing. "The meme thing is mostly over. Sure, there were pranks. People got a lot of fun from infecting their victims with pseudo-religious visions of Elvis or Princess Di. But now the drug cartels have muscled into memes as a way of delivering natural highs, the craze has died down. Besides, changing belief systems is a hard hack. I'd say that the virulent campaigns against genetic modification died out from natural causes, not from infection by some kind by imaginary supermeme."

He's right, of course. There are limits to what ordinary kids working in homemade labs can do. But in the heady atmosphere of the convention, with hackers partying to the limit and engaged in intense, fast-paced, jargon-ridden conversations, their tattoos and chromatophore bands flashing and blushing, it's suddenly easy to believe that even their most fantastic claims will soon come true.

THE MADNESS OF CROWDS

To answer some of your questions:

Yes, I really am Bill McAbe's older, not-so-smart, and much-less-famous brother;

No, I don't know where Bill is, but I'm certain that he didn't plant the bomb that blew up his apartment and killed his assistant, and I do think he's still alive: sue me if you think I'm prejudiced;

Yes, I do know why he disappeared. He told me everything, and toward the end I was part of it.

How do you know that I'm who I say I am, if what I'm going to tell you is true? Be patient, friend. I'll get to that.

ℋ

As far as I'm concerned, it began three weeks ago, when I got back from a disappointing dinner party, at which a very good friend of mine tried his worst to match me with someone totally unsuitable, to find my answer phone blinking. It was the manager of this club I happen to know. He said that he had someone in his office who claimed to be my brother. One of the security guys had

found him prowling around on the roof, and would I like to come
down and sort it out or would I prefer he called the cops?

I went right over, and it was lucky for Bill that this guy,
Stavros, a three-hundred-pound Greek sweetheart, happened to
owe me a favour after I had designed the club's wet room at cost
price. I got Bill out of there after only a half hour of kissing ass,
making all kinds of promises that it would never happen again. I
even got Bill's stuff back, although the security guy had stomped
on it pretty thoroughly, thinking it was some kind of recording
equipment; the club, a very discreet consensual sex place, is highly
sensitive about that kind of thing. Well, it was recording equipment of a kind, although it wasn't a video camera or a tape
recorder. Bill hugged the bag to his chest all through the ride
downtown to his loft apartment in Tribeca, for once in his life
clamming up—you know Bill, so you *know* how unusual that is—
and refusing to tell me what he had been doing up there on the
roof, fussing with his bleeding nose and saying that maybe he'd let
me know in a couple of days, providing the Samoan asshole who'd
kicked his stuff up and down the stairs hadn't compromised the
samples.

I didn't push it. I was tired, I had a headache from too much
wine and Stavros's cigar smoke. I even forgot about Bill's promise,
until I got a call three days later.

Bill and I both lived in New York City, and we saw each other
once a month for a pizza pie lunch at Hot John's, in the Village,
where Bill would suck me dry of gossip about the romantic world
of TV drama production and speculate a little too loudly about
which of the off-duty firefighters, cops and other municipal
workers who hung out in the restaurant would make a good
boyfriend for me. Yes, you know how Bill was. Like a Tourette's
sufferer, he couldn't keep his thoughts to himself; he had no inner
monologue, no censor, and he also had a filthy mind and a pretty
childish sense of humour. In many ways, he had never really
grown up—you only had to look at his apartment, the laboratory
at one end full of all kinds of scientist's toys, the living room at the

other full of all kinds of boy's toys. He had a bad, bad jones for gadgets, robots, and sci-fi props. He had the world's biggest lava lamp. I believe he was among the first to buy one of those silly-looking dumbbell/pogo stick people movers.

This time, though, he was all business, and we didn't meet in Hot John's, but in a coffee shop over in the East Village like a perfect little time-capsule of 1950s futurism, with streamlined chrome trim on its counter and stools and china decorated with black-and-white starscapes and rocketships.

He said, "You want to guess what I was doing on that roof? You can have three chances. Get it right, I'll pick up the check."

I said that I'd rather pay, to save time and to make sure that we got out of there alive—Bill is the meanest tipper I've ever encountered.

"I was collecting pheromones," he said, favouring me with one of his chipmunk grins. He never would wear his braces when he was a kid, and as a result he had an overbite that would cost tens of thousands of dollars to fix. Not that he didn't have the money of course, from the two dozen patents on his Spin Resonance Chromatograph and those other techy gadgets he invented; it just never occurred to him to spend money on something as mundane as dentistry.

Now *you* know what pheromones are, of course, but I had to suffer one of Bill's little Dick-and-Jane lectures on the way that chemicals released into the air in absolutely minute quantities could affect our behaviour; I had to watch his eyes roll when I essayed that they were like perfumes; I had to listen to his condescending and perfectly tedious explanation that we are very sensitive, at an unconscious level, to subtle variations in body odour, that the mix of complicated organic chemicals in our sweat is determined by the make-up of our immune systems, that it had been experimentally proven that girls prefer men who smell like their fathers ("Of course, you'll probably prefer men who smell like our mother," he couldn't help adding) because that means they have compatible immune systems and so will produce better children. I'm sure I've gotten some of this wrong, but you get the drift.

I asked him what this had to do with his little roof-top escapade.

"I told you. I was collecting pheromones. It's my new field. I'm getting some very useful results. You'll be interested to know, for instance, that the samples I collected from the air vent of that club prove that men like you are just like men like me."

"How alarming."

"Pheromonally speaking. You produce the same inducers as heteros."

I made the mistake of asking what inducers were, and was rewarded with another insufferable lecturette on the effect of pheromones on the parasympathetic nervous system, on brain chemistry, on human behaviour.

"As we smell," I said, "so shall we reap."

"Not bad," Bill said. He made a big deal about noting it down in his PalmTop, and said, ever so casually, "What are you doing next week, by the way?"

He knew of course. I was resting. The production company that made *City Girls* was in negotiation with NBC for a third season, so everyone, including their set designer (*c'est moi*), was on a break.

"How would you like," Bill said, "to go to Las Vegas? Top hotel, all expenses paid. If you say yes, I'll even pay for this coffee."

I thought that Las Vegas in February sounded pretty nice, even with Bill attached to the package. I thought, what's the harm? Really, how dumb can you get?

Because there was, of course, a catch. And of course Bill didn't tell me about it until we were there. After I'd told him, at length, how much I hated boxing, he shrugged, and said, "All you have to do is sit there, two or three hours, the equipment in the bag on your lap. It's just a pump that flushes large volumes of air through activated charcoal filters. I take the filters, bake off the organics, run them through the old SRC."

"And you can't do it because—"

"Because you know how much I hate crowds."

I couldn't argue with that. He'd always taken taxis, never the subway or the bus, even when he was a poor-as-a-churchmouse postgraduate student. It wasn't claustrophobia, and it wasn't that he hated people. It was just that large numbers of them in a small space freaked him out. That was why he got so interested in the whole pheromone thing, of course, but I'm getting ahead of myself.

Well, the fight didn't take three hours, or even two. I reeled out, my ears singing with the aftereffect of the atrocious rock music they pumped at full volume to get the crowd going, and Bill wasn't waiting where he said he would wait, and he wasn't answering his cell phone either.

Where he was, I learned, a couple of hours after I got back to our hotel, was in jail, for attempted assault on one of the contestants.

He was out the next day. He bailed himself for a cool hundred thousand, was full of his little adventure. While I was being battered by hard rock in the audience, he stood in the little crowd of autograph hunters outside the arena's freight entrance, waiting for one of the boxers to arrive. Somehow, he got past the man's handlers, and now he was looking at ten years for assault. With a cotton-wool bud.

"I wanted a sweat sample," he said, utterly unrepentant. "I have a theory about boxers, about people who like to fight."

"You could have gone to a gym."

"The guy is the heavyweight champion of the world. He's the alpha male's alpha male."

"He *was* the world champion," I said. "He lost in the first round. You're lucky he doesn't sue you."

"At least you got the sample."

"My ears are still ringing. And I don't think I'll ever get the stink of cigar smoke out of this suit. Which is Paul Smith, by the way, imported from London, England, not that it will mean anything to you. The least you can do is tell me what all this is about."

"I promise. Once I'm certain."

I know. Not at all like the run-off-the-mouth Bill we all know. He was very serious about this thing of his.

We flew back, Bill in First Class, me in Business (using my bicoastal air miles to upgrade the stowage ticket he'd bought me), and I didn't see him for two weeks, although he kept sending me faxes of newspaper stories. A massacre of Muslims by Hindus in India. A mob in England that burned alive an old man incorrectly suspected of paedophilia; after they set fire to his house, they drove back firefighters and police with stones and petrol bombs. A baying mob of Protestants outside a Catholic school...all kinds of human brutishness. Do you get the idea yet? No, nor did I, until Bill Explained All.

This time it was in a scruffy riverside park in lovely post-industrial northern Brooklyn. I took the "L"; Bill took a taxi. He looked terrible: red-rimmed eyes, a bum's stubble, greasy hair, a haunted expression, the jitters. We clutched cardboard cups of coffee and shivered in the breeze off the East River, and he told me what he had been researching, and what he had found.

He had collected samples from venues where aggression was literally in the air—from rush hour subway stations to my boxing match—and used his Spin Resonance Chromatograph to isolate and characterize a particular human pheromone. He told me that it acted like a highly specific shot of alcohol. It released inhibitions, made people reckless and heightened their tendency to behave violently. Not only that, but when you breathed in a dose, your body started manufacturing and releasing it too: it spread like a cold, a contagious madness that could turn any crowd into a blood-hungry mob that would attack anyone who stood out—anyone who didn't belong, anyone who was that little bit different.

"I found a version in chimpanzees, too," Bill said. "Specifically, in sexually active juvenile males who are subordinate to the alpha male. In the wild, young male chimps can be like teenage gangbangers. They rape any female chimp they come across, murder her baby, form a gang to go hunting monkeys... We're just like chimps, which is hardly surprising, because we share a common ancestor with them. So do gorillas, but gorillas live in family groups of females and their children and a single alpha male, and alpha males are less sensitive to the releaser. Alpha males, they're cool, they don't need to gang up with other males to show what they're made of."

"That's why you wanted to test the boxer."

"I had a better idea. Took a few meetings with CEOs of pharmaceutical companies; they're alpha males too. I spun them some bullshit, wore an adhesive plaster on one of my fingers so I could get a sweat sample when I shook hands. I found that CEO sweat is almost completely free of releaser, but most of their subordinates have low to medium levels. You ever notice how *calm* it seems, up in the executive suites? It's not just because of the thicker carpets and the better lighting. It's also because of the air chemistry."

There was more. Some people were highly sensitive to the releaser, but couldn't make it themselves—Bill was one of them, a wimp and proud of it. And Bill had broken down the releaser's structure and synthesized an antidote to it: an antagonist that inhibited the releaser's action on the human nervous system.

"The thing is," Bill said, tossing his half-empty coffee cup toward the river, "someone else has made it too."

He'd been taking control samples in what he believed would be neutral spaces—libraries, museums, a shopping mall. And he'd found the signature of the antagonist in the air of the shopping mall.

"Not as good as mine, but it does the job. Have you ever wondered why people zone out in shopping malls, in train stations, airports? Well, now you do. It's because someone is messing with your mind."

I said that it all sounded very X-Files.

"You don't believe me? Well, the reason we met here is that I've been followed, the last week. Everywhere I go. Don't worry, I'm pretty sure the taxi driver shook them off before we left Manhattan. I've always wanted," he said, "to tell a taxi driver to lose the guy on my tail."

"Who's following you? How do they know that you know?"

I didn't really have to ask how they knew that Bill knew. Once he had amassed enough data, he'd gone online, boasting to his colleagues, stirring things up in science newsgroups.

"The antagonist makes people less prone to violence," he said, "but it makes them docile too, suggestible, sheep-like. Completely lacking anger is as bad as having nothing but." He looked around for perhaps the fiftieth time in the ten minutes we'd spent together. He said that he had to go.

I wasn't one hundred per cent convinced, but I told him to be careful.

"Look after this," he said, and handed me a padded envelope and walked away.

That was the last time I saw him. The next day, his apartment and the apartments above and below it were wrecked by the crude but powerful bomb that also killed his research assistant. I don't think that was Bill, covering his tracks. If he ever made a bomb, it would be more carefully constructed than any of the Unabomber's. No, I think he stumbled on something someone doesn't want us to know about.

By now, I have no doubt that you're wondering how you can ever believe this preposterous story.

Well, for one thing, you're on the list that Bill gave me; you're an expert in the use of Bill's Spin Resonance Chromatography system. Go into any large shopping mall, take an air sample, and look for the signature of the organic molecule that's given in the attachment to this message. And don't try and trace this email—I sent it through an anonymous remailer, and I like to think that I've made myself pretty hard to find.

There was a big wad of cash in that padded envelope, enough to allow me to travel in style for quite some time, and there was something else.

Two little sealed glass vials, the kind you used to get poppers in, if you've ever done that scene. Each half-full of a colourless, oily liquid. One is the releaser. The other is the antagonist. One pure madness, the other a million-fold dose of universal peace—or the worst weapon of a brainwashing despotism.

So please. Look for that signature. Satisfy yourself that I'm telling you the truth. Think very carefully, and then go to the biochem.net newsgroup and post an answer to this question: should I destroy Bill's gift, or, like poor wretched Pandora, should I give it to the world?

THE SECRET OF MY SUCCESS

Murder was easier than I had thought it would be, even though Mark had been one of my friends. Cutting up his body was worse than actually killing him, but once I set my mind to it, it was only hard work rather than something impossibly disgusting.

Mark had owned a good range of barely used kitchen knives, but none of them, not even the big Chinese cleaver, was up to the job of jointing him. The tenon saw I'd found soon clogged its teeth with flesh and gristle; I broke three hacksaw blades on the big bones of his legs and had to shower and get dressed and go out, feeling slightly hysterical, and buy more from the ironmonger's around the corner on Brewer Street. I bought a cold chisel and a mallet, too, and a roll of twine and a pack of strong, green binliners. If you want a job done right, get the right tools for the job.

After I had finished, and showered again (I'd done the butchery naked, in Mark's white-tile and chrome bathroom) and dressed, I redeemed my BMW from the nearby NCP car park and loaded Mark's bled-out arms, legs, head and torso, wrapped in six pairs of binliners tied up with twine, into its boot. Although it was late in the evening, there were still plenty of people about in Soho, but not one spared me a second glance, even when I worked up a sweat wrestling Mark's heavy torso, in its slippery green wrapping, from doorway to car.

It occurred to me that the butchery wasn't strictly necessary; the police would find traces of blood no matter how much I wiped down the tiles. But they wouldn't know for sure that Mark had been killed, and it was good practice. I planned to kill again.

Have you ever read H.G. Wells's *The Time Machine*? If you have, once I've told you the story of my success you'll know why I did it. You'll know that it wasn't really murder when I killed Mark. It was the first blow in the war between us and them.

♓

It doesn't matter how successful you are: you always need more. You climb the jagged scape of your career, trampling on the hands of lesser competitors, busting a gut or wrecking your heart, shedding a marriage or two if necessary, and when you get to where you always wanted to be, when you've reached a pinnacle where you'll enjoy a clean uncluttered view high above those less fortunate, less gifted, or merely less ruthless than yourself, you see that you've merely climbed the first foothill of an endless range of mountains, and each is surmounted by smug bastards who seem to have got there effortlessly, parachuting in with the help of Mummy's money or Daddy's connections. Who aren't even aware that you exist.

But at first, while I was still climbing that first foothill, my own success was nothing but a series of lovely surprises.

At school, I'd always been good at both English and science. Science was what I liked working at; the English thing was like a sixth finger, a freakish talent. I was always top of the class in English, but I was useless at other languages (those in the top stream of English at the public school where I had a scholarship were supposed to do Latin, but I was so bad at it I was demoted to metalwork) and all the rest of the arts curriculum. I was a science bug who could write. I managed to argue my way into doing English, Biology, and Chemistry A-Levels at school, and then went on to do a zoology degree at Oxford because they didn't mind my rag-bag of qualifications. When I got my First, I toyed with the idea of doing a PhD, but couldn't see how I'd find time for the novel I really wanted to write.

So I came to London, and knocked around doing the usual freelance jobs, reviewing and interviewing for listings magazines, doing capsule reports of Filipino and Thai horror movies for *Sight and Sound*, writing mind-numbing corporate pamphlets and PR leaflets, tidying up abysmally literal translations of Korean electronics manuals. I worked every night and weekend on The Novel, which soon turned out to be not anywhere as good as I first thought. And then, during a spell of unemployment, I wrote another novel in eight weeks flat, a fat thriller about a computer expert who becomes entangled in a series of Internet-related murders and a political scandal, and I was taken under the wing of the first agent I tried.

And that's where my success really started.

Anne Shapiro was one of the top three literary agents in London. For some strange reason she approved of me at our first meeting, an exhausting inquisition in which she covered everything from my family background to my medical history, concluding at last that I had "potential". The quote-marks are hers; she talked not in English, but in heavily inflected Irony.

Anne was an American who had come over to London in the Swinging Sixties. She married a chemical industry baron in the Seventies, was widowed in the Eighties, and in the Nineties built up what was to become the most important literary agency on both sides of the Atlantic. She was five foot nothing with a bob of silver-blonde hair, so thin that you could see every bone in her face, and given to wearing well-tailored silk trouser suits and lots of silver jewellery. Although she seemed as fragile as cut glass, she had the vocabulary of a Liverpool docker with Tourette's syndrome, and the tenacity of a pit-bull terrier. She frightened the shit out of editors, who in London, in the Nineties, still fondly believed that publishing was a gentleman's game. At the start of face-to-face negotiations she would light a cigar with a diameter bigger than her wrist, daring the person on the other side of the desk or the restaurant table to ask her to put it out. No one ever did, not even the Hollywood producer we met in LA when we were flown out to meet the lovely people who had given us a large amount of money for the movie rights.

With Anne Shapiro on my side, the novel became the centre of a mildly intensive bidding war amongst publishers on both sides of the Atlantic. It did well in hardback and sold to fifteen other countries, including Finland and North Korea. The British paper-back sales were good, briefly touching the lower end of the bestseller lists, and selling through five reprintings in a year. Meanwhile, Anne secured me a contract with a TV production company to turn it into a six-part series, and just as I was polishing the final draft of the scripts, a few weeks before produc-tion started on the TV series, she sold the movie rights after a three-way auction. The option money for the winning contract was ridiculously generous, and it was given a green light for the fast track into production. Of course, I had to come up with a new plot, because the movie people liked the character but didn't want to remake the TV series, and I had to translate everything into an LA setting, but I was encouraged by the six figure advance and the promise of much more when the movie was made.

My fiancé and I (it was mostly my money, but Jane did the hard work of dealing with estate agents and solicitors) bought a decaying house at the edge of Primrose Hill for more money than my father had earned in his lifetime, and spent half that amount again fixing it up and kitting it out. We bought a BMW B3 Alpina and a sporty little Mazda. Jane planned to give up her job (she did publicity for my publishers, which is where we had met) when we got married. I had my own newsgroup on the Internet, alt.fan.oliver-slater. Everything should have been lovely.

But of course it could easily have been even more lovely, and that was the problem. As anyone who lives in London knows, location is everything. Primrose Hill is very nice, a village-style community full of actors and writers aspiring to middle-class bohemianism, with a beautiful park commanding views of central London at its edge. But our house was, strictly speaking, more Camden than Primrose Hill, within sound if not sight of the railway junction at Chalk Farm, and because we had no garage, we had to keep our cars on the overcrowded street. Soon after we moved, the cherry red paint of my BMW was keyed all the way down the offside. The people in the house opposite had obviously entered some sort of competition for the title Worst Neighbours From Hell, and from regular use of a high-powered sound system into the small hours of the morning were comfortably ensconced in the semifinals. There was vomit and dog-shit on the pavements. One morning, Jane opened the front door to find that a greasy-clothed, linoleum-skinned tramp had decided to make a kind of tent of cardboard and lice-ridden blankets on our doorstep. The house was nice enough for the moment, but there were places that made it look little better than the tramp's bivouac.

The exclusive square of double-fronted mansions in Kensington, for instance, where we went to a party for which Anne had passed on a couple of invites, and where things started going wrong.

Jane and I arrived in a slightly odd mood, a hangover from an argument we hadn't quite managed to have a few days before, after Anne had treated us to a delightful dinner at Damien Hirst's new restaurant. Jane and I had told Anne about our marriage plans, and Anne had urged us not to rush into having children.

"It doesn't pay to make too many life changes at once," she had said, fixing us with her ice-blue gaze over her glass of Puligny Montrachet. "You should wait a couple of years. Three at the most. You won't be disappointed."

Afterwards, Jane tried her best to start an argument. One of the reasons we were getting married was because we both wanted children, and Jane, bless her, was unbendingly conventional in this area. She felt that Anne's remarks had slighted her.

"She's taking over our lives," she said. "She has no right."

I tried to be reasonable. I tried not to take sides. All the usual mistakes blokes make in confrontations like this. Because of course the argument was really about territory. It was about *me*.

We were getting ready for bed. I was half-drunk, and halfway out of my trousers. I said, "Well, aside from my obvious genius, she is responsible for a lot of the lovely things that have been happening."

Jane gave me a hard, brittle look. I added hastily, "But of course that gives her no right to interfere. It's just how she is. She means well."

"You should start the novel you're always talking about," Jane said. "You were a novelist before she took you up."

The problem seemed to be that I had not taken off my shoes before trying to take off my trousers. I said, "Before I met Anne, I was an unpublished novelist."

"It would have been published without her help," Jane said. "Now, instead of a career, you're doing endless revisions of the same thing."

I had managed to pull my shoelaces into a hard knot. I said, "It pays well."

"Exactly," Jane said. "You're the one who earns money for Anne, not the other way around. Why do you think she made you take that medical before she signed you up? Because she wanted to be sure you weren't going to drop dead, that you were a good long-term investment. What's in her best interest isn't necessarily in your best interest, sweetie. She just sees the enemy of promise in the hall, and loss of her ten per cent."

"The enemy...?"

"'The enemy of promise is the pram in the hall'," Jane said. "Cyril Connelly." She had an English degree, and could always trump me in literary matters. She added, "Anne doesn't even have children of her own. It's well known that she married for money, but was cheated out of it when her husband spent it all on freezing himself."

And so on. Jane was trying to provoke me into defending Anne, so that she could accuse me of taking sides against her, so that we could have a real argument. I managed to dance around her jabs, and although nothing more was said, it was still smouldering away, like a fire in a tyre dump, when we arrived at the party.

It was given by another of Anne's clients, Tom Rose, author of several enormous bestsellers about an Englishman who worked for the CIA. One had just been made into a movie, with Patrick Stewart as the lead, and there was talk that this would be the first of a series of big budget action thrillers.

Tom Rose came from a family which had been in law for about two hundred years, and his wife was a Conservative MP; he was Establishment in a way I could never be, as quickly became clear at the party. A flunky in a 17th century frock coat, breeches and a powdered wig greeted us at the door. The bottle of champagne which I'd insisted on bringing against Jane's advice, was whisked away, still in its Oddbins bag, with our coats. Another flunky led us up a sweeping staircase, with two chandeliers burning high above, to the vast ballroom where the party was in full swing.

There were two bars, waitresses circulating with food on silver trays, a twelve-piece string orchestra, a mountain of shaved ice with foothills of caviar and streams of vodka, and naked people painted to look like statues standing in decorative poses in various alcoves. As for the guests... Jane dresses well, and she was wearing a new Ghost dress she had bought for the occasion, but every woman there was wearing either Prada, Westwood, Chanel, or (Jane told me later) unique creations from the new designer's store in Fulham, which was so select that only members of its exclusive club could shop there. And while I was wearing a brand new pistachio-hued Armani suit, all the other men in the room were wearing dinner jackets and white ties. Clearly, everyone knew everyone else, and they seemed to belong to a different species, one made out of a better kind of flesh. The women were as elegant as swans, the men hale and hearty, and muscular in all the right places. Everyone had healthy tans, immaculate coiffures and rows of gleaming white teeth which they showed constantly. I have good teeth—I have never needed a filling—but everyone here looked like they'd spent half a million pounds on getting theirs snowy white and even.

I have a traditional background for a writer: a solid, provincial, and utterly conventional lower middle class family. My father was a railway clerk in Derby, and my mother spent all her energy keeping our little two-up two-down immaculate. I had escaped via a scholarship to the local public school, and then to Oxford. You'd think I would have been overjoyed to have found myself a guest at a party like that, even if I did stand out like a parrot amongst a flock of penguins, but was I fuck. Although I had been looking forward to having a lovely time, the undercurrents of our ongoing non-argument were now running strongly through my mind, darkened by resentful envy towards all of the effortlessly immaculate people around me. Not only that, but there was no sign of Anne, and while we knew many of the other guests, it was only because we had seen them on TV, or in the fashion magazines or movies.

While Jane turned this way and that, exclaiming how well-preserved this fifty-year-old pop star looked, or how slender and unreal that supermodel was, I started drinking too much. I was coming back from the bar with two more monster gin and tonics, ready to make the sensible proposal that we should wait ten more minutes to see if Anne would turn up, and then beat it to the Groucho Club, when I saw that Jane was talking with the editor of a glossy men's magazine. From the way she was nodding intently, I knew that they were talking business, and rather than interrupt I downed one of the G&T's, set the empty glass on the tray of a passing waitress, and turned and pushed through the crowd to search for the loo.

At the far end of a marble-walled corridor, a group of men were standing outside a door that had to be the door of the bathroom, although none of them seemed to be in any particular hurry to make use of it; they looked as decoratively elegant as extras in a Merchant-Ivory film. One of them said something about telomeres, and then they looked at me and fell silent, no doubt wondering why some nutter in a green suit had wandered in off the street.

I was just plucking up the courage to barge past when someone put a hand on my shoulder and said, "You made it."

It was one of my university friends, Mark Ellis. We'd kept in touch after we'd moved down to London—he'd landed a job in a digital effects company in Soho—but I hadn't seen him in more than a year. His hair had been receding, and he had been rounding out from too many business lunches, but now he looked as spruce as the rest of the guests, tanned and relaxed in a dinner jacket and kilt—he was one quarter Scottish, and wore a kilt at every possible social occasion. His hair was thick and glossy and black, pulled back in a ponytail that, unusually, looked stylish and uncontrived.

"Thank God there's someone here I know," I said. "I feel like a gatecrasher. My agent wangled me an invite but she isn't here."

"Anne got in on the ground floor, didn't she," Mark said. And added, when he saw that I didn't know what he was talking about, "I have to say you've got guts, wearing that suit."

"And I have to say that you can fuck right off. No one told me it was a dinner jacket affair."

"And where is the lovely Jane?"

"Oh, sucking off some tosser of a magazine editor."

Mark laughed. He'd had his teeth straightened and polished. "Oh, you needn't worry about networking at this kind of bash. It's neutral territory. Outside, of course, we're all at each other's throats, but not here."

We talked for a couple of minutes, catching up. I commented on his tan, and he said that he'd been in LA for a couple of weeks. I told him about the script I was trying to write, and he told me that he had his own post-production company now; perhaps he'd get to do some work on the movie. It was a nice, grown-up conversation. Then someone at the other end of the hall called to him and he glanced at his wafer-thin Patek Phillipe watch and said he had to see some people. I assumed that he was off to do a couple of lines of coke or something similar; in a way, I was right.

"I'm really pleased you made it, kiddo," he said. "I'll give you a call."

And that's what he did the very next day, suggesting brightly that I come and visit him on Sunday; we could watch a new print of *The Life and Death of Colonel Blimp* he'd borrowed from the NFT, in his company's private screening room.

"You still have a thing for Powell and Pressburger, don't you?"

"Sure. I mean, yes. Yes, it would be cool. Let's do it."

I was nursing a killer hangover, and it was one of the brain-grey, brain-dead November days that are the curse of London winters. I'd carried on drinking at the party, moving from relatively harmless gin-and-tonics (full of health-giving minerals, quinine and, thanks to the lime slice, vitamin C), to hundred-year-old brandy. I didn't really remember the taxi ride back, and had a vague idea that I had thrown up when we'd got home. Jane had left for work without waking me; she was away for five days, shepherding a retired cricketer around the country on a publicity tour for his autobiography (called oxymoronically and inaccurately, since it had been written by a hack for a tenth of the cricketer's advance, *My Autobiography*). I spent most of the day on the sofa, watching crap cable TV and feeling sorry for myself, instead of working on the script.

I was still liverish the next day, and as I left the house for Mark's place I discovered that a dog, clearly an unfeasibly large dog on a diet consisting exclusively of vindaloo curry, had shat copiously on the doorstep, and a number of people, perhaps the crowd that inevitably would have gathered to look at this wonder of nature, had spread the stinky muck all over the pavement. The odour lingered in the car, suggesting that despite my tip-toe care I'd somehow managed to get some of the shit on my shoes.

I was skirting Regent's Park when my mobile rang. It was Anne; she asked if I would mind popping into her office. I cheered up at once. The last time we'd had an impromptu meeting was when she had given me the good news about the rights auction which had resulted in the movie deal. I found a parking space right outside her building, bounded up the stairs to her office suite and went straight in; because it was Sunday there was no one in the reception room, with its squashy sofa and well-lit display case with specimens of the books of Anne's clients, including my first and so far only novel, racked on perspex stands.

Anne was standing by the floor-to-ceiling window of her office, some kind of spray canister jammed in her left nostril. She sniffed hugely and turned and saw me, said that she was suffering from hayfever, and calmly stowed the canister in the mini-fridge in the corner. We didn't sit down; the meeting only lasted five minutes. The news was not good.

"There's a problem," she said, "with the studio. They've put the project on the back burner."

"But I thought they were fast-tracking it. The last time we talked, they were going to start casting. I thought—"

Anne dismissed this with a wave of her hand. "They've got some shit-hot new project. Fuck-ups like this happen all the time. Don't worry about it. You still have the option money."

"I was rather counting on the rest," I said. I wanted to sit down because I wasn't sure if I had the energy to remain standing while maintaining the fixed grin that had taken residence on my face. The thing with movie deals is that everyone knows about the big, headline-grabbing total, but you only get the full amount if the movie is made. But because the deal had been green-lighted from the start, I had been counting on getting that full amount so that I could pay off the huge mortgage on the house.

There was worse news: I still had to write the script. That was part of the deal, it seemed; I had already been paid for it, and the

movie people wanted their pound of flesh. And to be honest, I
hadn't really done very much work on the script. I was tired of
writing the same thing over and over again.

I tried to tell Anne about the novel I wanted to write, thinking
that at least I could get an advance for it. It probably wouldn't pay
off the mortgage, but perhaps it would reduce it enough so that
Jane's salary could cover the payments. I began to wonder how I
was going to tell Jane that she couldn't quit her job after all.

The idea for the novel had excited me when it had first
arrived—a big, roomy saga describing the rise of the media elite in
the Eighties and their successes and failures in the Nineties—but
now it sounded trite. Anne had turned to look out at the view of
Russell Square, its field of muddy grass with red buses crawling
along one side under the bare winter trees, and when at last I fell
silent, she nodded without looking around.

"I'm sure we can sell it somewhere," she said, "but remember
that your strength is in the thriller genre, Oliver. The secret of
success is to find something that works and stick with it as long as
possible. You have good genes. I'm sure you can redeem yourself.
Think about it."

And so I wasn't at my best when I arrived at the offices of
Mark's company, in a smart building on Soho Square. It specialized in digital post production, and had benefitted from the trend
for ever bigger and better explosions and stunts demanded by
American blockbuster movies. It could add computer generated
virtual actors in crowd scenes, enhance or simulate explosions, lay
snow over a landscape or add breath-smoke in scenes where actors
were supposed to be talking in freezing air. Soon enough there
would be no principal photography at all, Mark said, and let drop
that on paper he was a multi-millionaire.

"Of course, if I actually wanted the money, I would have to
sell all this."

"All this" was three floors of open plan offices full of work-
stations crammed with the latest hardware; even a Cray
supercomputer. Even though it was a Sunday, one or two people

were at work. They greeted Mark cheerfully; clearly, he was a good boss. And a good friend, too. I had briefly thought of going home, and the only reason I'd come here was that I couldn't face the idea of being on my own. If Mark noticed that I was a bit withdrawn, he didn't comment, and made sure that I felt right at home.

We watched *The Life and Death of Colonel Blimp* in the screening room, then went over to Mark's loft on Great Pulteney Street, where we played pool and drank a delightful brand of Czech lager I'd never heard of before, and then, in a spirit of post-modern irony, ate a Thai take-out and watched a hardcore porn video, *Edward Penishands*, he'd brought back from a recent trip to New York. In the middle of the various jiggling penetrations, and while Mark was off having a slash, I went over to the big red Westinghouse fridge to get another beer. And as I rummaged around, I found a slim grey canister just like the one I'd caught Anne using.

I was, to be frank, fairly drunk. We'd had a few drinks while watching the film, and we'd smoked a couple of joints, too. And while playing pool I'd been drinking at least twice as fast as Mark. On impulse, with the hazy notion that it might be some kind of designer drug, I plugged the nozzle of the canister into my right nostril and gave myself a little spritz. I just had time to register an oily, faintly bitter scent before I heard Mark coming back. Instead of putting the canister back in the fridge, I dropped it into my pocket.

I watched the rest of the video in a state of anticipation, wondering when the high would kick in, and what it might be like, but nothing happened. I went home half-cut and horny, and got all maudlin with Jane over the phone, pretending to be scandalized when she told me that the cricketer, currently appearing in a breakfast cereal commercial with his family, had brought along an eighteen-year-old girlfriend for company. I suggested that I could drive up to York tomorrow, but Jane said that after a signing and a radio interview they were going straight over to Bradford and then on to Manchester, where there would be another radio interview and a long evening signing session. "I'll be back on Wednesday, sweetie," she said. "Remember to do the washing up."

)(

I found the spray canister the next day, when I was putting away my jacket. On top of a hangover, I felt like I had come down with flu: scratchy throat, aching joints, unpleasant bouts of sweating and shivering. The ends of my fingers and toes hurt too, as if someone had inserted powdered glass under the nails.

Now I did what I should have done before. I read the list of contents printed on a square white label which was stuck to the base of the canister, next to a barcode strip.

TRC1, HAPa, SGSih, WRN3 retroviruses. Human lysosomal base. Keep refrigerated.

I didn't know what the alphabet soup was, but I knew about retroviruses. Everyone knows about retroviruses. HIV, which causes AIDS, is a retrovirus. Retroviruses burrow into your cells and get in your DNA and fuck around with it until it isn't yours any more. And I'd sprayed a whole mix of them up my nose, and now I had something like flu.

What I should have done was call Mark, confess, and ask him what the stuff was. After all, presumably he had been spraying it up his nose, too, just as Anne had been. She had said it was for her hayfever, but who had hayfever in November? And then there was that remark I'd overheard at the party, and the remark Mark had made about Anne. She'd got in on the ground floor through her husband, the man who had been deeply into genetic research before he died, and who was now cryogenically frozen, waiting until he could be revived and made better. With all this came the thought that the party had been some kind of test which I'd failed, and the collapse of the movie deal was the first sign of that failure. If they knew I had stolen this stuff, what else might they do? It was pure paranoia of course, but all writers have a streak of paranoia in them, and at that moment I was feeling particularly vulnerable.

So instead of phoning Mark, I called on one of my old Oxford pals, who was doing research in the University College of London. He'd helped me get some of the technical details right in my TV scripts, and I told him that I was doing research for a new novel and needed to pick his brains again. Then I made another phone call, to someone else I'd consulted when writing those scripts.

"I can tell you what one of them is," Colin said that lunchtime, after he had read the canister label. "WRN is a human gene associated with longevity. I suppose WRN3 is a variant. If someone put it in a retrovirus, then it must be for gene therapy, although therapy for what I couldn't say. I suppose the packaged genes would get into the blood system through the mucosal membranes, but I'm not sure how they'd target the right cells. Lysosomes wouldn't be my first choice as a delivery agent; we mostly use genetically engineered lymphocytes or embryonic stem cells now, and transplant them directly. Still, I'd be interested in looking at it. Where did you say you got it?"

Colin was turning the slim grey canister around and around. His long white fingers were stained blue with the dye he used in electrophoresis gels. One hinge of his black-framed spectacles had been mended with yellow biohazard tape, and he was wearing the same shabby green cagoule he had worn for three years at Oxford. He was a perfect example of what the upper class students had disdainfully called a northern chemist, but he was also a nice, straightforward guy, amused but not at all impressed by my success and sudden wealth.

I took the canister from him. We'd met in an Irish themed pub on Euston Road. It was half-full: a bunch of braying teenage clerks in cheap suits and football hooligan haircuts, clumps of students, some bewildered tourists in eye-hurting leisurewear, and the usual half dozen broken-veined, dry-haired, fifty-year-old alcoholics who are fixtures in just about every pub in London. I thought that any one of them could be a private investigator on my tail. By now I was more than a little bit paranoid; I'd had quite a morning, in Dalston.

When I stuck the canister in the breast pocket of my jacket, my thumb nail caught on a seam and hinged up with an excruciatingly sharp pain. Colin asked me if I was all right as I gingerly stuck the nail back down. Blood was leaking from the edges. It hurt like fuck.

I said, "Old DIY wound. Look, about this thing. I got it from a friend, but I can't tell you—"

"I might be able to run a sequence on it. Might be interesting..."

I got him onto another subject, and when he had finished his half pint of Caffrey's and his plate of pie and chips, he looked at his watch and said he had to get back to the lab. As we were leaving, I asked as casually as I could about telomeres.

)(

Afterwards, when I had used all the plasters from my BMW's first aid kit on my tender, loose fingernails, I sat and thought about the implications. The idea of introducing strange genes into my system was somehow worse than the idea of retroviruses. I had seen plenty of vampire flicks, and there was that strangely unpleasant movie, *Society*, in which a group of rich Californians turn out to be a species of slimy shape-changers.

My face was sore and tender. My joints ached.

Whatever I'd inhaled was changing me.

I gripped what I'd bought in Dalston. Its heavy weight made me feel better, gave me the resolve to call Mark on my cell phone. I told him what I'd done. He was relieved. He said, "I left a message for you. We were both pretty fucked up, eh? Drop it off at work."

I said I'd meet him at his loft, rang off, and drove straight to Soho. I had all kinds of questions to ask him, but I didn't get many answers.

When he opened the door, I held up the canister and said, "I know."

"You know?"

"I worked it all out," I said, and told him.

Mark laughed, and that's when things got a bit ugly. I showed him my new toy, made him sit in one of his antique Sixties chairs, and tied him up. At first he tried to bluff, and then he got angry. I got angry too, and things got out of hand. We had a shouting match that hurt my already sore throat. I have to admit I hit him a couple of times with a pool cue. I didn't learn much. He said that he didn't know anything about telomeres. All he knew was that he'd paid a king's ransom for the kind of stuff I'd stolen, and it had made him healthier than he'd ever been. It treated male pattern baldness, removed body odours, tightened up collagen to stop wrinkling. It was plastic surgery without scalpels or stitches; it was a health regime that actually worked, although it wouldn't work on me, apparently. Mark said that some kind of primer treatment was needed first.

Perhaps it wasn't working, but it was definitely doing something. I felt sicker than ever.

By this time Mark was in a lot of pain. He became stubborn and wouldn't tell me any more. So I killed him and dismembered his body, stuck it in the boot of my BMW, and drove home.

⽊

All the lights were on in the house, and the front door was open. I thought that Jane had returned early, and bounded in, calling her name, forgetting for a moment about the dismembered body in the boot. But the woman waiting for me in the living room was Anne.

"This is all my fault," she said, coolly ignoring my dishevelled, sweaty, wild-eyed state. "I shouldn't have brought you on so quickly." She gave a little shrug. "But you are so very promising, Oliver, that I couldn't help myself. So let's help each other now, okay."

"I gave Mark his spray back," I said.

"That's good. That's a start. Sit down, Oliver. Take some deep breaths. You look flushed."

She sat on the sofa and patted the space beside her, but I remained standing, my hand in my pocket. She didn't know it, but I was in control.

I said, "I know about the gene therapy."

She shrugged. "You've been under a lot of strain in the past few days, Oliver. You're worried about the movie deal. And I can see that you have a fever."

"You fucked up the movie deal as some kind of punishment because I didn't pass your test. What next? A couple of burly chaps coming to take me away?"

"Don't be silly, Oliver. There's no conspiracy. There was no test. Your deal fucked up because most of them do. There will always be more deals for someone of your obvious talent. Just finish the script and move on."

Which was perfectly reasonable in one sense, but crap in another, given that I had already killed someone involved in the conspiracy, even if he hadn't told me much about it.

Anne said, "I can fix up what's wrong with you. I can put you forward for the primer treatment, too, once you have enough money. This kind of thing will be available to everyone soon, but we'll have the edge because we have all the best scientists working for us. People like us will always have the edge. I'm on your side, Oliver, really I am. If you're a good boy, there's just a chance I might get you work on the script for the next Tom Rose movie."

That's when I shot her.

♓

It's amazing how cheap a gun can be, in certain parts of London. I met this guy, Fat Tony, when I was doing research for the TV series. I was introduced to him by a journalist friend. Fat Tony was a punisher. You paid him to hurt people. So much for a broken nose, so much for a broken leg. I could have hired the gun from him by the hour, but I bought it outright. I'm going to need it full time. Guns suit me because they deliver instant justice. You point, you shoot, it's done. Frankly, it's a good thing they're illegal; if they had been readily available, I would have been put away long ago for shooting to death surly supermarket checkout clerks, half a dozen magazine editors, the guy who charged me two hundred and fifty quid for taking twenty-two minutes to not fix my central heating, Scandinavians who hump their giant ruck-sacks on to the Tube, middle class idiots who insist on bringing their horribly behaved children into restaurants, every driver of a white van in the central London area, cyclists who assert their urban ecowarrior credentials by running red lights, and anyone, anytime, on Oxford Street.

So while shooting Anne might seem a tad impulsive, it wasn't difficult. And besides, I had seen her working her magic on editors and movie executives. I knew when she was lying. And I knew about telomeres.

Thanks to my neighbours' sound system, no one heard the shots. I didn't bother to joint Anne; she was small enough to fold into a couple of binliners.

After I had stowed the body in the boot, I tried to call Jane, but the hotel switchboard couldn't get an answer from her room. I love you, Jane. Don't look for me. I'm on a mission. I'm doing this for our unborn children.

Let me tell you about telomeres. They sit at the ends of our chromosomes and, by getting shorter each time, count how many times our cells have divided. After a certain number of divisions, there are no more telomeres, and the cell can't divide any more. If you restore a cell's telomeres, it gains the potential to divide forever—it becomes immortal. That's what happens in cancer cells—their telomeres don't shorten after each division.

In *The Time Machine*, Wells's Victorian Time Traveller ended up in 802,701 A.D., where the human race is split into two: the beautiful but weak, child-like Eloi who live in the gardens of the

surface; the strong, ugly, sinister Morlocks who live amongst the
subterranean machines. The Eloi were once the rulers, but became
prey to their former servants, the Morlocks. Now think of a
future where we ordinary people—with our rashes and pimples,
our bad breath and caries, our myopia and the rapid enfeeblement
of old age—will be the servants of Eloi who are strong and clever,
bred for success and virtually immortal. Who will be made strong
by things which will kill us.

Think of the rich and successful, with their perfect skin and
perfect teeth. Think of the movie stars who seem to get younger
every year. Think of the politicians…

They'll rule forever if they get the chance.

I'm in a Traveller's Lodge outside London, with my laptop
and modem. I have twenty thousand pounds in cash. I've dumped
the BMW. I've spent all night working on this; now it's time to
move on.

The fever's worse. My joints are swollen, and blood is leaking
out of my fingernails. My teeth are loose, and there are lumps
under my skin…

Once I've downloaded this to all the relevant newsgroups on
the Internet, I'm off to do my bit in the war of them versus us. I
wonder how many of them I'll be able to kill before the secret of
their success kills me.

THE PROXY

O z Hardy had been in the book trade
since leaving university. To begin with,
he scraped by on the scanty fees paid by
broadsheets and literary magazines for capsule reviews of arm-
breakingly heavy biographies of minor poets and obscure
nineteenth century politicians, but before he could graduate to the
less exhausting and more remunerative reviews of first novels, or
the steady but easy work of summarizing the virtues of paperback
reprints, he was forced to drop out of the reviewing game because
it took too much time from what had become his real job: a book-
runner.

He stumbled into the job through the contacts he'd made
when, every week, he staggered down to Charing Cross Road or
Chancery Lane with a holdall stuffed with the latest review copies,
for which he received half the cover price. A book-runner ran
after books. A customer would come into a secondhand bookshop and ask for some long out-of-print rarity, and if the owner of
the bookshop didn't have it in stock, he'd take the customer's
name and phone number, and add the title to his want list. Oz and
all the other book-runners ran around London searching for
books booksellers had promised to prospective customers, and

buying underpriced books and overlooked bargains and passing
them on, at a small markup, to those who better appreciated their
value. It was a little like bounty hunting, although hardly as
dangerous or exciting, and much more badly paid. Oz developed a
talent for sniffing out rarities in the marginal bookshops of
Tilsbury and Greenwich, in charity shops and in church sales, in
the bargain bins of department stores whose buyers didn't have a
clue. He sold on his finds and developed his own list of customers
with their obscure wants and desires.

But the Internet was bringing an end to the book-running
trade. You could enter the rarest title in an Internet search
engine and be presented, at once, with selections from the cata-
logues of half a dozen booksellers. You paid by credit card and
received your prize by post or by courier a couple of days later.
Collectors were burning through their want lists, and bargains
became harder to find because everyone knew the proper price for
everything.

Oz tried to adapt. He set up his own web site, specializing in
genre fiction because genre writers often had low print runs and
rabid fans, and used an Internet auction house for his other business, selling historical documents and autographs. The problem
was that anyone could now, in theory, sell anything to anyone
else. The auction sites on the Internet were like global yard sales;
Oz's profits were soon pared to the bone. The six months he had
spent selling, page by page, the autograph album of a particularly
tenacious pre-First World War stage door Johnny, soon seemed
like a distant golden age. His rusty Morris Minor comprehen-
sively broke down on the Westway, and he was three months
behind on the rent of his flat.

The day his life changed, Oz was in his flat, chair cocked back
and feet up on the desk next to the humming computer, listening
to the D'Oyly Carte recording of Ruddigore while sleepily
digesting a steak pie and two pints of Strangeways Ale after his
lunchtime session at the Branch, when someone rang the doorbell.
Oz threw open the window and looked down at the front door,

expecting to see one of the army of couriers—swarthy leather-clad bikers; wiry lycra-clad cyclists; off-hand van drivers in nylon windcheaters—who brought him stuff he'd bought over the Internet, or took away things he'd sold. Instead, he saw an old gent in a pinstripe suit, who lifted the horn handle of his furled umbrella from the bell push and looked up at him and said, "Mr. Hardy? I'd like you to find something for me."

※

Ten minutes later, the old gent, Colonel Leslie Salisbury, was explaining that Oz had been recommended to him by a mutual friend—Teddy Bannister, the owner of a secondhand bookshop in Islington.

"Teddy's an old chum," Colonel Salisbury said. "He said that you might be able to help me."

They had crossed the road to the Branch, where the Colonel had bought a pint of Strangeways for Oz and a double Bell's for himself. Apart from Ken the barman the pub was deserted, but the Colonel leaned so close Oz could smell the whisky on his breath, and whispered, "This is rather a confidential matter."

Oz said, "You have something special you want to sell?"

"Not to sell," the Colonel said. "To buy. And Teddy said you were the man to help me."

Oz said, "I quit the book-running business a while back, Colonel."

The Colonel drummed his bony fingers on the beak of his umbrella. "You don't have to search for this particular item. I know just where it is. But I do need your help to buy it."

The Colonel explained that his elder brother had squandered the family fortune, losing heavily in Lloyds syndicates and at Kempton, Sandown, and Cheltenham. After his death, the manor house had to be auctioned off to meet the debts and death duty, and the Colonel had sold much of the library to Teddy Bannister.

"But not everything, you understand," the Colonel said. "I kept my favourite volumes. And, of course, the Eccham Incunabula."

"The Eccham Incunabula," Oz said, trying to look as though he had heard of it.

"You won't have heard of it," the Colonel said, twinkling over the rim of his whisky glass. "The man who built Eccham Manor, Sir Toby Eccham, compiled it from a variety of ancient sources. He was something of an alchemist, but he also fought on the King's side in the Civil War. He walled up the Incunabula for safe-keeping, but he never came back—he was killed at the siege of Oxford. His sister's family—my family—took back the Manor after the Restoration. The Incunabula turned up again when my grandfather was extending the Manor. It has been a secret family treasure ever since, and I kept it through the recent troubles. But then I recently learned that it was for sale."

Oz said, "It was stolen?"

"My thought exactly," the Colonel said. "When I learnt that the Incunabula was for sale, I went straight around to my bank. That's where I keep it. Far too valuable, you see, to have in the house. No, it was safe and sound. I still have it. But so, it seems, does someone else."

"They must have a copy," Oz said.

"Not very likely," the Colonel said. "Only the immediate family knew about the Incunabula, and it has always been locked away. And what's advertised for sale is a printed volume, dated 1818. Made when the original was still walled up in Sir Toby's hiding place."

Oz sipped his beer. He said, "It could have been set from a copy made before Sir Toby hid the original."

"That's certainly one possibility," the Colonel said. "In any case, I hope the mystery will be solved once I've bought the damned thing. It's up for auction. That's why I came to you."

Oz was too honest for his own good. He said, "Why not bid for it yourself?"

"Because it is up for auction on the Internet," the Colonel said. "At somewhere called...just a minute..." The old man reached inside his jacket, took out a piece of paper and unfolded it and held it close to his eyes. "Haystack full stop com. My great-niece saw it and told me, and Toby told me that you conduct most of your business that way. So, young man, will you do it?"

Oz said, "It's simple enough. Your great-niece could—"

The Colonel laid a hand on Oz's sleeve. "Ah, but there's one other thing. I want you to be my proxy in this auction, and I also want you to find out about the person who is selling it."

)(

They agreed on a fee of a hundred pounds a day plus expenses; the Colonel handed over a five hundred pound retainer. He said that he wasn't such a silly old fool to trust everyone he met, but he liked the cut of Oz's jib.

"Not many people your age appreciate Gilbert and Sullivan," he said, "and not many have the sense to dress properly either."

Oz was hardly the showiest character in the book trade—Lawrence Ackroyd, for instance, wore a red leather suit and went about without a shirt even in the depths of winter—but people often commented on his clothes. That day, he was wearing a high-collared white shirt with a ruffled front, a white silk cravat, a red and gold waistcoat, a black jacket and black trousers with a black velvet stripe, and a practical pair of Doc. Martens. He habitually carried an ebony cane with a silver fox's head, which he had picked up for a song on one of the stalls in Camden Passage, and his blond hair was worn in a shoulder-length Richard the Lionheart bob.

It had started after he had joined the chorus of the Cornish Gilbert and Sullivan Society. He'd sung in *Iolanthe*, in *HMS Pinafore*, in *The Yeoman of the Guard*. He'd sung in *The Pirates of Penzance*, in Penzance. And he'd taken to wearing the clothes

of the period, cutting such an eccentric figure at school that he had
never been troubled by bullies. His parents were artists—his
father American, his mother English—who had moved from San
Francisco to a commune in Cornwall in 1970, two years after
Oz had been born, and Oz's adoption of Victorian formality
might have begun as a typical rebellion against his parents' values,
but it had lasted half his life, for so long that it was no longer an
affectation.

Oz and the Colonel shook hands on the deal and Oz went
back to his flat, fired up the modem, logged on to the auction web
site and found the relevant page.

The auction had been under way for more than three days and
was scheduled to expire at midnight; there were only eight hours
left. Oz initiated a proxy bid and entered the Colonel's ceiling
price—more than a hundred times the highest current bid. It took
him two minutes. He wrote down the email address of the sellers
and went off to catch a 38 bus.

)(

"Looks like they've got their own server, man," Gabriel Day
told Oz.

"How is that a problem?"

Oz was standing at Gabriel's shoulder, because Gabriel was
sitting at the computer on the only chair in Gabriel Day's studio
flat. The small room, in a housing association block on Rosebery
Avenue, was crowded with dead tech. Vocoders, Betamax video
players, video disk players, record decks, cyclostyles, ancient
computers, battered printers. Boxes of 8 inch, 5 1/4 inch, and 3 inch
disks. Shelves of gutted electronics, sheaves of wires, the multicoloured pips of transistors, the beautiful acorns and thimbles and
pods of electronic valves.

Gabriel Day was a fortysomething university dropout with a
greasy pony-tail pulled back from his bald patch, a permanent

hunch, and slab-like glasses with thick black plastic lenses. He specialized in fixing obsolete hardware, but had a sideline in sourcing obscure information.

He told Oz, "If they were using a commercial service provider to get access to the Internet, I could probably get their address through the subscriber list. Either with a simple hack, or even easier, with a little bribe to an under-paid clerk. But this, I'll have to lay it off on a real black-hat hacker. He'll use a trojan program to get into their computer through their email, and it'll look around for their phone number or find some file with their address."

"Will it take long?"

Gabriel sucked at his stained teeth. "Two days at the most. Why do you want to find them?"

Oz laid out the story over a cup of black coffee—Gabriel made good coffee in a battered electric percolator, but spoiled it by adding powdered milk if you wanted it white.

"It might be a scam," Gabriel said, when Oz was finished.

"I did wonder. That's why you might get your hacker friend to check the people making bids, too."

"In case they're fake bids, artificially jacking up the price for something which might not exist."

"Exactly."

Gabriel grinned, showing coffee-stained tombstone teeth. "Like the Australian virgins."

"There are virgins in Australia?"

"Some guy in Perth, man, offered virgins for sale through one of the net auction houses. He wasn't really selling virgins, of course. He was collecting names and addresses of everyone who made a bid. And then he posted them on his web site. It's the fourth wave."

"The fourth wave?"

Gabriel adjusted his heavy glasses with finger and thumb. "The first wave was hardware—actual machines, IBM, the telcos.

The second wave was software—that's what Bill Gates realized, that's why Microsoft beat out Apple, because Apple was as much about beautiful machines as it was about software. The third wave, that's now, that's concepts, dot coms, ideas about how to use the Internet to connect people and things in the real world. But soon there'll be the fourth wave: stuff that never leaves the Internet, stuff that only exists in cyberspace."

"Like virtual reality," Oz said. He had read some of the sci-fi books he sold: he knew about virtual reality.

"I mean fairylands, dreams, ideals. And scams, spoofs, pranks. Fairy gold, man. Looks like gold when you find it, but turns out to be cobwebs or leaves when you get it home. That's what this book might be. You could be chasing the grail."

"But you can find the grail's telephone number."

"No problem, man. Everyone has to live somewhere."

♓

"You have it?" the Colonel said. "I must say that's amazingly quick."

"We won the bid. Now you have to pay for it." Oz gave the details.

"That's the Queen's bank," the Colonel said.

"Yes, and they wouldn't give up the name of the account holder."

"I pay the money into this account, and the book will be delivered."

"To me, yes. I gave them my address."

"I'll do it right now," the Colonel said.

"Use a credit card. It'll go through at once."

"I knew I could rely on a chap like you."

"I still have to find out who the seller is," Oz said, "but I'm confident that I will."

♓

Although Oz was fairly sure that Gabriel's hacker would be able to dig out the grail's telephone number, he also planned to interrogate the courier who would bring the book to his flat once the Colonel had settled the bill. Couriers were physical extensions of the Internet, their routes an analogue of the Internet's web. The courier who brought the Incunabula would have to have picked it up from somewhere, and the right question (or bribe) might help Oz trace it back to its source.

So Oz sat in his flat all day, waiting for the courier. He checked the various auctions he was conducting. He got his accounts up to date. A can of oxtail soup took care of lunch. He waited until eight o'clock in the evening, then put his hat on his head, picked up his cane, and went out.

There was a lock-in at the Branch, and a game of five card stud poker at a penny a point, played upstairs on the tiny stage, amidst the props of the latest play, an adaptation of a minor but classic noir movie, *Detour*. At midnight, Oz was holding a pair of sevens and a pair of fives, and was pretty sure that Ken the barman was yet again bluffing on a high card pair, when he heard the throaty roar of a motorcycle. He threw in his hand, and clattered down the stairs and shouldered through the fire door just as the motorcycle roared past, heading back the way it had come.

It was a big black beast, its black-clad rider bent low as it raced past, raising a wind that sent litter swirling high in the air. Oz glimpsed the insignia on the motorcycle's tool box—an old-fashioned posthorn with a single loop of cord, white on blue—and then twin red flames stabbed from the exhaust pipes as the bike put on speed and flew across the bridge that arched over the canal, the throaty snarl of its engine rising and then cutting off as abruptly as if the motorcycle had hit a brick wall on the far side.

Oz walked to the crown of the bridge, but saw only the empty street stretching away beneath the double chain of orange streetlights.

The posthorn insignia wasn't the badge of any courier service he knew, but when he got back to the flat he found that the book had been delivered. Not to his door, but to his flat: to his desk.

The package sat on top of his computer. A big padded envelope, sealed with staples and parcel tape, his address printed on a stick-on label, with the name of the courier service in cursive script below. *Thurn und Taxis.* Befuddled by Strangeways Ale, Oz sat on his swivel chair for some time, looking at the package. After a while, he got up and went downstairs and examined the locks on the front door, and the locks on the door to his flat. There seemed to be fresh scratches around the keyholes, but he wasn't enough of a locksmith to know if that meant anything. But, indisputably, the book existed. It had been delivered.

♓

"You didn't open it," the Colonel said.

"No, sir. It's your package."

It was the next day, in Colonel Salisbury's tall, narrow house in a quiet Camden square. It was crammed with old furniture designed for much bigger spaces. The living room was carpeted with three overlapping Persian rugs, and two big sofas faced each other amidst a profusion of side tables on which stood art deco lamps with stained glass shades, vases, and family photographs in silver frames. Portraits in heavy gilt frames were hung cheek by jowl on the walls.

The Colonel did the thing with his eyes that made them look like they were twinkling, and said, "I knew I could rely on you, young man." He weighed the package in both hands, then turned it over and ripped the tab off the envelope and pulled out a slim octavo volume bound in faded red calfskin with stamped gilt lettering.

A silence fell as the Colonel stared at the cover, and at last Oz ventured, "It is the right book?"

"What? Oh yes, yes. Would you excuse me for just a moment...?"

After the Colonel had wandered out, not taking his eyes from the book, Oz sat in one of the sofas, sipping the driest sherry he had ever tasted, so pale it was almost colourless. He'd woken early, and had spent a lot of time on the Internet, where he had learned that the family of Von Thurn und Taxis had a stranglehold on postal services in Western Europe from the fifteenth to the nineteenth century. At the height of its power, it employed more than twenty thousand mail-boys, and its monopoly on mail extended from the Baltic to Gibraltar. But after the French Revolution, Napoleon allowed some of the German states to start up their own postal services, and by the nineteenth century nationalization of mail transport in most European countries shrank Thurn und Taxis's empire to a few German territories and cities—and even that rump had been lost after the family had supported the losing side in the war between Prussia and Austria.

Oz used half a dozen web search engines, plundered the Internet white pages, even phoned Company House; it seemed that no courier service by the name of Thurn und Taxis was registered in any European country. The family still existed—you could visit their palace in Frankfurt—but the courier service had expired at about the same time as the passenger pigeon.

A courier service which did not exist had delivered a book which should not exist.

Oz returned to the auction web site and after some poking around discovered that the same person (or at least, someone using the same email address) who had sold the printed copy of the Eccham Incunabula was a fairly active buyer and seller of antiquarian books. He made some phone calls, and at last discovered that Lawrence Ackroyd (he of the red leather suit) had sold the mystery man several items.

"All late eighteenth and early nineteenth century stuff. French, mostly, and mostly commonplace stuff in no more than fair condition. Hardly your sort of thing," Ackroyd added, clearly suspecting that Oz wanted to edge into his business.

Oz said, "I leave the gilt and leather trade to experts like you, Larry. But I have a friend who has something your client might be interested in."

"I'd be happy to take a look at it, but between you and me, I can't guarantee anything."

"You don't know your client?"

"I've never met the man. He keeps in contact by mail or by email, pays by banker's draft, and the books are collected by courier."

"Thurn und Taxis, by any chance?"

"I wouldn't know. I leave the books outside my door at night, and in the morning they're gone. If your client has something to offer, I'd be happy to help out."

Oz said that he would bear it in mind, called Gabriel Day, and learnt that Gabriel's tame hacker had found the telephone number associated with the email address of the mystery man.

"But it won't be much use," Gabriel said, "because it isn't real. See, the telcos keep back certain numbers. Fake numbers, the way every number in an American movie starts with the 555 area code. And this number, man, is from 555 land. I looked it up on this reverse directory I happen to have, and it doesn't exist."

"It's ex-directory."

"It's ex-everything, man."

Oz had examined every one of the time-darkened portraits in the Colonel's living room when the old man finally returned. He had the dazed look of a man who has opened his own front door one morning to discover a jungle or cratered moonscape instead of the accustomed street. He poured himself a sherry, drank it in one go, and said, "It's the same text, more or less."

Oz said, "'Things are seldom what they seem, Skimmed milk masquerades as cream.' Whoever sold you this has been buying old books, mostly incomplete or foxed volumes. But condition doesn't matter if all you want to do is take up pristine copies. You age them with tea, you bake them in an oven. I know this little maniac who can knock up a perfect copy of any modern edition overnight. He'll be able to tell if what you've bought really is nineteenth century."

"I don't want anyone else involved." The Colonel poured himself another sherry, and said, "Might there be more than one copy?"

"It's possible."

"I was afraid of that. And I'm afraid that I haven't been entirely frank with you, young man."

The Colonel crossed to the window and looked out in both directions, and then drew the heavy curtains and said, "Sir Toby Eccham was not just an alchemist; he was also a practitioner of black magic. The Eccham Incunabula contains descriptions of his ceremonies. Many of them involving dead bodies or parts of dead bodies. And molestation of children. Of babies."

Another silence, into which a clock under a glass dome threw three silvery chimes.

Oz said, "Every family has its black sheep."

"It doesn't matter to me, young man, but my nephew, you see…"

The Colonel mentioned a minor cabinet minister, well-known for his promotion of Christianity and family values. As far as the Colonel was concerned, it wasn't a political matter. He was an old-fashioned Tory and disliked New Labour because they had stolen the ideas of the Conservative Party (Oz, a socialist by upbringing and inclination, disliked them for exactly the same reason). It was a matter of family honour, the Colonel said; that was why he had to be sure that there were no more copies of the Incunabula.

"His daughter told me about the auction, and I promised her that I would do something about it. He doesn't know about this, and I hope he never does. But if a newspaper should get hold of this…"

Oz promised that he would do his best, and walked all the way home. It was raining lightly, and he turned up the collar of his raincoat and pulled down the brim of his hat, just like a proper detective. By the time he reached his flat, he knew exactly what he had to do. No more sneaking around. Time for some direct action. He hung up his raincoat and his jacket, rolled up his sleeves, and dialled the number Gabriel Day had given him.

It rang a long time. Oz sat in his chair, his feet cocked beside his computer, and listened to it ring. He was beginning to think that it would ring for ever when someone picked up.

A sound like the ocean roar in the seashell of his ear, and then a whisper, hoarse and curiously intimate.

"There's no one here."

The line went dead. Oz redialled.

It rang for five minutes, ten. At last a click and the sigh of distant waves. Oz said quickly, "I know about Thurn und Taxis."

No reply. Oz said into the roar of the sea, "I know what you're doing. I know why you're buying copies of old books." He said, "We need to talk."

The line clicked, and there was only the burr of the dial tone. Oz redialled again. The phone rang and rang, but no one picked up again.

♓

They came for Oz that night.

He was on the way home after sinking one too many pints of Strangeways at the Branch. They jumped out from behind a double-parked white van, two figures all in black, their heads swollen globes. Oz swung at one with his cane, but his arms were seized and something cold and wet, with a piercingly sharp chemical reek, was pressed over his mouth and nose.

The world receded. When it came back, everything was in motion. Oz was lying in a swaying, rushing metal box stroked by flashes of light. The back of a van, a van making speed. A figure loomed over him, braced against the van's sway. The swollen head was nothing more sinister than a black crash helmet, but behind the darkly tinted visor were two red sparks where the eyes might

be, and the fingers of the hand which lowered the wet cloth to
Oz's face were tipped with stout, curved claws.

The strong reek: the van's rush rushed away.

♓

Oz woke, his mouth dry, his head pounding, bathed in the cold
light of three wide-screen Sony TVs stacked on top of one another
like a piece of modern art, all tuned to a dead channel. Oz sat up in
stages and at last managed to get to his feet, fairly sure that he
wasn't going to throw up, dusted off his black jacket, straightened
his cravat. His cane lay at his feet, and he picked it up and tucked
it under his arm.

The huge room was lit only by TV-light. Bare concrete walls, a
poured concrete floor, no windows, metal double doors big
enough to admit a truck. There was a row of bookcases behind the
stack of TVs, and a ticking as of many clocks in the darkest corner,
beyond the caravan that sat on blocks in the middle of the dark,
lofty space, a streamlined aluminium cylinder like a spaceship
from a 50s B-movie. Luminescent TV snow sparkled on its side
like rushing stars. A thick cable ran up from its curved roof into
the darkness. Its windows were shuttered with black blinds and its
door was locked; no one answered when Oz rapped on it with his
cane.

The big doors were locked too.

There was a bog standard Panasonic video recorder on top of
the three TVs; on top of that was a silvery box from which half a
thick black glass disc protruded; and on top of *that* was something
like a reel-to-reel tape recorder that used inch-thick transparent
tape. All cabled into the back of the TVs, from which three black
cords rose up into the darkness overhead.

The bookcases were cheap fibreboard and white melamine
self-assembly jobs, but the books were anything but ordinary. Oz
squinted at volume after volume in the TV light. There were
leather-bound books in French and German and Italian. There

were books which should not have existed because they had never
been written. Charles Dickens's *Martin Sweezlebugg*. Raymond
Chandler's *The Poodle Springs Mystery*. J.R.R. Tolkien's *The Lost
Road*. H.G. Wells's *The Return of the Time Machine*. James
Joyce's *A Dublin Fairy Story*.

Oz thought that he'd been right all along, that the Colonel's
dissolute brother had let someone take a long look at the Eccham
Incunabula. He'd had debts, and there were scholars who'd pay
well for access to a suppressed book of the black arts. A copy had
been made, and it had fallen into the hands of these people. They
were forgers all right, but with a lot more style than most, for
they didn't just copy rare books; they also wrote new books…

Here was a book in what looked like Babylonian cuneiform,
but with pictures of what looked like airships. Here was a rack of
pornography: men and women; women and women; men and
men; men and animals; men and really *strange* animals…

The biggest book of all stood on a brass lectern, a folio volume
bound in heavy leather with iron corners. Oz heaved it open.

Fiery letters hung on pages of infinite depth, burning through
his eyes into his brain.

He slammed the heavy cover shut. The crash echoed around
the huge, stark room.

A moment later, lights came on all around the walls: the ordinary miracle of electric light, but horribly bright after the
flickering near-dark.

ℋ

The first thing Oz saw, through swelling tears and the fading
brands of backwards-slanting script, was that the clocks ticking at
the far end of the room were not clocks at all, but tickertape
machines. There were more than two dozen, standing under glass
domes like bird skeletons modelled in brass and Meccano, pecking
and clucking and scratching, busy with gears and pinwheels,

extruding henpecked ribbons of paper that made untidy nests as they spilled on to bare concrete. The smallest, elevated on a mahogany table, could easily have fitted into the palm of his hand; the largest was twice as tall as a man. There were other machines on a bench, things like teletypes, things with mirrors or crystal spheres, a tangerine iMac. Every machine was connected to a thick black cord, and all the cords ran up into the ceiling.

Oz's first thought was that Gabriel Day would definitely feel at home here.

His second was that these maniacs weren't forgers after all.

"You are a traveller," someone said.

"By your clothes we can see that you are not from this place," someone else added.

Oz turned. A man and a woman stood in front of the big doors. They were slight and slender, fine-boned and white-haired. They might have been brother and sister. They were holding hands, and dressed identically in black roll-neck sweaters and black jeans, like two beatnik elves.

The woman said (hers was the hoarse whisper Oz had heard on the telephone), "You said that you know about Thurn und Taxis. We do not know about you."

The man said, "If you were not so obviously a traveller, we would have disposed of you."

Oz laughed. He'd just come to a conclusion as crazy as anything in his sci-fi pulps.

The two looked at each other.

"I believe he looked in the Book of Urial," the man told the woman.

"If he looked too long, his mind will have been turned," the woman told the man.

Oz said, "People make all kinds of comments about my clothes, but I think this is the first time they've saved my life." He was trying to regain his equilibrium. It was like walking on to the stage: you had to leave your fear behind. He said, "I thought it was an elaborate hoax, but it's all real, isn't it? The books are real. Thurn und Taxis is real, too. I think it links all kinds of places together—including places which don't really exist."

"Of course they exist."

The two spoke together.

"I bought a book from you, on behalf of a client. It was a printed copy of a unique handwritten manuscript that was a closely guarded family secret. A secret in this world, in this line of history—but perhaps not a secret in other histories. My client is anxious to know whether you might be selling other copies."

The man said, "Is that why you contacted us?"

"That's how it started," Oz said.

"We sell unique items," the man said.

"You mean, no more than one of a kind?"

"We mean what we say," the woman said.

"Good. My client will be pleased to hear it."

The man and the woman looked at each other.

The woman said, "Travellers do not have clients."

The man said, "We begin to believe that you are not a traveller after all."

The huge metal doors swung back. The space beyond seemed as infinite as the sky. Figures were slowly advancing out of it, seeming to cover many miles with each step. It hurt Oz's eyes to look at them, and he forced himself to look away, to look at the man and the woman.

He said, "Perhaps I've read too much of my own stock, perhaps it's the stuff you dosed me with, or perhaps looking in that book really did drive me crazy, but I think that Thurn und Taxis didn't fade away where you come from." He was talking quickly. He felt that he was talking for his life. "Perhaps Napoleon didn't start to dismantle their empire; perhaps Napoleon never existed, or never became emperor of France. Thurn und Taxis kept growing, and grew bigger than the world. It buys quite ordinary items in one place, and sells them in another to collectors who want things which don't exist—at least, not where they live. I know how it works: I'm in the same trade. Christ, what are those things?"

The advancing figures seemed to be giants, but it hurt too much to look at them—like staring at a welder's torch—to make out any details.

The woman said, "In some places, people are not like you or me."

Oz said, "I want to help you. Do you think I'm the only one who'll be able to work out who you really are?"

"Most people do not ask questions," the man said calmly.

"You've been relying on the Internet to make deals with people who were happy to take your money and ask no questions," Oz said. "But the thing about the Internet is that it is transparent. Anyone can find out about you because anyone can see what you buy and what you sell. You've to set up a point of contact, and that allows anyone to find you. Anyone in the world. I'm the first. There'll be others."

The man and the woman looked at each other, looked at Oz.

Oz said, "Okay, perhaps I'm not the first to find you. But I'm the first who can help you. Do you know what a proxy is?"

The two looked at each other again. After a long moment, the great doors swung shut.

The woman said, "You told us that you are in the same trade?"

Ж

If anyone asks (hardly anyone does), Oz is in the import/export trade. He handles all the work himself, with computer and modem, telephone and fax. No customers ever come to his flat (a lot bigger than his old one, it has a fine view of Islington's toniest Georgian square). That isn't how he does business. No one visits his house except for the people who bring him things and take other things away, and he is careful never to see them.

His imports are exotic, peculiar, unique, one of a kind, but he earns exactly the same commission from exports as mundane as skimmed milk: a complete set of Jeffery Archer's first editions, the Athena print of the map of Middle-Earth, a Monopoly set, a 3-D postcard of Leonardo da Vinci's Last Supper, the London telephone directory for 1953...

I SPY

1 *spy for a living. That's why I know what you are. That's why I know what you do. That's why I humbly lay this confession at your feet.*

⋊

Childhood is supposed to be the happiest time of your life and once they have put it behind them for most people it is. They remember the good times. They remember Christmas and birthdays. They remember sunny days and freedom and laughter. But my childhood was a hell with no redemption. I grew up resenting the way my schoolmates were cosseted and aimed towards adulthood by caring parents. I had to find my own path. It was no easy one.

My father was a Polish ex-airman. He had fled the Nazis when the tanks rolled over the border in September 1939. He was not a coward. He wanted to get out so he could have his revenge on those who had destroyed his country.

He joined the RAF and flew more than fifty sorties against the Luftwaffe at the height of the Battle of Britain. After the war he

203

settled down and became an accountant. He was well-respected in the little Gloucestershire town where we lived. He was a prosperous small businessman. He was a war hero. But he was also a violent bully. He missed the certainties of war and hated the contingencies and random mess of civilian life. He became a martinet who exerted fanatical and rigid control over his family.

Everything in our little bungalow had its place and everything had to be kept spotlessly clean. Meals had to be provided punctually. His clothes had to be ironed and starched in a certain way and had to be laid out for him each morning in the correct manner. He spent most of his evenings at the British Legion club. He drank heavily and came home and beat his wife after he failed to fuck her. He stood in the doorway of the bedroom of his only son and cursed him and listed perceived transgressions and the punishments he would deliver. In this he was as methodical as in everything else. He devised a tariff of discipline which he carried out to the letter.

I hated my mother more than my father because she never complained or stood up to him. She explained away the bruises as falls. Our neighbours accepted this because she was so prone to narcolepsy and epileptic fits she was not allowed a driving license.

She was a mouse of a woman. Someone who should have protected me and could not even protect herself. She had no friends in the town. She was an only child and her mother was widowed. My father forbade her to have any contact with her meagre family. She was allowed out only to shop. My father would ring from the office at odd times to interrogate her.

I grew up fearful and quiet. I had been taught to speak only when spoken to. Any hint that I might be lying brought swift and terrible punishment. My father once broke a broom handle on my head because he thought I had stolen a ten pound note. He later found it on the bureau and beat my mother for misplacing it. The world was constantly thwarting him.

I had a concussion for three days. I did not mind. The world was pleasantly out of focus. Everything seemed an inch from my grasp. For the first time in my life my sleep was deep and dreamless.

My father was a burly man. Drink coarsened his face and added a swag to his belly but he remained hale and hearty until he died. He had excelled in all sports as a young man. Although he could easily have afforded a car he walked everywhere. He walked at the same fast pace whether it was raining or gloriously sunny.

I took after my mother. I was slightly built and short. My eyesight was poor. My father forced me to do Canadian Air Force Exercises each morning. He made me use Indian clubs to build up my muscles. They had little effect. He could circle my upper arms with his fingers. Once I tried to defend my mother because he was still beating her after she had been knocked unconscious. Blood was coming out of her ears. He threw me the length of the living room with a flick of his arm.

I learned how to evade the worst of my father's anger. I found many places to hide. Sometimes I spent the night away from home. The beatings I received upon my return were fearsome but they were a small price to pay for a respite from my father's drunken rages and the aching quiet of my mother's fear. I found that if I pretended not to care about the beatings my father would lose interest. In truth he was getting old. He had married late. He had been fifty when I was born. There had been another child ten years before that. My brother had died when only two months old. He had been my father's true heir. My father blamed my mother and often told me that I was a mistake. It was the only one of his cruelties that I believed long after his death.

I did not seek out friends. I was mostly left alone at school. I was too weird for the bullies to bother with and too scary for the other misfits. A few of the teachers recognized my intelligence and tried to draw me out but I refused to respond.

I turned in essays and other work on time but otherwise I drifted through school. There was nothing to hold my interest. I spent most of my time daydreaming. I drew elaborate patterns inside the covers of my exercise books. Classes dragged slowly towards release at 4.15 each afternoon. The school was a grammar school with public school pretensions. It displayed silver trophies in a glass cabinet next to the door to the headmaster's study. The names of the dead of two world wars were engraved on walnut shields hung in the assembly hall. The names of those who had gone on to university were painted on varnished pine boards that lined the main corridor. In its traditions and discipline I saw only a weak reflection of my father's regime. I despised it.

I spent most of my free time as a teenager reading science fiction and Marvel comic books. I read Alfred Bester's *Tyger! Tyger!* and Theodore Sturgeon's *More Than Human*. I read Robert Heinlein's *Stranger in a Strange Land* and John Wyndham's *The Midwich Cuckoos*. I loved Roger Zelazny's Amber series of novels. They were about an ordinary man who discovered that he was a powerful prince of a hidden realm realer than our own world.

I used this raw material to construct my own fantasies. I was an orphan of star sailors who had abandoned or lost me for complex reasons. I was an experimental subject unknowingly adopted by my parents and although I was outwardly an ordinary boy I would slowly realize my powers. I would be able to read minds or move objects by mental power. I would be able to see into the future and amass a vast fortune. I would be able to hypnotize girls and do whatever I wanted with them (the phrase *he bent her to his will* woke a particular thrill in me). I would found a new religion and be surrounded by loyal friends and beautiful compliant women. I would allow my mother and father to be employed in some lowly and humiliating position.

I read James Tiptree, Jr.'s story "Beam Us Home". My father did not own a television and I knew nothing about *Star Trek* but the story rang true at a deep level. For many weeks I dreamed that a great golden ship would one day sweep down out of the sky and hover over my town. Everyone would be tested and everyone but me would fail. I would rise in a beam of light to the wonder of all.

And then there were the comics. Their dramas were centred on weaklings or cripples who were imbued with secret identities and superpowers. Spider-Man—his alter ego a misunderstood teenage loner like me. Iron Man—a millionaire afflicted with a near fatal heart ailment. Thor—otherwise a cripple. The X-Men—mutant teenagers who hated the difference their super-powers bestowed upon them.

Unlike the X-Men I wanted to be different. I knew that I was better than those around me. I was better than the ordinary teenagers who had loving homes and went on dates and were good at sport. I could not believe that my suffering and my father's punishments were for nothing.

)(

Were you already living in the town? Did you select me? Were you moulding me through those fantasies? Were you beginning to turn me into your disciple?

I will prove myself worthy of you. I will show you that I am capable of deeds of true and absolute justice. I will show you how I triumphed over my father.

)(

I practised telepathy. I tried to control the flight of birds by willpower. I shuffled packs of cards and tried to guess their order. I collected coincidences and wondered if the whole world was a conspiracy. I imagined that it was peopled with actors in a drama centred on me.

I was sixteen. I cut an eccentric figure around town. I craved attention but was too introverted to seek it out. I thought that people would recognize and love my uniqueness. In this respect I was not unlike other teenagers.

In summer I wore an orange jacket and green trousers. In winter I topped this off with a quilted navy blue anorak. Like everyone in the '70s I wore my hair long. I did not often wash it. It was greasy and spangled with dandruff. I had thick-lensed National Health spectacles with thin blue metal rims. I cultivated a wealth of acne by long sessions of pinching and prodding at the bathroom mirror.

I was given no pocket money except for a few odd coins my mother managed to hoard from her meagre housekeeping. I spent her gleanings on second-hand Panther and Pan paperbacks at jumble sales. This left a little over for the bag of chips I shared with the pigeons in the little park by the church. After I had used up the public library I needed to steal to get my fix of pulp thrills. I stole Marvel comic books from the revolving wire rack in the newsagents. I stole Foursquare and Star paperbacks from Woolworths bargain bins. I wrapped my books and comics in plastic bags and hid them in various places in the bungalow's unkempt garden.

I did not know that comics and science fiction were popular culture. I knew nothing about popular culture. We did not own a television. My father kept the radiogram permanently tuned to Radio 4 and listened only to the evening news. I believed that the books and comics were schemes for an ideal world which would one day rise through the quotidian. I believed that they contained secret messages that only the illuminati could understand.

I began to patrol the town at night soon after I took up shoplifting. I was looking for secrets. I did my homework early and went out after my father left for the British Legion club. Sometimes I followed him. He revealed nothing. It was not until later that I discovered his secret.

But there were plenty of places of interest. I planned my excursions like military operations. I haunted the common. I made furtive raids on the perimeter of the American airbase. I walked the corridors of the hospital. I wandered about the yards of the factories that backed onto the railway line.

I picked up a pair of binoculars in one of the jumble sales. The magnification ratio was feeble and both lenses were badly scratched. It did not matter. I watched ordinary domestic routines through lighted windows. I knew where all my classmates lived and where their girlfriends lived. I watched them in bus shelters or chip shops or in the patch of waste ground where they drank Blackthorn cider and VP sherry. I knew where the older teenagers went in the woods above the town. I knew that the dairy regularly tipped unsold milk back into its tanks. I knew that stolen goods were distributed in the yard of the *Prince of Wales* pub by the bus station after hours. I knew where dope was sold and I knew who bought it.

I made notes on different coloured paper. I made elaborately coded dossiers. I believed that they held the key to all of the town's secrets. All I had to do was scry the patterns.

There were other rewards. Sometimes I glimpsed through half-drawn curtains a girl or a woman taking off her clothes. I saw Janice Turner take off everything but her bra and then she turned and with one hand reached behind her long white back and began to unfasten the strap and with the other switched out the light. She was one of the girls at the High School who were rumoured to "do it". She became the subject of my humid private fantasies for weeks afterwards.

Spying did not satisfy my need to know things. The sixth form had its own building in one corner of the school grounds. It was easy to bunk off school between lessons without being missed. I knew the routines of the householders and always carefully checked that they were out by telephoning them before going into action.

It was surprisingly easy to break into houses in those days. Very few people had burglar alarms or security locks. I avoided houses with dogs. People hid spare keys under flowerpots or doormats. They hung them on strings inside letterboxes. In summer they left windows open.

I took nothing. I wanted only to be in the spaces inhabited by ordinary lives. It was like being on stage in an empty theatre. I read letters and bills. I found diaries. I learned all their dirty little secrets. I printed my authority on the common-place domestic interiors through minor transgressions. I lay in the fragrant beds of teenage girls and masturbated with their underwear around my penis. I pissed in baths but washed it away afterwards. I walked naked around other people's houses.

Although I took nothing from the houses I broke into I some-times found rabbits and other small pets in sheds or out-houses. Once I found half a dozen new born kittens blindly moving over each other in a cardboard box lined with newspaper. I killed these helpless creatures in various slow and interesting ways using the dissection kit I had been issued for biology classes. I smeared their blood on my face. Sometimes I drank a little of it. The thick salty taste made me ill. I was not yet worthy. I left the remains of these small sacrifices in various places at the edge of town. I impaled them on bamboo canes or on branches of certain trees. I was marking the place as my own.

I returned to the sacrifices again and again. Sometimes I discovered that the corpses had been further mutilated. At the time I thought that foxes or crows had found them. Now I know that you were leaving signs of your presence.

ℋ

Are you lost or did you come here deliberately? Are you experi-menting with the town? Or did you come here because of me? Did I draw you here? Perhaps we are the first of a new kind of being.

You have much to learn about me. You should know that after dark the town is mine. I see everything.

ℋ

I was too unworthy to recognize any messages you left me then. I had not yet ascended to a higher level. I will tell you how I began that long climb. I will tell you how I killed a man.

I was still obsessed with Janice Turner. I broke into her house
several times and found her diary. I learnt the names of the men
she was having sex with. One was an American sergeant from the
airbase. She met him every Sunday evening. Her parents believed
that she was practicing the clarinet at a friend's house or that she
had gone to the cinema. In fact she was fucking her boyfriend.

He was a burly man with a thick mustache and a severe crew
cut. He drove a red Mustang. It had left-hand drive. The
American Air Force allowed their men to ship their cars over. His
name was Kowalski.

He had a flat in a big house at the edge of town. The relatives
of the old woman who died in it had sold its large garden to devel-
opers. Unfinished yellow brick houses stood where the orchard
and lawns had once been. These houses overlooked Kowalski's
flat and it was easy to keep watch from the outside.

One day I decided to break in.

All that week I had practised being invisible. It was a matter of
sidling along and not meeting other people's eyes. It was a matter
of concentration. I was sure that I could do it long enough to see
what Janice Turner and her boyfriend were doing. I wanted to see
Janice having sex. I wanted to see him fucking her.

I dressed in black. I rubbed coal dust on my face. The lock on
the front door was a cheap imitation of a Yale. I knew how to
open it using a slip of plastic. My heart was beating fast as I eased
inside. My chest felt very full. I was taking many small breaths.

It was very hot inside. It stank of cheap perfume and booze. I
could hear a TV roaring at full volume. There was a kitchen to the
right. The cooker was black with grease. The sink was full of pots
and pans and dirty plates soaking in grey water. The main room
was to the left. In a later era estate agents would call it a studio flat
but it was really a glorified bed-sit.

Candles burned everywhere. They were stuck to flat surfaces with their own melted wax. A gun lay in front of a half circle
of red candles on a side table. I picked it up. It was very heavy.
Its cross-hatched metal grip was oily and cold. It was real.

TV light flickered over the pull-down sofa where Janice Turner lay.

She was naked. Her white skin shone with sweat. Her thighs were slick. Her big sloppy breasts rolled on her ribcage as she looked up at me. Her eyes were glassy and black. She looked at me and my heart beat even faster. Then I knew that she was looking past me. She was looking at the half-open bathroom door.

Kowalski was in the bathroom. He was naked too. His back was to me. Black hair swirled over it. He bent over the bath. One end of a taut strip of cloth was in his mouth and the other wrapped around his arm. He had a glass hypodermic and was searching for a vein. There was old blood spray on the white tiles.

I must have made a noise because he turned. I stepped backwards. Despite the noise of the TV I heard the hypodermic clatter in the bath. He said something and reached for me and the top of the bathroom doorframe exploded in dust and splinters. The gun had gone off. I had not heard it but I felt the shock of it in the muscles of my arm. Kowalski was screaming. His hands were over his face. Blood squirted between his fingers. I shot him twice and he went down.

Janice Turner giggled. I dropped the gun and ran.

♓

I know now that you recognize me. I know that you have read this poor confession.

I first saw you running from one side of the high street to the other. You had taken on the appearance of a naked man. You vaulted a parked car and disappeared down the side of the library. You moved so quickly that by the time I zoomed in you were gone.

I saw you again four weeks later. This time I remembered to use the video. But when I played it back it showed only the street and its pools of light and shadow. You did not register. You have the true power of invisibility.

But I saw you.

I remember your face. It flashed ghostly white as you passed beneath a streetlight. I saw the round dark moonpools of your eyes. I saw the slather dripping from your pointed teeth.

You came again last night. I found your sacrifice. I hid it for you. It took all night but it is done. No one will find it.

You know me now.

You know what I am.

I wait for you to come to me. The others are like sheep. They are blind to our true nature. I am the only free man here. I am too tired and too excited to write more. Be patient. Tomorrow I will write about how I broke free from my father.

҉

There was a huge scandal after Kowalski's death. It was revealed that he had been supplying heroin to many of the personnel of the American Air Force base. He had injected heroin into Janice Turner's arm that night. She was convicted for manslaughter but the sentence was suspended.

At first I was scared and then I was elated. I fed on my fear and turned it to strength. After three days I knew that Janice Turner had not really seen me. I had been the invisible man. I had rescued her from Kowalski. I had delivered justice. I lost myself in fantasies in which Janice remembered what I had done and came to me in gratitude.

I grew bolder. I sneaked out of the bungalow at night and roamed the town. I broke into houses and stood by the beds of sleeping people. Sometimes they woke and stared at me in sleepy confusion, but they always went back to sleep. Sometimes I masturbated over them. I violated their dreams.

I was twice stopped by the police. I told them that I had been seeing my girlfriend. They drove me home in their patrol car and watched as I went in through the front door. I stole from the piles of change that people left on bedside tables and chests of drawers. I had stolen money in my pockets when the police stopped me. I bought a knife from the Army surplus store in Bristol. Its blade was as wide as my hand. One edge was serrated and one edge was razor sharp. There was a notch for cutting twine. I found a medical shop. I bought straight scalpel blades and heavy curved scalpel blades. I bought a surgical saw and heavy forceps. I said that I was a medical student. The shop assistant did not question me.

I left many sacrifices in the woods where now surveyor's tapes stretch between iron poles and yellow crosses of spray paint mark the trunks of trees which will be cut down to make room for new houses.

I left school that summer. I scraped passes in three A-levels without much effort. It did not matter. I did not want to go to university. In any case my father would not pay for it. He found me a job in the paper mill where he audited the accounts. I worked as a labourer on shifts. I volunteered for the night shift. I came home at dawn and slept for a few hours and then roamed about town. I read the novels of Philip K. Dick. I read Frank Herbert's *Dune* series. I came to believe that most people were zombies or androids. They were no more than machines. Only those who could pass specific tests were human. I had a sudden insight that felt so right everything in my life locked around it. I was the only real person in town because I had passed just such a test. I had murdered a man for true and absolute justice. I began to look for other tests.

I did not know about you then.

I did not know that you were my secret sharer.

I took to following my father. I found out his secret.

It was very simple and very banal. He was fucking his secretary in the lunch hour.

She was a spinster. She was only a few years younger than he was. She was heavily built and had a large mole by the side of her nose.

I watched them several times. They did it on the desk. They pulled down the blinds but in their haste they often left them askew. My father's offices were on the first floor over a butcher's shop. I watched from the flat asphalt roof over the refrigerated store in the rear extension. I was Spider-Man. I tingled with a premonition of absolute justice.

I knew I had to expose this crime. I made several sacrifices in preparation. My father brought in a pest control firm. He thought that there were rats in the building and that some had died under the floorboards. I sanctified the space and made it my own and then I confronted him.

He always locked the office door at lunchtime. One Saturday I stole his key and had a spare made. When I came into his office two days later he tried to rear up from under the weight of his secretary. Then she saw me and screamed and fell to the floor. Her nylon petticoat was bunched up around her flabby white thighs. Her grey hair hung around her face. My father's face was white and red. His penis deflated in little throbbing jerks. I stared at him and went out.

My father said nothing that night. He did not need to. We both knew I had taken away his source of power. He no longer went to the British Legion club. He drank at home. He drank a bottle of Teacher's whisky every night. He raged at my mother but no longer hit her. They were sleeping in different rooms. I realized that my father was an old man.

I came and went as I pleased. I left dead animals on the desk in my father's office. I dissected them to the bones and spread them on his blotter.

I saw my father's defeat as vindication of my power. I knew that I could use my power to do good. I would become an avenger.

Stolen goods were dealt openly in the *Prince of Wales* pub. I kept watch and learnt that one of the local police detectives was involved. He turned a blind eye and was rewarded with cash. Sometimes he brought in radio cassettes taken from crashed vehicles or jewellery taken from burglarized houses. He brought pornography confiscated from the sex shop in Gloucester.

I determined to expose him. It was my undoing. I overestimated my powers.

I broke into the shed at the back of the pub. Stolen goods were stored amongst crates of empty bottles and carbon dioxide cylinders. I taped pornographic pictures to the windows of the detective's car. I left a stack of VCRs on the step of his house.

Superheroes left villains tied up for the police to deal with. I thought that justice would flow naturally after the crime was exposed.

The police came for me.

I was framed. Stolen goods were planted in my locker at the paper mill. All the recent local burglaries were pinned on me. There was a false confession. The fact that I had been stopped twice in suspicious circumstances added weight to the charges. My father cooperated. I believe that he used his business connections to get rid of me.

I was over eighteen and considered an adult. I was given a five year prison sentence. Crimes against property were taken very seriously in the county. I was taken to Birmingham prison. My parents did not visit me.

Prison terrified me. Prison gave me discipline. Prison taught me that justice is arbitrary and administered by fallible men.

I had to watch myself every minute of every hour. I had to watch what went on around me. It was lucky that I already knew how to become invisible.

Most of the men inside were recidivists who wanted to do their time quietly. I learned to keep away from the few blowhards and troublemakers. The others left me alone. I was not worth bothering with.

I cultivated my isolation. I knew that I was a political prisoner amongst criminals. I read my way through the library. I listened to men talk. I learned how to hot-wire cars. I learned which alarms could be deactivated. I learned how to pick locks.

I still had a misplaced sense of justice. I learnt that one man controlled the flow of drugs through the jail. I snitched him to the warders. Two days later I was ambushed in the showers by two men and severely beaten. In a last flash of lucidity I recognized my assailants and then they were both wearing my father's face. I screamed and writhed under his blows.

The men who beat me were warders. No doubt they were the men who brought the drugs into the prison. This time I kept quiet. My nose and jaw and cheekbones were broken. I almost lost the sight of one eye. I had to have surgery to reconstruct my face. I recovered in hospital and was transferred to Wormwood Scrubs.

I did the rest of my time quietly. I was promoted to the kitchens and ate as much prison food as possible. It was much better than my mother's cooking. I exercised. My frame filled out.

I served three years of my sentence. I was taken into the chaplain's office a few weeks before I was released. He told me that my father was dead. He asked if I wanted to apply for compassionate leave to attend the funeral. I shook my head. I looked down at the institutional carpet to hide my dry eyes.

I had learned of several security firms which employed ex-cons. I got a job with one of them. It was run by a retired police inspector. The word was that he had retired because he had been caught taking bribes from sex shops in Soho. The pay was low. You had to buy your own uniform.

I loved it.

I was rotated through several low grade assignments. I stood night watch in an empty office block. I patrolled the grounds of a hospital. I patrolled an engineering factory. I took pornography from the workmen's lockers and burnt it.

I got a job in another security firm. I was working under a false name. The firm prospered. It won a contract to staff one of the new privatized prisons. I guarded prisoners between prison and court.

Five years passed and then I saw the advertisement which brought me home to you.

I knew at once it was mine. I applied. My references were good but I knew that they were irrelevant. My old sense of certainty surged back. I knew I was one of the masters of the world.

And so I returned home. I returned to you.

)(

The town has changed. There is a housing estate where beech woods once stood. There is a triple set of mini-roundabouts on the site of the old brewery. A bypass skirts to the west. Warehouses and supermarkets are strung along it. It could be anywhere. There is much unemployment and crime is high. The police do not dare patrol parts of the council estate at night.

There was a small riot in the town centre. Youths refused to move on after the pubs had closed. They sat around the market cross. They were drinking and shouting and playing ghetto-blasters. The police were outnumbered. Someone threw a petrol bomb. A police car was overturned and set alight.

The council responded by putting in a system of closed circuit television cameras. I am one of four security officers who keep permanent watch on the bank of TV screens in the little office in the council building.

I spy for a living. No one knows who I am. My face has been changed by the beating and by time. I keep my hair in a Number Two crop. I wear contact lenses. I am no longer skinny. I have followed my mother down the street several times. She did not recognize me. I keep watch on her.

I have visited my father's grave. He can no longer harm me. He is in my power now.

I keep watch on those of my former schoolmates who have not left town. The police detective still works here. I watch him. I watch everyone.

I spend my nights watching TV screens that glow with intensified black and white images of the streets of the town centre. I can pan and zoom on anything. A video recorder makes a time-stamped recording of any behaviour I feel is criminal or suspicious. I have an open line to the police station.

That's how I saw you. That's why I know what you are. That's why I know what you can do.

I last saw you four weeks ago. I was just coming on shift. I always arrive a few minutes early. Roland Miller was on duty. He is a scruffy and overweight young man. He had the radio tuned to a pop music station and was flicking through a tabloid newspaper.

I saw you on Camera Sixteen. I saw you run out of the scruffy bushes that line the patch of ground by the war memorial. You ran very fast and by the time I had slapped Roland's hand from the joystick and taken command you were already off screen. I switched through Cameras Fifteen and Twelve and saw you again. Roland was complaining loudly. I shut him out. I saw you run beneath the halo of a streetlight and the camera overloaded. I backed the sensitivity down but you were gone.

Roland did not see you. I ran back the videotape but there was nothing there.

Roland laughed at me but I knew then that I was the chosen one. Because I had practised invisibility I alone had the power to see you.

For the first time I deserted my post and went to see your handiwork. The pitiless white moon shone down on her. I marked myself with her blood and went back to work. I watched a police patrol car pass by without knowing she lay a few feet from the road.

I returned at the end of my shift. I took your sacrifice to the churchyard and buried it in my father's grave. No one will find it. My mother never visits the grave and it is in an overgrown corner of the churchyard.

I know that I have found someone worthy of my worship.

The woods are almost gone but I have left sacrifices in a belt of scruffy sycamores beside the ring road. I broke into my mother's bungalow and took back what was mine. I dug up the caches of my precious comics and books. They were swollen by

water and mould but burned easily once they had been soaked
with petrol.

I have sacrificed my childhood to you.

Now it is full moon again. I have left signs. Only you will
know their import.

My mother's head lies at the site of your sacrifice. In the last
moment of her life she knew who I was. I have had revenge for her
failure to protect me from my father.

I buried her body with your sacrifice.

My father's decomposed body lies amongst the faded poppy
wreaths on the steps of the war memorial. He is dressed in my
security officer's uniform. I dug him up a few days after I took up
my post here and I kept him in my flat. Now I know that everything was meant to be.

I have been purified.

I have cast off my past.

I wait for you. I switch from camera to camera. Moonlight
gleams on the windows of the shops along the high street. The
supermarket at the edge of town burns with a fever light. The trees
in front of the churchyard are restless. A group of teenagers are
drinking by the side of the town hall. I should report them to the
police. Instead I think that they will be the first sacrifice we make
together.

I know that I am worthy. I know that you will come to me. I
know that we will achieve a glorious synthesis.

Together we will change the world.

THE RIFT

1 *Ron Vignone*

He was standing at the very edge of the Rift, barechested in only shorts and hiking boots, kicking loose rocks down the steep slope. They clattered away, gaining speed as they rolled, beginning to bounce, bounding along until hitting a snag or outcrop and sailing out into the air, dwindling until they smashed into ledges or dry slopes of scrub far below, and Ron turned and looked into Ty Brown's video camera and yelled, "Virgin no more!" and danced along the edge and kicked down more rocks, feeling terrifically keyed up, the way he always did before a climb, like the anticipation of sex. He was slim and wiry, sweat glittering in the black hair which matted his chest, in the beard he'd started growing in the week it had taken them to get here, by light plane, by boat up a wide tributary of the Amazon, finally by helicopter from a loggers' camp.

The Rift stretched away for miles in either direction, the bluffs of its western edge overhung by forest, slopes and terraces and cliffs dropping away towards the perpetual mists which hid its bottom. There were plenty of loose rocks along the rimslope, dangerous to anyone climbing below them, and it took most of the day to get it clear and safe so they could think of beginning the first pitch. Ron and a couple of the other climbers wanted to do it right then, even though the light was going, but the Old Man, Ralph Read, said no, they had plenty of time to do this right. He made a little speech about the Rift, saying that it was one of the last wildernesses, speaking to Ty Brown's camera with the sun going down in glory over the Serra Parima mountains.

Ron, eager to get going, ready to penetrate this baby all the way to the bottom, told Matt Johnson in disgust, "The Old Man's just realized he's too old for this, I reckon. He fucked up on the first expedition, and he's lost his nerve. We'll be carrying him down."

Matt, who spared a word only when he really had to, so that most days you thought he'd been struck dumb, just shrugged.

They camped out on bare rimrock, with the two helicopters tied down against the wind which picked up after sunset, tents and piles of supplies and rope bags scattered on the stony ground and Coleman lanterns hissing out white glare here and there. It was the last time they would all be together.

In the middle of the night, Ron woke with a full bladder and moonlight shining through the fabric of the tent he shared with Matt Johnson. He went out and crabbed up a knob of rock that overhung the edge of the Rift. Far out and far below, the mist glowed faintly in the moonlight, looking like radioactive milk. Ron pissed into the void, and saw as he picked his way back to his tent that the science geek woman, the botanist, was watching him from the open flap of her tent. He grinned to himself. Maybe she'd loosen up before the trip was over.

The next day didn't start well: more rock kicking after the first easy pitch had been made, hard sweaty work crabbing along the sixty degree slope with the sun burning down and a hot wind blowing up from the Rift, while Barry Lowe and the Danes worked out the route. The Old Man had determined that the Danes would set the pace; the others would set up a relay for bringing down the supplies. And that was the way it went for the next three days as they descended into the Rift—the Danes forging ahead while Ron and the others worked like slaves moving supplies down to each new base camp, following pitches the Danes had made. The Old Man stayed up at the rim, keeping in radio contact with his number two, Barry Lowe; Ty Brown spent most of his time with the Danes, because that was where the action was, coming back up to the supply team's base camp each night breathless and elated.

The Danes were moving fast, Ron had to give them that, but they were using up rope, pitons and rock bolts at a terrific rate and outstripping all efforts to keep up with them. Even the two science geeks started to complain. On the third night, Amy Burton got on the radio and, with Ty Brown filming her, told the Old Man that she couldn't do any work because she was too busy humping supplies.

They were camped on a wide dry ledge more than a mile into the Rift, having spent most of the day following traverses that zig-zagged down a huge bluff, and then sliding down steep smooth chutes where temporary rivers of floodwater poured into the Rift during the rainy season. The bluff loomed above, blocking out half the sky; below, a forested forty degree slope stretched away to its own edge.

"You told him right," Ron said to Amy Burton afterwards, as they all sat around the camp fire. "Everyone should get their turn."

Burton pushed a lock of lank blond hair from her eyes. She was a stout, sunburnt woman in khaki shorts and a T-shirt and hiking boots. Like everyone else she smelt strongly of sweat and woodsmoke. She said wearily, "He got money from the UN because he claimed this was a potential world heritage park, but while I'm working as a sherpa all I can do is sight surveys."

"Maybe I can help," Ron said, thinking of an assignation off in the bush. A couple of the guys were staring at him, and he gave them the finger surreptitiously, then saw, shit, that Ty Brown was filming, and Barry Lowe was watching him too.

"We're all caught up in this mad scramble," Amy Burton said. "Like the most important thing is to get to the bottom."

"Well," Ron said, turning his head to give the camera his best profile, "that's the point, isn't it? This is about the last place we can go without finding someone else's camp litter. Don't you think that's important?"

He was trying to be reasonable, but she stared at him with disgust. She said, "Maybe there should be places where no one ever goes."

Ron said, needled, "Then what's the point of them?"

"Because," she said, "what happens when everything's used up?"

Barry Lowe chipped in then, with bullshit about how much the scientific work was appreciated and how time would certainly be found for it once routes had been opened up, speaking for the record, and Alex Wilson, the TV guy who was looking for some kind of extinct sloth, said he certainly hoped so or else the expedition was a pointless show of macho bravado. It became a fierce argument, with Ty Brown's camera capturing everything. Ron, sidelined and silent, felt anger tighten in his chest, kinking like a twisted rope until he could hardly breathe, and he got up and walked away to the far end of the ledge. This wasn't what he had signed up for, carrying supplies and nursemaiding a couple of science geeks, and as they all hiked along a narrow trail through the steep little forest the next day he tried to tell Lowe that, tried to explain that he wanted some of what the Danes were getting, the pure stuff of establishing new routes. Lowe told him that his turn would come, but Ron knew now that the Rift was fucked forever in his head, and that some kind of payback was due.

2 *Ty Brown*

He was exhausted every moment of the day, but exhilarated too, because he knew that he was getting something good here, a real drama unfolding in front of his lens. The expedition was slowly pulling itself apart. The Danes were moving too fast and the rest could barely keep up with them, and now Barry Lowe was worried that the rope would run out; none of the routes were as straightforward as the limited aerial surveys had suggested, making it necessary to establish many traverse pitches. Lowe had pleaded with Read over the radio to have more rope flown in, but Read wanted to press on because the rainy season was drawing near and he knew from the bitter experience of his first failed expedition that the Rift would be unclimbable then. And because the secret of the Rift was out, someone else, probably the Brazilian Army, would want to have a go next year. Meanwhile, the other climbers resented the fact that the Danes were the advance party and they did nothing but resupply, the two scientists resented the fact that they had had to virtually give up their work and pitch in to help, and the Old Man, Ralph Read, the grizzled charismatic climber who'd conquered every famous peak in the world, was reduced to an impotent god lost somewhere above, trying to run things through a bad radio link.

Communication was getting worse as they descended, the granite walls bouncing signals or simply swallowing them; no one knew what was below the perpetual mists because radar was bounced around the same way. The best guess was that the Rift was more than four miles deep. It had been completely unknown until Read had discovered it five years ago, although there were rumours of an expedition to this area a hundred years before, and the Indians who had lived in the forests below the massif before logging had displaced them claimed that all kinds of monsters lived there.

Ty had always thought that there wasn't much chance of getting an undiscovered beast on tape, although that was how he had got the commission; he was supposed to be filming Alex Wilson's search for giant sloths, and had hours of material of the cryptozoologist talking to Indians, examining tufts of greenish hair they produced, squatting with them to examine animal tracks, or staring meaningfully into the darkness beneath the giant forest trees. But now things were definitely taking on a human angle, which was what audiences loved. Finding some animal previously thought extinct was a two day thrill, but human conflict was a keeper.

Ty had cut his teeth as a second unit cameraman on nature documentaries. He'd spent more than a decade camping out in remote areas, spending days waiting to get just the right thirty second shot of a bower bird's mating display or a baboon caught by a leopard (that one, filmed on the fly and shaky as hell, had won an award). He'd started up his own company, accumulating library shots and filler work for films that went out on National Geographic or PBS to increasingly small audiences, but he knew it wouldn't last. Most people lived in cities; the only animals they saw in real life were roaches and pigeons (someone had won an award a couple of years ago with a documentary on urban pigeons; there was a joke in the trade that soon vermin would be the only species left to film). Nature documentaries were wall-paper, something to pass the time before the ball game started. And it was getting harder to find an animal species which hadn't already been filmed and that was sexy enough to get some atten-tion. There had been *three* documentaries last year about the last remaining Galapagos tortoise, for Christ's sake.

But now he'd lucked out: his first real independent feature, which had started out as a pretty straightforward quest-for-a-living-fossil twenty-three minute filler, was turning into something different. Just as well, because so far there had been no trace of any animals at all in the Rift, and it was just too big, too inhuman in scale, to film properly. You could descend all day, and when you looked back all you'd see was the last fifty metres of overhang you'd abseiled down, hiding the bluff you'd spent most of the day traversing and the forest above that you'd spent the previous day hiking through. Right now, for instance, he was following Barry Lowe and one of the climbers, a vain little Brooklyn Italian, through a stunted forest which wasn't much different from the understorey growth at the edge of what remained of the true forest, and you couldn't see that this was clinging to the side of a huge cliff because the skinny little trees were packed too closely together. He'd have to get some aerial shots afterwards, but it wasn't the Rift that mattered anyway.

They were carrying a load of rope and following some kind of animal trail which had been enlarged by the Danes (who weren't Danish) and marked here and there with red paint sprayed on a boulder or a tree bole; the rest of the party had returned to the previous base camp, to retrieve more supplies. It was mid-morning, the sun beginning to break through the canopy. They'd been descending for more than two hours when at last they came out of the edge of the forest. They abseiled a smooth dry chute to another ledge, then abseiled again, this time down a vertical cliff to more stunted forest, taking a lot of time to get all the rope bags down. And then they hiked for an hour through more forest to where the Danes had made camp yesterday afternoon, by a boulder field and a series of pools; Ty had taken some good footage of Kerry Dane unselfconsciously swimming in her under-wear in the biggest pool.

But the Danes weren't there, although they had told Ty they'd wait.

The climber, Ron Vignone, dumped the three big blue nylon bags of rope in disgust and flopped back on them and stared up at the sky; Lowe switched on his radio and tried to contact the Danes. He got through after a couple of minutes of switching channels, but had scarcely established contact when the radio squealed and went dead. He couldn't raise Read or the supply team either, although he tried every one of the channels, and at last said they'd rest up and unpacked his Coleman stove and brewed some tea. He was big and blond, a strong, capable climber, affable in a baffled, English way and not too bright, very much Read's right-hand man. He was drenched in sweat, and his face was badly sunburned despite the fluorescent orange sunblock he had smeared over his nose and cheeks. He thought it might be best to wait until the rest of the party brought down the supplies, and then press on and catch up with the Danes the next day, but Ron Vignone said they would have gotten even farther ahead by then.

"Well," Lowe said, "they'll have to stop sometime. They'll run out of rope."

"Yeah," Vignone said angrily, "and then they'll start free-climbing and where'll we be? They'll run off with this fucking expedition if someone doesn't do something. I'll tell Read that if you haven't got the balls."

"The Old Man knows about it," Lowe said. He was trying to calm Vignone down, but his bland affability only riled the climber more.

The two men tossed it back and forth for a few more minutes, with Ty filming. Lowe tried the radio again, but succeeded only in running down his batteries. So they decided to go on while it was still light, and picked up the baggage and went on down through the boulder field, following the red splotches the Danes had help-fully sprayed here and there.

Half an hour into this, they saw the bird.

They were following a boulder-filled trail, almost certainly a stream in the rainy season, between two stands of forest towards a drop-off half a mile ahead. The bird flew straight across their path, so low that Vignone, who had the lead, threw himself flat. Ty managed to swing his camera on it: vaguely pigeon-shaped but bigger than a pigeon, dusty black plumage and a naked red head. It flew clumsily, crashing into the nearest trees and scrambling away through tangled branches. Ty thought he saw claws at the angles of its wings; then it was gone. A black feather floated down and he picked it from the air.

Vignone jumped up. "Did you see that fucking vulture go for me?"

"It was only a crow," Lowe said.

"They don't have crows in the Amazon basin," Ty said.

"A fucking vulture," Vignone said, and dusted himself down and went on, jumping from boulder to boulder with a careless agility.

It hadn't been a vulture either.

A couple of hours later, they caught up with the Danes. There was a short drop at the end of the boulder-filled trail, and then a series of pools stepping down between huge water-carved rocks, strange tree-ferns growing in pockets of soil on top of the rocks and shading the pools so that it was like descending through a green water chute. Most of the pools could be waded; the water was warm, and it was very humid. The only really deep pool could be crossed by clinging to a blue nylon rope bolted to the curved flank of a huge boulder while using a second rope as a kind of tightrope, and then swinging around the corner onto a knife-edge of slippery black rock that lipped the pool (Ty, made clumsy because he had to hold his camera away from the rock, scraped his arm badly). Then there was an easy descent over cobbled boulders to a forest of fern-trees, the air hot and humid under a low roof of stiff green fronds, the scaly trunks of the fern-trees covered in creepers and bromeliads, blackflies and sweat bees a torment. They came out of this, and there were the Danes camped at the edge of a wide apron of rock.

The Danes weren't Danish; they were an Australian family who spent their lives adventuring. They'd sailed a yacht around the world, trekked through the Himalayas, spent two years trying to save one of the last coral reefs off Belize. Ken (who had a bit of Aborigine blood and never let you forget it) and his wife Kerry were both in their early forties, super-fit and very competent; their son, Sky, was seventeen, the youngest member of the expedition, and one of the best climbers. He and his parents worked together in a close-knit team.

Vignone started in on them almost straight away, of course. He'd been working himself up to it on the descent. He told them that they were taking the best of the climb and turning everyone else into their bearers, that they were being selfish and wrecking the spirit of the expedition.

"Now hold on, mate," Ken said. "Don't you think that's a bit harsh?"

"We're doing what we were asked to do," Kerry said. She put a hand on her husband's shoulder. She was taller than him. Her blond hair was tied back from her tanned, lined face.

"I'd say we're doing a fair job," Ken said to Lowe, who shrugged uncomfortably, his face turning redder under its sunburn, and mumbled that there was a bit of feeling amongst the others, and maybe it would be a good idea to make a camp here and wait.

"And not rip on?" Ken said. "That's crazy. You can see what comes next. This beauty could be twenty miles deep for all we know."

They were at the top of a cliff that dropped into a narrow band of forest growing along the edge of another cliff. And so on, a series of cliffs and forested set-backs that stepped away towards the permanent mist cover, the banded bluffs on the far side of the Rift only half a mile away. Ty had taken a panoramic shot of it in the last light; now he had switched on the camera's floodlight and was filming the argument, swinging from face to face and hoping the microphone caught it all.

Vignone wanted the Danes to go back and join the resupply team while some of his climbing friends took their places; the Danes didn't see what was wrong with pressing on; both parties wanted Lowe to make a decision, and Lowe didn't want to. He tried using the Danes' radio to contact Read, but without any success, then said it would be best to wait, they'd done fantastically well and it was time to rest up and plan the next part of the descent.

"We've hardly begun to crack it," Ken Dane said.

"If you hadn't set up so many traverses," Vignone said, "we'd be much farther down and we wouldn't be so short of rope."

Which started another argument as the air darkened around them, until at last Vignone said that he was making the next pitch right now and would camp out alone, glaring at Lowe when the Englishman said mildly that it wasn't a very good idea.

"I want some fucking climbing," Vignone said. He was already sorting through one of the rope bags, paying out blue nylon cord in neat loops.

Sky said that he'd go with Vignone, but Vignone said he would solo it; the rock was dry and craggy. So after the wiry little man had put on his harness and climbing shoes and fixed the rope to the edge of the cliff, Ty filmed the first stage of his descent in the dusk, with Sky watching beside him. Sky was taller than his parents, his blond hair shaved close to his skull. When Vignone disappeared into a chimney and Ty turned off the camera, Sky said thoughtfully, "There are all sorts of weird things out here. I hope that guy doesn't run into any of them."

"I saw a bird today," Ty said. "A very strange bird."

Ken Dane said that there might be anything down here, there were hundreds of kilometres of forest after all, and his wife said, "This kind of place would make a fine reserve, don't you think? That's partly why we're here. You people make so much noise you've scared off all the wild life—even we can hear you, sometimes. But we've seen a few things, moving away from us. There are some big animals down here. Ron has let his pride overrule his caution."

Ty knew that a jaguar could crush your skull in its jaws while you slept, or an anaconda could ease you into its gullet without waking you. Wild pigs could knock you down and strip your bones in a couple of minutes. There were dozens of species of poisonous spiders, and snakes, and scorpions. The campfire seemed very small in the huge darkness of the Rift.

Sky said, "I should go down there maybe."

"It's too dark now," Ken said. "We'll check him out first thing."

Ty told the Danes about the bird, and showed them the black feather he'd caught. It was greasy, and had a pungent, musky odour.

"Dr Wilson will be pleased," Kerry Dane said.

They all woke a little after dawn. Ken and Sky Dane abseiled down the cliff to check on Ron Vignone; Ty Brown and Kerry Dane and Barry Lowe were eating breakfast when father and son came back, and dumped Ron Vignone's torn sleeping bag in front of them.

3   Dr Alex Wilson

There was so much fuss about the missing climber that Ty Brown forgot to tell Alex about the bird until the evening after the search.

Alex wasn't too worried about Vignone. It was well known that he had been pretty pissed at the way the Danes had charged ahead of everyone else; Alex thought that he'd probably gone off to get some glory of his own. Foolish and selfish, yes, but that was all it was. He'd left his sleeping bag behind and it had been torn up by animals. There was no blood, no trail; any animal dragging away a human body would have left both. No one would listen to Alex's opinions though, and Lowe insisted on wasting the day searching the long narrow forest.

Ever since they had begun the descent into the Rift, Alex had been possessed by a kind of smouldering fury mixed with anxiety—the whole expedition had been turned into a circus, a race for the bottom at all costs, and he was helpless to stop it. The search for the missing climber was finally a chance to look around, but Alex was paired up with a taciturn climber who took the search seriously, and the noise the others made probably scared off every animal in the Rift: he saw nothing and returned in a bad temper made worse because the botanist woman, Amy Burton, was brimful of enthusiasm. The forest was a relic community, she said, full of cycads, gnetophyte vines and ancient species of pines;

even something she was pretty sure might be a species of cycadeoid, a group which was thought to have died out tens of millions of years ago, although she couldn't be sure because it had not been bearing any cones. She wanted Alex to help her do some quadrats right there so that she could attempt to determine species diversity, but he refused of course, and tried to explain that diversity best correlated with number of bird species—what was the point of counting plants or insects when it was easier to look for birds?

"At least we can count plants," Amy Burton said. She was a defiant, dumpy woman, her T-shirt sweat-stained and her dishwater blonde hair ratty around her face. Alex pointed out that when it came to preserving ecosystems, rare animals were essential in raising a media profile, and she walked away, flushed with anger.

Alex turned to Ty Brown, who had been filming them, and said, "I hope you got all that."

He was pissed with Ty, too. The cameraman had become obsessed with silly little spats and disputes when he should have been concentrating on Alex's work; after all, the bulk of the sponsorship had been raised to look for rare or previously unknown animals. But like most naturalists Ty was contemptuous of cryptozoology. He saw it as monster hunting, searching for Bigfoot or the Loch Ness monster or dinosaurs in the Congo, when really it was nothing of the sort—well, it was true that Alex had collaborated with Read in a search for Bigfoot in the Sierras a couple of years ago, but that had just been to raise his profile so he could get money to do some real scientific work, something a snobby academic like Amy Burton, with her university sinecure, couldn't understand. No, cryptozoology was just what it meant: the study of hidden animals. Even today, with ecosystems all over the world in poor shape and even the most remote forests being cut down, new species were turning up all the time: an ungulate in Vietnam; a parrot in Venezuela; a big flame-kneed tarantula in the Sonoran desert. It was quite possible that some of the large mammals which had been wiped out by human invasion of North America had survived in remote areas of the South American rain forest; there had been indisputable sightings of giant sloths by loggers; Alex was pretty sure that the hair samples he had obtained from the local Indians would yield DNA for testing.

He was so riled by the dumb argument with the Burton woman that at first he ignored Ty when the cameraman said he'd seen an odd bird the day before, but then Ty produced the feather and described what he'd seen, and Alex's anger melted away because even before he saw the brief blurred video clip on the camera's tiny screen he knew what it had to be, and that this would make his name and end forever the hard scrabble for funds and the contempt of lab-bound scientists.

On the other side of the camp, Lowe shouted and clapped his hands for attention, saying that he'd finally made contact with the Old Man, and he was already on his way down.

4   *Ralph Read*

It was all falling apart, and the injury to his knee was almost the final blow. He'd come here to prove that he was still who they all thought he was, Ralph Read, the Old Man, Himalayan veteran back when Katmandu hadn't been full of bad German cooking and American hippies, before the real explorers had run out of world to explore, before it had become so small and used up. Last time he'd been up Everest, escorting some film actor and a documentary crew, he had been horrified by what had happened to the beautiful mountain: the queues of fee-paying novice climbers waiting their turn to strike for the summit, the litter, the piles of shit, the toilet paper and food wrappers blowing around, the discarded oxygen and propane cylinders, even dead bodies lying in the ice, everyone too preoccupied with getting to the top or too exhausted to bury them properly, let alone bring them down. He had helped do that to the Mother Goddess of the World, he real-

ized—the horde had followed in his footsteps. She was ruined.
And now his life in ruins too. It was the Rift, the bitch of the Rift.
All mountains were women to Ralph; he had seduced them—
ravished them—with the same inexhaustible energy with which
he had pursued real women. And the Rift was no different, except
they had to conquer her from the top down, but she was hard, the
bitch, too hard for him. The Old Man: old and fucked up.

Perhaps it was because of the dirty secret, he thought, the
thing no one else but he knew, the way he'd found out about her
and then pretended she was his discovery when all along she'd
been someone else's. Like many of the old style mountaineers,
Ralph was a deeply superstitious man. Back then you relied on
yourself and your own good luck, not on piton guns and free-
running carabineers and nylon rope, on oxygen and lightweight
sleeping bags and radios—good Christ, people even took portable
phones up mountains now, to call up the rescue services when
they got in trouble or ran out of soup. No, you had needed skill
and luck in the glory days of climbing, before technology all but
factored luck out of the equation, and luck was an intangible gift
that had to be carefully cultivated.

But now he'd blown it; he should have known on his first
expedition into the Rift, when he had tried to follow the route of
the Victorian explorers and had been caught by an early start to
the rainy season and had almost drowned. And now this, a man
lost and his knee fucked and Alex Wilson babbling in his face
about some stupid bird—Wilson had never understood that at the
heart of the expedition was the need to conquer, to claim, to show
that the Rift's wilderness could be matched and overcome by the
human spirit.

It was all just too bad: bad luck.

It took Ralph a day to descend to where the expedition had
stalled, far longer than he had expected. He had always known
that he wasn't up to forging the path all the way down, but he
thought that he could make the last mile or so, wherever it was
below the perpetual mists, be the first to the bottom. So he waited

at the rim, ostensibly to co-ordinate the supply lines and the advance party, but even that went wrong very quickly—the Rift's granite walls scrambled radio signals, and the helicopter pilots refused to descend within her walls because of unpredictable updraughts and katabatic winds dropping over the edge. So in the end he'd decided to go down early, and just as well, because half-way down, when he finally made contact with Lowe, he learnt that one of the young climbers had gone missing and Lowe was in a panic about it. The man was a good second-in-command, but lacked the backbone to make decisions in a pinch.

Ralph had trained rigorously for the Rift, but he was too old; no amount of training could get him fit enough. His arms were still strong and he could bench press twice his weight, but his lung capacity was half what it had once been, and his legs were giving out. Even though he was helped by two climbers, the descent took far too long, and then he banged up his knee.

He had been all right abseiling down the easy pitches—the equipment and gravity took care of that—but there were far too many traverses and far too much walking, and then there was a tricky move around a big boulder at the edge of a pool, something that in his prime he would have managed easily. But he hurt his knee badly making the move, and hurt it again when he landed half in water, half on the pool's rocky rim, and it quickly swelled even though one of his helpers put a pressure bandage on it. He insisted on going on, although every step jammed a red-hot needle under his tender kneecap, at last having to be supported on either side by his helpers down the boulder field, then lowered in a sling down the cliff like a sack of potatoes, sweating like a pig and itching with prickly heat, the muggy air like gruel in his lungs.

So when he finally arrived at the camp, he was exhausted and almost in tears, from the pain of his injury and from the shame of his failure, not at all ready to deal with the pandaemonium which erupted around him almost at once. Lowe was desperate for advice while at the same time pretending that he done everything he could; the other climbers all wanted to give their opinion; and Alex Wilson was babbling about some bird someone had spotted.

Ralph waved them all off, demanding in his stentorian voice that he be given some hot chocolate and perhaps something to eat and certainly somewhere comfortable so that he could put up his knee. That gave him a breathing space, and at last he was seated on a pile of rope, turning his good profile to the glare of the light clipped to Ty Brown's video camera, one big hand wrapped around a steaming tin mug, the other stroking his bristling beard, for all the world like a monarch and the climbers his supplicants, Wilson skulking at the back with the botanist woman, the two of them exchanging furious whispers like plotters at the edge of his court. He got the story out of Lowe, silencing with a glare anyone who tried to chip in, and knew it was bad. The expedition had been strung out too thinly—he'd let the Danes set the pace and they had gone off without any regard for the difficulties of resupply. Despite the money they'd brought, bamboozled from some long-haired bleeding-heart pop-singer millionaire, it had been a mistake taking them on, they simply weren't team material. And it was clear that his guesses about what supplies would be needed had been hopelessly inadequate. At this rate they'd run out of rope in two or three days, and they were nowhere near the bottom yet. But he had to try and salvage what he could.

Ralph asked for silence and made a pretence of thinking, but he had decided what to do almost at once. Divide and rule, the only way. So he told them that the climbers would be organised into two teams, taking turns to forge new pitches or work on resupply, scavenging rope if necessary. The Danes, who had already done so much good work, would have the important job of looking for the missing climber... for a moment he couldn't remember his name. Vignone, that was it, Ron Vignone.

"He's probably gone off on his own, but we need to make sure he isn't lying up somewhere with a broken ankle, eh?" He looked around at them all, beaming with patriarchal benevolence.

Lowe objected of course, because Ralph had undermined his authority, such as it was. He especially didn't like the idea of scavenging rope from pitches higher up. "What if we need to ascend quickly? If someone gets hurt or the rains start early?"

"We've plenty of good climbers," Ralph said. "I'm sure they can re-establish the routes quickly enough, especially as the pitons are already emplaced."

"I don't know," Lowe said. "Some of those overhangs are rather—"

"I chose my climbers well, I hope," Ralph said. "I'm sure they're up to the challenge."

And of course they all nodded, either because they were as full of piss and vinegar as he had been at their age, or because they didn't want to admit their fear; once you let your fear show you're finished as a climber.

"Well then," Ralph said, and smiled at them all and lit a cigar, even though he was still short of breath in the soupy air, and asked Ty Brown, "I hope you got all that, young man. It's a pivotal point in our little adventure."

Alex Wilson came forward, stepping amongst the climbers, and said, "What about the bird?"

Ralph had forgotten about that detail. He blew a plume of cigar smoke and said, "You and the young lady there can help look for Ron, and perhaps you'll find this bird too."

In his opinion the whole thing would go faster without having to nursemaid a couple of scientists. Perhaps this really would work out after all. Of course, losing a team member was unfortunate, but it was excusable as long as they reached their goal. A necessary sacrifice.

Wilson wanted more, of course—he wanted everyone to look for the confounded bird, and the botanist woman backed him up even though the two of them had previously been like cat and dog. Wilson babbled about relic populations, about the importance of a living fossil that might resolve the debate about whether or not birds had evolved from dinosaurs. "If I can find a fertile egg, I can determine whether its digits are reduced according to the theropod pattern or that of modern birds. And dissection will show whether the lungs are bellow-like or flow-through. It will be the discovery of the century, believe me," and so on, playing to Ty Brown's camera until Ralph cut him off.

"We still need to get to the bottom of the Rift, so we must push on."

Wilson was so wound up he was actually quivering with indignation. "But the science—"

"Science and exploration go hand in hand here," Ralph told him. "Now, I think we've had enough talk. I'm sure we all need some rest. We have a lot of work to do, but I'm confident you are all up to it."

But later, he was unable to sleep. The expedition was falling apart, a man missing and almost certainly dead, and he had staked everything on a last throw, a desperate race for the bottom that would only succeed if his luck held. He lay awake a long time, thinking of the notebook he had discovered, the diary of a member of a Victorian expedition which had penetrated several miles into the Rift before being chased off by a fierce tribe of Indians, the clues it provided enough to pinpoint the Rift on photographs taken by a Russian landsat so that he could claim it for himself, and himself alone. Read's Rift. It had a certain ring. He had never told anyone about the notebook; no one but he knew about the indigenous tribe or the other things. The relic bird was nothing compared with the claims of the Rift's first explorers, but of course he couldn't tell Wilson about that, just as he couldn't reveal that he knew that a lost tribe of Indians lived here.

And so no one was armed except for himself. He had brought his ex-army Webley .45. He hoped upon hope he wouldn't have to use it, but he was beginning to believe that he had turned things around, that his luck would hold.

He was wrong.

)(

5   *Amy Burton*

"At least we can get some work done," Alex Wilson said *sotto
voce* to Amy the next morning, as the two parts of the expedition
got ready, one to descend further, the other to retrieve ropes from
higher up. A sentiment which managed to shock her even though
she had already decided that, this side of snake oil sellers, dieti-
cians and shampoo manufacturers, Wilson was quite the most
amoral person masquerading as a scientist she'd ever come across.
A man had gone missing, for God's sake; he might be dead, and all
Wilson could think of was his pointless quest. Well, perhaps she
shouldn't be surprised. It was common gossip that Wilson's PhD
was nothing of the sort, merely an honorary doctorate from a
mid-West college dazzled by his series of lost world TV documentaries, and it seemed to Amy that he was both horribly
arrogant and desperately insecure. She'd kept away from him as
much as possible, given that he kept trying to pick fights with her
on specious grounds, and fortunately he'd spent more and more
time arguing with the cameraman, who proposed following the
new lead team rather than filming Wilson searching for his bird.

Meanwhile, Ralph Read sat on his throne of rope bags saying
nothing yet trying to look as if he was still in command. He was
pale under his tan, sweating heavily, and massaging his bandaged
knee when he thought no one was looking. After Amy saw him
take a swig of something from a silver flask, she assumed her best
no-nonsense voice and told him she'd take a look at that knee, and
he gave in after a token protest.

"I've no objection to being ministered to by a comely young
woman," he said.

"Bullshit," Amy said, for she harboured no illusions about
herself—she was a dumpy, pear-shaped thirty-five, a handmaiden
to science with a poor career profile because she loved field expeditions far more than the publication mill or the petty rivalries of
university departmental politics. Her father had worked for the
CIA in Central America in the sixties, when half the governments

had been in the pay of the United Fruit Company, and although she was irredeemably left-wing in the classic pattern of anti-parental rebellion, she loved her father for the camping expeditions on which he'd taken her and her brother—that was where she had developed her passion for botany, and where her life had been shaped.

She got rid of the poorly knotted bandages by judicious use of her Swiss Army knife; Read winced as she probed his knee with expert fingers. It was in bad shape, misshapen and swollen with internal bleeding, the skin a shiny black. She treated it with novo-caine cream and splinted it, and told Read that he should really be taken back up.

"The expedition needs me," he said. "I'm quite comfortable, and I'm sure the radio will work better down here. Thank you," he added. "It does feel better."

"In this climate it'll become gangrenous if you don't get proper treatment," she warned him.

"Oh, a little gangrene is nothing," he said, with only a ghost of his usual braggadocio. "I lost two toes on my first assault on K2."

Before they left, Amy had two of the climbers rig up a sunshade for the silly vain old man, and then the expedition divided with noisy banter. The Danes got up from where they had been squatting and drifted into the forest—a strange secretive bunch, but Amy quite liked them, despite Ken's aggressive assertion of his one-eighth Aboriginal ancestry. Ty Brown went down the cliff with the lead party; Alex Wilson ascended with the rope scavengers to search for his bird where Ty had seen it yesterday. Amy shouldered her backpack and made herself scarce before the old man tried to persuade her to stay and keep him company rather than wandering off into a dangerous forest by herself.

Amy didn't think the forest dangerous at all, although it was spectacularly strange. With cycads as the primary growth, it really was the kind of place where you expected to be confronted by a dinosaur, and she was certain that several of the plant species she saw were new to science—either relic species or genuinely unknown. If she could have her way, the expedition would abandon all efforts to get to the bottom and concentrate on doing some real science, but there was no chance of that while Read was still its leader. He was interested in nothing but climbing. He'd even called this place a rift for God's sake, when it was nothing at all like a rift valley: it was a canyon, probably formed on a fault line and deepened by irregular uplift and water erosion, perhaps even the collapse of an underground water course.

The narrow belt of forest stretched for more than a mile to either side of the camp, slashed by smooth rock flood channels. It was like the cliff forests which had been discovered in Canada, a refuge for dozens of species which could obtain precarious footholds in its diverse range of microhabitats; and it was also an island population, its environment both geographically isolated and physically distinct from the rain forests around the massif which the Rift bisected, an evolutionary laboratory where species could explosively radiate to fill empty niches.

Amy passed through the forest which had been searched yesterday, descended a long gentle grade of tumbled rocks, an old rockfall overgrown by creepers and ferns and moss, and rambled on through the unexplored lower terrace of the forest. She sketched and took meticulous photographs with a scale always in the foreground, took samples of leaves and cones and flowers and placed them in plastic bags with a dusting of camphor powder to kill bugs, carefully documented each photograph and specimen. She took species counts of gridded areas too, and assessed growth habits as best she could.

And always she was filled with wonder at the treasure house through which she wandered, a last wilderness that even now was being despoiled by the expedition. Although she hated to admit it, she knew that Wilson was right about the bird; if it was a living fossil, a close relative of the ancestral species of modern birds, surviving as coelacanths had survived in the deep waters off East

Africa before they had been fished out, then it really was a fantastically important scientific discovery. Yet the forests were important too, although Wilson couldn't see it—that was the problem with zoologists. They were so focused on their big mammal star species—pandas or tigers or blue whales—that they often didn't see the importance of the infrastructure of plants and fungi and insects and even bacteria that made up the habitats where the mammals lived. The primary mistake of zoos and many conservation bodies was to believe that by saving a rare animal they had somehow preserved the most important member of a vanishing habitat, but without the thousands of unacknowledged species which coexisted with it, it was no more than a trophy living out the last of its days in sterile captivity. More enlightened programmes held that everything in a habitat was important; they took cores or sweep samples, tried to calculate and define biodiversity. That was why Amy's work was so important.

In this way, the day passed quickly, until she discovered the standing stone.

In fact, she walked right past it without really seeing it. It was only when she was taking a photograph a little way off that she really saw what it was, and went back with her heart hammering, suddenly full of apprehension.

It was a columnar piece of native granite a dozen feet high, perhaps originally flaked from the cliff by weathering, but someone had set it upright in the thin laterite soil and shaped its base into the crude likeness of a pregnant woman. It reminded Amy of the ancient clay figures discovered in prehistoric cave dwellings. She walked around it, noting brown, wilted flowers at the base, and a pile of rotten figs, and started to take photographs, the click of the camera shutter and the whine of the motor suddenly very loud and obtrusive in the watchful green of the forest. She was just putting the camera back in her pack when she heard a faint crackle far off, as if someone had stepped on one of the dried cycad fronds which everywhere littered the ground.

Heart in mouth, she lifted the pack and backed into a stand of feathery mimosa, settling down on her haunches, her eyes skittering back and forth as they tried to distinguish movement in the green shadows.

There! A tall figure drifting silently down the path she had followed. Amy almost burst out laughing, for she saw at once who it was. He was quite naked, and carried something before him—a bright wreath of orchids, which he placed with awkward yet touching reverence at the foot of the standing stone.

When Amy stood up and stepped from her hiding place, he jumped almost a foot in the air and then she did laugh, and after a few seconds he did too.

"Well, you caught me I guess," Sky Dane said, with a rueful grin.

"I didn't mean to." Amy wanted to ask where his parents where, and where his clothes were, too (although he was so unselfconsciously naked that he was clad, as it were, in his dignity). Instead, she asked him about the standing stone, and who might have carved it.

"I mean," she said, "no Indian tribes would work something like this in stone. It isn't in their tradition."

"Not in their tradition, I guess, no."

"But there is a tribe living here."

"Sort of."

"And you know about them, you and your parents."

"Sort of." She stared at him and he did blush then, and added, "We've seen signs here and there. We travel fast, faster than the others suspect, so we've had time for a bit of exploring. We saw one or two things. There's an old cliff dwelling half a mile up, made in a cave under an overhang? They must have lived there a fair old time because the ashes from their fires are more than ten feet deep, but my dad reckons that no one has lived there for thousands of years. We found some glyphs carved in the rocks, too, although you have to have the eye to see them."

"Who are they? Do you think they took the climber?"

For a moment Amy had the horrible thought that perhaps the Danes had murdered him—but no, Ty Brown and Alex Wilson had been with them.

Sky said, "They killed him most like. It's what Indians do with intruders on their patch. Look, are you going to tell about this?"

Amy said carefully, "Is it important that I don't?"

"Not when you get back. In fact, it's important you tell people, because of the government rules about undiscovered tribes. We can give you stuff about what we found, photos and the like. But I mean, you won't tell the others now."

"I don't see why—" Amy started to say, but got no further because that was when the shots rang out in the distance.

Two shots, close-spaced, echoing off the cliff above. A third rang out just after Amy started to run, chasing after Sky's fleet figure, his buttocks glimmering in the green gloom as he raced away from her.

It was a long run, across the old rockfall and through another mile of forest. She arrived at the camp covered in sweat and out of breath, mouth parched with fear. Sky, now wearing shorts and a T-shirt, was tending to a man who lay on the ground clutching his thigh—there was blood running between his hands, soaking his shorts. Ralph Read stood at the edge of the drop, propping himself up with a tent pole and menacing the air with a huge antique revolver.

"They ran, by God," he shouted to Amy, fierce and exultant. "By God how they ran!"

"Here," Amy told Sky, "let me look," and knelt by the wounded man.

It was one of the young climbers, Matt Johnson. His face was grey, and slick with sweat. He told Amy, his voice tight with pain, "They came at us while we were hacking through forest a couple of terraces below. I don't know where the others are."

Amy glanced at Sky and said, "Tell me later," and pried his fingers away from his thigh and saw the slim arrow shaft that stood up from it, fletched with dyed red feathers. She probed

around it, determined that the head wasn't in the bone, and told
Matt Johnson what she was going to do. "It will hurt," she said.

"It already hurts."

"You had better hurry there," Read shouted. "The buggers
will be back."

Amy twisted up her handkerchief and gave it to Matt Johnson
to bite down on, then cut the shaft in half with her knife and with
one quick hard motion pushed the remainder of the arrow
through the meat of his thigh. Blood gushed as the arrow-head
broke through the skin on the far side. Its point was flaked stone,
neatly socketed in the shaft. She got a grip on blood-slick stone
and drew the rest of the shaft from the wound.

Matt Johnson looked at it and shuddered and said, "Jesus
fuck."

"Don't faint on me now," Amy told him, hoping he wasn't
going into shock.

"It isn't so bad."

"You're lucky it wasn't poisoned," Sky said.

Amy washed blood from the young climber's wounds, sprinkled antibiotic powder in them and packed them, and wound a
bandage tightly around his thigh. A little blood soaked through,
but the arrow seemed to have missed the major vessels.

Ralph Read had been hobbling up and down at the edge of the
cliff, yelling into the radio, cursing, switching frequencies and
yelling some more. Now he threw the radio aside and drew his
revolver and fired three times at something below the cliff edge,
each shot a tremendous shocking noise. "Here they come!" he
shouted into the echoing silence, and broke the revolver open and
thumbed brass cartridges into its chamber, closed it, and started to
fire again.

Amy reached the edge of the cliff and looked down just as the
arrows started to fly up, dozens of them twinkling at the peak of
their ascent and then slipping back down the air. Ralph Read
began to shoot into the trees from which they came, the revolver
bucking in his hand. Amy thought she saw shadows slipping

through shadows beneath the cycads along the edge of the talus slope at the bottom of the cliff, and then Sky pulled her away.

"You must go!" Sky yelled, but she hardly heard him, half-deafened by the revolver and the hammering of her heart. He tried to drag her across the rock apron towards the cliff and the fixed ropes, but she pulled back.

Ralph Read was leaning on the tent pole and reloading his revolver, a wild and grim expression on his face. He glanced at them and said, "I'll keep them off until you reach the top of the cliff. I can't climb with this blasted knee, but you can lower a sling and get me up that way. Go on now!"

Sky said, "He's right. I'll stay and help him. You go. And remember to tell the authorities that there are Indians living here!"

Matt Johnson had already climbed into his harness, and now he helped Amy get into hers. She hadn't realized how scared she was until she tried to do up the buckles, all thumbs. She said to Matt Johnson, "Can you climb?"

"I can always climb. I got back, didn't I?"

His face was still grey with shock, and his hands were trembling, but he got her harness fastened and roped her to him and they started the climb, leaning out more or less horizontally and walking up the face of the vertical cliff of hard red-black granite. The harnesses were fixed to the ropes with jumars, metal clasps which slid up the rope but not down, and although these made the climb easier, Amy's arms and shoulders were soon burning. There was a traverse thirty feet up, along a narrow ledge to the chimney that led up through a big overhang. Matt Johnson started to spider along it. He had to use his legs as much as his arms, and Amy heard his gasps of pain. Then he was at the chimney and paid out the belay rope, and it was her turn. Just as she started the traverse, her clumsy hiking boots slipping on the ledge, her hands cramped around the rope, the greasy granite an inch from her nose, something clattered beside her. An arrow. More lofted towards her, small deadly things that struck the rock on either side and dropped away. Then she was at the chimney and hauled herself up with Matt Johnson yelling encouragement. When she was lodged safely in it, rock on either side, she dared look back.

Below, Ralph Read was standing by the piled equipment in the centre of the rock apron, firing first to one side and then the other. Arrow shafts stuck out from his torso. Figures were dancing at the edge of the cycads, seemingly dressed in shaggy hides. She could not see Sky. Then the belay rope tightened. Matt Johnson was climbing on and she turned and followed him and saw no more.

6   *The Danes*

What can you say about the Danes? They are not Danish but Australian. They are a tightly bound unit, mother and father and son. They have their own rituals, their own body language. They are bonded together so tightly that nothing can pry them apart— not Ken's occasional infidelities, not Sky's occasional moony girlfriends, whom he mostly ignores because he needs nothing more than his family and their way of life.

They had a long palaver after Ralph Read's speech, realizing that they had reached the crux of their private mission. "We'll look for this cludger," Ken said, "but they certainly murdered him, and they don't want us to find his body or they would have just left it."

Sky, who loved horror movies, said, "Ate him, I reckon."

"Now we don't know that," Kerry said. "The evidence for cannibalism was only found in grave sites, and it was probably ritual."

"It's what they do in the New Hebrides," Sky said.

"These people aren't anything like that," Kerry said.

"They murdered him and stuffed his body somewhere," Ken said. "And they'll probably kill the rest of the climbers, too. It's a shame, but there it is. It isn't their fault these bastards came blundering in."

"That's just why we should tell Read what we know," Kerry said, but Ken vetoed that. "That bugger Wilson would chase after them," he said, "and so would Read. The two of them went looking for Bigfoot together, remember. So we can't let them know what's here; the poor people would be turned into circus freaks."

They talked some more, but it was decided. The next day they went their separate ways into the forest, and when the inevitable happened, Read's revolver shots ringing out into the Rift and finally ceasing, they met up in a prearranged spot several miles south of the campsite.

Even when part of other expeditions, the Danes always had their own agenda. It added spice, as Ken liked to say, and spice was everything in life. He didn't mind that people said they were hippies, relics from a lost age, that he was trying to keep his youth alive through adventure. It was all part of the cover for the half-world they inhabited. There were others like them, keeping the secrets of the world safe, a disorganized conspiracy that somehow worked most of the time.

They had been allowed to join the expedition because they had wangled money from a pop star to look for new tribes of Indians. There were still plenty to be found in the Amazonian basin, even at this late stage in its exploitation. The forests really were very extensive and very close grown. A hundred people, the size of most Indian tribes, living off the land in a small area, could stay hidden until some prospector or logger stumbled into them by accident. Just a couple of years ago, a jaguar hunter had been murdered, shot with an arrow, when he had encountered a hunting party of a previously unknown tribe, and a subsequent aerial survey had spotted the tribe's huts, almost invisible beneath the close-knit forest canopy. Like all recently discovered tribes, it had been left alone; the early Twenty-First Century was as toxic to these Stone Age indigenes as poison gas. The whole area had been declared off-limits.

That was what the Danes hoped for here, and they were pretty certain now that this was a very special tribe indeed.

They met at the standing stone. Sky was naked again, as were his mother and father. Sky had smeared the green juice of berries on his face and bare chest. He had knotted a black T-shirt around his head to hide his blond hair. He told his parents what had happened, and Ken nodded and asked what the botanist woman had seen.

"They didn't come into the open until she was halfway up the cliff," Sky said. "I reckon she didn't see too much. But one of the climbers got away too, and I don't know what he saw."

Ken scratched at the pelt on his chest. He was a stocky man, with a broad nose and a shock of wiry hair. "Well, it's a risk," he said, "but not a bad one. The others will be too scared to look around much."

Sky thought about how Amy had found him, and her questions, but kept silent. He trusted her; she had been the only one who had tried to understand this place.

"They'll think it's just Indians," his mother said. "They don't have the imagination for anything else."

"We'll wait here a while I reckon," Ken said. "When the fuss has died down we'll see what's left of the supplies, and then we can begin."

They sat in green shadow a little way from the standing stone. "They ran from everyone," Kerry said dreamily, leaning against her husband.

"It was the first great extinction," Ken said. "They were killed just like my people were killed when the Europeans came to Australia. They were hunted for sport because it was easier to think of them as animals than accept that people come in many different forms. *Homo sapiens* has done a lot of harm in its time, but that was the beginning of it all."

"Some got away," Kerry said. "Think how far they came! They were pushed further and further from Africa."

"Or Java," Ken said.

"They must have been the first to cross from Asia to Alaska," Kerry said, "but the modern humans followed and pushed them farther. Until they ended up here, with the other relic species."

"Something's coming," Sky said, and at the same moment the first of them stepped out of the darkness between the cycads.

"Steady," Ken said. "Remember, we're not like the others."

The figure that confronted them was small and stooped yet muscularly broad, and covered in a reddish pelt. Its feet clutched the earth; one leathery hand clutched a sapling whittled into a spear. Little eyes glinted under the shelf of its brow; its nose was broad and bridgeless; there was no chin beneath its wide mouth. It made no signal, but suddenly there were others behind it.

Sky and Ken and Kerry slowly got to their feet. Naked, they held out their hands to show that they had no weapons, that they were no threat, and waited for judgement.

ALIEN TV

efore Alan Smith could get into the convention, he had to endure a few minutes of low farce at the registration desk. Although Howard had promised to arrange a day membership, the woman behind the desk, wearing an ExoCon 8 T-shirt, with a soft toy of an alien fastened to her shoulder like a pirate's parrot, couldn't locate Alan's badge. She called over a colleague and they riffled through a printout and searched the boxes under the desk with an increasingly harried air. At last, the woman found him listed as "Friend of Howard Hutton", misspelled his name in purple Magic Marker on a blank badge, told him to wear it at all times, and, before he could protest, pushed the pin through the lapel of his brand new Cerruti jacket.

So Alan was feeling more than slightly pissed-off as he went around the desk and display boards that blocked the top of the broad flight of stairs, but then he saw the sports-bar-sized screen at the far end of the big lounge and it was as if eleven years had dropped away. The screen was tuned to alien TV, of course. Not the compilation channel which played on cable, which flipped from one programme to the next every thirty seconds, but the real, live, uncensored thing.

It was one of the panoramic views, looking out over a valley wooded with parasol trees towards low, eroded mountains, the mountains blue against the indigo sky, the crowded caps of the parasol trees (reminding Alan of the umbrellas of shoppers jostling through the city centre in the cold Easter rain) dark violet mottled with glittering cyans and purples. Ruins of a tower stood salt-white in the middle distance; half a dozen aliens were dipping and weaving above its jagged top.

Alan had seen the first decoded clips released by NASA when he and Howard had been engineering freshers and best friends at Cambridge, both of them science bugs from provincial city comprehensives, intimidated by the gilded arts students and the ancient rituals of the university. Alan, a sci-fi fan, had been more interested than most because here was the wondrous reality that his beloved science fiction novels, with their gaudy covers, clumsy prose, and stagy melodrama, had only approximated. Aliens living on a desert world half the size of Earth with a moon as big as Mars, twin planets really, only fifty light years away. Aliens simultaneously transmitting a thousand different TV programmes, saying hello to their neighbours. But it had been Howard who had dropped out of engineering to take astronomy and biology instead, Howard who had systematically collected and digested video tapes and NASA press releases and scientific papers, who had submitted articles about the aliens to popular magazines, who had, just before graduation, struck gold, and published a three-page piece in the colour supplement of one of the Sunday papers. After university, Alan had joined an international company specializing in mass transit systems, married, and started a family. His sci-fi collection had been sealed in a carton which moved with him unopened through various postings until it had been lost somewhere between Bangkok and Munich. Meanwhile, Howard had drifted into the freelance journalist scene in London. He had come to Alan's wedding and had once visited Alan in Paris, his first posting, but gradually they had lost touch. Then, a month ago, Alan had found one of Howard's books in an airport bookshop. Howard's email address had been printed at the end of the brief preface, and on a whim Alan had sent him a message. Howard's response mentioned that he was going to be a guest at a convention in Liverpool; Alan had a meeting with the city council that same weekend. The coincidence was irresistible; they had arranged to meet.

Alan had stayed in this hotel two years ago, during a corporate hospitality jaunt to Aintree, and had been amazed by the brazenness with which the city's unofficial hostesses, in their tight, short, white dresses and bleached hair and artificial tans, had mingled with the race goers in the big lounge which, with its chandeliers and tall gilt mirrors, was a replica of one of the Titanic's passenger lounges. But there was no sign of that cheerful rowdiness now, although there were plenty of people sitting on banquettes around tables or in circles on the carpet. The lights in the big chandeliers were on, even though it was the middle of the afternoon, and the room had the dowdy, exhausted look of a twenty-four-hour fast food joint. Alan walked slowly down its length towards the big screen and its strange alien panorama, but saw no sign of Howard. Most of the conference delegates were men tending towards forty or older, a sizable percentage with beards and straggly hair, most wearing T-shirts or denim jackets and baggy jeans or sweat pants, the uniform of students twenty years ago. They talked animatedly or hunched together over laptops or palmtops; no one was watching the screen. There was a comradely buzz of conversation, a stale smell of beer and cigarettes. The ashtrays were overflowing; the tables were cluttered with empty glasses and bottles. It was like a cross between a computer fair, a science convention, and an all-night party.

Howard wasn't in the bar to one side of the lounge either, or in the "real ale bar" to the rear. Alan felt a mixture of amusement and frustration. It was so like Howard, famously absent-minded and always late for lectures, to have invited him and then to have forgotten all about it. Alan looked at the pocket programme he had been given along with his badge. A panel on starship design, another on alien behaviour, a third on possible translations of alien glyphs. Howard was giving a talk later in the evening, on the timeline of the aliens' history, but it was scheduled to start after Alan's flight was due to leave. Alan stood in the back of the room where the current programme item was being held, someone showing slides and speculating about caste relationships in one of the nonflying species domesticated by the aliens and used as both labourers and a food source, but he couldn't spot Howard amongst the rows of intent people and slipped out.

And saw Howard coming down the stairs on the far side of the lounge, talking with a heavily made-up woman in a business suit and followed by a man with a professional video camera up on his shoulder. Howard was better dressed than Alan had expected, in suit, tie, and polished brogues, his wiry hair short and neat, a bit of a paunch stretching the front of his shirt, but otherwise Howard, the same square white face, the same gold-rimmed spectacles, the same grin when he saw Alan coming towards him as he said goodbye to the TV people.

They caught up over gassy pints of beer in the bar. Howard still had the same braying laugh, the habit of adjusting his spectacles by pinching their bridge between thumb and forefinger. Their frames had marked his damp white skin. He still bit his nails, Alan saw, but his fingers were no longer inkstained. Screens banked along one side of the bar were showing various channels of alien TV. Howard kept glancing at them, their light sliding over the lenses of his spectacles. He had brought a paperback copy of one of his books, and signed it with a cramped yet fastidious hand.

"I still remember what you said when the first clips were shown," he told Alan.

"I remember how pissed everyone was."

NASA had released the clips at six o'clock Eastern Standard Time, eleven at night in Cambridge, pub closing time. The TV lounge of the college had been crowded with raucous undergraduates drinking from cans of lager or beer.

Howard said, "And we were drinking coffee."

"So we were. God, yes. The only sober people in the room. And that woman, what was her name? The mature postgraduate."

"Eileen O'Neil."

"Right. She said that it was like the first moon landing."

"It was more important than that," Howard said.

"Well, it was a long time ago, anyway. Eleven years. Jesus."

"It's still important," Howard said.

There was an awkward silence. Alan asked about the publishing business, genuinely interested in how Howard managed to scratch a living.

"I get by," Howard said, with an evasiveness that might be mistaken for modesty if you didn't know him better. He had never liked talking about himself; Alan had known him for two years before he realized that his parents were divorced. He still stooped, as if mortified by the presence his height lent him.

"It's amazing," Alan said. "I mean, that you can make money with this."

"It was the biggest thing in a thousand years," Howard said. "The public interest didn't last, but there are still plenty of people all over the world studying the aliens. Your company keeps track, I bet. Most big companies do. And the people here keep track too."

The response was so smooth that Alan wondered if it was the kind of soundbite Howard gave to TV people. He said, "Of course we keep track. We'd be foolish not to."

All the big discoveries had been made years ago, of course, but, like its competitors, his company still monitored the alien TV broadcasts, using AIs to sift out anything potentially interesting. Otherwise, people watched alien TV about as much as they watched, say, QVC. A few watched all day; some watched for a few minutes with the same kind of inert fascination (how long *can* that guy talk about car wax? Just *what* is that freak thing doing?); most, like Alan, caught a few seconds while flicking past late at night, in the usual hunt to confirm that, yes, there was nothing worth watching on any of the two hundred cable channels.

Howard said, "There's a lot more to it than stealing their technology. Exobiology, behavioral studies, language, history, just to begin with." He ticked them off on his fingers, hunched forward in his chair so that his knees brushed Alan's. Alan pulled his chair back a little, but Howard didn't notice. He said, "The aliens have been civilized for at least a million years. They want us to know all about them, and the amount of information in their broadcasts is phenomenal. Of course, companies like yours look for stuff to steal, and universities have research programmes, but alien TV is like astronomy. Most comets and novas are still spotted by amateurs, and there's plenty of room for amateurs to make valid discoveries by watching alien TV. We pick up the stuff no one else bothers to watch. AIs are programmed to sift data in a limited number of ways, but the human mind is infinitely flexible."

Alan laughed. The same old Howard, earnestly pedantic, hoping to win any argument by sheer weight of words. He said, "You don't have to convert me. I used to watch that stuff as much as you."

"It's still just as much fun," Howard said, glancing at the screens as he leaned forward to pick up his pint. "We could watch a thousand years and still have things to learn."

Alan laughed again. "You sound...evangelical."

"It's what I do," Howard said. "You might think that I don't have a proper job, but this is it. I'm off to the States later this year. They hold a big convention every year, over the Labor Day weekend. Five thousand people from all over the world."

"And do they find anything? Anything important, I mean."

"If you mean commercially important, no. But that's not the point. It's the sense of wonder, like your old science fiction books. One of the other GOHs here used to be a science fiction writer, in fact."

"GOH?"

Howard grinned and said, as if confiding a clue to a secret code, "Guest of Honour. It's great for egoboo, but it's also nice to meet your readers."

They had another drink, and Howard insisted on showing Alan around the dealer's room. There was a stand for a company selling the satellite dishes and decoders needed to access the raw alien TV broadcasts that were relayed from the joint NASA-ESA radio telescope. Trestle tables were loaded with racks of data needles containing thousands of stills and hours of edited video sequences, magazines, self-published theses as thick as bibles, computer programmes for image capture and analysis, models and sculptures of aliens and alien buildings, maps, field guides to the flora and fauna of the alien planet and its moon, exquisitely detailed dioramas of landscapes, even a table of tattered sci-fi paperbacks.

Howard chatted knowledgeably to the dealers, signed copies of his book proffered by deferential fans. This was his element— more important than alien TV to these people was the culture they had created around it. Howard had never really grown up, Alan realized. Still the same fascination with trivia, the same selfish irresponsibility. He wanted Alan to stay around for his panel, and said that afterwards the convention committee would take them out for a meal in this really great Greek restaurant, but Alan made his excuses. In truth, he felt a touch of claustrophobia, surrounded as he was by the products of tens of thousands of hours squandered on simulated scholarship no one would ever read. The last thing he needed was to be trapped in a taverna with a bunch of obsessives.

"We should keep in touch," Howard said. "I've always said companies like yours could learn a lot from us."

"It's not really my field," Alan said carefully.

"But it touches on everything. You know," Howard said earnestly, "I still remember what you said when we saw the first broadcast, that nothing will ever be the same again. You were right. Alien TV changed us, and it's still changing us."

"I said that?" Alan felt now that he was being manipulated, that Howard wasn't interested in him because of their old friendship, but because of his connections. He said, knowing how feeble it sounded, "Listen, Howard, it was terrific to meet up again, but I really do have to go and get ready for my flight. Don't let me hold you up."

But Howard followed Alan out through the revolving doors into the rain, and was still talking about the importance of his work as Alan got into a taxi. "The beauty of their world," Howard said. "And ethics, and philosophies we can't even dream of. The intangible that stands behind the tangible. By using their technology without understanding them, we're changing ourselves in ways we can't predict!"

He had to shout the last, because Alan had shut the door and the taxi was pulling away.

Ж

Alan went back to his own hotel and packed and called his wife, then took the elevated train (a subsidiary of his company ran it) out to the airport. He sat in the bar until his flight was called, chatting with a couple of structural engineers whose company also had a share in the construction of the space elevator. The feeling that he had escaped from some suffocating dream slowly left him; after the second drink the whole unfortunate episode began to take on a comic aspect, and before he left he managed to make a couple of jokes about it to his new companions.

Nairobi was only an hour away by scramjet. Alan looked out of the port (every seat was a window seat in business class) and drank a gin-and-tonic and ate chilly peanuts while the blue-white curve of the Earth turned below. His wife was there to meet him in the crowds at the airport, and she drove him through the dusty streets out to the compound where they lived. It was evening here, still very hot. The elevator stood against thunderclouds to the northwest, limned by blinking warning lights, vanishing into the bruised sky like a *Land Of The Giants* version of the Indian Rope Trick. Alan's firm had just won the contract to build and service the huge elevator cars, each as big as a ten-storey office building, that would shuttle between the Earth's surface and the terminal in geostationary orbit.

Later, after he had given his son and daughter their presents and helped the nanny with their bathtime, and picked over an unwanted dinner, Alan sat in his big leather chair in his den, sipping a gin-and-tonic, restlessly flicking through the channels on his screen. And there was the alien TV compilation channel, one of them facing the camera or whatever they used, gesticulating with half a dozen limbs, including the bright red thing that looked like a long spiny penis, then *flip*, an aerial shot of one of their roosts, hundreds of tall thin spiky towers studded with openings and platforms and ledges that reared up out of scrubby desert with tens of thousands of aliens swooping and gliding at all levels, *flip*, a view across the rolling green grassland of the aliens' big moon, with the alien's planet a blue-white chip stuck in the dark sky, *flip*, aliens clustered around some huge half-dismantled machine under a tented roof of gauzy material, *flip*, hundreds of ape-like creatures working in a flooded field, *flip*, a wide canal running across a red desert, *flip*, *flip*, *flip*...

What did it matter exactly how old their civilization was; whether or not they were on their way here to eat us or conquer us or sell us the squidgy things they sometimes rubbed over their bodies; whether the formal battles they fought, hand-to-hand aerial combat above the vast natural amphitheatre of a shield volcano, were over religion or whether red- or blue-banded squidgy things were best? They were aliens. What they did was inexplicable. Only the few broadcasts which featured the universal language of physics and mathematics were comprehensible, and only what human minds and hands did with the knowledge gleaned from those broadcasts was important. The space elevator, the use of artificial photosynthesis to end world hunger, the extension of human lifespan, pinch fusion, the ceramics used in scramjet motors, monomolecular films: all developed from clues gathered from watching alien TV, but developed by people.

Alan had been lucky enough to live through those few months when everything in the world had changed utterly and forever. But it was not possible to recreate the excitement of the first months after alien TV had started, the banner headlines, the thousands of hours of speculation on TV, the T-shirts and dolls and instant books, the bombing of a NASA ground station by Catholic extremists who claimed alien TV was a conspiracy by an alliance of Zionists and atheists. Briefly, it had been something everyone had to have an opinion on, but then the media had moved on to the next thing which had caught the fickle public imagination. The world had moved on, leaving alien TV to the research and development laboratories, university academics, and obsessives like Howard and his T-shirted friends.

So why, with the screen flickering through a series of otherworldly images, did Alan feel as if he had lost something? Why did he feel a spurt of envy at the thought that Howard was still possessed by a secret which had once possessed him, but which he no longer possessed?

He sipped his gin-and-tonic and watched alien TV until his wife called to him. He flicked off the screen and dutifully went up.

BEFORE THE FLOOD

The two men, one middle-aged and one young, are squashed together behind the pilot of the little Bell helicopter. They wear fat ear defenders against the roar of the helicopter's engine, and blue FBI windbreakers, and are talking over the intercom link. Below, dry, rounded hills dotted with scrubby junipers speed by. It is summer, late in the afternoon. Deep shadows lie in the saddles between the hills.

"I'm not sure if I want to do this."

"You're already doing it, John. You're doing fine."

"I left and I didn't ever want to come back."

"You're being a great help to us. Don't think we don't appreciate it."

"That's a double negative. How am I supposed to take reassurance from something couched in a double negative?"

"I mean that you're doing fine."

"I don't feel fine. Are you sure he's dead?"

"We're pretty sure. You just have to look—"

"I've never seen a dead body before. Isn't that odd? I mean, I'm thirty-eight. You'd think I would have seen a dead body by now."

"You'll be fine, John," the younger man, the FBI agent, says.

John Kosik looks through the perspex bubble of the helicopter's cabin at the dry red hills of Utah. He does not feel fine. He left this behind for a very good reason, and now, seven years later, he is back because Michio's followers are either dead or in flatline comas, and the FBI want to know if Michio is amongst them.

The helicopter lands near a white, fat-wheeled all-terrain van waiting on an unpaved track at the top of one of the hills. John asks why they aren't going all the way in the helicopter, but the young FBI agent merely shrugs and says, "Procedure."

As soon as they have climbed out, the helicopter dusts off, turning away into the sky with a hellish roar. John hunches against the downblast of its rotors. The hot dry air stings his sinuses; the smell of sun-baked rock and juniper needles brings back a flood of unwelcome memories. He says, "You think he's still alive! You're afraid of him!"

"We're pretty sure he's dead," the agent says, leading him by the arm towards the van. The driver has already started the motor.

They drive fast along the switchback road, a banner of dust trailing behind. John knows this road well, and feels unwelcome memories stir. There is the cluster of notices, pockmarked with old bulletholes, warning people that this is private property; there is the long chain-link fence Michio had built around the three thousand acre compound. The gate is smashed down. The road climbs through a stand of pinon pines to the crest of the ridge, and there is the deep valley, spread beyond the white crescent of the dam and the cluster of towers.

"Look at those things," the young agent says. "Just like alien TV."

At first glance, the towers *are* just like the towers of the roosts depicted on one of the panorama channels of alien TV: tall and thin and organic, twisted like half-melted taffy, fretted with windows and ledges. But they are coated in black piezoelectric polymer, and their lower flanks are studded with big screens which all, judging by the synchronous movements that march ant-like across them, seem to be tuned to the same channel of alien TV.

"I don't watch TV any more," John tells the agent. "Not alien TV, anyway."

"I used to, when I was a kid. It gave me weird dreams."

"I mean real alien TV, not the commercial channel. The raw material, not the edited highlights."

John knows that if you have been trained to watch them properly, the alien images can tangle with mythopoeic images hardwired in the human cortex. They can give you seriously weird bad dreams. That was what happened to everyone in the early days of the colony, but John got out. He escaped. He had not seen any dead bodies, no, but he knew people had been killed that night, when the madness took them and he woke a kilometre downstream, naked, with someone else's blood under his broken nails and in his mouth.

He escaped, and tried to put the past behind him. There was reconstructive surgery, a nervous breakdown, a slow recovery. The dreams of things stalking him at night, the paralyzing visions of people's faces melting into animal masks, the fear of crowds, all slowly left him. He married, took a job in a college in New Hampshire, teaching English. He has a daughter, two years old, an amazing gift of hope and renewal. Seven years, free and clear. And then the FBI came for him, and he realized that he hadn't escaped after all.

The young agent is asking him something, asking if he is okay.

"A touch of travel sickness." Yes, because he is travelling back into the unwelcome past.

The van speeds down the switchback road into the valley, through the shade of pinon pines and tall blue eucalyptuses, and out into the hot blast of the late afternoon sunshine. The tamed river trickles over and around sandstone boulders. FBI vehicles are parked on a wide gravel apron in a bend in the river a little way downstream of the towers. RVs with microwave antennae and satellite dishes on their roofs, SUVs, and a boxy armoured car with mesh over its slit windows. Beyond is the white dome of a pressurized tent. People are moving about purposefully. The whole place has a circus air.

John says to the agent, "You were expecting trouble."

"Of course. But it was all over when we got here."

Still, as he follows the young agent towards the tent's white dome, John can't help noticing that the FBI men and women are wearing bulletproof vests under their windbreakers, and that most are armed with pistols and rifles. The local agent in charge of the investigation, Buck Gilmore, is waiting outside a kind of airlock tunnel that leads into the tent.

Gilmore is a tall, powerfully built man in a white shirt with pearl buttons, blue jeans and cowboy boots, thinning blond hair brushed back from his craggy face, blue eyes that seem to search John's thoughts. "We appreciate this," he says. "How was the trip? Can I get you anything? Soda? Water?"

"Let's just get it over with," John says.

He is very afraid, but it is not so bad once they go inside. The tent is pressurized and air-conditioned, noisy with fans and pumps. Harsh lights glare atop tall metal poles. The sharp smell of ozone and disinfectant overlies something sweetly nauseous. Those in comas are laid out on metal-framed cots, monitor screens over their heads, stands from which hang clusters of IV bags beside them. Their chests rise and fall in time to the tick of respirators that pump air through the tubes taped over their mouths. The dozen or so dead lie on the floor beyond, on green plastic sheets that John suddenly realizes are open body bags, with packets of documentation by their heads.

"Take your time," Gilmore says, but John wants to get this over with and moves quickly between the rows, forcing himself to look carefully at each empty face. First the living, all of whom have been altered to some degree, far more than he ever was. All are very tall and thin; some have had their faces reconstructed to look like the aliens' bony masks; a few seem to be wearing tattered capes—huge flaps of skin extending from shoulder blades to hips and wrists. There are no children, a blessing. And then the dead, their dry eyes looking up at him from half-closed lids. The dead are all unmodified. Their torsos are marked by deep slash wounds mercifully washed clean of blood.

When John reaches the end of the last row, Gilmore says, "Nothing?"

"I don't think so." He recognizes no one, neither Grace nor Hunter nor Roanne, or any of the other original colony members. He says, "The plastic surgery is more extensive than it was when I was here."

It was done by a colleague of Michio's, Eden Galich, a paediatric surgeon who learnt how to do the cosmetic surgery Michio required from textbooks and experiments on willing volunteers. The scars down John's sides and back itch reflexively.

Gilmore says, "It's more than plastic surgery. They were hiring a team of body designers on a regular basis. There are forty-seven here. There should be forty-eight. Most have had talons implanted, which wiped out their fingerprints. And dental records are useless in more than half the cases. DNA will tell, but it'll take time."

"You think he's still alive."

Gilmore's sharp gaze transfixes him. "Apart from these people, you are the only one to have spoken with Dr Perl since he set up this community. Would he have killed himself?"

That was one of the first questions John was asked when he was interrogated during the flight from Boston to Salt Lake City. He gives the same answer now. "I don't know. I don't think so. Please, can we go outside?"

Gilmore lights a cigarette and says, "Let's go stroll by the river. You think about what you've seen and tell me anything that comes to mind."

He has someone bring them bulletproof vests. They are light but rigid, cased in blue nylon. Gilmore shows John how to do up the buckles at the sides. They start to walk upriver, towards the towers. Two sharpshooters start to trail after them, rifles slung on their shoulders, but Gilmore dismisses them. Men and dogs are working through the pinon pines on the far side of the river.

John asks, "How did it happen?"

"Someone used a mobile phone, shouting for help. We think it was Alice Paley, one of the recent recruits. When the local police arrived, they came under fire at the perimeter fence. Someone was shooting from a position in the trees. They responded, and when the shooting stopped they went in. And then they called us. Most of Dr Perl's people were laid out in deep, unresponsive comas. The rest were dead, scattered down river or along the road. My best guess is that there was a dispute. Perhaps some of the people here wanted to get away, and while they were being hunted down the police arrived. Then there was a Jonestown scenario, except the followers here didn't drink cyanide-laced orange juice, but injected themselves with a cocktail of drugs. The medical examiner says their higher brain functions are destroyed. The question is, why didn't they simply take poison?"

John thinks that Gilmore has it about right, except that the dead weren't trying to escape. He says, "You probably know more than me. I'm sure you kept an eye on this place—you know how many people lived here, for instance."

Gilmore draws on his cigarette. He says, "Dr Perl's methods weren't exactly legitimate, but I'm given to understand that some people in government are interested in the results. Monitoring was pretty low key. No infiltration, no bugs."

"We used to do an intensive search for cameras and transmitters every so often," John says, remembering. "We always found one or two."

"Well, they got better at finding them. So I really do know very little about it. I'd appreciate it if you'd tell me what you know."

John wonders uneasily what Gilmore already knows. Does he know about the madness from which John fled?

Gilmore sits on a boulder by the water's edge, lights a second cigarette from the butt of his first. The sun is setting behind the towers, and their shadows tangle across the boulders of the half-dry river bed. The screens glow brightly with the light of another world, all showing the same jerky aerial perspectives of vast fields stretching away under an indigo sky.

The FBI agent blows a riffle of smoke, crosses his legs at the ankles. "Tell me about it from the beginning," he says.

John is too nervous to sit. He says, "The idea was to live like the aliens as much as possible. Michio said that we would be like pioneers, discovering new territory inside our own heads."

"Was this when the project was set up?"

"No, afterward. After it was shut down and we came here."

"Back up a bit," Gilmore says. "Start at the beginning."

The alien broadcasts were first picked up twenty years ago, a thousand compressed TV channels transmitted in the so-called water hole frequency range, between the natural emissions of free hydrogen and hydroxyl radicals. Alien TV provided vast amounts of detail about the aliens' home world, with its big moon and vast desert basins, their technology and their agriculture, their domesticated slave species and their cities, their physiology and anatomy, but there was nothing in the thousands of hours of TV about their psychology, not even something as simple as the reason why they had started broadcasting.

In human beings, the impulse to tell stories is very strong: society is woven from shared fictions, personality from long term memories laid down by the narratives of our dreams. Life without memory is no life at all, and memory without narrative structure is no memory. Every newly discovered Stone Age tribe in the rainforests of Brazil or Borneo has its origin myths, its stories explaining where people and animals and diseases came from, explaining why the world is the way it is. And all myths, even those of the most isolated tribes, share common roots: mythopoeic symbolism is derived from the hardwiring of the interface between sensory nerves and the cortex. The storytelling impulse is the foundation of human consciousness. Even artificial ways of thinking about the world—

mathematics, science—are strongly marked by the narrative arrow.

But the aliens appeared to lack any overt narrative ability. They had no fiction or drama, no music or organized religion; their mathematical system was non-deductive, lacking any conception of proof and derivation, relying instead on powerful heuristic techniques. Michio Perl, a medical researcher with degrees in psychology and social and biological anthropology, was the leader of a research group that was attempting to discover underlying narrative structures in alien TV, using cluster analysis, statistical evaluation of association between images, vector analysis of framing and tracking, and a host of other techniques. Progress was slow. While tangible benefits were flowing from analysis of alien technology, accelerating advances in material science, fusion technology, medicine and many other fields, the aliens themselves remained as opaque as ever, and public interest in them quickly waned. After eight years, at the end of an interminable series of reviews, the team's funding was withdrawn.

John told Gilmore, "You have to understand that Michio was very persuasive—a true charismatic. He moulded us from the first, and he responded to the crisis with what seemed to be magnificent idealism."

"And so he led you here, into the wilderness."

Michio persuaded the movie producer, Abner Bronson, to gift them a parcel of land. The colony, as Michio renamed his team, liquidated their assets and provided the labour. They stole—liberated was Michio's term—the computers, screens and other equipment from the institute. They built the first cluster of towers while living in tents through the baking summers and freezing winters, existing on welfare food and the occasional bounty of a deer or a horse. They recruited new members from vagrants, itinerants and runaways, using a technique of sexual enticement, flirty fishing, borrowed from a late twentieth century cult. They dammed the river, which was prone to flooding, and channelled its flow through a sluice to generate electricity. They built hang-gliders and microlights so that they could imitate the flight patterns flocks of aliens wove above their roosts.

Gilmore smokes two cigarettes while John summarizes the colony's history. Now he lights another and says, "You never spoke out against your colleagues after you left."

"I wanted..." John is struck by dizziness, as if he is somehow falling into the past. He sits down hard on warm stone. He says, "I thought I'd put it all behind me."

Gilmore sees his distress and says, almost kindly, "You'll be done here soon enough. If he's alive, I doubt he's here. There's an APB out for him. If he's alive and out there, we'll pick him up soon enough. We'll have to search the towers anyhow, of course, and that's going to be some job. They're lousy with crawlspaces, passages, nests of tiny rooms. Each one a real maze."

"I know," John says, looking up at the towers. "I helped build the first of them."

There are many more towers than he remembers. The original colony was a cluster of half a dozen towers no more than three or four storeys high, but this is dwarfed by newer structures, twenty, thirty of them standing on either side of the river, some more than a hundred metres tall, the lower parts of their black surfaces studded with screens. All the screens are playing the same scene, aliens flying low above vast irrigated fields where hundreds of individuals of one of the slave species flee in disorder...

John says, "He's still there."

Gilmore has masked his blue eyes with mirrorshades; these flash when he turns to look at John. He says, "In the towers? Damn, I knew it was a good idea to bring you here. How do you know?"

"Because I spent years studying the aliens, and Michio has spent even longer trying to think like them. Because—"

A siren whoops; John whirls around, his heart racing. A dozen ambulances are ploughing down the trail towards the FBI's encampment, blue lights twirling. "It's okay," Gilmore says. "We're evacuating the coma victims."

"No," John says. "No, I don't think you should do that."

Gilmore grins. "Another hunch, Dr Kosik? You still haven't explained—"

"The dam. Did you search the dam?"

"Sure we did. Found two of the dead there. You think—"

And the sharp thunder of an explosion echoes down the valley. Birds loft from the trees as a geyser of water and concrete dust shoots into the air. John begins to run towards the nearest of the towers. Gilmore runs after him, shouting questions lost in the roar as the river's flow suddenly surges, white water swirling and smashing around boulders. Then with a dull rumble the dam, weakened by the explosion, gives way. A wall of water and debris pours down the valley, smashing into trees, swirling around the towers. The base of one of the towers nearest the dam crumbles under the impact and the tower drops straight down into the tawny water.

When John and Gilmore reach the nearest tower, the flood is swirling around their waists. It rises rapidly, chasing them up the narrow steps of the helical staircase. John stumbles and is almost dragged down, but Gilmore grabs him under his arms and pushes him on. The worst of the flood is already subsiding. They walk around and around the stairs, lit by beams of sunlight that strike through narrow window slits, and climb out onto the platform that crowns the top of the tower.

They are fifty metres above ground, their clothes soaked through and steaming in the hot sunlight. John is shaking with reaction. He has banged up his left knee, and sits with his feet dangling over the edge of the big round platform while Gilmore paces the perimeter of the tower, talking into his phone. Below, muddy water filled with the debris of broken trees chases around the feet of the towers. The screens flicker eerily underwater, still showing the loop of the alien hunt. Downstream, the big tent has vanished, washed away by the tidal wave. Ambulances and RVs are smashed up against trees and boulders. People are shouting to each other, their voices small and distant. A dog barks and barks and barks. Upstream, a diminishing spout of water pours through the gash in the dam's white crescent.

Gilmore folds away his phone and says flatly, "You know."

"I'm not sure..."

"You'd better tell me, mister. I'm not sure how many of my people have been hurt, and I know for a fact my five hundred dollar boots are fucked."

"I know what we used to do. We imitated as many of the aliens' overt behavioral patterns as we could—the flocking dances, the so-called aerial combat rituals, the hunting of certain slave species. Michio insisted that these would encode the aliens' mythic impulses, just as Mircea Eliade theorized that true human myths were codifications of shamanistic rituals, rituals which narrate the creative activity of supernatural beings and constitute the paradigm of all significant human acts. Michio wanted us to think like aliens, and for a while it seemed to work. But I think he was wrong."

Madness overtook the colony when enactment became reality, but John cannot bring himself to tell Gilmore about that. It would implicate him in murder. Gilmore is staring hard at him, and he looks away. He says, "I think all this happened for a reason. I don't think the people who were killed were running away. They were hunted down."

John has a sudden memory of riding a hang-glider in the strong thermals above the cliffs downriver, swooping towards prey clumsily splashing through water. The muscles in his arms spasm; dizziness almost makes him topple over the edge of the platform. He scrambles back, shaking, his gorge rising in his throat. His hands have become fists; his nails are dug into his palms.

Gilmore says, "It happened before, didn't it? They hunted you. Or wait, fuck. You had to have surgery after you left. You were one of the hunters."

"All of the dead were slaves," John says. "That's why they weren't modified. That's why the TV pictures—"

He stands up and points, because a hang-glider has dropped away from the crag above the broken dam and is swooping towards the tower.

Gilmore turns and says, "Son of a bitch," and snaps open his shoulder holster and pulls out a little automatic pistol. He braces himself as the hang-glider rushes straight at him, manages to get off two shots. Then the hang-glider's shadow looms overhead and the pilot swings in his harness and rakes Gilmore from neck to belly with his clawed feet. Gilmore spins around and topples backwards off the platform, a surprised expression on his face.

John lunges after him, but he is already gone, and the hang-glider is circling back. John waits, every thought cleanly erased by shock, as the hang-glider drops towards the platform at a steep, stalling angle, the pilot running forward two or three paces and shucking his harness, the hang-glider's white diamond tipping up behind him.

"The prodigal returns," the pilot says.

It is Michio, of course, but so transfigured that John knows him only by his voice. Hairless and starveling thin, ribcage expanded with a lattice of bones sharply defined against the leathery skin, folds of skin linking arms to hips, arms and legs extended to inhuman proportions, fingers and toes armed with thick, curving talons. Only the eyes, embedded in the bone-white mask of the face, are human.

"Why did you do it?" John's hands are raised defensively, and it takes a conscious effort to lower them.

Michio's eyes show amusement. It is difficult not to think of him wearing a mask: the mask that is his face. He towers over John. He says, "I could not let them be taken away. The rebirthing was not complete."

"And the flood has completed it? You'll have drowned them all."

"Better that than allow them to be taken away before the transformation is complete. But I doubt they've drowned. They're in sleep so deep they can survive without breathing for quite a while. Water is life, John. That was one of the first things we learned. Why did the FBI bring you here? Are you a judas goat come to lead me to slaughter?"

"They didn't know if you were amongst the dead."

"Only a few died, John. Those unworthy. The true believers merely sleep, and in their sleep they will ascend to the next stage."

"They're brain dead."

"They will rise again. They will carry on my work."

Michio steps past John with a curious gait forced upon him by the disproportionate length of his thigh bones. He looks down at the flood. The setting sun casts his shadow a long way down the valley. He turns and says, "I have learned so much since you left, John. We have become so close to them now, and the rebirth will be the final stage."

"Your methods are...flawed. Everything you've done here is tainted because you are human. You change the body, but you can't change the mind, you can't change the structures of the brain that underpin consciousness."

"You're wrong, of course," Michio says lightly. "That's why you were forced out of our garden, but you've obviously been rationalizing it."

"I left."

"You failed and fell. But you have returned, and perhaps you can earn my forgiveness."

"If I'd known you were alive," John says, "I wouldn't have come at all."

He always knew that Michio was mad, but he did not allow himself to understand it until that awful day when the colony divided itself into hunters and hunted, masters and slaves.

He says, as steadily as he can, "The only success we had was to merge a little of the alien with all that makes us human. But the human is stronger—it always will be. You've changed your appearance, but not the neuronal wiring that underpins your self.

This flood is a primal human mythic symbol, the submergence of the old in a brief return of primal chaos, followed by reemergence and regeneration."

"No." Michio is still amused. John hopes it is a good sign. "It is a fundamental ritual of the aliens. I played it out on the screen for you, but you do not understand."

"We can't know what it means. We never did learn anything. They could be killing those slaves who by planting the fields have learned some forbidden secret about the crops. Or they could be simply culling excess workers once the work is done. There are a hundred explanations. We can't know which one is right."

"When you've lived as we have lived," Michio says, "you would know which is right. You would be transfigured, as I am transfigured. I faced death, John, and was reborn."

"Like every mythic hero. Don't you see? Your story isn't alien. It's human."

Michio cocks his head and looks off into the empty blue sky. He says, "I've done things you can never imagine. People don't understand the true nature of alien TV. They merely mine it for technology, or treat it as mindless entertainment. But I've looked deeper than anyone else. I've seen what it really means, John. There's a great and terrible beauty waiting to be born." He turns, the bone-white mask unreadable. "The survivors are regrouping. Time to go, I think."

For a terrible moment, John thinks that Michio means to kill him. But Michio steps past and shrugs into the straps of the hang-glider. "Tell them," he says, and runs straight over the edge of the platform.

John shouts after him, but Michio is already stooping low and fast over the flood, drawing a ragged fusillade from the surviving FBI agents. Then he catches a thermal from the southern side of the valley and begins to rise, turning and turning, rising above the tallest of the towers and still rising high into the darkening sky, lost in the glare of the setting sun as the helicopter clatters over the ridge to the north. John sees the sharpshooter leaning in his harness at the helicopter's open door, and turns away. He does not want to see Michio's last fall.

When he looks back, the helicopter is the only thing in the sky, the roar of its rotors echoing off the towers. John strips off the bulletproof vest and flaps it over his head and as the helicopter turns to him he wonders if Michio might have grasped some kind of hidden truth after all. Perhaps alien TV is slowly and subtly changing the human psyche in ways yet unforeseen. He wonders whether the colonists will awaken from their comas as Michio has promised. And if they wake, how will they have been transfigured by their long sleep? He wonders what kind of world his daughter will live in. And wonders what kind of story he will tell his rescuers.

A VERY BRITISH HISTORY

I t's about time someone produced a proper history of the space race. After all, here we are in this year 2001, with two permanent colonies on the Moon, and outposts on Mars, Mercury, and the moons of Jupiter and Saturn. Not to mention close to a hundred low Earth orbit factories, hotels, laboratories, and solar power farms, and the even dozen habitats orbiting the L5 point between Earth and the Moon. Why, at the Aldermaston Jet Propulsion Laboratories they're building the first robotic interstellar probes, and blueprints for multi-generation arks capable of transporting colonists to new Earths around other suns are already on the drawing boards. We've had plenty of readable, thoughtful but rapidly dated pieces of space boosterism by enthusiasts like Clarke and Asimov and Sagan. We've had far too many dry-as-dust official histories written by committees, and a plethora of self-serving, ghostwritten autobiographies by minor rocket scientists and second-string astronauts. We've had more than enough heavyweight commentaries by the likes of C.P. Snow, Norman Mailer, and Gore Vidal, which, although ostensibly about the first men on the Moon or the Second American Revolution or the race for the outer system, are really about the authors' egos and hangups. And we've certainly had enough quickie pieces of crap knocked up from press releases by sci-fi hacks and penny ante journos, and more than enough half-baked manifestos cranked out by greedy shills masquerading as space-age messiahs (I can dig George Adamski's for-real craziness, and chortled my way through Baudrillard's *The Space Race Did Not Happen*, but *L. Ron Hubbard*?).

Yes, it's about time that we had a proper history of space colonisation by a real historian: rigorous, heavily researched, determinedly fair-minded, leavened with some cerebral wackiness, and big enough to do some serious damage if you dropped it on your foot, even here on the Moon. A capstone to the first instalment of space exploration. Of course, it could only have been written by a Brit.

So here it is, Professor Sir William Coxton's *A Brief History of the Colonisation of Space* (University of Oxford Press, 858 pp (with another cccxxvi pages of appendices, references and an exhaustive index), £75.00). And I'm very pleased to tell you that, despite the dry semi-detached style, for someone like me, who lived through part of this, it's the Real Deal. It makes you kind of proud to be in it, even if not much more than a footnote (page 634 if you're interested).

But I should warn you that despite appearing to bend over backward to be fair-minded, Sir Bill is never shy of elevating the contributions of his own country above those of the States and the former Soviet Union whenever the opportunity arises, as might be expected from someone who has, after all, benefited from the touch of the Queen's sword on his shoulder. Sir Bill isn't an actual aristo, having been born into a coal-mining family in a Yorkshire village which is, as far as I can make out, more like one of the hard-scrabble towns in Kentucky than the landscaped acres of some ancestral pile. But like a lot of heavyweight Brit academics, he's far more pro-establishment than most of the actual establishment, and despite the many hours he spent in the archives, and the many more hours he spent interviewing the surviving principals of the keynote dramas (he even wasted a couple of hours talking to yours truly), he's prone to a certain partiality.

As shown by the fact that he doesn't begin his story in the usual places—Tsiolkovski's schoolroom, Goddard's machined fireworks—but with the race for Peenemünde at the end of WW2. Sir Bill is famous for his theories on hinge points in history, and has edited a fat book of counterfactual essays in which historians imagined what might have happened if, for instance, that ur-student radical Gavrilo Princip's revolver shots had missed Archduke Ferdinand and his wife in Sarajevo in 1914. And here he spends a lot of time arguing that, as far as the space race is concerned, the capture of the Nazi rocket scientists is the crucial hinge point in the history of space exploration. In fact, he's so consumed by this notion that he wastes a whole chapter specu-lating about what would have happened if the Brits didn't get there first. But I'm not going to depress us all by arguing the details of Sir Bill's imaginary account of the failures of nerve, the overriding requirements of the military-industrial complexes of the USA and the former Soviet Union, and the political, budgetary and managerial blunders that might have aborted NASA's exploration of the Moon and prematurely curtailed the slower but in many ways more ambitious Russian space program. After all, none of that actually happened, and even if the US army had managed to get to Peenemünde before the Brits, it still might not have happened. In the end, I'm pretty sure that Sir Bill's coun-terfactual is just one more of his ploys to convince us all that only the Brits were fit to be the first true space pioneers.

So we can skip all that theoretical gloom with a clear conscience, and get our teeth into the meat of the book. The story of the British army's capture of Peenemünde has been told many times before, but Sir Bill spices his account with an extensive reimagining from the point of view of a certain Sergeant Stapledon, who claims to have led the mission and who remained to his death (Sir Bill interviewed him ten years ago) sorely pissed off that he was written out of history by his superiors. It's exciting, full of hectic detail, and permeated with the intricacies of the British class system (Sergeant Stapledon was, like Sir Bill, a committed socialist, and ignored the order of the day because he despised his officers as effete fops).

It was because of Stapledon's initiative, Sir Bill claims, that the space age began in the ruins of Europe at the end of the Second World War, when the Brits won the race to capture the secrets of the V-2 bunkers. Winston Churchill cannily arranged a swap of a few of the debriefed German personnel and a number of V-2s for American atomic technology, while spiriting much equipment, several half-completed V-3s, and a large contingent of technicians led by the formidable Werhner Von Braun, to the new rocket ranges at Woomera in the Australian outback. One of Churchill's last acts before the postwar election was to secure the future of the Woomera facility by encouraging engineering luminaries such as Barnes Wallis, Christopher Cockerel, and Frank Whittle to work with the Germans and, in Churchill's words, "extend the British ideal of freedom and fair play towards the stars". What he was about, of course, was building a new British Empire.

The next half dozen chapters dig deep into the crazy stiff-upper-lipped heroics of early Brit space pioneers, who defied death atop barely tested rockets for the glory of King and Country. Sir Bill is no sentimentalist, but it's easy to detect a sneaking admiration for those rocket boys in his account, which in taut, laconic prose captures the reckless mood of volunteers who, like Battle-of-Britain Spitfire pilots, made almost inevitable death seem like no more than an awfully big adventure: boys who could never grow up. The most famous of them all, Maurice Gray, now retired and tending his beehives and rose garden in Devon, still sounds like a fey mix of Peter Pan and Christopher Robin, a boy laughing lightly at inconceivable death, the British version of a zen master.

These were necessary heroics. While the Russians were racing to launch the first satellite, using big chemical multistage rockets designed by their own native genius, the legendary Chief Engineer, Sergei Korolev, and the Americans were developing a military space program centred on the X-series rocketships, the British were concentrating on true manned space flight. The first man to ascend beyond the tropopause, to a height of more than twenty miles, was sixteen-year-old Maurice Gray, in a helium balloon in 1955; he also broke the current airspeed record by breaking the sound barrier when he plummeted nineteen miles back to Earth in free fall before opening his parachute. This was quickly followed by several suborbital lobs of RAF volunteers atop modified V-3s in 1956 and 1957, but after several fatal crashes of the two stage A.20, British scientists became dissatisfied with mere chemical rockets and decided to develop a more powerful atomic technology, despite a couple of hair-raising (and hitherto suppressed) accidents which could have rendered most of Australia uninhabitable for a thousand years.

Meanwhile, the Russians were the first to orbit a satellite in 1957, swiftly following that with a capsule containing a dog, and then a capsule containing a man, and with the X-20 the American Air Force developed a reusable chemically powered space plane which achieved orbit in 1960. But even as the two superpowers vied for military and political supremacy in Earth orbit, Britain's space program looked further, developing a reusable space ship using the highly advanced White Streak atomic motor, whose power both the Russians and the Americans grievously underestimated. In July 1962, two Brit scientists, Savage and Kingston, landed on the Moon, where they spent an entire Lunar day, two weeks, exploring and collecting rocks before returning to a hero's welcome.

The American government's space program remained strictly military. But the brilliant and ruthless entrepreneur Delos Harriman, spurred on by the British example, started a commercially funded space program in the States, and in 1970 finally reached the Moon using conventional multistage chemical boosters. Sir Bill's account of Harriman's achievement is curiously muted; it's clear he doesn't think much of the Yankee mix of rabid capitalism and pioneer individualism. And of course the British, using their atomic technology, had already reached Mars in 1968—here, drawing upon extensive interviews with the protagonists, Sir Bill deftly improves upon Patrick Moore's classic account, in *Mission to Mars*, of how the first expedition was stranded because the motor of their craft was damaged on landing, and of how they survived for a year before a second expedition rescued them.

With the Moon and Mars secured by the British government and American free enterprise, the Russians turned their attention to the inner solar system. Only recently, after the fall of the communist state, has the tragic fate of the first manned expedition to Venus been revealed. No one who has heard the recordings will forget the screams of the two unlucky cosmonauts as their descent capsule was cooked and crushed in Venus's infernal atmosphere. There's no derring-do here: only horror. What had been intended as a coup de theatre to trump the British expedition to Mars became a tragedy which was hastily covered over, and Sir Bill has cannily exploited the recent openness of the new Russian government to secure at first hand accounts of the Venus disaster. The first Russian landing on Mercury, four years later, in 1972, was of course more successful, establishing solar powered robot mining facilities and a rail gun which within a year began to launch back to Earth packages of refined precious metals, immensely enriching the Russian economy, and starting in earnest the race to commercially exploit the Solar System.

By this time the British had established a permanent colony on the Moon, and a dozen expeditions were exploring her surface in powerful tractors. Early space suits, which had borrowed their design from deep sea diving outfits, heavily armoured and with pincers instead of gloves, had given way to more comfortable suits based on the indestructible cloth invented by Sidney Stratton, with integral life support backpacks instead of heavy metal air cylinders. There was also a semipermanent scientific station on

Mars. After the disappointment that the fabulous canals of Lowell had been no more than optical illusions and wishful thinking, the British Geological Society was busily exploring vast canyons, craters, and volcanoes, and drilling deep for signs of life in the Martian crust. In 1977, to celebrate the Queen's Jubilee, a British climbing expedition planted the Union Jack on top of Mount Elizabeth, the largest volcano in the solar system.

All of this was no longer under the control of the military, but was funded by a mixture of public subscription, commercial money (especially from the BBC's Relay Chain satellite network), and money earned by transporting material for American and Russian projects—just as in the old British Empire, the new colonies were largely self-funding. Meanwhile, British atomic-powered space ships were carrying out the first surveys of the moons of Jupiter and Saturn. Life was discovered in Europa's salty sub-ice ocean in 1982; the first expedition landed, if that's the right word for a descent to a surface covered in liquid ethane, on Titan in 1988.

While British expeditions are bringing back treasures to the Science Museum, and the British government has built an extensive spaceport in Ceylon to service almost daily flights to Earth orbit and the Moon, the official US space program is still recovering from the political and economic fallout of the Second American Revolution. The Lunar colony founded by Harriman's company had been taken over by the feds in 1977, and used as a dumping ground for dissidents after Nixon was elected to his third term as president. In 1979, a revolt by the imprisoned dissidents led to the foundation of the Lunar Republic and the fall of the Nixon government after a brief bombardment of the American mainland with rocks launched by the Lunar rail gun. Sir Bill's account of the revolt, the former Lunar prison's declaration of independence and the brief war, quite rightly highlights the way mainstream history (heavily influenced by Heinlein's colorful but disapproving popular account in *The Moon is a Harsh Mistress*, whose claims that libertarian heroes were suppressed by evil socialist radicals and drug-crazed hippies would be pitiful if they weren't, thanks to the movie version, still so widely held) has unfairly dismissed the discreet but vital help given by the British Lunar colonists to the former prisoners. For as this writer can affirm from personal experience, the phlegmatic Brit scientists were surprisingly sympathetic to us hepcat hippie rebels.

After the revolution, some of the rebels, including William Burroughs and Jack Kerouac, chose to return to Earth, but this wasn't, as Sir Bill claims, a split in our ranks, merely a natural shake-down amongst a bunch of highly creative and mostly anarchic individuals. Many others, including Ken Kesey, Allen Ginsberg, Neil Cassady, Tom Hayden and Noam Chomsky, stayed on to found a new republic that attempted to marry the artistic impulses of many of its members with the technology required for survival. Very soon, we in the New Lunar Utope became expert at building habitats from scratch, and furnishing them with self-sufficient closed ecosystems; something we developed by ourselves by the way, despite Sir Bill's crude hints that we were dependent on British expertise. It just wasn't so, Bill: we had to learn to develop efficient closed-loop systems quickly or perish, and as this veteran of Ken Kesey's magic bus tour of the Martian highlands can affirm from personal experience, it was all down to good old Yankee ingenuity.

After the fall of Nixon and the election of Ronald Reagan, detente with the Russians swiftly followed, and the end of the Cold War has led to a welcome diversion of funding from the US military space program to the construction of habitats and factories and solar power farms in Earth orbit and at the L5 point between Earth and the Moon. It's a healthy sign, surely, that the habitats are not the transplanted whitebread suburbias of NASA's drawing boards, but are designed by the New Lunar Utope as diverse multicultural centres for any artistic and scientific community which can afford the one-way ticket out of Earth's gravity well.

Meanwhile, the Russians have consolidated their exploitation of the vast resources of Mercury and have begun to mine many near-Earth asteroids. After the fall of communism, Mercury declared itself an independent republic, and dozens of mining communities scattered through the asteroid belt have declared their autonomy too. Sir Bill's explication of the political links between the former Soviet mining stations and the Free Lunar Utope is enjoyably disapproving. He's forced to admit that the British hegemony is now strongly compromised by plans to extend the alliance to the outer reaches of the Solar System by sling-shotting seed colonies past Venus towards the newly discovered planetoids of the Kuiper Belt, and his speculation that the Free Lunar Utope and the Autonomous Space Republics have transformed the comet fragment Neo-8 into a multi-generation starship aimed at Tau Ceti reeks of panicky paranoia.

It's understandable that the Brits are nervous. It turns out that the bustling Solar System hasn't become the new British Empire after all, and it's natural that they don't want their tremendous investment in the first robot interstellar probes—due to be launched within the next two years toward the eight extra-solar systems with Earth-like planets discovered by the Newton space telescope on the far side of the Moon—to be upstaged. But hey, whatever happens, and here I'm in complete agreement with Sir Bill, we can only look back fondly and admiringly on the writings of the first prophets of the Space Age, and marvel at how timid their once outrageously optimistic predictions now seem. Let a thousand flowers bloom!

CROSS ROADS BLUES

The first time Turner heard Robert Johnson play was to a vast crowd in Washington, D.C., December 5th 1945, the night the desegregation bill went through, and just three weeks before Johnson was assassinated. The second time was on what was supposed to be a routine archive trip, June 3rd 1937, a jook joint just outside the little Mississippi town of Tallula, and it was something else.

Afterwards, Turner hung around outside, an anonymous still point in the crowd that, slow as molasses, dispersed into the hot dark night. The music still thrilled in his blood. Songs he'd known only as ghosts in the crackle of a few badly worn 78s or as no more than titles in charred files from the fire-bombed office of an obscure record company had one after the other ripped through the heat and noise of the crowded juke joint, so much sound from one man and one guitar, driving the whoops and pounding feet of the dancers, that Turner doubted his state-of-the-art Soviet recorder had been able to capture one tenth of the reality. Turner had once played a little guitar himself, enough to know that what the old bluesmen said about Robert Johnson was true. Even before the New York concerts, the years in prison on a trumped-up murder charge, his letters and his protest songs, the Freedom Marches and the Segregation Riots, near-canonization after his assassination, he had been the best of them all.

The hard little capsule planted under the skin beneath Turner's collarbone, where the grain of Americium hung suspended in its Oppenheimer pinch, tingled. He should have cut out and closed the Loop when Robert Johnson had finished his set. Get in, do the job, get out. Don't give the paradoxes any chance. But Turner had heard raw truths in Johnson's songs; for the first time since he'd been brought home after the Peace Corps had been disbanded, he felt alive again. Before he closed the Loop, he wanted to meet the man whose music had cut him deep.

The sandy yard and dark road in front of the jook joint were empty now; only Turner and three men sitting on the sagging porch were left. The men, all in various degrees of drunkenness, were passing around a chipped enamel jug in the yellow light of a couple of kerosene lanterns, talking in low voices and glancing sidelong at the stranger in the dark suit (it hung oddly around Turner, and the suspenders which held up the trousers were gouging his shoulders), clean white shirt (soaked in sweat), and polished two-tone shoes (which pinched like hell). He strolled over to them, casual as he could, wondering if one of them was the man whose recollections about Robert Johnson, told to a field researcher in some twenty years time, had brought him here. His pulse in his throat, his mouth dry, he asked where Robert Johnson was.

One of them said, "He out back somewhere."

Another added, "With a woman. Comes to women, Bobby Johnson's like a snake in a henhouse."

The third wanted to know who was asking. Turner gave his cover story of being a talent scout, named a large New York record company. It was sort of true.

The man, burly and barechested under bib overalls, fixed a mean look on Turner. "Never heard of no gentleman of color working for no record company before."

"Bobby Johnson, he already done got himself a deal," the first man said. He was the oldest of the three, his face a map of wrinkles like drying mud, his eyeballs yellow as ivory, his nappy hair salt and pepper. He peered at Turner and said, "You got yourself seventy-five cents, Mr New York, you can walk into Mr Willis's dry goods store tomorrow and buy a record of his 'Terraplane Blues'."

The second man, skinny and mournful, said, "I heard he been on the radio in Detroit, singin spirituals. Shit, he been round this country a couple three times now."

"Race records are a big thing in New York," Turner said, already in deeper than he'd intended. "That's why we're very interested in Robert Johnson."

"What they know bout the blues in New York?" the old man said. "You go tell your boss that down here is the rightful home of the blues, no place else. Why, I play harmonica myself. I get the blues real bad sometimes."

The mournful man said, "Bobby Johnson, he got 'em worse of all."

"He got a mojo hand, no mistake," the old man said, and drank from the enamel jug and smacked his lips.

"They say ol Legba gave the boy a lesson in the blues, in exchange for his soul," the mournful man said, and there was a hush as if an angel had passed overhead.

The old man took another drink and said, "Well I don't know if that be true, but I do know one time Bobby Johnson couldn't play a lick to save himself. I got the story straight from Son House. Bobby Johnson, he could play harmonica right enough, but he was always fixin after playin gitar. Hung out every joint and dance and country picnic there was, pesterin the players to give him a chance, but he was so bad it wasn't even funny. Anyhow, he went away maybe a year, and I don't know if he went to the crossroads with ol Legba or not, but Son House told me when he came back he was carryin a gitar, and asked for a spot like old times. Well, Son was about ready to take a break, and told

Bobby Johnson to go ahead and got himself outside before the boy began. But that time it was all changed. That time, he tol me, the music he heard Bobby Johnson make put the hair on his head to standin.'"

It had the air of a story told many times. There was a silence, and then the mournful man said, "He near to burnt down the place tonight, and that's the truth."

The old man said, "Son House tol me Bobby Johnson tol him a man called Ike Zimmerman taught him how to play, but what truth's in that I don't rightly know."

Turner, whose first name was Isaac, felt an airy thrill.

The burly man in the bib coveralls hauled himself to his feet, using as a support one of the posts that propped up the corrugated tin roof that sloped above the porch. He pointed at Turner and said, "You fools tell this stranger whatever's on your minds, an you don't know who he is."

"He tol you he scouting talent, Jake," the old man said. He told Turner, "You come on down to Mr Willis's dry goods store tomorrow, Mister New York, I show you stuff on the harmonica you ain't never before heard."

"He ain't no scout," the burly man said. "He got the look of the law about him." He came down the steps towards Turner, a mean glint in his eyes.

"I'm just passing through," Turner said, and raised his hand to his chest, ready to collapse the Oppenheimer Pinch if he had to.

"Don't pull no gun on me," the burly man said, half-angry, half-fearful, and swung clumsily at Turner and turned halfway around and sat down with comic suddenness.

The door of the jook joint opened. Yellow light fell across the yard. A slightly-built man in a chalk-stripe suit stepped out, a guitar slung across his back, a fedora tilted on his head. It was Robert Johnson. He looked directly at Turner and said, "Why, Isaac. You come back. I always wondered if you would."

⛢

Robert Johnson soon disengaged himself from the three hangers-on, refusing a drink from the enamel jug but somehow acquiring a crumpled pack of cigarettes. He took a long swallow from a half-pint bottle of whiskey he took from his jacket pocket, and passed it to Turner. The bootleg whiskey was as raw as his songs. Turner managed not to cough, passed the bottle back, and Robert Johnson took another swallow and lit a cigarette and held it jauntily in the corner of his mouth. "Well all right," he said with satisfaction, and exhaled a riffle of smoke.

They stood in the warm dark, looking at the lights of the little town across a rough pasture where the unfathomable codes of fireflies winked on and off amongst the weeds.

Robert Johnson said, "When I saw you back there, Ike? Thought for a moment I'd been wrong all along about who you were. Thought you were the devil after all, come for my poor soul."

He spoke with the grave care of the profoundly drunk, although he didn't look drunk at all.

"I'm not who you think I am," Turner said.

"You're not no devil, that for sure. Never forgot what you taught me, Ike, and never did figure out why you did it. One of the boys on the porch said you were a talent scout. That just a line you spinnin, or you in some other business now?"

"I just came to hear you play."

"I was good, wasn't I?"

"Better than I'll ever be."

"I learnt a lot from you, Ike, and I'm still learning. That barrelhouse shake-up ain't nothing to my best. I got stuff that'll put some real upset in your backbone. Tomorrow, when I'm not so drunk as I am now, I want to play them for you."

There was nothing Turner would have liked better. He said, "I have to move on tonight."

"Yeah? Maybe I come along with you."

"That really isn't possible."

"It ain't?" Robert Johnson looked sideways at Turner when he didn't reply. "I guess you don't have to tell me where you goin or where you been. You look good though, Ike. Not a year older. Me, I been through some bad times and some good times. I lost me two good women and a baby, I travelled all over this land like a vagabond, I been in jail, I been ridden out on a rail, but I got my singing put down on record, and I'm fixin now to be famous."

"I heard some of it in your songs."

"Got to tell it in my songs. Got no other way."

Robert Johnson drew on his cigarette. His fingers were so long they seemed to run back to his wrist. Under his sharply creased suit, his white shirt was open down to his navel. He looked both easy and dangerous.

He said, "I get to thinkin sometimes that there's somethin missing in them, maybe I need to make the beat better. Not just louder, but more insistent. I remember when I was a little kid, down around Banks, the cotton fields there? Way the croppers sang the old worksongs as they picked. I try to put that in, but my ol gitar ain't enough."

Turner shrugged. He was inside something so deep he didn't know which way was up.

Robert Johnson laughed. "I guess them ol days are gone, teacher. I guess I got to figure my own way now. But it's hard, you know? Sometimes the days just run by me, it seems, can't seem to catch hold of anythin lasting."

"Your songs will last," Turner said. It was true, but none of the songs Robert Johnson had sung tonight were the songs he'd be remembered for.

"Maybe so." Robert Johnson said it softly, and exhaled a last riffle of smoke into the dark air. He took a swig of whiskey and said, "You heard I got recorded? It could happen again, if I can get me to Dallas in a couple of weeks."

"You'll be there."

Turner's colleague, Bill Frankel, would be there too, aiming his equipment at a warehouse room above a Buick showroom that had been made over into a makeshift recording studio.

There was the sound of a car approaching, muffled in the humid night air; off across the dark fields, headlights pricked the night. Someone on the jook joint's porch said, "Shit, here comes ol Sheriff Wiley, looking to see if we wants trouble."

"I have to go," Turner said. The last thing he needed was a policeman asking him what he was doing with a tape recorder that wouldn't be built for thirty years.

"Believe I'll fade too," Robert Johnson said. "Real nice seein you this one more time, Ike, and I'm wonderin if you can help me out here. I got so busy with a lady friend I missed gettin paid, I'll have to wait til mornin, and I done spent the money people put in my gitar on this good whiskey we shared. Meanwhile me and my lady friend are lookin for a room to stay, only we lacks the necessary you understand..."

)(

Turner gave Robert Johnson all that was left of the little money he'd been issued and walked a little way into the dark field and used his magnet to disrupt the Oppenheimer pinch. The flash decay of the grain of Americium caught inside the pinch, an element that wouldn't exist until it was created by the Fermi Lab's cyclotron in the late '50s, was the hook by which the Loop machinery reeled him back from still-segregated mid-Depression Mississippi to 1963.

Washington, D.C., early spring, the Potomac pewter in rain-dulled light, cold rain drifting across the Mall's acres of grass, hanging heavy on the blossoms of the cherry trees and clinging to uniforms of the marching bands that were practising beneath them. Nearly thirty years separated the ends of the Loop: it might have been a thousand. In 1963 there were two African Americans in the Supreme Court, a dozen in the Senate, more than fifty in

Congress. The president of Harvard was African American; so was the Secretary of the Interior and the commander of the US Army Air Force Corps. And the first African American President, Adam Clayton Powell, was in the White House. Hastily sworn in on a plane a year ago, after Kennedy had been shot at the beginning of his campaign at a second term, all his dreams of a newer stronger America, an America that finally would count in the world, spilling out with his brains on the tiles of that kitchen in the Ambassador Hotel while his widow knelt over him in a cross-fire of flashguns. Powell was a good man, no question, and the first African American President counted for something any way you looked at it. But Powell was more interested in expanding the Welfare and Federal Work program budgets than the international scene. Kennedy's finest legacy, the Peace Corps, had been suspended—feed our brothers and sisters in Harlem, in Watts, in Roxbury, white and black and coffee-coloured, and their children will be strong enough to really help the world, Powell had said— and that was what had brought Turner back from the refugee camps in Madagascar to his old job as a Loop rider, held open for him since he'd dropped out two years before.

Most of Turner's friends thought that he spoke out against Powell's policies because he resented the disbanding of the Peace Corps; only a few knew that he had always been an interventionist, that his father had died in Mexico in '49 during the disintegration of the support of the Christian Democrat guerillas against the Marxist government, twenty thousand Americans lost and Turner's father one of them. America had a chance to become a world power during the Mexican revolution and had blown it, and now it looked like it would never come round again. For all her size and wealth, America was a sleepy backwater compared to the British Empire or the Communist Axis. Powell seemed set on making sure that was all she ever would be.

Turner deposited his recordings and underwent debriefing with Bill Frankel and the rest of the team. He didn't mention that he had waited to meet Johnson, and never talked to anyone about that mysterious encounter. Robert Johnson had known him, yet before that moment they had never met. It could be that later on Turner would Loop to some earlier part of the singer's life, but there was no point in worrying about the way the future could tangle with the past, and so Turner tried to set the mystery aside. If it had happened it would happen, that was the way it was, no use brooding over it.

Spring wore into summer. Turner Looped to pre-earthquake San Francisco to gather data for someone studying immigration patterns and interracial tensions, got beaten up by a gang of Chinese, and was put on light duties while he recovered. But he chaffed at doing background work in the Smithsonian's musty stacks. He was a rider, not a historian, and besides, the old restlessness which had prompted him to join the Peace Corps had been awakened by Robert Johnson's music. So he took a month's vacation and spent it at the family farm, mowing the fields which his stubborn but frail mother should really give up. When he came back, the first person to knock on his office door was Bill Frankel, bearing half a dozen LP records. They were the transcribed recordings of early period Robert Johnson, Turner's own jook joint recording amongst them.

The LPs were newfangled '33s, and Bill Frankel had a little trouble setting up the record player he'd brought along to play them. A wiry man the same age as Turner, with a shock of prematurely grey hair, he had been promoted to team leader while Turner had been with the Peace Corps, and was still unsure how to treat his old colleague. He hardly said a word as he fussed with the balance of the player's complicated tone-arm, and Turner smoked two cigarettes and looked out of the window at the office workers sunbathing away their lunch break on the Mall's browning grass, suddenly and unaccountably nervous.

"I think we're about ready," Frankel said at last. "All in all it turned out very well, except for the attempt to bug the second hotel session."

"You used what, infrared vibratometry?"

"The first time it was fine. The second, 1937, drapes were drawn across the windows to keep out the noise of the traffic, and the sound was too muffled for anything but lyric transcription. Columbia want to put out some of the recordings, did I tell you that?"

"Really? That's good, Frankel. Who gets the money?"

"Not me, unfortunately. The Smithsonian, and Robert Johnson's relatives. I have a release I need you to sign later. But now: hush."

Crackle and hiss, the sudden loud noises of a crowd, handclaps and foot stamping, a fiercely-strummed guitar sounding like a barrelhouse piano and slapped bass all in one, a strong high clear voice carrying over this furious rhythm, singing about feeling around on the floor for his shoes, feeling he got those old walking blues.

And Turner was back in the jook joint with its garish murals animated by the reeling light of kerosene lanterns that swayed above the bobbing heads of the dancers, standing at the front of the feverish crowd, watching Robert Johnson in his shirt-sleeves, eyes closed as he sang and hollered, slashed and hammered at his guitar. He came to himself only when his forgotten cigarette stung his fingers and he dropped it on the office's institutional carpet.

Robert Johnson's first session of that lost night, more than twenty minutes long, took up all of one side of the LP.

Bill Frankel smiled as he flipped the black disc over. "He was something else, right?"

"Oh yes..." And Turner said no more; Bill Frankel had lowered the needle to the groove, and Robert Johnson sang out again.

ж

Columbia Records issued an LP set of Robert Johnson's early songs. Turner bought it and played and replayed it, played the lost songs back to back with the familiar protest songs on which

Johnson had built his fame, the songs which had helped lay the ground for desegregation, the songs hundreds of thousands had sung in unison on Freedom Marches across America, the songs half a million people had sung on the Mall in Washington, D.C. the night the bill for desegregation had gone through. Turner had been six years old. His father had lifted him on to the wide shoulders of his Army greatcoat, where he had swayed above a sea of packed heads receding into darkness and sleet flurries towards the high stage from which Robert Johnson's steely voice rang out…and the next year Turner's father had gone to Mexico and vanished there.

Turner played the lost songs again and again, brooding over them in his two-room apartment, sometimes lost in memory, sometimes trying to figure out why they sounded so much more powerful than the later works. There was the driving beat, and the way Johnson sounded like two or three people playing at once, but that wasn't it, or wasn't it entirely. There was something else, some vital spark the protest songs lacked. A directness, a human nakedness. If the protest songs had relied on familiarity as much as their message (and how many in the crowd that night had dwelt on the words as they sang with Robert Johnson, him elevated on a high stage, alone in crossed spotlights?) how much better would they have sounded if they had the passion of the younger Johnson's songs of failed love and lost salvation?

Einstein had said that it was impossible to change the past, that time's arrow was set in only one direction, fixed and invariant. You did not change the past when you visited it, but became part of its preordained pattern. And no one doubted Einstein, or at least officially, for otherwise the Loop facility would not have been built. But there were plenty of rumors amongst the Loop riders that inadvertent changes had been made, that some small change could tip the momentum of the past into a new course: why else were precautions so stringent, training for the Loop so elaborate? While Turner played and replayed those lost songs, he dreamed of a world where Robert Johnson turned to protest early in his career, becoming part of a movement that urged America to enter the war in Europe and help defeat the Nazis, or at least gave her the resolve for a full commitment to the counterrevolution in Mexico. No debacle, perhaps a world role after all. It was possible. After all, he'd met someone who had changed the world, and hadn't that meeting changed him?

It might have remained a dream, if a group of dissident musicians in Britain hadn't taken up those lost songs, and made them into something new.

Before the year was out, the four members of the group, the Quarrymen, were the most famous men in Britain. They called themselves rock and rollers. Two guitarists, an electric bass player, and a drummer, belting out a crude but vigorous mutation of the rhythm and blues that had been popular in Chicago before the Marches. The music caught fire in the hearts and minds of Britain's disenfranchised youth. For all the British Empire's solidity, for all its wealth, there were millions of unemployed in the Mother country itself, out of work and on the dole because South African and Indian slave labor was so cheap. The Quarrymen's mutated blues articulated their grievances. There were riotous scenes at Quarrymen concerts, and a dozen imitations sprang up to be idolized in turn: Blues Incorporated; Blues by Six; the High Numbers (who quickly changed their name to the Who); Little Boy Blue and the Blues Boys (who just as quickly became the Mannish Boys).

In the States, British rock and roll was available only on incredibly expensive imported discs, but Turner bought everything, even got hold of a bootleg tape of a Quarrymen concert: the audio quality was incredibly poor and the band's playing was all but drowned by the screaming of their fans, but he heard again the electric rawness that he'd responded to when he'd heard Robert Johnson singing in the jook joint outside Tallula. If this transatlantic facsimile could wake Britain's lost generation and begin a cultural revolution that the British government was powerless to stop (too slow to stamp out the movement at birth, its random banning of concerts now seemed petty and foolish), what could the original do? Turner hunted out his old guitar, and knew why Robert Johnson had recognized him that time.

)(

There were only a few times and places where Turner could be sure of meeting the young, untutored Robert Johnson. He lucked out on the first, outside a little town east of Robinsonville in Mississippi, on a humid Saturday afternoon in August 1930.

Someone had thrown a rent party at their shack. It stood on a gullied rise above a sweep of cotton fields, one of dozens straggling along a dirt road: a tin roof, unpainted clapboard walls raised on bricks to keep the termites out. It had rained earlier and promised to rain again, and the shack was packed out; people spilled over the porch, stood around on the muddy ground while Willie Brown and Son House played inside. Others clustered under the big shade tree hung with kerosene lanterns, where hooch was being sold and a mess of pigs' feet was stewing in a big black kettle.

Turner sat on damp grass a ways off. His guitar was with him, in a canvas sack. He'd seen a young Robert Johnson go inside the shack an hour before, knew he'd soon come out humiliated, after having borrowed a guitar from Son House and made a fool of himself. Turner had verified the story from House himself.

He'd been there all day, had plenty of time to wonder at what he was doing. The Loop operator, a friend of Turner's, had been easy enough to bamboozle, but Turner knew that the altered destination would show up in the records. Right at that moment he didn't care. He was here to teach Robert Johnson how to rock and roll. He was here to remake history into something better.

He was so keyed up that he had to keep going off in the bushes to take a leak, and he almost missed the moment when Robert Johnson came down the steps, shouldering through the people with his head down, his swagger broken-backed. Buttoning his

fly, Turner picked up his guitar and headed after the young man as
he set off down the red clay road.

The road curved around the edge of an untidy cemetery;
Turner cut through the crowd of leaning crosses. It was twilight,
and the sky was heavy with purple clouds; a storm was rolling in
from the south like an omen. The road was crossed by another at
the cemetery's far corner, and it was there that Turner caught up
with Robert Johnson, meeting him beneath an old magnolia tree
just as the first heavy drops of rain began to fall.

♓

Four weeks went by, mostly on the road, as Turner taught the
young Robert Johnson the hard-driving rhythmic techniques he
had heard his older counterpart use. Turner was careful to use
only old standards in his teaching, for where would the songs
come from if Robert Johnson learned something Turner had heard
him play? The origin of Turner's adopted name was enough to
give him a headache. He called himself Isaac Zimmerman, of
course, because that was the name of Johnson's legendary teacher.
But who had chosen the name? There was a very young, very
obscure white folk singer by that name in Turner's own
time...but Turner had only found that out because he'd been
trying to trace Robert Johnson's mythical teacher, not realising
that all the time he was on the track of himself.

But there was little time to wonder about metaphysics. While
Turner taught him how to play blues guitar, nineteen-year-old
Robert Johnson taught Turner how to ride the blinds. You could
hitch a ride to almost anywhere on the railroad, Robert Johnson
said, except Alabama. He refused to go there; he said that it was
the land of death.

It seemed half the nation was on the move in those dog days of
the Depression, but even in the hobo jungles, alongside railroad
tracks, in boggy hollows, in junk-filled clearings in shabby
suburban woods, there were always at least two campfires

burning, separate gatherings of black and white. Turner and Robert Johnson sang for their supper, and sometimes white men would hang at the edges of the black encampment, transfixed by the music—but it was not they who fed the musicians.

Four weeks. It was not enough time. Turner managed to teach Robert Johnson the rudiments of his craft, but although the young man was an avid pupil, practising twelve hours a day until his extraordinarily long fingers bled on the strings of the Gibson guitar (which had been Turner's father's, who at that moment was alive and not yet married, and, strange to think, younger than Turner himself), he was still only a shadow of what he would become.

Robert Johnson knew how much he had to learn, and sometimes he would weep in frustration, but he played on while the tears ran down his cheeks, driven by a passion that awed Turner. At nineteen he'd lived through more than men three times his age: he'd had three stepfathers; his wife had died in childbirth. He burned to redeem something from that world of hurt. If only there was enough time, Turner knew he could teach him the brutal rhythms that drove the rock and roll of the Quarrymen; but there was not enough time.

They rode a boxcar into the Big Easy, and Turner spared a few of his antique dollars to pay a week's rent on a room. There was no furniture but a couple of mattresses and a broken chair, and flying roaches big as sparrows emerged after sundown, whirring into walls and smashing into the glass of the lantern. Bobby Johnson was beginning to master his craft, but the city held too many distractions. One night Turner came back to the room to find Bobby and the guitar gone; the young man turned up the next day and admitted he'd pawned the Gibson to get enough money to afford a night in a cathouse.

"I got needs, Mr Zimmerman," he said, his face averted in shy shame, his narrow shoulders hunched. "I got needs same as any man I guess, but sometimes they're just plain stronger than me, and that's the truth."

He was so comically contrite that although Turner was angry he easily forgave the boy. It wasn't a matter of money—Turner carried a dozen gold rings ready for pawning when the need arose—it was the waste of time. He redeemed the ticket on the guitar and told Bobby Johnson he'd done enough practising. It was time he tried working a streetcorner solo, playing the guitar instead of the mouth-harp with which he had, until now, accompanied Turner.

So Robert Johnson made his professional debut as a blues guitarist on a corner of Canal Street in the middle morning of a hot heavy September day. Turner hung about in a storefront across the street, watched the small crowd gather, heard snatches of Bobby Johnson's hard-edged but trembling tenor above the chugging of passing automobiles, the rattle of streetcars. Mostly, the boy stayed close to the small repertoire he'd established, from old time blues like "Heart Made of Stone" and "Stack O'Lee" to newer numbers like "Pony Blues" and "Birmingham Jail," making a stab at a couple of Bing Crosby's latest hits along the way. But a couple of lines floating through the gap between a streetcar and a Model T raised the hairs on the back of Turner's neck, Bobby Johnson singing about a kindhearted woman who studied evil all the time, a stray verse from Robert Johnson's late repertoire, ringing out clear in the muggy heat of that New Orleans morning. It drew Turner from his doorway to the kerb, his heart lifting. And someone pushed through the crowd towards him: it was Bill Frankel, looking incredibly young in a seersucker suit and a wide-brimmed boater, saying, "Come on now, Isaac, I believe it's time to go."

"I'm not done here," Turner said. He was trembling, he didn't know if it was fear or shock. "He isn't much beyond being a good blues singer, and he has to be something else."

"You haven't changed anything yet, Isaac, and we're taking you back before you can. I don't know what you were planning, but it can't be allowed to work."

"If you've been here a while you'll know why," Turner said. He talked too fast, stumbling over words. He knew this would be his only chance to explain himself. "Here and now I'm just another nigger. I could get thrown in jail, just talking to a white man like you here on the street. What I'm doing is bringing the end of segregation closer, ten years ahead of time. When I'm done with Robert Johnson he'll be singing in Carnegie Hall all right, but in just one or two years from now, not ten. And then, when the European War comes, America won't be caught up in civil unrest over desegregation. That'll be over, and everyone will be able to move forward together, help America find its place in the world!"

"America has its place," Frankel said. "And they won't be ready for Robert Johnson in New York until they are ready. Nothing you can do can change that. It's time to close your Loop. More than time."

Turner felt something fly out of him. "I don't suppose you're alone."

Frankel's glasses flashed full of sunlight as he shook his head. "Don't make me call them, Isaac. Let me do this for you."

Frankel steered Turner back into the doorway. He had a magnet in his hand. Just before he clapped it over Turner's Oppenheimer pinch, Turner looked back for a last glimpse of Robert Johnson. But a streetcar was rattling by, and he couldn't even hear the last of the boy's song.

♓

There was a trial, but it was held in camera, and nothing got out to the press. Turner was sentenced to ten years and served his time in an open prison. It wasn't too bad; he adjusted to it with a Loop rider's ease. That's what Loop riders mostly were, not historians or physicists but actors, chameleons. He worked on the farm and had a cell to himself, there was TV and a gymnasium, and the library was well-stocked. Most of the prisoners were white-collar

offenders, spiced with a sprinkling of political prisoners from the
bad old days when Hoover had tried to bring down Kennedy.
Mostly lesser minions—Hoover and his inner circle were
brooding in the high security Army base in Alaska—but there
were two of the notorious "electricians" who had bugged
Kennedy's rendezvous with Marilyn Monroe a few hours before
his assassination, which ill-conceived revelation had caused
Monroe's suicide and finally brought Hoover down.

Turner kept his nose clean and got out after only five years. It
was 1969. His mother had died six months ago; he'd attended the
funeral in handcuffs. The one-time movie actor Ronald Reagan
was in the White House after a landslide victory over Adam
Clayton Powell, who in his second term had been discredited by a
string of sex scandals. The Soviet Republics had made good
Kruschev's boast of landing men on the moon before the decade
was out. The Quarrymen had just split up after their second tour
of the States. Lennon had taken up with a Japanese avant garde
artist and had moved to New York and applied for American citi-
zenship; he said that he was tired of revolution, and that the States
was as good a place for retirement as Eastbourne. On the same
spring day that Turner was released from prison, a general election
in Britain returned the first Labour government in forty years; the
day after his victory, the pipe-smoking premier was photographed
backstage at a rock and roll concert, shaking hands with Paul
McCartney and the members of the Mannish Boys and the Who.

The next day, Turner was sitting in a plush steak restaurant in
Alexandria, the neatly preserved Colonial suburb of Washington,
D.C., talking to an earnest, newly-minted Army captain.

The captain came to the point after they had been served
coffee. "We're very interested in what you tried to do, Mr Turner.
We believe it has great potential. If you can help us, we can help
you. You're still a trained Loop rider. You can operate in the field.
You know the era." Which in his rich mid-Western twang he
pronounced "error".

"Are we talking about the 1930s?"

"We certainly wouldn't want you to go back further than that. There's enough potential for paradoxes already."

The captain had small, deep-set green eyes and a boyish crew cut. His gaze was candid, and his manner was disarmingly frank, but all the same Turner sensed a certain disingenousness. He sipped his cappuccino, enjoying the tang of sprinkled nutmeg, waiting for the man to get to the point. He'd learnt to be patient in prison.

The captain said, "You're not the first person to try to use the Loop in the way you did. To our knowledge there were at least three other unsuccessful attempts."

Turner tried to hide his spark of excitement. "What did they try to do?"

"None of them were as subtle as you. One wanted to change the outcome of the Civil War by building tanks for the Confederacy. He got as far as showing Lee his plans, but fortunately Lee thought he was a madman. And then they caught up with him and closed his Loop." The captain leaned closer. "We don't condone freelance efforts, you understand, but we do think that use of the Loop for nothing more than historical research is an absolute waste of a unique and powerful resource, one we have been trying to exploit since its development. Einstein made a big deal of saying that God does not play dice with the Universe, but he knew that the Loop could be used as a weapon; so did Szilard and Oppenheimer, and they made darn sure that it wouldn't be. It's our edge over the rest of the world, and it is used by academics for trivial reasons. A terrible waste. Ideally, we'd send troops back to Mexico, turn the war right around, but the power expenditure makes it impossible. What you wanted to do, though, now that was interesting."

Mexico. Of course they would know about his father. Turner said, feeling that he was leaning above a great drop, "Who exactly is interested? The Army?"

"America had several chances to take the lead in shaping the world, but they were all squandered, just as the chance to use the Loop for some good has been squandered. My father served in the Expeditionary Force, Mr Turner, in the Marines. He was killed in the retreat, won a posthumous Silver Star because his company held back Rivera long enough for the rest of the 2nd Division to be properly evacuated across the Rio Grande. It wasn't the Army that lost the war, it was a failure of political nerve. Perhaps you don't realize it, but now we have someone in the White House who has more nerve than any we've had since. Oh, I'm not saying Powell was a bad President, but he had no international vision."

"I heard Reagan's speeches, Captain North. We did have TV in prison."

"Then perhaps you heard how he likened America to a shining city on a hill. An ideal we strive towards. An example for all the world. The communists might be able to put a cosmonaut on the Moon, but they still need American grain to feed their people. The sun might not set on the British Empire, but in England they still have slums dating from Queen Victoria's reign. Our country has a vast wealth of natural resources that should be used to enrich Americans, not traded for Soviet computers or British jet airplanes."

"I remember that Reagan said something like that in his inaugural speech. And I remember his speech in *Casablanca*, too, the final scene at the airport. Where he says he's an American, not a European."

"Rick Blaine said that, not Ronald Reagan. Don't confuse movies with reality, Mr Turner."

"Unlike Reagan, huh?"

"You don't have to like us, but it would help, because we can be very useful to you." Captain North smiled. "Like you, we think that something in Robert Johnson's life may be a critical branch point. If he goes down one road, if he goes to New York and performs at Carnegie Hall, you get the history we're living in right now. If he doesn't play there, if he goes down another road, he won't become a focus for the desegregation movement, and perhaps America will look outward instead of inward, and enter the war on the side of the British, before Churchill is deposed, before the Yalta Treaty. We'll be the ones who beat the Nazis, not the Russians; we'll be the world power, big as the Brits. Maybe even replacing the Brits. Of course, whether you or I would know we had changed history is a bit fuzzy, the scientists aren't agreed on how much carries over. I said we knew about three unsuccessful attempts, who knows how many *successful* ones there were? Well, I guess we can't, but the important thing is that we do know that history *can* be changed."

Turner said, "I wanted desegregation to happen earlier, not later."

"The best of all possible worlds. I understand. But we subjected your idea to games theory analysis, found too many problems with it. Our scenario is stronger, much stronger. And besides, think about it, Mr Turner, aren't we all of us in this country second class citizens in the world? And aren't you an American before anything else?"

"Of course," Turner said, "you could just have him killed."

The captain's gaze flickered for a moment. "It's a viable scenario, and I'll admit that we studied it, but the President isn't happy about signing an executive order to eliminate one of the most famous men in recent American history. Also, there's a theory that history has a certain momentum; if we did eliminate him and it was in any way botched, we could risk turning him into a martyr, as much a cause celebre for the bleeding heart liberals as the New York arrest and his protest songs. Branch-point analysis tells us that our best shot is to keep him away from the Carnegie concert, keep him in obscurity down in Mississippi."

"How do you propose I help, Captain North?"

"When you were traveling with him, Mr Turner, just how much influence did you really have over Robert Johnson?"

</p>

〉〈

Robert Johnson said, "Now see, Ike, I've done with all this rehearsin. I'm not no Shakespeare actor or any such thing. I play the blues. Way I do that, is go out and *do* it."

Turner blotted sweat from his face with his handkerchief. It was hot in the empty storefront, the close wet heat of Memphis's summer. "We've been through this already, Bobby. What you're doing here is something so new you have to get it just right. It's like a Fourth of July rocket. Either it rushes up and explodes, or it just sits there and no one'll take notice of it."

Robert Johnson sort of leaned on the guitar slung around his neck. Electric cord ran back from the pickup inside its hollow body to a buzzing valve amplifier. The cord twitched as he swayed to and fro impatiently. "We can't tell if we got it right less we play it to people. And you know I've never been one to fix in one spot too long. I been here two months now, wouldn't have stayed longer than two weeks if you hadn't shown up. I'm not saying that this idea of yours is no good. I like it. But it's time to get it *movin.* That right, boys?"

Behind him, the drummer started up a slow beat, and the trumpet player bent long notes over the top, a parody of the funeral march opening of "Love in Vain," the slow beat of the train leaving the station, two lights on behind. A couple of the hangers-on began to clap in time. The bass player, a fat balding man, sat to one side, his big woman-shaped instrument keeled at a low angle, its head in his lap. He took a swig from a bottle of beer and wiped his lips, watching Robert Johnson and Turner face off.

Turner forced himself to swallow his anger. He had to stay calm to stay in charge. Things weren't going quite as he'd expected. He'd been Looped to Memphis, where the Army's research had discovered that Robert Johnson would be blowing the money Vocalion had wired to him, the last of the fee for laying down more tracks with Don Law. Turner had managed to prise him away from the cronies his money had attracted, get him sober, put the proposition. To Turner's surprise, he'd accepted at once.

He'd been thinking along the same lines, he'd said; after he'd been through Chicago and heard what was going down there, he'd wanted to get his own band together, but Vocalion saw him as a Delta blues singer and that was all she wrote. But if Ike Zimmerman told him to do it, and if Ike Zimmerman had the money...

It had slid together sweetly and easily. They'd found a drummer and a stand-up bass player, had Robert Johnson's Gibson modified for electrical amplification. The trumpet player had been Robert Johnson's idea, put a little plaintive edge in it, he'd said. And because there was a thriving black business community in Memphis, it had proved easier to find a place to rehearse than Turner had anticipated. Ever since 1914, Boss Crump had used the black vote to get his hand-picked candidates into office—blacks had been given back their franchise, and regularly returned fifty per cent of the poll. Black leaders co-operated with the white political machine in return for favors, and by 1938 a substantial proportion of medical and educational budgets were aimed at blacks: the black section of Memphis had paved, well-lit streets, and parks and libraries. Turner had no trouble renting out an empty store a block away from Beale Street. A couple of payments kept the local cops away. And Turner made sure that Johnson didn't get too much money, enough for drinks and women if he wanted, but not sufficient to subsidize his new-found drinking buddies. Still, that hadn't stopped him getting in trouble once or twice; he'd even been thrown in jail after he'd been picked up for vagrancy when playing a street corner for spare change, an old habit Turner couldn't break him of.

Turner said now, "You sure you're not in trouble, Bobby? Or one of your women isn't?"

"There's maybe a couple of boyfriends lookin out for me, but that ain't nothin new. What is, I got to hear of an offer today. Some white guy wants me to give a concert. In New York."

Turner felt as if his insides had been haled away. Here it was. Here was the crossroads.

Robert Johnson said, "I hear he wants me to go up in a few months. He'll buy me a train ticket, put me in a good hotel, and have me play the Carnegie Hall. You know it? Is it a good place to play?"

"One of the best."

"So I'm thinkin we should try out what we're doing on the road, see if it works out, or if I should stay with what I was. I mean, that's what he wants, this guy, he wants me as Robert Johnson, Delta blues gitar man. And the best is what I am, too. But what I'm asking here is, Ike, do you think I should go?"

Turner's blood softly thrilled, the way it had when he'd heard Robert Johnson play in Tallula. Here was the place where time's highway branched: one road leading to Carnegie Hall and jail and the letters and protest songs that had fired the Freedom Marches; the other to at least twenty more years of Boss Crow, war, and perhaps, just perhaps, the elevation of America to the world stage. He felt like he was falling right where he stood as he said, "I think we should take this thing of ours on the road."

Robert Johnson's face split in a wide grin. "I knew you'd see my way of thinkin," he said, and swaggered off to his band, saying, "All right, boys. One more time, with feelin."

And as the band swung into the slow burn of "Cross Roads Blues," Turner tried to believe that he could feel the change, the switch. But all he could feel was the music.

♓

Turner had spent an entire week setting up the dates for the tour, but it nearly came to grief on the first night, when an amplifier blew ten minutes into the first set; Robert Johnson had to revert to his solo act, and very nearly wrecked that, too, he was so nervous. He got blind drunk afterwards, and the next morning he was still so drunk Turner and the bass player had to carry him between them to the train.

But from the first moment of the second concert, everything swung into place. The crowd stood in a trance as Robert Johnson, gas light hitting him under his chin, led the band into spaces they'd never been before. It ended with an apocalyptic reading of "Hellhound on My Trail," Johnson singing with the fevered defiance of one who knows he's already damned, underpinned by the rock-steady rhythm of drum and bass and mocked by the trumpet's counterpoint as he told his tale of being driven across a world with no respite, pursued by demons real and imagined; then in a space of silence he sang with tender regret about how he had discovered too late that all he needed after all was his little sweet woman to keep him company, and the drums came down, and the trumpet and his guitar screamed like devils harrowing him into darkness. When the lights came up the crowd stood there for a long minute before they remembered to clap. But Robert Johnson was already gone.

He wasn't backstage with the rest of the band, and when Turner looked for him in the smelly little dressing room he found someone else waiting there: a tall lithe man with a shaven scalp, his skin so dark it looked blue-black in the yellow light of the unshaded bulb, who uncoiled from the chair and bounded to his feet before Turner could ask who he was, put a hand on Turner's chest, over the place where the Oppenheimer pinch was lodged, and said, "Don't be foolish, or I'll Loop you without a thought."

The man's gaze locked with Turner's. In the distance, the crowd was stomping and shouting for an encore. Turner said, "What did you do with Bobby?"

"Robert Johnson? Why, nothing at all. And I won't, as long as you keep on keeping him from New York."

Turner felt a surge of relief. Ever since the band had set out on the road he'd felt that he was being watched, and it was good to know it wasn't in his head. He said, "How did you like the show?"

The man took his hand away. He wore his dark double-breasted suit like a costume. A smile came into his face as if he'd flicked a switch. "Don't try to be smart with me, Turner. Just do your job, and I don't have to do mine. Keep Robert Johnson under control until December, and then you can go home." He picked up his hat and carefully set it on his head, smiled again, and was gone.

⅗

The band rode the train across the country, playing each night in a different town, moving on the next morning. And each night it was as if the band was playing as much for itself as for its audience, testing the boundaries of where it could go, crossing and redefining each line it found. Turner, who knew what the English white boys had done (or would do), knew they could never come close to this; not even Lennon on his anguished solo LPs came close. He had set out to do what he'd been asked to do, he was keeping Robert Johnson from his appointment with history in New York, but he'd unleashed something else. He was scared that it would make Robert Johnson as famous as the Carnegie concert, but he'd lost control. It was as if he'd cut down a levee, and they'd all been swept away on the flood.

The band played two long sets each night, grabbing a few hours sleep in their hotel or rooming house, grabbing a few more hours rest on the train to the next town and the next concert, nerving themselves up with whiskey and amphetamines for each show. Turner kept looking over his shoulder for his shadow, but saw no trace of the man. They'd been on the road a month now, and Robert Johnson wasn't ready to stop. When Turner suggested that they take a break, put together some new songs and think about starting a new tour in the New Year, he said, "You don't know what it's like up there. I'm gettin to where I've been tryin to get all my life, and I know I've got you to thank Ike, but I'm beyond anythin you can do for me now. I got to see for myself how far I can go. Maybe we should take ourselves to New York after all, blow Mr White away at the concert."

Turner argued with him for an hour, sweating hard as he tried to talk him out of it. In the end, Robert Johnson shrugged and said, from his distance, "We'll see how it goes."

After each concert Robert Johnson would sit alone awhile with a bottle, smiling and returning the banter of the backstage crowd, polite but distant. Later, he'd find a woman and he'd be gone. Turner couldn't get close to him; no one could. A few times, Turner had to bail him out the next morning; once he'd been badly beaten—a tooth gone, one eye swollen shut—by some guy cut up over the girlfriend he'd lost to Robert Johnson's charms, but he told Turner not to worry, and sang that night as strongly as ever. This is the world we're in, he sang, where terror and beauty walk hand in hand. If it only was different, couldn't we have a time, babe? Then Robert Johnson found they'd been booked to play in Birmingham, Alabama, and flat-out refused to go.

"I'd rather go to Hell than Alabama," he said. "Alabama is death for people like us, Ike. Especially people like us who dare to try somethin different, somethin new. They don ever want anythin to change down there, they happy with how things is, every white man a king, every black man his slave. It's death."

And that was that, they had to pile off the train at the next stop. Turner was relieved. He hoped that they'd lost their seemingly unstoppable momentum; he'd have a chance to argue for a rest, find a place to rehearse, lay low. He'd have to pay off a string of disappointed promoters, starting with the one in Birmingham, but money wasn't the point. Captain North had made sure he had plenty of money.

The band spent the night in the station; Turner bribed the stationmaster to keep the waiting room open. The next morning, he found that Robert Johnson was gone.

)(

At first, Turner was scared that his shadow had caught up with them and murdered Robert Johnson, but by the end of that frantic day he discovered that the singer had walked into town, staged an impromptu concert in front of the hardware store, and got on a bus. Turner chased after him across country; for two long weeks he was always just ahead, a rumor, a ghost, and then Turner caught up with him at a house party at Three Forks, some fifteen miles outside Greenwood, Mississippi, on a dirt road that ran between unfenced fields.

It was the end of August, swelteringly hot. Turner got a lift with half a dozen men crowded into a rattling open-topped Ford Model T, saw the lights of the clapboard house far off in the blue bloom of the night; as the car drew up, he heard the stomping noise of dancing inside the house, Robert Johnson's high, harsh voice cutting through it. A young man with a guitar slung over his back stopped Turner on the porch, said that he'd come all the way out here because he'd seen Robert Johnson play with his band in Little Rock, and wanted to see him play again.

"I play the blues real good," he said. He swayed, holding on to Turner for balance. He was blind drunk. "Not good as Mr Johnson, no one can touch him, but I plays real good. He tellin everyone he goin up to New York to play. You need someone else to play in your concerts down here, you asks for Honeyboy Edwards—"

Turner shook the man off and pushed inside the house.

The heat outside was oppressive; inside it was even worse. People packed out a front room stripped of furniture, stomping and clapping and hollering along to Robert Johnson's song. He sat on a stool at the back, swinging his big Gibson guitar back and forth, singing a couple of verses and then carrying the rhythm by rapping the body of the guitar with the knuckles of his left hand while he took a swig from a half-pint bottle of whiskey before picking up the song again. When he saw Turner he grinned, and shouted that he would be done in five minutes. Turner pushed outside. He was wet through with sweat. Couples were whirling around in the yard. Men sat on parked cars, drinking. The young musician, Honeyboy Edwards, leaned against the trunk of a cottonwood tree, being copiously sick.

Although the noise from inside the house had hardly diminished, Robert Johnson appeared at Turner's side. He had sweated through his shirt, his guitar was slung under his arm, and there was a fresh half-pint of whiskey in his hand. He spun off the cap and took a swallow and offered it to Turner, who shook his head.

"You're mad at me," Robert Johnson said. "I don't blame you, but you got to understand I got to do what I got to do. I got to go play for Mr Hammond in New York because it puts a cap on this part of my life. He want a Delta bluesman for his concert. He get the best. Then I come back here, and we set the world on fire."

"You won't come back," Turner said.

"You got to trust me," Robert Johnson said, and took another swallow of whiskey, offered it again to Turner. "Takes a drink with me, Ike. This is fine smooth stuff, real mellow. Given to me by a fellow that purely loves my music."

Turner knocked the bottle aside and grabbed hold of Johnson's narrow shoulders. "You have to listen to me, Bobby! You won't come back because they won't let you get there! But if you come with me—"

Johnson shrugged away. "This more of your conjure stuff, Ike? You sayin you know the future?"

"I know it's a wicked world. Come back with me. Please."

Robert Johnson shrugged. "Don't I know how wicked the world is," he said. "Listen, I gots to play for these people, then we sit down and we talk."

"Come with me now, Bobby. Before it's too late."

"Aw, Ike, I'm just havin me a little fun here. Like the old days, remember, when I played back of you?"

The dancers inside clapped and howled as he sat down and started to play again. Turner stood just inside the door. The music flew past him into the darkness. Robert Johnson was slowing things down now, swigging whiskey at the end of each song, toasting the crowd. He had just started the lazy lope of "Come on in My Kitchen" when he suddenly stopped and bent over and clutched at his stomach. Sweat was dripping from his face. He took a few deep breaths, took a swig from his half-pint of whiskey, and started in on "Stones in My Passway," and for a moment it seemed as if everything was all right.

Turner, pressed in on all sides by the restless crowd, only caught a glimpse as Robert Johnson collapsed again. Someone in the crowd shrieked, and a terrible anguished howling took up the note, as if the pit of hell had been opened right there in the packed, airless room. It was Robert Johnson, writhing on the floor and screaming like a gutted dog. Turner tried to struggle forward, but the panicking crowd surged back and forth like a sea struck by a squall. Someone yelled for a doctor and someone else shouted something about poison whiskey and someone else was laughing, a tall very black man laughing right in Turner's face, his hand coming down on Turner's heart.

Ж

Bright sunlight, hot and vivid on the white sidewalk, flaming on plate glass windows. Turner nearly fell off the curb, and a green boat-shaped automobile with upswept tailfins blasted him with its horn, the driver yelling something about damn drunken heathen niggers through the swirl of dust as he pulled away. There was a peeling sticker on the wide chrome bumper. *Nixon for President.*

Who the hell was Nixon?

Turner made it across the pavement, found a little shade in a doorway and sat down and rested his head on his knees. Somewhere down the hot white street a radio was playing rock and roll, but he didn't know any of the songs. His brain felt like it had been slammed to mush inside his skull.

He sat there until the cops came to move him on. There were two of them, one young and skinny, with a drooping moustache and collar length hair, the other red-faced, his belly hanging over his Sam Browne belt. The radio was playing something Turner recognized now.

The fat cop pulled Turner to his feet, said, "I'll be goddamned, but he don't smell drunk."

"Maybe he's on acid," the younger one said.

"Ain't no niggers fool enough for that, that's for your young rich white assholes."

"Hell, we was all of us on anything we could get, in Nam."

"I swear that fuckin war's all you talk about. You ain't there now, and this nigger sure ain't fightin the Viet-Cong." The fat cop slapped Turner a couple of times, not hard. He said, "Wake up now. No nigger should be sittin outside of Ray Dillon's funeral parlor. You fixin to die, boy, your own kind'll take care of you."

The song the radio was playing was a Robert Johnson song, "Cross Roads Blues," but it was being sung by some white English boy over a howling wind of virtuoso electric guitar.

Turner said, "Please, officer, can you tell me who is that on the radio?"

The fat cop scowled. "It seems we got one of those educated niggers on our hands here. You're in the wrong place if you are."

"The band, please, I need to know." He'd Looped back, but he didn't know where. Someplace where rock and roll was played on Southern radio stations, someplace where there was a war, America fighting a war...

The young cop said with a smile, "You're a Clapton fan, boy?"

"Fuck that shit," the fat cop said. "Let's get Martin Luther King here down the station."

Turner let himself be manhandled across the sidewalk. He tried to cling on to the hope that at least Robert Johnson had not died in vain, that America was raised up after all, a shining citadel of freedom fighting a just war for the sake of all the world, but as the cops bundled him into the hot smelly squad car he knew that he was in Alabama now.

For Lew Shiner

AFTERWORD

By Paul McAuley

The design of the back of the British two pound coin includes an interlocking circlet of differently-sized gears. It may have been intended to be an homage to the once mighty British engineering industry, but whoever designed it clearly didn't know much about basic mechanics. A careful count reveals that there are nineteen gears, and as anyone with a smidgen of common sense knows, an interlocking gear-train with an odd number of components will jam rather than turn smoothly.

Despite the best intentions of its author, editor, copy editor and proof reader, a novel is a large and complex machine that will almost inevitably contain by omission or oversight at least one odd-numbered gear-train (I've always thought that the best definition of the novel is 'a long piece of fiction with a mistake in it'). Although novelists may aspire to perfection, the very nature of the form means that they can never quite attain it. But because novels are such baggy monsters, they can work their magic despite the odd glitch, whether it's a factual error, like the use of near-sighted Piggy's glasses to start a fire in *Lord of the Flies*, an error in continuity, like the pockets a naked Robinson Crusoe stuffs with salvage, or misuse or overuse of a word or phrase. A short story is far less forgiving of error than a novel because there's far less room for mistakes, but for the same reason, the very best short stories have the potential be quite perfect, like little machines in which every component is smoothly meshed into a flawless whole.

It's one reason why the short story is such a beguiling form; you begin each one with the hope that this time it really will come out good, that this time you'll be able to capture that elusive moment of inspiration and deliver it whole and fresh and alive, that this time it will flow on its own melting. In an introduction to a collection of his journalism, John Updike suggested that if writing a novel is like striking out into the ocean of literature, then writing criticism is more like hugging the shore. To borrow and extend Updike's metaphor, writing a short story is like surfing. More likely than not you'll wipe out, but once in a while the perfect wave will come along.

It's unlikely that any of the short stories collected here are close to that ideal, but I've resisted as much as possible the temptation to enter into an improving collaboration with my younger selves. Only two stories have been reworked: one because the circumstances of its production precluded the final polish of copy editing; the other because the treatment of the character about whom the story revolves doesn't now satisfy me. Otherwise, apart from the odd squirt of oil in the punctuation, a quick tightening turn of one or two loose syntactical bolts, and the occasional scrape of the file to remove the burrs of misprints, they remain as published. For in addition to the possibility of perfection, the short story is also a beguiling form because it captures a single moment or turning point. It is what it is. To revise it is to not to improve it, but to change it into something else. These little machines are what they are. I hope you enjoyed them.

Some brief notes:

THE TWO DICKS

Philip K. Dick is possibly the only authentic genius to have worked almost entirely within the science fiction genre. Like all geniuses, every novel he produced is indelibly imbued with his deeply humanistic world view, and *The Two Dicks* is both an homage and (I hope) a celebration. I owe the title to my friend Russell Schechter, who writes under the *nom de plume* of Jay Russell; go check out *Brown Harvest*, his mordant and very funny homage to boy detectives.

RESIDUALS

Science fiction stories are more often than not about ideas, and writing about ideas lends itself far more easily to collaboration than writing about character and situation. I can't now remember whether it was Kim Newman or myself who had the original idea (what happens to heroes after they've saved the world?) for this one, but it came up in one of those conversations writers sometimes have when they've exhausted the perennial topic of the Evil That Publishers Do, and it clicked with both of us. There are probably as many ways of writing a collaborative piece of fiction as there are writers willing to have a go at it; this one was written in alternating chunks, and we both took a turn at polishing the draft. Writing a collaborative story in the first person is odd but interesting; the resultant voice is neither Kim's nor mine but grew out of the story itself, and while many of the pop culture references come from Kim, and much of the setting comes from me, I'd be hard pressed now to tell you whether a particular sentence was one of Kim's or one of mine.

17

Traditionally, the CVs of writers, particularly male American writers, are supposed to be stuffed with all kinds of oddball stints of manual labour. Blame Hemingway, I guess, who often wrote standing up because he thought that writing should aspire to the condition of work, and believed the old canard that you should only write about what you know. Personally, I think that sympathetic imagination is at least as important as experience, but the setting of this story is derived from one of my few stints of manual labour, when I worked in a paper recycling factory in the summer between leaving school and starting university. It wasn't quite as harsh an environment as 17's, but it did have its own peculiar ecology, which I've only slightly exaggerated.

ALL TOMORROW'S PARTIES

This is a kind of pendant to the Confluence trilogy; a self-contained excerpt from the back story of a very long-lived posthuman character that riffs on the juvenile philosophy of certain Californians uncovered by Ed Regis in his rather wonderful *Great Mambo Chicken and the Transhuman Condition*.

INTERSTITIAL

An end-of-the-world story that takes off from the theory that life had survived at least one bottleneck caused by a runaway effect that created a snowball Earth, and ends in the kind of conflict between the military and scientists that powered most 1950's sci-fi movies, with a tip of the hat to *2001: A Space Odyssey*.

HOW WE LOST THE MOON, A TRUE STORY BY FRANK W. ALLEN

Short stories are an endangered species; the great veldts and rainforests of the periodicals where they once flourished have shrunk and are shrinking still, and the wisdom of the market place is that original short story collections don't sell unless they are themed. In the wrong hands, this can lead to ludicrous collections of stories about magic cats, but if the editor is savvy enough to keep his mind open and his theme sufficiently indeterminate, these kind of anthologies can be great fun. There are few editors more open-minded than Peter Crowther, and I had a lot of fun writing a story that was an excuse to tour the Moon, and most especially visit a particular place where history was made in front of a significant fraction of the world, including me. Armstrong and Aldrin's EVA occurred in the small hours of the morning, British time, and my unsleeping mother woke my brother, sister and me up to watch it, something for which I'm eternally grateful.

UNDER MARS

This story was written for Peter Crowther's anthology of stories about Mars. *About*, not *on*, that's the key to this story about finding the lost dreams of Mars in a theme park that really isn't in any way like D*s*e*l*nd.

DANGER: HARD HACK AREA

A couple of years ago, one of the editors of the science journal *Nature* (some would say *the* science journal; it's where Watson and Crick published their paper on the structure of DNA) thought it would be fun to ask a bunch of science fiction writers to contribute short stories speculating about the future of science. *Very* short stories; space in academic journals is always at a premium, which is one reason why scientific papers often read like those old-style telegrams. It was an interesting technical exercise, and I didn't mind at all that after 20 years of doing actual research I finally got my name in *Nature* with a spoof report on a science conference. No, not at all.

♓

THE MADNESS OF CROWDS

A *jeu d'esprit* about human behaviour that didn't quite make it
into my novel *White Devils*.

THE SECRET OF MY SUCCESS

"Let me tell you about the rich. They are different from you and
me," F. Scott Fitzgerald wrote in his short story 'The Rich Boy' to
which Ernest Hemingway famously riposted, "Yes, they have
more money." Now they have better plastic surgery too; and in
the future…? Some in the genre will try to have you believe that
it doesn't matter if a novel or short story is badly written as long
as the idea is good. Nonsense. There's no excuse for bad or lazy
writing, just as there's no excuse for polished prose with
absolutely nothing to say. This story reflects my increasing
interest in getting the narrative voice right; in this case a bit of
ventriloquism involving the kind of writer I'm too old-fashioned
to ever be. It also reflects a move I made from Scotland to
London, where I learned that there's a good deal more to
publishing than writing the best book you possibly can, and
having the occasional lunch with your editor or agent. For more
on this, I recommend George Gissing's *New Grub Street*; sadly,
things really haven't much changed since it was first published in
1891.

THE PROXY

Another theme anthology story – this time about the internet. Rather than write something obvious about virtual reality,
chatrooms, or sex, I thought I'd write something about the
area where the internet most usefully interacts with reality:
shopping.

⋇

I SPY

This story about a science fiction fan who takes everything far too literally was written for a horror anthology edited by Stephen Jones (the alien invasion story occupies the uneasy boundary between horror and science fiction), and is set in a town that has a passing resemblance to the Cotswold town where I spent most of my childhood. Things are always worse in reality than in fiction—even horror fiction. The last time I visited the place, a drive-through McDonald's had sprung up next to the bus station.

THE RIFT

Another theme anthology story. What can I say? This time I was asked for a contribution by Ellen Datlow, as much force of nature as Hugo-winning editor. The theme was endangered species, but like most of the stories in the anthology, *The Rift* is really about *what* endangers them. And if you don't know what that is, go take a long look in a mirror.

ALIEN TV AND BEFORE THE FLOOD

It's a tradition of Novacon, a science fiction convention held every November in or near Birmingham, that the members of the convention receive a booklet containing an original piece of fiction by the guest of honour. These two linked stories were written for Novacon 28; the hotel in which the first story is set is based on Liverpool's magnificent Adelphi, which contains a replica of the *Titanic*'s stateroom; five years after writing the second, I'm beginning to think that it contains the seed of a novel.

A VERY BRITISH HISTORY

This alternate history celebrating the long-lost British space programme grew out of my childhood fondness for the science fiction novels of Patrick Moore, the astronomer who is better known as the host of *The Sky at Night*, Britain's longest-running TV programme. By one of those lovely coincidences that are far too neat to be believably incorporated into a piece of fiction, David Hardy, the British space artist who painted the covers for some of Moore's novels, later provided the illustration for my PS novella *Making History*.

CROSS ROADS BLUES

This story has been substantially revised since its original appearance. Since then, there's been a lot more research published about Robert Johnson and the scene he briefly dominated, and I'm pleased to be able to get the chance to correct a few factual errors. The main changes are not to do with fact, however, but with voice: when I reread this story I wasn't happy with my first attempt to capture, no matter how obliquely, the voice of an African-American blues singer from 1930s Mississippi. I hope it sings a little more truly now. That history may have changed if Robert Johnson lived to perform in New York is of course no more than a conceit, and part of his reputation is, unfortunately, built on his untimely murder. But after you strip away the gloss of myth, the music remains, and if you don't already know it, I urge you to check it out.

ACKNOWLEDGEMENTS

With thanks to editors Peter Crowther, Ellen Datlow, Gardner Dozois, Henry Gee, Gordon Van Gelder, Maxim Jakubowski, Stephen Jones, and David Pringle, and to Kim Newman, for allowing me to include our collaboration in this collection.

"The Two Dicks" first appeared in *The Magazine of Fantasy and Science Fiction*, 2001.

"Residuals" by Paul J. McAuley and Kim Newman first appeared in *Asimov's Science Fiction*, 1997.

"17" first appeared in *Asimov's Science Fiction*, 1998.

"All Tomorrow's Parties" first appeared in *Interzone*, 1997.

"Interstitial" first appeared in *Asimov's Science Fiction*, 2000.

"How We Lost The Moon, A True Story By Frank W. Allen" first appeared in *Moonshots*, edited by Peter Crowther, DAW, 1999.

"Under Mars" first appeared in *Mars Probes*, edited by Peter Crowther, DAW, 2002.

"Danger: Hard Hack Area" first appeared in *Nature*, 2000.

"The Madness of Crowds" first appeared in *Asimov's Science Fiction*, 2003.

"The Secret of My Success" first appeared in *Interzone*, 1998.

"The Proxy" first appeared in *The New English Library Book of Internet Stories*, edited by Maxim Jakubowski, New English Library, 2000.

"I Spy" first appeared in *White of the Moon*, edited by Stephen Jones, Pumpkin Press, 1999.

"The Rift" first appeared in *Vanishing Acts*, edited by Ellen Datlow, Tor, 2000.

"Alien TV" first appeared in *Alien TV*, Novacon Publications, 1998.

"Before the Flood" first appeared in *Alien TV*, Novacon Publications, 1998.

"A Very British History" first appeared in *Interzone*, 2000.

"Cross Roads Blues" first appeared in *Interzone*, 1991.